DON JAIME

Tales of Jim Tuck
Book 4

DAVID A. ROHE

January 2021

Paperback: 978-1-966652-82-3
eBook: 978-1-966652-83-0
Library of Congress Control Number: 2025906103

Historical Fiction. Main characters are real. Stories as told to author by Jim Tuck.

Ordering Information:

Prime Seven Media
518 Landmann St.
Tomah City, WI 54660

Printed in the United States of America

Table of Contents

Acknowledgements v

Foreword vii

Chapter 1   Trouble in NYC 1

Chapter 2   Away to Madrid 69

Chapter 3   Life Back to Normal 100

Chapter 4   The Land of Spaghetti Westerns 124

Chapter 5   In Jim's Words 137

Chapter 6   When Dougie Met Jim 150

Chapter 7   Delights and Disasters 170

Chapter 8   New Chapter 236

Chapter 9   Newspaper Man 255

Chapter 10 Family Man 259

Chapter 11 Shift to Warmer Places 280

Chapter 12 Return to the States 320

Epilogue 387

Acknowledgements

I have three friends who have helped, stimulated, corrected and supported this writing, particularly this final chapter of Tales of Jim Tuck, book 4. These people who were intimately involved with Jim during the period between 1963 and 1978 included his wife, now widow, Margaret, his daughter Irene and his young friend, Dougie Chowns. Margaret and Irene have provided documents and memories; Dougie, memories and a chapter, and all three encouragement during my "lulls". I have attempted to take particular care with the history part of this historical novel to be true to these lovely people. In addition to his chapter, chapter 6, Dougie provided the watercolor used for the book cover. It is his memory of the Granja la Maja where Jim lived in Valdeolmos.

I also want to express my great pleasure in the fact that I got to work with my granddaughter, Emma Rose, who designed the cover for the book, utilizing Dougie's artwork. What a talent she is, and a beauty as well.

Last but not least is my great friend, Raymond John Hope, who relieved my bleary eyes for an editing, finding 9 more needed corrections in the process. Well done, mate.

DAR

Foreword

Jim Tuck was actual. I grew to know him in Augusta, Georgia from 1982 until his death in October 1989. He was born in Woodstock, New York in June 1916. At least that is what was on his passports.

That Jim was actual is not what drives me to tell his stories. It is the reality that his stories are both outrageous and common. Like many with genius capacities, he had grand appetites along with human frailties. That combination is what drew me to write about him. His tour with the Flying Tigers in China and his time in Zamboanga as a newspaper manager have already been recorded, with embellishments, in Book Two, Zamboanga Times, of this four-book series.

I said Jim had genius capacities. They were demonstrated in his being a polymath. His capabilities were demonstrated in his successful enterprises, among them being a writer for publications like The New Yorker, producer for New York plays, an organizer of a cook-off by chefs from the Big Apple's finest restaurants, and a marketer for a South American coffee cartel. He also was a blue collar contractor, rehabilitating dilapidated tenements in Manhattan. He started the first one with his wife, Marta, to provide a home for their family of three. He expanded this work so that it became his main source of income in New York. As far as I know Jim had no design or construction experience prior to diving into the business of reconstructing old apartment buildings.

That was Jim's way. Get an idea, examine the assets and constraints, decide what to do, then do it. That was the system he used since hastily leaving home, and school, at the age of 15 and joining the Merchant Marine, undoubtedly lying about his age to qualify. At 17 he traveled through Mexico on horseback, making a living boxing for prize money. When he was 19 or 20, he went to California to write screen plays. He wound up learning to fly instead. That's when he made his way to China where he was a "volunteer," read mercenary, in the Chinese Nationalist Army as a member of the Flying Tigers. His journey continued when he started an illegal airline in the Philippines. Those misadventures led to a stint in newspaper management at a local paper in Zamboanga, Mindanao Island in the Philippines. After Zamboanga, he returned to California to find his true love and marry her. Not settling for long, he returned to the Merchant Marine during World War II

After the war, he returned home to Woodstock to support his growing family and write for the local paper and other publications. Eventually he took a marketing job for a South American coffee consortium. Finally, at the start of this book, the fourth in the series of 4, we find him living and working in New York City.

Since Jim incessantly entertained grand ideas and ambitions, he was almost always in trouble, some life threatening, and many leaving a lot of people pissed off. He never escaped notice. In some ways this may have been by design, as he craved to be admired, noticed, but not necessarily liked.

Jim Tuck was one of the most complicated people I have ever known. I was a good listener when he talked about his life. That is why he probably told me as many stories as he did. He almost always embellished. Like many, I got to the place where I discounted most, if not all, of what he told me, only to discover later that I had doubted way too much. For this book I have attempted to figure out fact from fiction. There are many who have personally participated in these events and who are still around to read them. I have tried to be true to the actual history. Jim's unembellished story holds sufficient interest.

DAR, 13 January 2020

CHAPTER 1

Trouble in NYC

"**G**oddamn their rheumy eyes and syphilitic brains!" BAM! The open hand slams the table.

"Jeem! What are you doing?" Marta strolls in from the kitchen, wiping her hands. She slides them onto her husband's tense shoulders.

"Those slimy IRS bastards apparently think it's a good opportunity to pile on. Here's their letter demanding back payroll taxes. Payment required within 30 days."

"Here, let me see," and Jim hands her the letter while her other hand continues to quietly massage his tense neck muscles. While she is reading, she can feel the tension beginning to release. Jim rolls his head around on his neck, beginning to relax, "It says immediate payment within 30 days or contact this office," Marta says.

"'Contact this office,' my ass! What am I going to say, 'Sorry, folks, but you'll just have to get in line?'"

"Of course you don't say that. You call, make an appointment, go see them and make a deal. They want money, not buildings, in exchange. They make deals for term payments, many times. We only get in trouble if we ignore them, yes?"

Jim is no longer slumped over the table, surrounded by papers, his adding machine, black bakelite telephone and a picture of his dogs, the two boxers. He turns and gathers Marta about the waist, pulls her onto his lap and slips his hand under her skirt. That's when the door flies open and their daughter, 17-year-old Xochitl comes striding in with the two boxers on leashes, Sancho of the lolling tongue, and Pancho the younger. "We're back! Great walk. Two poos, one each, seven pisses, four for Sancho and three for Pedro. The block's theirs for sure. Whew! Did I interrupt something, in the living room no less?"

Marta springs to her feet, flushing slightly and Jim just grins. "Marta is just soothing the savage beast. Got some bad news from the IRS and I was protesting a bit. So she intervened. That was a quick tour of the block."

"Not all that quick. You were just having too much fun to notice. When's dinner? I need to go get supplies for school."

Marta quickly replies, "What's the hurry? It's the middle of August. No school for at least three more weeks."

"OK, you caught me. Max and several of my friends are going out to get theirs this evening and I wanted to be there. Juanita, for sure, will be there. We're going to Woolworth's, spend time at the lunch counter, a couple of Cokes, who knows what, and get school supplies. Yes?"

"We see," says Jim. "Another reason for a party."

Xochitl, a senior this year, shares her mother's beauty. Marta named her daughter after the language of Central Mexico where she was raised. Xochitl's name means "flower."

"Poppa, it's our last year. Last go round. We gotta take every chance we can get. Don't you understand?"

"Never having done this end-of-high-school thing, no, I don't quite understand. But sometimes you just have to adapt. So when's dinner, Marta?"

"It's at six, one hour more. You can help with the preparations, chica. Set the table and uncork the wine. Let Poppie finish his work here. You can put the dogs in the back, downstairs."

"K." And away she goes, unleashing the boxers as she makes her way to the back stairs.

"You try to control yourselves, OK," Xochitl chimes, with a cheeky grin.

Jim lights another cigarette and nods as Marta turns and heads back to the kitchen. Just as she passes the door the phone rings. Jim answers, "Tuck. Yeah, what? **They what?!**"

That brings Marta right back out of the kitchen. "What is it?"

Jim raises his hand to shush her and his eyes look wild, his breathing labored.

"Jeem, calm down!" Again his hand comes up and he gives her a look she has never seen. Pure animal rage is flowing like magma from his face.

"After everything we have done for that lazy lot of incompetents, this is what we get as thanks? They think they have me in a corner, do they? I'll call you back tomorrow!" He slams the phone into its cradle.

Marta waits silently for Jim to speak.

"That was Frankie, the crew foreman. The crew thinks they are not getting a big enough piece of the pie from this project and want a dollar an hour raise or they are striking, or slowing down production, until they get it. You realize what this means?"

Just then Xochitl flies into the room heading toward the kitchen, senses the smoldering space between her mother and father, and stops dead in her tracks. "What?"

Silence. "Nothing for you to worry your pretty little head about, pumpkin."

"Poppa, that response might have been OK seven or eight years ago. I'm 17 now. I'll be leaving, probably after this year. Don't you think it's time to include me in all the family stuff?"

Jim is quiet, glances at Marta who shrugs, half smiles at her daughter, and walks calmly into the kitchen.

"OK, pumpkin, here's the situation: You know we have two construction projects on at the moment, and have had for a couple of months. They are more than we have taken on before and money has been very tight. Today we received a notice from the IRS that our back payroll taxes are due within 30 days, or whatever. We have signed rental agreements, with deposits, for six apartments that are supposed to be completed in six weeks so tenants can move in. Construction is behind and Frankie, the crew foreman, just called to say the crew are ready to strike if they don't get more money. We have been so short of cash that I got a short-term loan from Tony Sylvano. I was supposed to pay it back with the first month's rent on the apartments. All in all, we are up shit creek, sweet pea."

"You think Frankie and Tony are working this thing together?"

Jim just sits quietly, looks at his baby girl, and has a large wake-up call. She's not a child anymore. That brings a half smile to his face and he just nods. "That's a distinct possibility. You know, Tony's mob family has its fingers in a lot of pies here in Manhattan. You'd think his holiness the pope was in charge. Still, your mom and I need to do some figuring. As bright as you are, this thing is not your concern, young lady. So go set the table, K?"

She smiles, glad that her father is treating her more like an adult. She trusts that her dad and mom can sort this out. They've been in tight spots in the past, though they rarely shared them with her. She just knew. Xochitl heads to the kitchen.

Jim lifts his tumbler of red wine and heads out the back door of the first floor apartment. Out the back there is a small balcony with a metal grid floor that overlooks the postage stamp garden a half story below. The dogs come bounding up the stairs on his arrival, toenails clicking on the metal stairs. Sitting at the table, he puts the glass down and begins to massage the large dogs behind the ears, over the shoulders, deeply up and down their backs, first one dog, then the other. If dogs could purr, Sancho and Pedro surely would.

Stroking his dogs helps Jim's brain to click, mulling alternatives, calculating constraints, until finally the outline of a plan starts to emerge and he sits back for a long sip of wine. The ice cube is not melted; it clanks against the wall of the glass signaling Jim to take his empty glass to the kitchen for a refill.

"I need to talk to you," he says to his wife as she is ladling soup into bowls.

"You can see I am busy, Jim. What is so urgent to interrupt me now?"

"Xochitl can finish that. I need to talk now while these ideas are still fresh. Come on!" and he takes the ladle from her, hands it to Xochitl. "You can finish this, right? I really need to talk to Mum."

"Sure. I'll come and get you in a minute. Back porch?"

"Yep, thanks, bud."

Jim refills his glass, takes Marta by the arm, guides her out of the kitchen and through the apartment to the back porch. The sun is much lower now behind the surrounding buildings and the temperature has dropped a couple of degrees, making it almost bearable. "Listen, I think we are in too deep and need to get out."

"What do you mean? What is the choice?"

"OK, here's how I see it. We have a situation that looks like it will only get worse. Tony's note is due in a month, the IRS wants their money in a month. First month's rents were supposed to start in a month, two weeks before the tenants move in. But now, the workers are slowing down or striking. If we arrange to pay them more, we run the risk of this project becoming a hobby not a money maker for us. We can't afford that. So I'm thinking it's time for a change of scenery."

"What change of scenery? You want to plant trees back here? Huh?"

"Now just listen for a minute, will you? We must make some decisions and I need your help." With that,

Jim cracks a smile and his eyebrows raise up. Marta melts.

"OK, I am listening. What are you thinking?"

"I think our experiment with real estate has run its course, at least in New York. We need to relocate. But we need finances to make a change. Our priority should be to pay off Tony, then get cash and move somewhere the IRS can't get to us. That means out of the U.S."

Marta is sitting quietly, then lets out a deep sigh. "Move away from here? Forever?"

"Whether it is forever or not I don't know just now. What I do know is that we don't want Tony for an enemy. There is little I can do for the work crews since I am tapped out at the bank, And, if we default on the rental contracts because of the apartments not being ready, the renters have every right to back out, which I suspect they will. That would leave us with nothing to pay Tony. That is, very much, not good, right?"

"That is right, but I think the workers must be supported, don't you? You do not want to be the wicked imperialist overseer, do you?"

"This wicked imperialist is out of money, out of time, and out of luck, except for bad luck. We have to make a big change if our family is to stay together."

Suddenly Marta is very quiet, still. She whispers, "You think it is really this bad?"

"Yes, so I need your wisdom to help make a plan. Can you help?"

It is very quiet on the balcony, a small bird is singing in the garden below and there is evening traffic noise, muffled by the neighboring buildings. Jim lights a cigarette, waiting for Marta to respond. With his raspy breath, Jim asks, "What ideas have you come up with?"

"I'm not sure, Jeem. It all seems so uncertain."

Jim smiles his large smile, leans forward and takes Marta's hand. "Here are some ideas for getting some of our money from our properties. We trade the deed for one property for the loan from Tony. He can sell it and make a little more than the amount of the loan, or take the rent each month and make regular money for years. Then we sell the other rental property, that is operating for income to us, for cash that we will need to live on. For immediate cash, we sell the air conditioners just installed in the two buildings under construction. Then, I think we should move to Spain."

Marta's head jerks up, her shoulders lift up and she says, "Spain? Really, Spain? I love it, Franco or no Franco."

"Yes, Spain. We speak Spanish well enough, not Castilian, but intelligible. I think that I have a contact there at the air force base."

"But who will buy the other building, who will buy air conditioners, what about the dogs, what about Xochitl and school?"

"Poppa, dinner is on the table!"

"Coming," replies Marta. "We must do more talking after dinner."

"Yes, we must."

Dinner was quieter than usual. Marta and Jim simply ask Xochitl to clean up afterwards. She senses tension, and, while she'd like to bicker, Xochitl does not complain. Jim collects a bottle of red wine and a single glass. Marta prepares a pot of tea. Together they adjourn to their sanctuary, the balcony.

It is dark now and Jim's voice resembles more of a growl than a murmur. He begins: "I think we have at most two weeks to get ourselves organized and out of here."

"But won't we lose just about everything if we leave that quickly?"

"We'll lose a lot more if we don't. Look, we have to get Tony paid. You know what happens if we don't. The workers, your beloved workers, have just made that impossible, unless we liquidate some of our assets. That would make it nearly impossible for us to support ourselves here in New York. My writing doesn't bring in enough to compensate, and neither does your fabric art.

All our money is tied up in the construction projects, and they have just gone to shit. We have a great network here in New York, and I think it is time to use it to get us away from here with as much of our assets as we can. Otherwise, we are in real danger of losing it all, and more. So, rather than think about what we will lose, let's start thinking about what we can keep, and how. Agreed?"

Marta puts her teacup down, rests her chin in the palm of her hand and just gazes moodily at Jim. Finally, she sits up, flashes a smile and says, "OK. Here's what I think we do. We have two buildings giving income from rent. I agree we sign one over to Tony and sell the other. If we have two weeks left, that is not long enough to make much money. So someone must sell it for us."

Jim starts to grin. Leaning forward, he says, "We also have 51 air conditioners that have just been installed in the two buildings under construction. They are brand new, it is summer, so they are worth something. We can find someone to take them all for a bargain price."

"Won't that ruin the new buildings for selling? What about the IRS bill?"

Jim just shakes his head and says, "We just dump those two unfinished buildings. We can't get anything for them the way they are anyway. Let the bank have them since it's their money that is mostly at risk. As far as the IRS is concerned, screw 'em." Jim growls out this last statement with more than his usual gruffness. "And, look, some of these ideas mean this whole plan has to be completely secret. Just us. OK?"

"OK." Jim and Marta turn to see Xochitl leaning on the open door frame. "Kitchen is all cleaned up."

"Well, young lady, you seem to find yourself in the middle of things. I presume you are aware of the seriousness of our situation, yes?" Jim is frowning, but calm.

"I think I do. I did not hear everything, but it seems we are in a very difficult place just now, and it seems you've decided that we are leaving, right?"

"Right. But difficult is the mildest way of describing it. We are in the shit, dangerous shit. If anyone else finds out about our plans, we're screwed. Clear? Not just financially, but we could be hurt physically."

Xochitl's face is a mask. Her breathing gives her emotions away. "Come here and sit down, bud. You're already in for a penny. Might as well be in for a pound."

There is no smile, but Xochitl's shoulders relax a bit. As she sits, Marta asks, "Do you want a cup of tea, or a glass of wine?"

"Glass of wine, please," and Marta leaves to get another glass.

"Look here, pumpkin, we are really stuck between several rocks and a hard place. In order to get ourselves out, we are going to have to divest ourselves of nearly everything we own and walk away. That means your last year of high school will be somewhere else. Understand?"

Xochitl nods and asks, "By divest, you mean get rid of, correct?"

"Correct." Marta comes onto the balcony and hands Xochitl her glass, a real wine glass. "We will sell some stuff, trade some stuff, pack a little of our stuff, and walk away from the rest."

Xochitl pauses as she pours a full glass, then asks, "What about Pedro and Sancho?"

"They will come with us wherever we go."

Marta looks at Jim, eyebrows up, but he just nods and says, "The dogs are coming." Marta shrugs and walks away.

"When do we leave?" asks Xochitl.

"In the next two weeks."

"Whew! That's quick!"

"Yes, it is. And it is necessary. And I have to tell you that if anyone finds out what we are up to, we're sunk. Understand? That means not a hint to anyone, particularly any friends. When they start talking about plans for this school year, you have to go along with no hints at all. This is not a game. Not even a little bit. There is very real danger involved, threat of arrest is the least danger I am talking about. Understood?"

Xochitl's glass is suddenly half empty as she nods, "Yes, Poppa. Understood."

"Good. That makes everything a lot easier since Marta and I don't need to try to hide anything from you. You will be a great help in planning and making this thing happen."

Xochitl is very quiet, then says, "This is scary, but quite exciting as well. What do you want me to do?"

"Well, first, we need a plan. We need to figure out how to sell as much as we can as quietly as we can. Our destination is Spain."

"Wow!"

"Yes, Marta likes that idea too. But we need to get the dogs over there as well. That will be your first task. How about we put you in charge of exploring options for getting the dogs to Madrid? Find out how much it will cost to transport them and then what the logistics are, if there are certification requirements for traveling dogs, etc. I suggest going to the Battery and checking out some of the shipping agencies there, talking to the airlines, whatever other options you find."

"I'll start with one of the expensive pet stores downtown to see how they do it."

"Marvelous idea. Just stay vague enough that your plans are unclear, OK ?"

"Right."

"Off you go."

"Now?"

"We are not in a position to be waiting, young lady. Stores are still open and the vet's office is open late. Get going. We need to be out of here pronto. Now go!"

"Yes, **sir!**"

"No need to get snippy. We're a team, right?"

Xochitl nods and she's off.

"Now for our tasks, I'll contact Tony and Ray Lombard."

"Why Ray?"

"He is running into supply shortages for his construction projects. Ray has air conditioners on back order and he is pulling out his hair. Saw him the day before yesterday and I'm pretty sure he will take all of ours off our hands, if the price is right. Maybe we can get a premium out of him, even though they are no longer in their boxes. We'll see."

Marta ponders this, then suggests, "I'll go see Wong Kai at the restaurant. We will need a confidential power of attorney for the sale of the other building, and he is the best candidate I can think of."

"Agreed. It will cost a fair amount, but I agree it will be worth it."

"What do you think a good fee should be, not that he and I will discuss that. He will probably want to settle that detail with you anyway. But just in case."

"He'll probably start at 15 percent, we'll counter with 10 percent, then settle on 12 percent or 12.5 percent of the purchase price. The trick, of course, is knowing the actual purchase price when we are in Spain, which is the reason for using Kai. I trust him to be truthful. OK, off you go. I'll get on the phone."

Marta's charm will be a great asset for getting Wong Kai's attention this time of the evening. His restaurant is not elegant, but extremely busy, particularly with the Chinese community. Kai, being both chef and owner, is running, literally, from 4 p.m. until the restaurant closes at midnight. First in, last out. Jim and Marta hold privileged positions in the local Chinese community. Wong Kai trusts them and considers them friends. They are the only friends he acknowledges outside the Chinese community. Even among fellow Asians his close friendships are few.

As Marta leaves the apartment, Jim picks up the phone and dials. "Yeh?" the voice on the other end mutters.

"Tony Sylvano. Jim Tuck."

"Ooo ya wan?"

"Tony, now, or I'll come rip off your fuckin' head."

"Ooo the 'ell ya think yer talkin' to, asshole?"

"A dead man, if Tony's not on this phone in 10 seconds, capiche?"

"Ah'm not…"

"Now, shithead. You're not listening."

Silence, then a click and, "Sylvano."

"You got some new help on board, eh? I didn't recognize the voice and cooperation was slow."

"Eddie's not bad. A nephew from Jersey, fillin' in. I'll introduce you some time. You got a need?"

"Yeah, I gotta need. How about the diner at 10?"

"Can't. It's my kid's birthday and we'll still be celebrating. This sounds like you're in a hurry."

"It's time to make some changes, and when it's time, it's time. You know how it is."

"OK, Jim. Say 11:30, the diner. I'll bring Eddie to introduce, so there can be better communication."

"Whatever. If we're good, then maybe we won't need too much more communication, eh?"

"Now you're sounding mysterious. You in trouble? We havin' any difficulties of the financial kind that I need to know about?"

"We're good. Nothing I can't handle with an intelligent man like you. See you at 11:30."

Click.

The rotary dial is turning again and suddenly a man's voice answers, "Lombard Holdings, how can I help you?"

"Ray, it's Tuck. You alone?"

"Just the usual office staff. Receptionist is in the can. What's up, Jim?"

"This is between you, me and the lamppost, but I have a line on 51 air conditioners at below market price, available in 5 days. Thought you might be interested."

There is a long pause on the other end, then, "Is this something we can discuss now, or do we need to meet.?"

"Meet. When, where?"

"How about Thursday, 10 a.m. at the racket club?"

"How about now, at Willie's, up the street from the Wisconsin Diner? It's in your neighborhood."

"Whoa, whoa, whoa. What's the rush?"

"This is a time-limited opportunity. You want it or not. If not, I make my next call as soon as I hang up."

"Don't get your panties in a wad. OK, OK! I'll head over to Willie's now. I'll be waiting."

"Not if I'm there first. See ya in a few." Click.

Jim rummages through the folder for the construction of the new apartments, and selects the warranty materials for the air conditioners, most of which have been installed into the windows. There are six still in their boxes, awaiting the attention of the slowed down workers. He stuffs the warranty certificates into a separate folder and gets up only to sit down again and open the file cabinet. He examines the folder for rental properties, selects one title and inserts it into the folder with the warranty certificates.

There's a taxi a block up the street and Jim is in front of Willie's 10 minutes later. No sign of Ray yet so Jim walks in, nods to Willie in the kitchen, points at the far corner booth to the waitress and sits himself down. Not a fan of iced tea, Jim settles for Willie's coffee, asking for the pot to be left on the table. Shortly, Ray comes in the door, does a 180 degree scan and spots Jim's booth. Patting the seat next to him, Jim invites Ray over, then fills the other cup from the pot.

As Ray sits, he notices the folder on the table beside Jim. "That's what you were talking about?"

"That's it, these are they. You are several air conditioners short and, as you may have surmised, I am the one with the air conditioners. These are the warranty documents for the lot." Jim slides the papers out in a stack, leaving the property deed and title unseen in the folder. "They are all new, most have been installed, with six remaining still in their boxes. None have any use time on them. There are 51 of them. What do you say to $700 each?"

"I'd say you are out of your friggin' mind. Why in the world would I pay market price for used merchandise?"

"Ray, are we having a meeting here, or are you just working your mouth? We are here, this is an opportunity for you arising out of my misfortune. We talking, or am I walking?"

"Look, this was your idea. Don't get your panties in a wad. We're talking, so talk!"

"I have about said my piece except this, and this is strictly confidential. One week and I am gone. A perfect storm of calamities has descended upon my family and I am implementing remedies, one of which you are the beneficiary, OK? So $700 is a bit high, you say. What's reasonable?"

Ray sits, holding his coffee cup, watching as Jim assesses the situation. Then he nods and says, "$550 each, delivered."

"$530 and you come get them."

"Done."

"OK, here's the deal. The workers are threatening a strike, or formal slow down, if I don't cough up another dollar an hour over their current contract. They are in with the mob, and looking forward to a bigger payday. I owe the family some money. The contractor knows it and figures now is a good time to put the squeeze on me. Of course, sharks can immediately tell when there is blood in the water. I can blow them off for a week, no more.

"Now here's my plan so far: exactly 6 nights from now - exactly, mind you - you have a crew assembled to extract the installed conditioners. Here's the warranty papers for them, including the six still in their original boxes. We start at 12:01 a.m. and finish by 6 a.m. So you have to have enough guys available who can do the work. They'll be humping it in any case. Five nights from now is September 1st, agreed? Oh, and fifty percent down, tomorrow. Meet me here at Willie's, coffee, 10 a.m."

"Let me see the warranty papers."

"Sure. Here's half. Better yet, take any 24 you want. Go ahead."

Ray shuffles through the pile, counting until he gets 24. He puts two of them up to the light, examining the watermarks in the paper. Looking at the fine print, Ray folds the stack once long ways and shoves them back into the empty folder. "So you sell off the air conditioners from two current projects to get a bit of liquidity. Then what do you do? How do you expect to finish construction?"

Jim says nothing, just sits and fidgets with his folder, anxious to leave.

"You're not finishing are ya? You're taking a powder. Am I right? What the fuck's goin' on? I ain't never seen ya quit. I'm not wrong am I?" Jim is a stone, glances up from the table and fixes Ray a stare worthy of Medusa. "Where ya goin'? Ya know the wise guys can find you anywhere, and, I mean, anywhere. I know you're into them for a reasonable figure they won't forgive."

Jim glances up at Ray, gives him a half grin and looks back at his cup on the table.

"What!? What!?"

"The first, at midnight - pick up at the two sites. But first, 10 a.m. tomorrow, cash, no checks. Right? No one knows you bought 'em, no one knows I sold 'em, no official transactions. That means no tax deduction for the expense. You can do the math as well as anyone. What you save in the cost of the a.c. units far exceeds any tax benefit. See ya, Ray." And Jim is out the door.

Ray sits there another minute, shifting his head side to side..

With time to kill before meeting Tony, Jim decides to walk awhile. He strides down the street to the corner, turns left and slows his pace. At the next light he turns to the right and waits for the crossing light, looking back occasionally to see what's behind him. Ray doesn't appear to be following. The light changes and Jim heads down the street three blocks. He comes to a small park consisting of eight trees, all mature, and an empty bench.

Sitting, he checks out the crowd and sees no one he knows. He relaxes for a moment and leans back, placing the folder on the bench. Hands behind his head, Jim looks up through the branches into the darkened sky. It's early fall weather in New York. He has not felt like enjoying it until right now.

Relaxation comes slowly: ankles crossed, shoulders relaxed, eyes at half mast. The traffic noise disappears, just like fan noise at night, and he drifts off, remembering all the drama of his last seven years in New York City. It hasn't been a bad run. It is the longest he has been anywhere since he was a kid growing up in Woodstock. As he is remembering tasks and triumphs, his memory slides right back to Marta. What a woman. No other like her anywhere. Somehow she is able to appreciate his affection while discounting his infidelities. Love of his life is a cliché, and, like most cliches, it is true. Adding to her loyalty, she has the ability to discern solutions to complex problems. A woman of such varied talents - from construction to silk painting - Marta is a marvel. His affection is genuine, even if his protestations of fidelity are not. Somehow she knows what's important, appreciates it and discards the rest.

Jim's belly is complaining again. So he rouses from his reverie into the street light over the sidewalk and ambles toward the Chinese restaurant. Marta is likely to have been there by now with their proposal. Maybe he can kill two birds with this one stone, that is, get a bite to eat and discuss terms with Kai. No time like the present.

"Jeem!" Kai greets him at the door. His apron is crisp and white, shoulders are rounded, and his step seems livelier than usual "You here also. Marta came today.

There was interesting conversation, yes? Now you are here to change it all, eh? Plans are changing, no?"

"No. Plans are the same. I am hungry and have another meeting later, so I decided I better have some good food to make the good deal. Deals on empty stomachs are never good ones, true?"

"Ahh, very true. I must make that another advertisement. Come, come. Sit. What you want? Red wine with what?"

That brings a smile and Jim says, "Red wine with whatever the special is today. No need to decide. It is all good. Then, after I eat and you have a moment, you can tell me what you are thinking?"

"Good, good. Yes, say what I think, eh?"

That brings another smile, this time at the irony of the likelihood of figuring out what Kai really is thinking. Kai rushes off, waving his right arm at Jim to signal the waitress's attention. Then he shouts through the open kitchen door so the order is there before he is. Moments after Kai disappears, the waitress materializes by Jim's side and places the glass of wine with a floating ice cube in front of him. Jim thanks her and she retreats to the service kiosk and starts cleaning cutlery.

Even after six months, he still does not know her name, but thinks she is Filipino. He manages to slip in a few of his limited Philippine words, which invariably delights her. Zamboanga seems a lifetime ago and a million miles away, but it retains a significant emotional part of his heart. Marta may be the only person in New York who is fully aware of his sentimental side. Xochitl may understand later. Some scattered friends may realize it. But, in New York City, Marta is it.

Jim finishes the dumplings and is into his third glass of wine when Kai settles into the seat next to him. Looking Jim squarely in the eyes, a highly unusual gesture, Kai says, "You have great difficulties now, eh?"

"Yes, great difficulties. You said Marta spoke to you this afternoon?"

"Yes. Marta spoke quite a lot and I have been thinking quite a lot."

"I have been very busy today and have not been home to speak to her. Did you and Marta come to any conclusions?"

"I think that you two have great difficulties and I decide that I want to help, if I can. We did not discuss exactly how to help. Can you tell me?"

"We must sell the property on 137th street. It is completed and fully rented with one open apartment. We must leave the USA immediately. So we must find a trustworthy person to sell the property and deposit the money into our bank. We think the person doing this task should receive a fee, a percentage of the net selling price after fees are paid. Can you do it for us, for a fee?"

"I suspected this was what Marta was wanting to discuss, but we did not arrive at such specific information."

With that Kai leans back in his chair, relaxing from his tense, forward leaning position. He strokes the wispy beard on his chin. "I believe I can help with this. I know the property on 137th Street. It is a fine building. These are difficult times, but can you tell me how much you think the net money will be?"

"I suspect there should be between $30,000 and $40,000 equity in the property, after paying the lawyers and retiring the mortgage. Since it must be a fast sale, it may be less."

"You are a very open man, Jim Tuck. I never can receive such information from any of my Chinese business associates. Maybe from family, but not friends."

"As you said, Kai, these are difficult times, and I don't have time to waste trying to be clever. What do you consider a fair fee for doing this business?"

"Well, first, I suggest the percentage should be of the total sale price of the property, and perhaps eight percent would be good."

"We are having a good discussion, aren't we, so I can tell you up front that I can't afford eight percent of the gross price. I must take cash with me to live somewhere else. If there is not enough cash, then my family suffers. It must be a percentage of the net sale."

"And from somewhere else you can trust that the information sent to you is true?"

Jim now leans back, mimicking Kai's relaxed posture. He looks him in the eye. "With almost no one. I can trust the information coming from you, but I will have ways to check."

Kai smiles a bit, the corners of his mouth rise and his eyebrows as well. "So, we are almost family, but with a little checking, eh?"

That makes Jim grin and nod his head.

"If the fee is to be of the net sale then it must be fifteen percent."

Jim's smile sags, leaving him with a sardonic expression, "Eleven percent and no more."

Kai's eyebrows jerk up, his shoulders noticeably stiffen and what smile remains has disappeared. He raises his shoulders. "Fourteen percent and no less."

That brings a huge smile to Jim's face, obviously unsettling Kai."It seems we may be getting somewhere. 11.5 percent of net sales," Jim says.

Kai leans forward again, on guard and slightly frowning. "Jim, you say we are friends, yet you do not act friendly."

"We are friends, Kai, and this is business. As soon as we have a deal, I will write it up at home and bring it to you tomorrow, along with a signed power of attorney authorizing you to sell the property in our names. I know that good business makes good friends. We can find a solution that is good for both of us. How about 11.5 percent?"

Kai relaxes a bit, looking down at the table top. Then he looks up. "13."

"12," says Jim.

"12.5 percent," says Kai, and Jim extends his hand to shake.

Kai looks at it briefly, then takes Jim's hand. "This is the number you thought of already, correct?"

Jim smiles and says, "This is good wine. I will have to remember it when Marta and I come with the papers, either tomorrow or next day. Is there a better time for us to come?"

Still grasping Jim's hand, Kai says, "Tomorrow is bad, too busy. Next day."

Jim nods, "Next day it is. This time, when customers are less?"

"Yes. See you then." Kai hastily gets up and moves on to conquer the next task..

Jim swallows the rest of his wine, smiles and stands up. He just stands there for a moment, taking in the scene. Checking his watch, he heads to the back where the restrooms and pay telephones are. After stopping in the john, he puts a dime in the pay phone and calls Marta.

"Allo?"

"It's Jim. Just talked to Kai and got the deal settled. Thanks for getting it going. I suspect it may not have been easy for you to deal with him. He is a bit of a traditional man."

"Oh, yes. Traditional man, for sure, but a gentleman. So what did you decide?"

"He will broker the deal and deposit the receipts for what we thought, 12.5% of the net sale price."

"Oh, we did not think much about net or gross when we were talking. That's better, for sure. That was good. Is he OK with this deal? What do you think?"

"The 12.5% was his figure, after going back and forth a bit, and he seems OK. I think he is happy with the deal. I trust him anyway. Plus we shook on it and he's been here long enough to know what that means. We're coming here this time the day after tomorrow with the papers. We can have dinner here as well, OK?"

"Sure, you know I like his food. Are you coming home?"

"No, I am meeting Tony in half an hour, so I'll head over there. I guess I'll be home about one."

"That's late. You've been going strong all day. Tony doesn't get started until afternoon, you know. Can you deal with him like this?"

"Have to. Gotta do what ya gotta do. Don't wait up. I'll be home as soon as I can."

"Te amo, Jeem."

"Si, yo tambien, mi corazón."

Hanging up, he heads out the door to walk the few blocks to the diner. Along the way a wino lurches out of a doorway, burps in his face and asks, "Gotta buck, bud?"

"Nope."

Another poorly dressed man leans out of the doorway, flashing a knife. "You sure? Might want to reconsider."

Jim doesn't even pause, walks right into the drunk in front of him and decks him with a right cross. As the fellow hits the sidewalk, Jim swings to his left, pivoting on his left toes, catching the thrusting right wrist of the knife-wielding bum and pulling him through the arc. As the surprised fellow starts his counterclockwise twist, Jim's right hand, heel first, connects with the bridge of the fellow's nose. Pop! The cartilage is separated from the bone, blood is spurting everywhere and the knife is on the sidewalk. Fully planting his right foot, Jim's left instep connects with his assailant's softish belly and "whoosh," there is no air left in the lungs. It's over before the two fellows have had a chance to react. Jim continues his stroll down the street, first remembering to collect his fallen folder..

"That actually felt good. Wonder if Tony knows these assholes are operating in his neighborhood," is Jim's thinking as he rounds the next corner and walks to the neon sign over the door to the stainless steel facade of the diner. It's only 11:15, but Jim likes being early, especially when dealing with Tony and his "friends". The diner does not have a liquor license so Jim goes for the coffee. Jackie knows to leave the pot on the table, two cups and lots of sugar packets. Filling his cup, the empty one on the other side of the table, Jim leans back and settles in for what he hopes is a short wait. His adrenaline is pumping enough that there is no chance of dozing off. Just as he is reminiscing about the encounter down the street, the double door opens and Tony, all 275 pounds of him on a 5 foot 11 inch frame walks through, light blue polo shirt inside a dark blue blazer, khaki trousers, loafers with white socks and his hair perfect. The door doesn't close all the way because a tall, slender, pimply faced fellow comes in right behind. The second fellow can't be over 25, probably much nearer 20 and is looking left, right, jittery. Tony spots Jim, sees the fidgeting fellow's antics and quietly offers suggestions. Calm is instantly restored, no more fidgeting, head slightly down but his chin is still above Tony's head. The transformation lets Jim know who the young fellow is, causing a small smile that is immediately smothered. Jim stands as Tony approaches the table.

With his right hand out and an ironic smile, Tony reaches Jim with, "So, here we are. Ye're lookin good. Don't see any dents or damage. What's the rush on my kid's burtday? Oh! And dis here's Eddie. Say hi, Eddie. This is Mr. Tuck."

Eddie does a bit of a shuffling 2 step, smiles with one side, but continues to slouch. "Hi, **Mr.** Tuck."

Bam, a meaty hand smacks the side of Eddie's head. "Stand up straight! Whataya doin? Ya keep on wit dat smaht mout and ya's walkin back!"

Rubbing the red area on the side of his head, Eddie straightens a bit and says, "Sorry. Didn't mean nothin. Just tired I guess. Sorry, Mr. Tuck. Won't happen again. Promise."

Jim says, "It's OK. Relax, alright? Lets sit down and get a little calm, OK? Forgot we were having a guest." With that, Jim raises his hand and a single finger requesting another cup that arrives practically before his hand is back at his side. "Thanks."

"Here, let me pour. Glad we could make it this evening, Tony. I gotta tell ya that everything that goes down here has gotta stay between us, OK?" With that, Jim's gaze fixes directly on Eddie.

"Sure, sure! No problem. Eddie's a bit young, for sure. But he ain't no idiot. Family or no, he knows what happens if quiet does not end up quiet." All through this little exposition, Tony's eyes are locked on Eddie's. Eddie does not dare look away, for fear of another whallop, can't help a fidget or 2, and just nods. "Good. That's settled. Now, what's on your mind.?"

"OK. Straight to it. I owe you $37,000. That loan was very helpful for getting these last 2 projects nearly finished. However, the gods have not been kind and the projects won't finish, not with Marta and me anyway. But, I can satisfy the note to you with this." Here, Jim opens the folder and extracts the deed to 85 137th St. "This is an apartment complex that is full, rents come in monthly from reliable folks, not a dead beat among them. I can sign this over to you tonight, you can register it tomorrow. The rents will pay off the full amount in a year, or you can sell the building for 4 times the annual rents, as you know, and get more than the amount of the note. So, signing this over either gives you regular income for years or quick cash for an amount more than the note." Jim hands the deed to Tony.

Taking the papers, Tony is looking at Jim then asks, "But you use these rents for your own income, right? What ya gonna do? This don't make sense."

Recognizing Tony's ability to play dumb and his likely role in the strategic strike by the builders, Jim's poker face has never been needed more. Raising his eyebrows a fraction, he says, "Look, several small disasters have just come together to make one large one landing on Marta and me today. It's been building for a while, but now she and I realize we gotta make a move. So, when ya gotta move, ya gotta."

"Move," says Tony, with only the hint of a smile. He'll make a tidy profit off this adventure. Eddie is quiet, not fidgeting. Tony examines the deed and puts it on the table.

"What do ya say?" Jim is examining the half smile on Tony's lips, realizing the calculation going on in there, keeps quiet while Tony decides.

"So, I take the building. It's mortgage free, right?" Jim nods. "And that settles the debt." Another nod. Quiet settles around the table for a minute. "Done," and Tony's hand comes out. Jim takes it, takes the deed and signs it over to Tony and extracts another paper from the folder.

"Sign right there, bud, and we're done."

"Wha's this?"

"Just verification that I've satisfied the note. Good business keeps good friends, right?"

Tony looks at the paper with 3 typed lines on it and a place for a signature at the bottom. Jim raises the pen and offers it to Tony.

"Wha! My word ain't good enough for ya? We shook on it, right?"

"Your word has always been good enough for me, Tony. Sometimes, others can get involved, and may not have all the relevant information before making hasty decisions. It's happened, right?"

Silence, then Tony nods, takes the pen and signs the receipt. Smiling, he returns the pen and leans back. Jim slides the deed over to Tony. "Sorry 'bout the troubles, Jim. You's a good guy. We done good work together. Hope ya comes out OK." With that, Tony stands, as does Jim, shakes hands again, turns and is out the door with Eddie scrambling to keep up.

Jim sits back down, slides the receipt into the folder then is up and ready to leave when Tony comes back in the door. "Say, there's a couple of winos on the ground, next block, look a bit beat up. Ya see anything on your way here? This is my street, and I gotta maintain some order around heah."

"Haven't seen a thing, Tony," and Jim slides right by the 275 pounds, out the door and to the left, away from the scene down the street. "Later, mate," and Jim waves a farewell.

It's close to 1a.m. when Jim quietly closes the apartment door behind him and walks into the well lit living room. Marta puts down her tea cup and stands to give Jim a hug, one that he returns long and strong. Still wound together she turns her head, raising her eyebrows in question.

"It's all good, so far. It's good." Jim disentangles himself and hands Marta the folder.

Sitting back next to her cup, she opens the folder and reads the receipt, and the few notes Jim has from his meeting at the restaurant. Nodding, she puts the papers back and says, "Where do we have a safe place for these?"

"For now, they'll just be here in the apartment, maybe under your pile of fabric. Monday, they go to the safety deposit box at the bank. Kai will have to have power of attorney for that, too, if it needs opening while we are gone."

Marta nods and hands Jim the folder. "The wine is on the counter."

"What else has happened around here?" Jim is on his way to the kitchen as he looks back over his shoulder talking. "Did Xochitl have any success with dog transport?"

"She got some good information. I'll tell you when you come back out."

A pop from a cork and the tinkle of an ice cube falling into a glass comes from the kitchen, then Jim reappears with tumbler and glowing cigarette.

"First of all, that was a very good idea to have Xochitl be in charge of the dogs. She loves Sancho and Pedro probably more than either of us knows. She went to many places yesterday including 2 pet stores, expensive ones, the vet office and then called a shipping company and an airline when she came home. One pet store and the vet office told her the same thing. The other pet store people were just rude so she left right away. The system requires the dogs have immunizations before shipping. The best and least expensive shipping company is apparently Allied, the same company that moved our furniture. They ship overseas and have a specialty department just for shipping animals safely. Shipping straight to Madrid by boat and truck is the recommended way, and the quarantine period in Madrid will be waived if the vet makes the proper papers about the immunizations. The airline can take the dogs in travel crates if they come with us. We are flying, right?" Jim nods agreement. "The vet is open tomorrow, oh, look at the time, I mean today, so we can get the immunizations done today. Only the shipping company or the airline would have the information where the dogs are going, not the vet office. From the time the dogs are on the ship until they arrive is 3 weeks if the best ship is used. One is leaving in 10 days from the battery. So, we can send the dogs and be there when they arrive."

"How much?" is the growled response.

"Not so much. Only $850 for both dogs, by ship, $700 if they go by plane."

"What?! You're joking! That's more than getting us there, either way!"

"Jeem. Thees is important, no? You want to take the dogs, we all want to take the dogs. Xochitl worked very hard to get this information. Now you want to complain! Behave yourself!"

Jim sits, growls, takes a long pull on the wine, then a longer pull on the cigarette. "Arrgh! We'll make it out of here, but busted and poor as church mice. Aaaargh!"

Marta just sits and watches since she knows she has the upper hand, that Jim would never leave the dogs behind, and that the verbal storm will pass shortly. She lifts a piece of lined tablet paper and gives it to Jim. "Xochitl took the time to write everything down for you to read when you got home. Here. Our daughter did a good job."

Jim just looks at the paper until Marta waggles it in front of him, then reaches and takes it without looking at it. Folding it once longways, he deposits it in the breast pocket of his shirt and takes another swig from the glass. Finally, the shoulders start to come down and he says, "Tired. Got another big day tomorrow. Coming to bed?"

Marta gets up and slips her arm around Jim's middle, giving him a small pinch on what used to be his waistline. "Lets go. You can praise Xochitl in the daylight. Right?"

"Aargh!"

Breakfast is fairly quiet until Jim's second coffee is down. When his cup is again sitting on the table, he says to Xochitl, "So, Marta showed me what you were able to accomplish yesterday. Fairly impressive. I'll admit being put off by the cost quoted you by both Allied and the airline. Have you checked other shipping companies?"

"Sure. I checked 2 others, and they cost more. The airlines are about the same. Also, the only maritime company recommended by both the vet's office and the first pet store was Allied. So, seems a no brainer to me. What we going to do, leave the dogs here?"

"Don't go getting your knickers in a twist. I didn't say that. You hear me say we're leaving the dogs here?!"

Marta gives out a large "Harumph!" and both Jim and Xochitl look her way. "We have lots to do. Once things are done, you two can bicker as much as you want. Jim, you said already Xochitl did a good job, right?"

Silence, then "Right."

"Xochitl, do you really think Jim would leave these dogs here? I know they are precious to you. Do you think they are less precious to Jim? Really?"

Silence, then, "No."

"So, this arguing is not useful, at all, yes? It just gets in the way of doing things we have to do. Enough!" With that she provides each of the 2 with her patented Marta stare and both Jim and Xochitl look away first. "Now, what are the things we must do today? I think getting the dogs to the vet for immunizations should be done today. What do each of you think we should do today?"

"I have to call Frankie. Gotta put the bastard off long enough for us to make it out of here. We are due at the restaurant for dinner, but that's tomorrow evening. Xochie, what do you think needs doing for the dogs?"

Xochitl refuses to let it show, but she really enjoys being asked. "One of you will need to go to Allied with the immunization certificates, if we are shipping them by sea. They won't book a cargo for me since I don't look the part. Too young."

Marta nods and agrees, "Good idea. Jeem, I think you are the best one to go."

"Agreed. I look old enough. But, I think we need to think about this dog transport a bit more, as well as ours. Hold off on your evil looks for a minute, and just listen. OK?"

Marta and Xochitl slump a bit with exactly the same thought, 'Oh no, what now?'

"OK, look, it is less expensive to send them by air, right. Besides that, I need to be out of here very quickly, since I am the one that will be hunted, by the construction crew at least, maybe by process servers from the IRS or the banks. So, I need to leave in a week, but there are tasks needing sorting by someone still here, like cashing out our assets, arranging the power of attorney for Kai, arranging any sea freight for stuff we can't take on the plane. I think we should travel separately. Marta, you finish the financials and shipping sea freight, I go on ahead with the dogs on the plane, get us a car in Paris and transport the dogs from Paris to Madrid. We'll schedule a flight for the 2 of you for a week later and I will meet you in Madrid with a place to stay. I will telegraph Tony Arizza today to start working on accommodation. That way, one of us will be with the dogs all the way, the essential details are accomplished and I am out of the firing line for pissed off folks. The construction project will be terminated September first when they find the air conditioners gone. I need to be gone then. It would be really nice if we all were, but I don't see how everything can get finished and we all leave in a week. There, that's what I have been working on instead of sleeping. I realize this is not the plan you thought was in place, so what do you think?"

Xochitl assumes Marta's previous posture causing Jim to smile, then says, "I don't know what to think. I don't like us not all together. Momma?"

Marta is very quiet, examining the contents of her coffee cup, then looks up, one corner of her mouth curled up, "I agree, even though I also don't like traveling separately. Pedro and Sancho will do better if someone they know is there immediately on arrival, rather than having to live longer in kennels. It will be nice to know a place for us to stay is waiting for Xochitl and me in Madrid. So, I agree." With that she looks at Xochitl, who has tears starting in the corners of her eyes, reaches over and takes her hand. "It will be OK, chica."

Xochitl looks from one to the other, then nods. Straightening her slumped shoulders she gets up from the table saying, "I can get the dogs to the vet if you give me their Kennel Club papers. Poppa, I assume you will be calling the airline, right?"

Jim's smile is reward enough, and the nod sends them all scrambling to get the list of chores accomplished for the day.

Shots delivered to the placid dogs, Xochitl heads back to the apartment to drop them off, then catches a bus to Woolworths. Jim folds the immunization certificates and heads to the airline booking office. He and Marta have already taken an inventory of the apartment, noting those items that MUST come with them to Spain. This list is not extensive, but is still more than they can take on the plane, so will get shipped by sea. While Jim is making the airline bookings Marta will be arranging the shipping of the household goods at Allied shipping lines.

Allied offices are facing the Battery, near the docks at the south end of Manhattan, the shipping piers just around the bend and up the East River. The offices are utilitarian, business like, not fancy, but functional. Marta inquires at the desk and is led to a clerk at a separate desk to the rear. Looking up, the middle aged, long-serving grey-headed man says, "Whataya got?"

Not seeing any chairs nearby, Marta goes two desks over and claims a vacant one and sits down. Manny, the grey-headed clerk, has watched the performance, leans back and smiles as Marta says, "My family and I have about 1 and a half cubic meters of household good as cargo for Madrid to depart on your ship in 9 days. I brought my checkbook to pay the freight. What you got?"

Manny, the shirt-sleaved, long-serving clerk, reaches into a desktop filing slot extracting a multipage form saying, "I got your sign up sheet right 'chere. Name?"

And they are off and running. Fifteen minutes later Marta is out the door with the three sheets of shipping forms and $450 lighter in their bank account. The crate will be on its way by noon on departure day. Not bad for a quarter hour's work.

The unexpected efficiency at the airline booking office has given Jim a few hours of "free time" that he decides to use by heading to Ray and then the construction site. Instead of calling Frankie, he'll see him in person, just to practice his ability at restraint. A quick call from a phone booth allows him to check what Marta was able to accomplish and update her with his current information, and his immediate plan. She is already back home, but offers to go by the hardware store and get them to deliver the materials they need for constructing the crate for their treasures. Phone back on the cradle, Jim heads to see Ray, collects the cash, confirms the date and time for air conditioner transfer then to the subway which will deposit him 2 blocks from the construction project. It's still an hour before he was to call Frankie. Good. There are advantages to surprise.

At the construction, Jim stands across the street in a shadowed doorway and watches for about half an hour. What he sees reinforces all decisions he and Marta have made. There is considerably more discussion than production going on, every trip up stairs or down is very deliberate, two people are carrying things easily carried by one. His temper rising, Jim decides it is time to go into action. Exiting the doorway, Jim dodges a horn-tooting taxi and heads across the street calling out, "Frankie!"

The stout, clipboard carrying, cigar smoking fellow with grey at his temples wearing a yellow hard hat turns abruptly with a vague smile that vanishes just as quickly, shades his eyes and puts down the clipboard on the trestle nearby. "Yeah, Jim, whatcha doin heah? Thought yous was callin!"

Jim's posture tells the story, long deliberate strides, head forward, shoulders hunched, arms vigorously swinging, eyes clearly focused on his target, Frankie. "Got the time, this is better for what we got to say." The voice is a booming box of gravel. "Over to your truck!"

The meeting is noticed by everyone within the entire block, everyone within earshot. That includes the entire workforce who have halted their desultory charade. Frankie glances to his left, not wanting to take his eyes off the bull charging at him and gives a perfunctory, "Keep woikin yous guys. Whadaya think this is, a holiday?" He's talking as he is edging toward his company panel van with the logo of a smiling, happy building on the side.

Meeting at the work side of the van, Jim jerks his thumb to the side indicating they should move to the far side, away from the eyes of the interested crowd. At the other side, Jim leans in, looking slightly up at the taller, beefier Frankie, lowers his volume and starts his prepared remarks, "What the fuck you pullin here, asshole? We have a contract, and your worthless crowd of social misfits is doggin it. I've been watching from across the street and I've done this work, myself, with Marta. You know it, and you know she and I could have gotten twice as much done in the past half hour than your band of loafers have done. You know I have rental agreements that will get canceled if this job doesn't come in on time. You also know I have financial obligations depending on those rental agreements. Now, you and your motley crew are wanting to change the deal, squeeze me for more money. What the fuck is going on?"

Frankie has been leaning back into the side of the van, looking slightly down at a seriously deranged face and 2 clenched fists. He is well aware of Jim's reputation, even heard rumors about an encounter last night, recognizes the precarious position he's in and stammers a bit with, "Look, Jim. Don't go gettin' all huffy at me. I'm just the messenger, ya know. The guys have been havin' extra expenses an all, coming all the way over here, some of 'em from Staten Island an' all, ya know that ferry ain't cheap. They just figgered ya could afford a bit more an' they say they need it, an' all, an…"

"Shut the fuck up. Who you think you're talkin' to. Some upper crust Long Island idiot from the Hamptons?"

Frankie, slides slightly to his left, shifts his weight back and forth foot to foot, then straightens slightly with, "Look. They ain't askin' for no big changes, are they? No! Just a little more an hour, for what, anudder munt. You got it. I know it, you know it. Why you all aggervated?" This last is delivered with a slight supplicant posture, well practiced.

Jim is perfectly in tune with Frankie's performance, but does not let up with his own. He and Marta are prepared to comply with the demand, which will mean one week of inflated paychecks before he is away. That week will, hopefully buy him a safe exit for parts unknown to Frankie, Tony, the IRS, everyone except Kai. So, this performance has to be good, and the cave-in to demands appear reluctant in the extreme. It'll be fine if Frankie is a bit intimidated. Actually, it's OK if he's a lot intimidated. Gotta get some satisfaction out of it. "Aggervated!? What the fuck is that word?! I'm not 'aggervated'; I'm pissed as hell. Why did you think you got this contract in the first place? Huh? Because your labor costs were below everyone else's, and you guaranteed, GUARANTEED MIND YOU, to bring the project in on time. You're the foreman on the job. What's your job, eh? WHAT?"

Frankie starts dancing foot to foot again, not looking Jim in the eye, stammering, "I know what the job is, fer crissake. Whadaya think I am, stupid or sumpin'?"

"Stupid would be a step up. You're squeezin' me, and you know it. I am not enjoying myself. Ya noticed?"

"Yeah, ya doan look real happy. Can ya calm down a minnit so we can talk heah? Huh? Calm down, OK?" Shift, shift, foot to foot, head slumped, hands fidgeting. Now, it's not much of a show. Anxiety is starting to creep into the performance.

Jim notices, takes a half step back and tilts his head to one side. The scowl stays right where it was, but there is less edge to the gravel coming out as he says, "What!? I don't look calm? I'm calm. See, see how relaxed I am? So, talk. Tell me something that will keep me calm."

"OK, Jim. Yeah, we gotta contract, for sure. I gotta reputation ta consider, heah, ya know. People around heah expect me to bring projects in on time, fuh shuah, so I am not happy these jerks are doin' whut theys doin'. Not happy at all. Do I look like a happy man? Whadaya think?"

"So, what are you going to do about it?"

"Whut can I do? I can't go find anudder crew dis late in the process. Dese guys know dat, so theys takin' advantage. Theys burned a bridge wid me fur shuah, but dats da fyuchah. Dis is now. Cancha give me sumpin to give 'em to smood dis ting ovah? Sumpin, maybe a liddle less than what dey said, but sumpin."

The negotiating has started and Jim smiles internally. He's thinking fuck 'em, while he's swaying, "So, what do you think they'll take. You know these guys, I don't. What?"

Frankie's shoulders visibly relax, his head comes half way back up and almost a smile shows at the corners of his mouth. "I figger dey'll take 50 cents an hour, instead of the dollah I said on the phone. Dey tole me a dollah, but I got a feelin' half'll do it."

The scowl stays on Jim's face, with difficulty. He steps back and turns slightly away while performing the contemplation 2-step, lean to the left, eyebrows up and down, lean to the right, wiggle calculating fingers as the complex formulas are apparently whirling around in his head. He slowly turns back to face Frankie again, a look of resignation comes across his face, then stern eye contact with, "That's robbery, and you know it, but I think we can just manage it, if the project comes in the week before scheduled. No overtime involved, just busting a few humps, and 50 cents an hour it is."

Frankie is obviously humble while a YES! is reverberating in his head and says, "I tink that sort of motivator will get the job done, and a week ahead of schedule."

"Good, write it up and bring it to me this afternoon before 5. I gotta go out after 5 so be there on time. Write it and sign it, 2 copies. I'll sign it and give you one. Marta won't be happy." He just had to throw that zinger in because he is fully aware that Frankie knows of Marta's advocacy for any workers. "Be there, before 5, right?"

"Right, Jim. Ya got it, no problem."

Jim turns, walks left down the block and dives into a taxi. Frankie, once Jim is out of sight, turns and fist pumps in the air to a chorus of cheers from the gang. Then he bellows, "We got tuh get dis ting done a week aheada schedule. I put in enough slack into da ting to allow for dat. But, ya gotta get off yous asses to get it done. Get ta work!" With that, the energy on the site lifted considerably, men split into their teams some actually jogged upstairs to resume their tasks, and the 2 man carrying teams split into singles each carrying twice what 2 had carried before. The industry of the place is as impressive as the smile on Frankie's face. The other guys were obviously impressed with their accomplishments as well. It was a happy work site this sunny August morning.

At the apartment, Jim finds Marta has cleared the walls stacking the art and photos into piles, and has started on the books. The living room shelves are cleared with the go or no-go categories in their stacks, empty crate in the middle of the floor. As the door slightly slams behind him, Marta wipes a wisp of hair from her forehead and gives Jim a large smile. "You want to check these stacks of books to be sure I saved the ones most important to you?"

"Sure, but first, come here." With that he opens his arms and Marta marches right in. A long embrace with a kiss is followed by a quick review of his meetings, at the airline office, showing the plane tickets, and the fact he went by the construction site and those results. Marta lets him know the schedule for the household goods being shipped while she snuggles within his embrace. The paperwork can be reviewed later.

Retreating slightly, she looks at Jim and asks, "So, you sure Frankie believed you, and we have a deal?"

"I imagine the place is humming right now. I saw Frankie start sweating a bit, and was willing to contribute a little more to his anxiety if needed, but it wasn't necessary. They think they have a great deal going. When you have a chance, can you figure the new wages total and go ahead and cut a check to Frankie to cover it for this week? The deposit money for the air conditioners is in the bank, so the check should be good. Might as well start getting real numbers into what we have available." They break their embrace and Jim looks around the room again with, "You've done a lot already. We may be packed by this weekend."

"I was hoping we could be. I do not like rushing last minute, you know."

"I know. OK, should I start on books in the bedroom?"

"Sure. Then look at these piles I did and we will start filling the crate."

The packing is underway. The furniture will stay right where it is. This building will be going to the bank anyway. Xochitl's room is left for her to sort. No one wants that level of aggravation resulting from messing with her things. Packing continues right through the afternoon until time to clean up and get ready for Frankie's visit. Xochitl is not expected until late tonight.

Tap, tap, tap. The knock is light. It is 4:45, so Jim suspects who it might be. Opening the door, he smiles seeing Frankie in a sport coat, no tie, regular shoes rather than work boots. "Marta, Frankie is here. Can you put the pot on?" It is already boiled, so the act is still being applied.

"I will, hi. Frankie," comes from the kitchen.

"Hi Marta," is returned, from the foyer. The frosted glass door to the living room is only cracked open, so the chaos in there is out of sight.

Jim indicates a move to the left, and the 2 men head down a corridor toward the back of the apartment and the deck in back. The back door to the living room is closed so they ease out onto the deck and each take a chair. Clicking sounds precede the dogs launching themselves up the stairs, stumps of tails wagging furiously, and Frankie's khaki trousers are immediately slobbered upon. "DOGS!" And both sit. "Sorry about that mate. They obviously like your company, but now they've messed up your nice outfit."

"Not a problem, Jim. Not a problem," as Frankie takes out a handkerchief and starts wiping himself down.

Marta appears with a tray of coffee and tea, a fresh coffee cake, cups, saucers and a smile. "Hello, Frankie. I am happy to see you." The winning smile melts any difficulties Frankie had been anticipating, he takes coffee, 3 sugars and a bit, cream and is stirring while Jim pours his coffee and Marta pours her tea.

Marta says, "We have not talked much since the construction started. Do you think it is good?"

"Oh yeah. The guys are bustin their humps. It will be done early, like I told Jim."

"Is this because they now are making more money? Jim told me about the deal."

"The extra little bit sure helps their attitude. Sure does. Yep. That was good."

"I remember when the project started that they seemed very happy to be working. It was strange, then, that they suddenly were not happy any more. Do you have any idea what made them unhappy?" This last is said with as angelic a face on Marta as Jim has ever seen. He's thinking there may be acting in her future somewhere.

"No idea what happened, Marta. The times are getting tough lately, so I guess they just felt they needed a bit more money."

Jim is nearly choking on his bit of coffee cake, but manages to get it down without coughing, then says, "Whatever. You have the agreement in that folder, 2 copies?"

"Sure. Right here," and he pulls out two copies of the 1 page document for Jim and Marta to read. It is simple enough, not needing more discussion, and both Jim and Marta sign them, as does Frankie. Jim hands Frankie his copy and they stand.

Normally, Marta, being Marta, would give a big farewell hug, but this time she extends her hand with half a smile on her face as Frankie readies to leave. This stings, since he recognizes the difference for what it is. He has always enjoyed Marta's company. They have actually known each other since the first tenement she and Jim renovated, 6 years ago. Nevertheless, he then extends his hand to Jim, who shakes it, turns without comment and starts for the door. "I'll see you to the door," says Jim.

"I know where it is."

"That's alright, I gotta be polite, right?"

"I will come, too," says Marta. "It is only correct when a friend is leaving, no?"

Frankie stops, looks at Marta, slightly shakes his head with a wry half smile, and gives a small nod. The 3 make their way back down the corridor to the front door and Frankie exits, turning back briefly and Jim salutes him with a wave of his copy of the agreement. Frankie lifts the folder in returned salute, and heads down the front steps and is away. Jim turns, closes the door and tears up the agreement, tossing it into the waste basket in the living room. A half smile crosses his face as he says, "Back to work."

Marta comes up, snuggles into his arms and they just stand among the chaos for a moment before she says, "I was not happy with Frankie. It was not fair."

"He knows. You told him, loud and clear. Now, lets do some more packing. We won't be doing any tomorrow evening. We have Kai, remember?"

"Of course I remember. You start on the filing cabinet, OK? I am in the bedroom." And they are back at it, hardly noticing the interruption.

The last of the day passes, well occupied with preparations and packing, so by that night the place looks almost completely torn upside down.

The next day packing resumes.

Xochitl has started on her things, her pile for the crate double in size to Jim and Marta's, and Jim's tone unforgiving about getting it whittled down. Xochitl complains, somewhat bitterly, to a face of stone. She recognizes it and starts reworking what is essential. Through fits and spurts all day the apartment is reorganized into departure and remaining piles. Things are progressing quite nicely.

Time for Jim and Marta to go. Xochitl is out again. She's obviously feeling the separation already. As Jim and Marta close the door to their apartment, they stop and look at the slightly organized mayhem inside, the shipping crate half full, the dogs moving carefully through the rubble sniffing at everything slightly anxiously. "You boys guard the house, OK?" With that reminder from Jim, they close the door and head downstairs to get a taxi.

"We are doing well, Jeem, eh?"

"We are, given the circumstances. We'll make it. This meeting with Kai is important, but I want to enjoy the meal as well. Last one." With that, Jim glances at the driver, who is apparently not attending to the quiet conversation in the back.

"It is OK, Jeem, we are quiet and he is not listening." Marta smiles her best, it melts Jim as usual, and they settle into the seat for the ride.

Kai meets the taxi at the curb, pays the driver himself and ushers Jim and Marta into the restaurant. Jim never had that happen before, with Kai, and the novelty is a bit unnerving. But, Kai smiles as he points to the table and there is a chilled bottle alongside the table with the aperitifs already set out on the 2 places. "Please to sit down. Marta, I should help you."

"This is a little much, Kai. Aren't you very busy this evening?" Jim is looking around and most of the tables are occupied.

"Oh, busy enough, but this is important evening, and each customer who orders the Peking Duck has this service. This not so strange service, no. Are you upset?"

Jim smiles one of his best saying, "Not at all. I am happy, but not used to this. Thank you." That produces visible relaxation from Kai who retreats toward the kitchen, even though he is in a fine suit and not his apron.

The dinner is one of the best they have ever had, the service is perfect. Kai stops by the table during the serving of tea following the meal. "We can talk more here or maybe in the private dining room. What do you like Jim?

"I think there is not much to say so we can talk here. Will your staff be surprised if you are sitting with us?"

"I think no because I have told them this is your special night, and I am responsible. Even if they think it is strange, they will say nothing. No problem, correct?"

"Correct. Is here OK with you, Marta?"

"For sure. I think Kai should have tea also."

"Sitting is good. Drinking tea is not. It is different, so I will not drink tea."

"Fine. As far as I am concerned, the details of our deal are that you organize the sale of the building, you receive 12.5% of the net after expenses, deposit the remainder in the bank and message us once the deal is finished and the money deposited. Here is the deed to the property. It is without a mortgage. Marta will bring the paper listing you as power of attorney for the sale and for access to the safety deposit box at our bank where there are important papers that must stay here in New York. She will bring it next week once the lawyer has completed it. And, here is the master key to the building being sold." With that, Jim slides a tidy packet to Kai who slips the packet onto his lap.

"That is what I remember also. I did not know about the safety deposit box, but that is no problem for me. Is the contact detail for you in these papers?"

"No. I will let you know when we have those details available. For now, you will be the only person in the USA with that information. Is this clear?"

Kai slightly bows his head with, "Perfectly."

"I will contact you here at the restaurant either by phone or by letter once we have those details for you. For now you can know that we will probably contact you from Spain."

There is no change in facial expression as Kai says, "Fine."

"I leave in a few days, Marta and Xochitl will come one week after. They will not be at our apartment, the one you know. They will be in the city making the final arrangements including the paperwork from the lawyer. She will call you when she has the papers to arrange for you to collect them. Perhaps you can come to her to get the papers, OK? It may be safer than her coming here where people know her."

The expressionless nod is all Jim receives from Kai, then the faintest of smiles.

Jim stands, takes Marta's hand and looks at Kai saying, "A true friend is indeed worth more than gold."

Kai has stood and offers his right hand to Jim who takes it wordlessly with a smile. Then Jim and Marta turn and leave the restaurant. At the entrance, the receptionist smiles and says, "I hope your dinner was as you expected."

Jim stops briefly with, "Beyond words, young fellow, beyond words." With that, he and Marta leave one of their favorite places, probably for the last time.

Xochitl is home listening to music when they arrive. "Hi. How was dinner?"

"Excellent. Kai outdid himself tonight. What a way to go out. How was your evening?" That is delivered with a wry smile.

"What's that look about? We went back to Woolworths, then to Times Square. I told them I was getting my stuff later, that's all. They all looked at me like I was brainless or something. I think Jerry is suspicious, but he got nothing from me. Promise."

"I certainly hope so. Jerry's uncle is Tony Sylvano and he's the last person I want knowing anything. Kai's lips are sealed I am certain. Would you agree?" His eyebrows go up toward Marta questiongly and she nods vigorously.

"Oh yes. Kai's quiet, for sure. Do you think the vet and the shipping and airline agents are OK?"

"Sure. What do they know? Next, it's the air conditioners. That's in two days. I got that organized, I'm pretty sure. I'll double check tomorrow. In the meantime, we have tons to accomplish here. Xoch, you got your room partially taken care of, right?"

"Already started. All the posters are down and my clothes are in 3 piles, here, go and maybe. Artwork is still a question. How much room do we have to pack stuff?"

Marta stands and takes Xochitl by the hand leading her over to the crate. "Everything left to take has to fit in there."

Xochitl looks, steps back slightly and tilts her head toward Jim. "You're kidding. My stuff has to fit in that space? Isn't there another crate?"

"No. Your stuff, my stuff and Marta's stuff has to fit in there."

"Aw! Come on! You can't be serious."

Jim stands slowly, and moves to beside Xochitl. "Deadly serious. This is not a game, Xoch. We are making a clean getaway, for the rest of our lives. Because it is necessary." His eyes are not smiling, his voice is an octave lower than usual, barely audible.

Xochitl's head droops, and tears are at the edges of her eyes, but she will not let any fall. Her head comes up. "Fine." With that, she gives Marta a peck on the cheek and walks firmly into her bedroom, solidly shutting the door.

Marta looks at Jim and he simply says, "She'll be fine."

"I know that. It's just hard, you know."

"I know. And now, so does she. Let's get to bed."

Two days of strenuous packing and pretending follow. Jim has confirmed the schedule and arrangements for the air conditioners, the dogs' air travel crates are confirmed, plane tickets in hand, shipping company confirmed for collecting the sea freight crate. The household crate is closed and labeled. Jim's flight to Paris is looming. But first, tonight, the midnight requisition of air conditioners. The first half of the sale price has been deposited with some of it going toward plane tickets and visas. The rest of the cash will be paid just prior to the launch of the extractions tonight. That will get deposited tomorrow, or maybe taken with them. Jim looks carefully at Marta and says, "I think it would be good if we changed my plane ticket to tomorrow. Frankie will find the air conditioners gone in the morning and be over here in a second. The crate leaves at 7, we can leave right after. I can head to the airport with the dogs, you and Xochitl take your bags and head over to Henrietta's apartment. Her offering it while she is away was one of the luckiest breaks ever. You have the key, right?" Marta dangles a house key on a short leather thong, swinging it back and forth in front of Jim's eyes. "Gotta be gone before the crew arrives at the work site."

"Give me your ticket and confirmation and I'll call the airlines while you are out. We can take the air conditioner cash with us on our trip?"

"We'll have to split it between you and me, maybe with Xoch as well, so no one is carrying more than the maximum allowed. It will be OK." That brings a small smile from Marta.

As 11p.m. approached, Jim was dressed in his best dark, unobtrusive clothes, long sleeves and all, even in the heat of the New York summer evening. Holding the packet of remaining warranty certificates, he gives Marta a hug and she quietly wishes him godspeed. Xochitl has already gone to bed so her best wishes have already been applied. As the door closes, Marta is on the phone to the airlines.

A quick march to the corner and he spots a taxi on the other side of the street. A whistle and a U turn gets him on his way. The address he gives is two blocks from the work site, just for safety sake. The street is deserted as he watches the departing taxi and reverses direction, turns right and heads down the parallel street to the construction. The plan is to get there at least half an hour early to watch for watchers.

Mid block, he enters an alley perpendicular to the main street and walks the block. At the corner, he peeks around the edge of the building and sees... nothing. At least nothing interesting to him. The street has a few parked vehicles on both sides, the area fronting the construction site is clear of vehicles, there does not seem to be anyone loitering about. Nothing. Slouching against the building, Jim settles in to wait.

Ten minutes later, 15 minutes before midnight, a flatbed truck comes slowly up the street, left to right in front of Jim, who slides into the shadows. The truck parks directly in front of the building and a car parks beside the truck. While Jim watches, Ray Lombard exits the driver's door of the car, 3 men exit the back and 1 the passenger door while Ray is telling the driver and

2 others to get out of the truck. Eight men, each with a small tool belt are milling about on the sidewalk, then 2 men unhitch the rolling dollies from the bed of the truck and leave the restraining straps dangling on either side. It looks like they are prepared, so Jim saunters out of the alley and up to Ray.

"Good timing. As far as I can tell, no one else is around. Be sure the guys know to keep the noise to a minimum, OK?"

"They know. What the fuck you think this is, amateur hour?"

"That's exactly what I think it is. Never mind. Here's the keys. There are unopened boxes on the second floor. The rest of the machines are already installed, but the installation is quick removal. They are heavy, so don't drop any. You break it, you still bought it. Got it?"

"Why you such a hard ass tonight? 'Course we got it. Gimme the keys."

"Just a bit touchy, that's all. Been a bit of a rough week, if you know what I mean. Relax. I am guessing we are in and out in an hour, right?"

"Good guessing. I'll move my car. Ed, here's the keys. Six boxes second floor, unopened, the rest are in the windows. We got an hour, OK?"

"Won't need it. Let's go guys."

With that, the dismantling of 45 air conditioner installations gets under way. Jim has to admit, he's impressed. There is hardly a peep out of the group, the group works like a well oiled machine. The truck is half full in 20 minutes and Jim says, "Shit, should have had your guys on this project from the start. They work well together."

"They been a team 5 years now. Took a while, but Ed keeps 'em in line, they get paid well. It works."

Another 20 minutes and the driver is securing the load to the bed of the truck. Jim and Ray meet in the alley, Ray handing Jim a fat envelope, Jim handing over the remaining warranty certificates. Jim makes a serious but cursory examination of the money and it seems accurate. No flashing cash around here. A hand shake, nod, and Jim reverses direction heading back down the alley, turns left at the street, crosses the street and hails a cab. He's back at the apartment in two hours and ten minutes from when he left.

Marta is still up, reading in the living room, when Jim unlocks the door and enters. Looking up, she asks, "Is it OK? You have not been away too long?"

Jim waves the envelope at her, drops it in her lap and the keys to the construction site on the table.

Marta is busy counting, finishes, smiles and says, "I called the airline and changed the flight. It is the middle of the week now, so I don't think the flight will be full. The dogs are also set to go.

"Good. I'll get up early and feed the dogs. Where is the anti-anxiety medicine for them?"

"In the medicine cabinet in the bathroom. One pill only, each one, yes?"

"Yes. I will be careful."

"I know. Just nervous I think. This is a very big thing, Jeem. I never did a thing like this before."

"I know, and we have been a splendid team, even Xochitl. Now we are on the last laps. We are OK. The shipping truck will be here at 7a.m. The household crate is ready, right?"

"All closed up, labels applied. The dogs are sleeping now. I think everything is ready."

"Right. I am up at 6. Going to bed. We're away tomorrow. Better let Xoch know tonight, OK?'

"Sure. Good night. What time do we go?"

"I suggest we are out of here before 8. What do you think?"

"Good. Goodnight. I'll talk to Xoch."

The family has exited the apartment, nearly exhausted from the frenzy of the morning, 5 til 8 a.m. and are closing the backdoor to the airport limousine that is taking Jim and the dogs to the airport, loaded to the gills with luggage, people and animals. Marta and Xochitl will ride back into the city to Henrietta's apartment after seeing Jim off at Idlewylde. The backdoor slams, the engine starts and as the limo pulls away, Frankie's truck with the smiling building logo pulls right in behind, coming to a sudden stop. Since the windows on the limo are tinted, Jim turns full face toward the rear window to see Frankie launch himself out of the driver's door of the truck and leap 3 steps at a time up to the entrance of the apartment building. He's frantically banging away at the call button for the Tuck apartment as the limo turns right around the end of the block and they are away. Jim smiles ever so slightly at the image of Frankie frantically banging away at the buzzer. Finally he turns forward on the seat, grasps Marta's hand in his and gives Xochitl in the jump seat opposite his full JT smile. The boxers are lying in a heap on the floor with their leashes in place, snoring. Away they are, Idlewylde Airport, here they come.

The airport is crowded, the flight to Paris is on time, but not for an hour and a half, so waiting seems forever. After the hectic check-in process, the leading of the dogs into the baggage processing area to their travel crates, checking their water, they are back to the departure lounge. This is the same area Xochitl and Marta will come to for their flight to Madrid.

Jim's patience has always been a thing in short supply and he fidgets, starts getting short with Xochitl until

Marta runs her hand over his shoulders and whispers in his ear, causing a sudden relaxation and a short nod from Jim. Xoch walks the short distance to a kiosk where she buys gum and a candy bar, things she never usually buys, and returns to their seat near the departure gait. "How long is your ride to Paris, Poppy?"

Jim gives her a quick glance, to which Marta responds with a solid nudge in the ribs. "Eight hours, Bud. It's still eight hours, like it was 7 minutes and 30 seconds ago." Two solid nudges and a grunt and he is still again.

"Do you have a pain, Poppy? You're grunting several times lately."

"Y--, grunt, no, not really just a bit nervous about getting going is all." Marta nods.

"OK. I understand. It does seem like forever, doesn't it. Oh well. Rome wasn't built in a day, right?" Smile, Jim squirms under Marta's gaze, everyone settles just as the announcement for boarding the flight to Paris. One last look around, hugs and kisses for Xochitl and Marta, with Marta's extended, hand the attendant the paper boarding pass, down the stairs, and Jim is gone from sight. Marta gently grips Xochitl's hand as they turn to retrace their steps to find the waiting limo.

CHAPTER 2

Away to Madrid

Eight hours and 15 minutes later Jim lands in Paris, negotiates customs and immigration, collects his bags and wends his way to the special baggage area to retrieve the dogs. From previous trips to the city, Jim gives the driver the name of a moderately priced hotel that is advertised as pet friendly and not far from the main attractions of the city. Buying transportation to get to Madrid is the priority for the next two days. The city lights are enough to keep him alert, given the late local hour and fatigue that is settling in. Just the details of checking in, getting to his room after walking the dogs in the nearby park keeps him going for a while. Then it is sleeping-in the next day, park-walk again, feeding the dogs on the grass, rest period, time out, whatever you want to call it. He has finished with the first leg of the journey. He realizes he has a pretty good team. The next two days he mostly spends his time buying the family transportation, for Paris to Madrid and beyond, a 1961

Volvo 404 sedan, dirty white. Getting the car purchased, for cash, serviced and loaded on the second day made his departure later in the afternoon, so he barely made it to south central France before stopping for the evening.

Jim had telegraphed Tony Arizza in Madrid, at Torrejon Air Base, prior to departing Paris, but had not received a response before leaving. He had known, for almost a year, of Tony's presence in Madrid, actually still in the Air Force. They had only exchanged 2 letters when the shit hit the family finances fan, and Tony had not seemed a priority contact at the time. He was now. So, that first evening, Jim chose an accommodation where guest services would probably be better, and they were. After checking in, Jim sent another cable to Tony, giving him his current location and the recommendation that Tony keep that information to himself. He also asked Tony to scout for suitable accommodation that will take a couple of dogs as well as the family, and gave Tony a rough ETA for his arrival with Pedro and Sancho. The message included a shortened version of the day's overall travel plan so Tony could better anticipate who he would be looking for. Jim went to bed that night without a response.

First thing next morning there is a quiet knock on the door. Jim answers it and the bellman hands Jim a pink message envelope. Tip passed, Jim closes the door and opens the message. Tony is there, in Madrid, looking forward to everyone's arrival, is not certain how long he will be stationed in Madrid but not to worry. "Safe travels." When Jim met Tony in Manila he had been a Captain in the US Army Air Corps. The telegram is signed off as Colonel Arizza, USAF. Nice level to retire at, Jim is thinking. Must be about time for retirement for Tony. It was 1939 when Jim and Tony had last engaged, to Jim's definite benefit. Twenty-four years ago. Long time. At least Tony is now closer to his Basque roots. "Five days and I'm there," is running through Jim's head. Not rushing. Still, looking forward to it.

September in Paris is grand. The tourist crowds have thinned considerably with schools starting, families needing to be home, the August escape for the French completed. Finding a suitable car took Jim and the dogs into interesting neighborhoods; buying the car was an adventure in itself, but successfully concluded.

For once, Jim decides to take the scenic route, which is less direct but allows visiting Barcelona first as well as following Jim's stomach. He has always enjoyed French food, and has planned the trip through the French countryside to sample as many different regional specialties as he can pack in. Then there is also one night in Barcelona which will definitely be worth it. The second morning he receives the directions from Tony to Calle

Lagasca in the area known as Salamanca in Madrid, which satisfies his need for directions in Madrid. The rest is following the maps through southern France, then east to the border and Barcelona. Barcelona to Madrid is a full day's driving, but with the address, maps and local assistance he's confident, and more relaxed than he has been in years.

Barcelona is everything Jim hoped and anticipated, and the twisted drive to Madrid is complemented by the scenery. Arriving in the bustling city almost feels like deja vu, back in New York, except it isn't. A city map, 2 stops to ask specific directions and finally he is driving in the last rays of evening sunlight heading north on Calle Lagasca, back windows wide open with the dogs heads hanging out, examining buildings for street numbers. Going slowly enrages some of the commuters trying to get home, which is dutifully ignored. Driving past a patisserie there is a roared TUCK! Jim jolts the car to a halt, examines the patrons and suddenly sees a vaguely familiar face emerging from one of the tables. Mother of God, it's Arizza!

Tony bounds over to the passenger side of the car that is blocking serious rush hour traffic, stoops down and says, "Right at the alley, park in back." A quick rub of Sancho's head, Pedro is hanging out the opposite window, and then Jim gives a thumbs up and relieves the pressure building behind the car by inching forward then turning right.

Gratefully extracting themselves from the car, each of the three stretches and wiggles. Pedro does a firm rub along Jims lower leg, briefly entangling himself with Sancho's leash. Jim locks the car and heads back to the street with both dogs out front, slightly straining each leash. The reunion with Tony Arizza is Latin in the extreme with hugs, kisses on both cheeks, hand shaking and constant jabbering on Tony's part. Jim's usual discomfort at tactile closeness is put on hold as he genuinely appreciates seeing the man who helped extricate him from a Manila prison. What a lifetime ago, but the grey temples and energetic fitness belie Tony's age. Tony leads Jim to the table he has been occupying, making room for the dogs by extracting one of the chairs, pointing to a chair for Jim.

Sitting down, there is an extended silence as they take in the scene from each perspective. Jim leans back, stretching his legs out straight with Pedro on the left and Sancho, tongue lolling out of the side of his mouth on the right, each head near Jim's hip, getting the Tuck rub but Jim doing the purring. Tony is grinning at the scene, never having seen Jim with animals before. Finally, Jim and Tony start talking simultaneously, laugh then Jim raises one hand offering Tony the floor, so to speak. "This is just too much, too much. Many days I have wondered what you got up to, how you fared after Manila. I did get the package delivered to South Manila by the way. And here you are, with these amazing dogs, your women arriving tomorrow. Carmen is so looking forward to meeting Marta. I am completing my time with the Air Force, here at Torrejon Air Base. I hope to be around a couple more years, then home to Bilbao. Good duty here, even if it is a bit boring. The natives are a bit touchy about so many Amereicans occupying their territory and I get involved about once weekly with some dust up, but so far it's good duty. Haven't flown in 3 years, riding a desk into the sunset. OK. Your turn." He looks at Jim with eyebrows raised in expectation.

"Thanks for running that errand. I assumed it got there, but had no way to confirm. After leaving Manila, I spent a bit of time in Zamboanga. "

Tony smiles then, "I realized that you may not have made it all the way back to the States as planned. There were reports of suspected contact with this unruly American, mostly through Pettit Barracks, but not much more. Seems there was some excitement involved later, not sure what that was about."

"I'll fill you in about some, not all, of it later. Eventually, I made it back to California, Los Angeles, met Marta through a mutual friend and have been around a bit before the three of us landed in New York city where we've been for several years. Xochitl is in her senior year at high school, Marta has a boutique fabric painting business. We had been doing well until this year when things pretty well went belly up financially. So, we decided on a change of scenery, and both Xochitl and Marta love the idea of Spain, even though they've never been here before. Marta's family was poor in the mountains of Mexico. She essentially escaped to Los Angeles, where we met." Just then the waiter approaches Tony and asks if his friend wants anything. Jim automatically responds with a request, bringing a smile to both Tony and the waiter.

Over dinner, 25 years of personal history pass between Jim and Tony with Jim's hands feeding his face or stroking the dogs. Tony remembers his version of Jim's removal from Manila, with Jim noting his objections here and there, Tony skims over a career in the Air Force that he expects to finish with retirement in 5 years or so. Jim cruises through Zamboanga, barest minimums of the necessity of his escape, describes meeting Marta in Los Angeles, then it's merchant marines until the war is nearly finished, move to Woodstock with a new family, marketing for a South American coffee cartel, shifting permanently to New york (he thought), entrepreneurship and producing, then restoration of buildings; finally

Madrid. A few of the details come out, after the first bottle of wine is empty, but much is left unsaid. Finally, Tony asks about Xochitl and school.

"She's a senior. Supposed to graduate this year. I understand there is an American school at the air base. Do you know about it?"

"I know where it is, never been inside, but it is supposed to have an interesting bunch of kids there. We can go see it, talk to the people running it, see what you think. Probably Monday after they arrive?"

"Sure. We have plenty to do but that's near the top of the list. You seemed to think there was a possibility of a place for us to stay, to rent here in town, some place that'll take the dogs?"

"Just up the street, actually. That's why I suggested we meet here in my telegram. The rent seems reasonable for Madrid, plenty of room with 2 bedrooms, it has its own fence which is convenient since we are still locking ourselves in for curfew every night."

Jim's eyebrows lift with the question that explodes out of his mouth. "Curfew!? What curfew? I didn't know anything about a curfew!"

"Not to worry, Jim. So far, it has not really gotten in the way of the expat community getting whatever done they need to do. Just a bit of a pain in the ass after 10p.m. until 6a.m. You'll have a door key and a key to the lock on the gate in the fence. I'll show you everything. Don't worry. And relax a bit, OK? It really is not a big deal. Let's head up the street and I'll show you around. It's a nice neighborhood, lots of interesting things nearby. Certainly better than your accommodation in Manila." Bump, and Tony gives Jim a small whack on the shoulder to loosen him up. "The women still arriving tomorrow?"

"Scheduled ETA for 2 p.m. We'll see. I'll get them from the airport."

"Well, you guys are on your own tomorrow, and then Saturday we'll take a bit of a ride to the countryside. There is an interesting town, not far, that is classic, and I understand there is property for sale you might be interested in. Plus, Saturday is a bullfight." Big smile, ear to ear on Tony's face.

The next day, Friday, is sleeping in until the dogs insist and Jim gets them walked in a fairly large park near the apartment. He leaves well ahead of time for the 2 p.m. arrival, leaves Pedro and Sancho in a well ventilated car, making sure there is plenty of space in the trunk for the luggage. The wait outside customs and immigration becomes interminable. He is not dealing well with the test and has started a concerted fidget just when the doors push open and out come Marta and Xochitl. Xoch does a quick skip to go with the involuntary screech, Marta sways her hips and smiles ear to ear. The hugs are immense then Xochitl launches into a blow by blow recitation of the honking man in the seat in front who is not to be outdone by the hell spawn behind who is kicking, thrusting against, battering the back of her seat. The child needing exorcism finally falls asleep, until honking man starts up honking again, awakening the beast behind who immediately wails in protest and launches into Xoch's seat. The nine hours were best forgotten as soon as possible. Marta's smile is permanent. Xoch's travelog is interrupted while she loves up on the dogs at the car and the bags are stashed into the trunk. Once on the road away from the airport, the story returns, and Xochitl as drama queen is born. Marta holds Jim's hand, stroking between the fingers and hums quietly. Jim has already gotten intelligence from Tony about a decent restaurant for dinner this evening, and that is where he stops, arriving very early for continental dinner, but not wanting to try to unload at the apartment and restart. Best to use the momentum available and have everyone crash once they get there. At dinner Jim goes over the facts of city life under Franco, curfew, procedures for into and out of the apartment, what's available in the apartment, Tony coming in the morning to take them to the countryside and a bull fight. Both Marta and Xochitl squirm at the mention of a bull fight and Marta is firm in avoiding that spectacle in favor of exploring Madrid on a Saturday morning. The matter settled, they finish dinner and head to the apartment. Crash is exactly what they do.

Saturday, and the ride for Jim and Tony to Valdeolmos is not long, 45 minutes at the most from the edge of town. Once out of the city the road was paved, but 2 lane. As it arrived near Valdeolmos it became a dirt track or road, graded for sure, but bound to be a challenge in the rainy season that starts in October. The day is warm, the air in the town is dusty, particularly around the bull ring. From the ring you can look up the hill and see the cathedral of the ascension. Tickets to the bullfight are inexpensive enough and the place is full. Many of the people have flasks of red wine with them causing Jim's mouth to water a bit.

The slaughter of the bull is classic, traditional and appreciated by the crowd, but Jim finds his attention waning in the afternoon sun and recommends a change. Leaving the bullring, Tony says it is easiest to just walk and they head into the center of the town. The plaza is hazy with the smell of the warm dust in the air. In the center is a small fountain and a spigot with a few women and children gathered there collecting water. Jim notes, "It's 1963 and these people still don't have running water?"

Tony says, "When we came into the village, did you see the small monument either side of the road with the cluster of bound arrows? It was metal and rusty, one each side of the road."

"Saw them. Aren't they phalange symbols? Those were Franco's people weren't they?"

"Right. Well, this village, Valdeolmos, was Republican, opposing Franco and the rebels, and after the civil war, and second world war, the government put those up as a reminder to these folks about who won the conflict. These folks aren't likely to get municipal running water in Franco's lifetime."

"Whew! They can carry a grudge, eh?"

"Right you are. Now, look across the open area, See that 2 story house with the rough front door? Good sized place."

"Yep. What about it?"

"I hear it's for sale. Has been for a while. Word is that the owner has influence with the locals and can get access to water from the well in the plaza for the house for anyone buying it. It's been up for sale for a while, I hear. Might be able to get it cheap. Granja la Maja."

"The goddess's farm? Where's the farm?"

"Used to be all around but the village made inroads, the owners stopped trying to farm dry land, etc. etc. Wanna go see?"

"Sure. We're here. Why not?"

It is a short walk over to the house where they peek into the windows set into solid brick walls 2 feet thick. It's dark inside, obviously unoccupied. There is a wall enclosing the rear of the property which appears sizable and trapezoidal in shape, maybe a whole acre or more. Walking back around to the front, an elderly gentleman shuffles over to them and asks if they are relatives of the owner, mentioning a name. Tony explains that his friend has just arrived in the country and is looking for a place to bring his family. Does the man know how to contact the owners? The man says a few people just leave a note at the front door and it gets to the owner, but not many do it. A few years now and no one wants the place. This is all in rapid fire Spanish that Jim manages to get most of and takes a small notebook from his back pocket. Tony provides a ballpoint pen and Jim prints a short note in Spanish saying he may be interested in talking with the owner about buying the house, leaving the address and telephone number where the family is staying in Madrid for a reply. Folding the paper he presses it into the crack at the edge of the door above the level of the door knob and they leave. The old man has stood by watching the process and nods as they leave. They wave in response and head back to the car. There is a note with a name and telephone number wedged into the gate of the apartment building fence when Tony and Jim arrive back in Madrid.

Marta and Xochitl's day of exploration and negotiating the traffic in Madrid was all Marta had wanted it to be, and more. She is beaming as Jim enters the apartment with Tony. "Jeem. Jeem, thees is the BEST place. I LOVE it!" She hasn't been this animated for years and Jim is smiling ear to ear, and waving the note at her.

Xochitl goes for the paper, but Jim teases by snatching it away and the animated dance flows around the lounge. Tony heads to the kitchen, which is relatively bare, except for several large bottles of red wine in the pantry, takes down four glasses and pours. The refrigerator is only recently plugged in, probably Marta's settling in, so there is no ice. It is survivable. Returning to the lounge, he gets people's attention and distributes the glasses. "Espania!"

"Espania!" is roared back by the other three as the glasses are raised and drained. Rich, full bodied red wine of some varietal they don't know goes right down, no trouble.

Tony returns to the kitchen with the empty glasses for refills and Jim opens the note. The house owner has gotten there before Tony and Jim, probably phone call from Valdeolmos. Translated it says that the owner is living in Madrid and just happens to be available tomorrow if Tuck would care to meet. There is no mention of price. Marta looks at Jim with head slightly tilted as if questioning, "So? Explain." Jim describes the trip to Valdeolmos, and concentrates on the house, leaving out details of the bullfight. As he talks, Marta's smile widens, Xochitl gets fidgety and Jim can see the excitement is rising. "So, shall we talk to this guy tomorrow? There is a Madrid phone number here. Should I call?"

Both Xochitl and Marta look at Jim as if his head is on backwards, Marta spreads her feet, stomps the right and puts on a fake scowl. Jim laughs, caresses her cheek and Tony appears with four refilled glasses. Taking their glasses, Marta and Xochitl ask at the same time, "Where do we eat?"

Tony recommends a place, says he'll go get his wife, Carmen, and meet them there. It's a long walk, but nice weather. The only constraint is curfew, so the family decides to drive. Parking is as bad as in New York, but the food is excellent, the three women are deep into conversation, Spanglish is used allowing Xochitl nearly full participation. Jim and Tony talk mostly about property prices and the evening passes very quickly. Forty-five minutes prior to curfew they break up the party, the Tucks stopping at a small convenience store on the way to the apartment to get some breakfast food, and the momentous day is finished, almost. There is a phone call to make, about the house in Valdeolmos, and the night awaits Jim and Marta, in exotic Madrid.

Xochitl is up early next morning, dresses and slips out the door. Restless, and her body still on New York time, she wants a chance to explore without the restraints of parents. Shutting the front door of the apartment building quietly, she skips down the front steps and has the key in her hand for the latch of the front gate bordering the walkway. Before she can unlock and lift the latch, a large man in army uniform steps in front of her and starts bleating away in rapidfire Spanish. Jumping back startled, Xochitl recovers and then the red starts rising along her neck and into her cheeks. "What the fuck are you talking about? Who the hell are you anyway. Get outta my way!"

The man steps forward, looks at Xochitl and asks her name in Spanish, which Xochitl understands easily enough. "None of your damned business! What's your name?"

With that, the man slips the rifle off his shoulder and is prepared to threaten Xochitl when from the steps there is a gravely sound resembling a voice and the soldier looks up, lowering the gun. He goes into a long explanation, semi tirade, gesticulating with his free hand, pointing at Xochitl until finally, Jim raises his hand and descends the stairs. Explaining that Xochitl is his daughter, that they arrived day before yesterday from out of the country, that she is a high school student and that they now live in this neighborhood, most likely to be seeing this protector of the people again soon. The fellow stands slightly more erectly, dips his head in acknowledgment, gives a slightly glaring nod to Xochitl and shoulders the rifle while walking down the sidewalk. He looks back once, then continues his progress down the block.

"In the house, Xoch."

"But…"

"In the house."

They retreat together. "It is just now just 6a.m. You tried to leave before curfew was finished. We talked about curfew. Did you think we were kidding? What in the world were you thinking? This is not the USA. He could just as easily have shot you if you exited the grounds before curfew was up. Teenagers and young people instigated the recent unrest here. Understand?"

Xochitl slumps into the sofa, Marta is standing in the bedroom doorway pale as a ghost. Jim is standing over Xochitl not at all amused. Finally Xochitl looks up, a tear trickling down her cheek, nods and says, "I forgot. Actually, I remembered, but then forgot because I was excited to explore. Sorry, Poppa."

Jim sits next to her. "No harm this time. Good lesson learned. Franco is a fascist, he's a dictator, and there is not really a rule of law here, not like we're used to anyway. Treading softly is the watchword, OK, Bud?"

"OK."

"Still want to explore? Curfew's over."

"Kinda over the exploration need, actually. Think I'll have a cup of coffee, or a glass of wine, actually." As she stands, Marta comes over and hugs her quite a long time, then lets her go and slips her arm around Jim's waist.

"She is sometimes too independent, or too strong opinion, I think."

"Sometimes. She'll learn, for sure. Which reminds me. Next item on the list is school. Tony gave me the number at the American School at Torrejon. Maybe we ought to call tomorrow and make an appointment."

"Good idea."

"According to the phone call last night, the house owner will be here at 11a.m. I think Torrejon is for tomorrow afternoon. OK?"

"That is good. I will make something to have with coffee at 11:00. Do you have an idea how much this house will cost?"

"No, not right now. I think leaving the owner to first come up with a figure is the best plan. Tony didn't have any idea either since it is so far out of town. We haven't even seen it inside. It may be a dump. We'll talk price, a bit, today, but make a plan to go see it, all three of us. Making something for the meeting is a good idea. I will call Tony and ask if he knows someone we can talk to about Madrid property prices for the Valdeolmos area. It's better to have some comparison, even if it is out of town." With that, Marta retreats to the kitchen and Jim sits in the seat next to the phone table, dialing Tony.

Eleven O'clock comes quickly and there is a bell ringing in the hallway. Jim and Marta stand in the lounge, and head to the door. Xochitl has gone out anyway, having recovered from her fright and reprimand, promising to be back by 1:00.

At the front door is a middle aged man, dressed trimly if inelegantly, medium height, medium build, medium everything, except that his English is impeccable. Shaking Jim's hand with the introduction, nodding to Marta, they move from the hallway to the lounge where scones, and jam, and coffee are sitting on the low table in front of the sofa.

"Ah, these look wonderful. Did you make them?"

Jim responds, allowing Marta's modesty to reign, "She did. Her idea, of course, ever the sweetener of any deals. We are very happy you were able to come over so soon. We only arrived in the country a few days ago, but are planning to settle here long term, so we are interested in finding a suitable place to make a home. My friend knew of your house in Valdeolmos and we, he and I, had a quick look yesterday. May I ask why you are selling such a classic old home?"

"Of course. My wife died 3 years ago. She and I shared that home for 20 years. Now, I am alone. Valdeolmos is a wonderful place for a family, a lonely place for a person alone. I have many friends here in Madrid, I own a home here as well, alone I certainly do not need 2 houses. So, I sell, or try to sell, one of them."

"My friend, Tony, said he thought it had been for sale for a while."

"Yes, it is a marvelous house, good quality, but in a dusty village with few visitors, and not close to the important sites in Madrid. I have talked to a few people who seem interested, but never follow through. I know I am a terrible salesman saying all this, but it is true."

"We would like to see the house sometime. Can we make a schedule?" Marta is seriously examining the body language and facial expressions of the owner as he talks to Jim.

"Si. We both want to see the house," comes from Marta, with a glance from Jim.

The owner looks from one to the other, nods, and says, "Is today too soon? I am free all day."

"Normally, today would be fine, but we have other plans for today, so I think tomorrow would be better."

The owner nods and says, "Tomorrow is fine. I recommend earlier in the day, when there is more activity in the village. Can we say 9 O'clock in the morning? That is more than halfway through the morning for villagers, but still plenty of people around.. It requires at least 45 minutes to drive during the day."

"Nine a.m. it is then, tomorrow. I think my friend, Tony, will not be there, but the 3 of us will." The front door opens, "Oh, here is my daughter, Xochitl, back earlier than expected. Xochitl, this man owns the house in the village of Valdeolmos and is selling it. We have an appointment to see it tomorrow morning."

Closing the door behind her, Xochitl nods toward the owner, smiles, and says, "I assume we are all going, right? Is Tony going?"

"Yes, for the three of us, no for Tony. We will leave about 8:15 in the morning, correct, sir?"

"That is when I will leave myself, to be at the house by nine, yes."

With that, Xochitl exits to the kitchen, Jim and Marta stand and show the owner to the door. "Until tomorrow at nine. Hasta la vista."

The owner automatically responds with, "Si, manana." With a smile and a wave he is down the steps and gone.

Marta closes the door behind them and says, "Is this going too fast, do you think?"

"Only if we do not pay attention. The house looks solid on the outside. It is obviously old, it is interesting, has a bit of land with it, and I suspect if we are going to get people to come visit, it will be there. Interesting places bring guests to out of the way places, si?"

Marta smiles and gives Jim an affectionate peck on the bristly cheek. "Si. Why did you tell the man we are busy this afternoon. It is Sunday. We are not busy."

"This is a negotiation. We keep as much control as we can. Going today would look like we are way too eager. Softly, softly,"

Marta finishes it for Jim, "catchee monkey."

They join Xochitl in the kitchen where she is making a classic peanut butter and jelly with potato chip sandwich. Both parents mostly hide their mortification. The three of them discuss the upcoming visit to the high school. Tony will be there to guide them through the massive base to the high school and introduce them to the principal. The Torrejon trip will occupy Monday afternoon and provide Xochitl some insight into what sort of peers are available for her to associate with in Madrid. It's exciting and scary at the same time.

The drive to Valdeolmos the next day is along ever more narrowing roads until near the edge of town the pavement runs out and all is dusty. The rainy season hasn't quite started yet. It is September and a bit late, but expected soon.

Slowly winding through the town, the car slows to a stop in the plaza near the fountain in the middle. Jim points out the cathedral on the hill, the adobe colored wine drinking establishment next to the bread store and then turning he points out the house they have come to see. Just then, a car drives up to the front of the house, parks and the owner appears, walking to the front double doors. Jim slowly rolls the car forward and parks next to the owner's car and the family climb out, waving to the familiar figure.

"Welcome to Granja la Maja. I am happy to see you," is with a full, genuine smile. He unlocks the door, opening it wide and invites the Tucks inside. It is a bit gloomy inside until he walks to the end of the corridor and opens the door to the back at the end of the hall. Light floods the area, and it has an instantly warmer feeling.

The tour does not take long as there are not that many rooms. On the left of the corridor are, first, the large bedroom on the left, then the kitchen next with a small room behind it. On the right are three rooms, first the living room or lounge with fireplace, then a bedroom, and finally a small room that stores spare furniture. Out the back is an outdoor toilet and bathing room, old fashioned, no water. The sink in the kitchen has a drain, but no faucet. Upstairs is a large room in an enlarged attic space with windows and flooring throughout. Some odds and ends of junk are scattered about as if forgotten during an exit. In the backyard, which is entirely surrounded by a wall, there is a sizable structure, mostly dilapidated, at the far end of the yard, with a fairly large open area in the middle. Just outside the back door is an ancient well, that actually has water at the bottom. The surrounding walls are above head height, offering some privacy, but no real security. It wouldn't take much to breach them.

Back in the house, a few chairs are gathered to allow sitting and discussion. Xochitl doesn't have a chair, so she explores the plaza while the discussion ensues. Marta is first to bring up the apparent lack of water available. The owner responds that the village is under the control of the Madrid authorities and they have not decided when to bring municipal water to the village. Jim notes, "But there is a public fawcett in the square. Where does that water come from?"

"That water is from an artesian well, has never run dry, and is protected by the village people. Everyone uses it for their water at home, to drink and bathe and whatnot."

"Artesian water is usually good, comes from higher up somewhere. Any idea where it comes from?"

"The local people have tried sometimes to discover the origin, but no one seems to know. They just use it, thankfully."

"So, that water has its own pressure from the artesian system. Do you know who makes the decisions about who uses the water?"

"Yes, the alcalde, or the person everyone calls alcalde, decides. But really, everyone knows that the water is for everyone, so no one has to ask permission."

"Why hasn't the house tapped into the well in the backyard?"

"To bring that well water into the house requires an electric pump. Also, that water is not such good quality. Maybe for watering plants it is OK, but I do not think it is good for drinking or cooking."

"Well, then I think the first thing to think about is how to have water inside this house, and that communal source in the plaza seems to be the most likely answer. But, I imagine permission to tap the artesian system and pipe water to the house must be requested. I think," and here Jim looks firmly at Marta for confirmation, receiving a nod that the owner notices as well, "that if we can solve that problem we would like to talk more about the price of the house. How much were you thinking of asking, by the way?"

"I can find the alcalde this morning, I think, and ask him about the idea of a pipe to the house. I am interested to hear what you think you can afford to pay for the house."

Jim sits back in the chair, realizing he may have his hands full in this negotiation, but forges on, "Why don't you see if you can find the alcalde, and when you come back, we can talk some more?"

The owner rises from his chair, nods to each of Jim and Marta in turn, and leaves through the front door, leaving Jim and Marta to discuss. "How cold do you think it gets here in the winter?" Marta, ever the practical mind rises and starts toward the living room.

"It's dry country, elevated, so I imagine it can get chilly, for sure. Why?"

"Because, as far as I can see, this fireplace in the living room is the only heat in the house."

They are standing in the living room, which is good sized, looking at a seriously large fireplace that has remnants of many fires about it. There is a serious amount of soot stain blackening the mantle and out of the corners of the fireplace, the floor of the firepit is swept clean and there are andirons in place, cast iron apparently. The bricks and stone are pitted around the interior of the firebox, and the stone hearth is well worn. It would provide a lovely environment on a cold evening, but you'd have to stay close.

Looking again through the other rooms they note that there is a single electrical outlet in each room with conduit exposed on the wall where the wiring is laid. The house has obviously been modified, electrified, in the past. The construction seems to indicate it is seriously old, with thick, solid masonry walls, deep window wells, ancient appearing woodwork and doors and window frames. It is a small fort. There would obviously be room available for the family, but some serious upgrading is needed. Fortunately, they've done it before, just never in such exotic and unfamiliar surroundings.

Sitting in the living room, they hear someone enter the front door, stand and the owner enters with an erect older man with a full head of nearly white hair. He is introduced, with a fair amount of fanfare, as the alcalde, which adds another inch or two to the older gentleman's height. He nods. Jim and Marta make appropriate polite greetings in Spanish, which brings a smile to the alcalde's face and general relaxation occurs around the room.

As they sit, the owner starts the conversation about the history of the fountain, the fawcett, in the center of the plaza. He pauses to allow any corrections necessary from the alcalde, who remains silent for now. Finally, the owner mentions the fact that the house, the Granja la Maja, is a fine old house, one of the earliest ones built in the village. Everyone nods, then he starts talking about the possibilities of further modernization as suggested by Jim and Marta, and the possible sale of the house. Silence follows, until Jim stands and walks to the nearest window, speaking in Spanish, "I have been many places in my life, from the USA, to Mexico, South America, Asia, but I do not think I have ever found a lovelier village."

Marta stands and joins Jim looking out the window, smiles, and turns to face the alcalde, and also in Spanish, "I agree. This actually reminds me of my home in the mountains of Mexico." She continues smiling in spite of the horrid memories associated with her childhood. The smile, as usual, melts the countenance of the alcalde who speaks.

"I understand you have a child?"

Marta responds, "Yes, our daughter Xochitl, who is exploring around the village while we talk. She is 17 and will finish her last year of high school here in Spain. We will be here a long time." Smile.

The alcalde rises, nods and beckons the owner to follow. There is murmuring out of sight by the front door, then silence. The owner reappears, smiles hugely, and says, "There is no difficulty to tap the community water and bring a pipe to the house."

"That is good. I think we can talk seriously about buying your house. Would you like to talk here, or back in Madrid?"

"I suggest we talk here. Is it acceptable to speak in Spanish?"

"Of course. I think you were about to mention a price you thought was fair." Jim's ever mobile eyebrows rise with the inferred question.

"Ah, I see you have experience in negotiations, Mr. Tuck. Well then, let us remove pretence. I want $35,000 US dollars for the house and land.

Jim sits down, leans back and beckons to Marta who sits beside him. "That is a bit more than we anticipated, particularly this distance from the city. We expect to do some work to the place, as you can imagine, and I must put that expense into the expected cost, you see. But, dispensing with pretense, I hope an offer of $20,000 would not insult you."

Leaning back in his chair, the owner extracts a large cigar from his breast pocket, slowly clips the end, strikes a match and slowly lights it. After a long puff, exhaling the smoke above his head, he leans forward saying, "This is a negotiation. Each is attempting to obtain the best result from it, no?" Jim and Marta nod simultaneously. "So, there can be no insult sent or received if we are having no pretense. $20,000 is too low, that is certain, but I think we can reach agreement."

"I agree. I think we can find a figure that we are both happy with. I believe we can come a bit higher, but must reserve our finances since we have no other source of income now and are living on the fixed amount we brought with us. If $20,000 is too low, how about $22,000?"

"$28,000 would sound much better."

"Can we agree on $25,000?"

The owner leans back in his chair, cigar deep in his mouth, the burning end suddenly glows brightly and a cloud of smoke escapes around the cigar. Removing it from his mouth he slowly stands, looks at Jim and extends his hand.

Jim rises, takes the proffered hand and gives it a solid grip with a smile. Marta is now standing, slightly bouncing from foot to foot until the owner faces her, slightly bends at the waist, takes her hand and kisses the knuckles ever so lightly. "It is a great pleasure to know you will bring such grace and beauty to my beloved home. My wife would be very happy. We can meet at my bank with the lawyer to complete the transaction. I suggest day after tomorrow, if that is good for you. I expect your honor will be demonstrated in completing the transfer without the need for a deposit. Am I correct?"

Jim takes his hand in another handshake and says, "It is. If you will write the name and address of the bank, we will be there, day after tomorrow. May I suggest 11 a.m?"

"Agreed." With that, the owner writes the details on a slip of note paper, hands the paper to Martta, turns and is gone, without a backward glance.

""Looks like we are residents of the village of Valdeolmos, Marta. Lets find Xochitl and tell her."

"Yes, lets."

CHAPTER 3

Life Back to Normal

The family is met at the airbase gate by Tony, guided to the school where introductions are made. Being US citizens they get a discount on the tuition and while these negotiations are being conducted, Xochitl explores the remodeled Barracks that is now the Madrid School, as it is commonly known. It used to be in town, but moved to the base since there are so many military dependents attending, a few Spanish kids, and a polyglot of others from around the world. School is school, but this might actually prove to be interesting.

Xochitl's enrollment, with Tony's help, was relatively simple. Surprising, since it involved the US military, but giving the Valdeolmos address as home, being US citizens and Xochitl's official high school transcripts all smoothed the process. The Valdeolmos address was still not actual since there will be renovations and the family was still on Calle Lagasca, for now. School was starting in 2 days and Jim and Marta would simply drop her off at school on their way to Valdeolmos to work on the house, leaving in time to pick her up before she had to wait too long. It's working out.

The running water was into the kitchen sink and the bathing and toileting room, a flush toilet installed and connected to the sewer and lighting installed in the downstairs rooms, hooked up to the electrical system. A fuse box was installed and the electrician tested the wiring for faults, fixing one in the kitchen. A new gas stove is installed that uses bottled gas from Madrid, and the bench tops rearranged creating an island in the center of the room and better space for more than one person to work there. Jim and Marta enjoyed cooking together at times. Other times, not so much. A railing along the stairs to the second floor was installed and all the internal doors were refinished. Jim and Marta accomplished all these with the exceptions of the electrical and plumbing work.

The professional help cost a fraction of what it would have in New York, and the quality, from Jim's practiced eye, was first rate. Despite the lower costs, Jim and Marta were beginning to squirm a bit at the rapid reduction in their bank account. The last cryptic message from Kai indicated that there may be a buyer for the New York apartment building, but not certain at all, and even when there was a successful sale the finances would not be available for another 2 or 3 months. There was enough money for frugal living for about 6 months, but they were going to have to do something soon.

That's when Jim came upon a nearly perfect solution, mostly by accident. He and Tony were sitting in a small cafe, drinking wine with snacks when a voice came across the room, "Arizza! That you?" Behind the voice came a fellow about 6 foot 4 with bright red hair, seersucker suit, patent brown leather shoes reflecting the lights, with floral tie and arms out wide.

Tony rises with a large smile, "Ben! Ben Erlichton!" The 2 collide beside the table embracing as long lost friends. After several slaps on each back and amazed "What the fucks!" Tony extracts himself and introduces Jim who has risen to his feet.

Ben turns from Tony and broadcasts his largest smile on Jim with, "Nice to meetcha!" that rings off the walls.

Jim's, "Likewise," response is considerably less strenuous, but he is nonetheless smiling anyway. There is no way to avoid it.

Releasing his iron grip on Jim's hand Ben says, "Sit, sit," just like it is his table. He pulls out a chair and sits opposite Jim, to Tony's left.

As they sit, Ben waves at the waiter and gestures something that seems to have meaning to the fellow and turns back to the table. "I haven't seen you," addressing Tony, "for at least 9 months."

"Eleven," says Tony. It was end of October last year, remember? Or did that night wipe your memory?"

"Ha! Nothing could wipe that one. Just did not remember the date, but the evening was unforgettable." Turning to Jim, he says, "This lad is magic at creating festive occasions, and that was one I will never forget." Turning to Tony, he continues, "How you managed to get the entire officers club for the whole night, I'll never know. And the dancers. Whew! What an evening!"

Jim's eyebrows go up, "Dancers?"

"Just a little entertainment I was able to round up, last minute. Madrid has some of the most beautiful women in the world, and talented too.!" The last is delivered with a bit of a crooked grin from Tony, one eyebrow up. "You remember, Ben, that when those futures paid off, we were suddenly in a position to organize something special. Until then, we were planning a dandy event, but got to really upgrade it with the additional cash on hand."

Jim's face suddenly is more mask-like as his attention is extremely focussed. Tony notices, and leans back. "Ben, here, dabbles in a few financial products, and every now and then we get lucky, eh Ben?"

"Eh, Tony. You ever dabbled in the futures market, Jim?"

"Now and then. I had an account back in the states, but usually never had sufficient capital to make a serious dent or return."

"I have various clients, here in Madrid, who invest fairly regularly. They come from all sectors, even military." With that he makes a smiling glance at Tony. "I am, what you might call, an equal opportunity investor. Nearly any amounts are a go, nothing too big, or too small. Know what I mean?"

Jim is quiet for about 20 seconds, an eternity in a conversation, then says, "What futures are being traded at the moment?"

Ben settles into his chair, lights a cigar and after the first smoky billow says, "There is anything here you can get in New York, but I suspect the best bet right now is orange juice. It is likely to go up a lot, and soon, due to the crop loss in Florida. Hurricane season was unkind to the state this year."

"Heard about that. I can get you $500 tomorrow. Agreed?"

"Sure, but you certain that's all you want?"

"Testing the waters, Ben. Testing the waters. Deal or no deal?"

"Deal. Of course it's a deal. Like I said, none too big or too small."

"Where and when?"

Tony has been watching, just nods his head with a smile thinking, "That's the Tuck I knew."

Ben says, "Might as well be here as anywhere. No wine at the office and the scenery is better here. Eleven a.m., K?"

"Here at eleven it is," and with that Jim rises, shakes hands with both men and strides off.

"Your buddy is abrupt, I'll say that for him."

"He's just like I remember him 25 years ago. Older, but acts just the same. Thinks, decides and goes. He'll be here. Make sure you are, with the paperwork. This could be very good, Ben. Don't fuck it up."

"Whah! You know me better than that. I have never stiffed anyone you have brought me, right?"

"Just sayin. Tuck has a good side, and a not so good side, depending. Know what I mean?"

"Gotcha. You gonna be here tomorrow?"

"Nah. Meetings tomorrow. I'll call ya. Later, Ben." With that, Tony is also away and Ben sits back down, ordering another glass of wine.

The futures transaction is made, but Marta is there as well this time. She has seldom participated in any of the investment activities, except for the tenement purchases. But, this time, when the family finances are at stake, and they are already running short, she needs to be involved directly. Jim has worked overtime convincing her that this test purchase is a good trial. They will need money before the apartment building sale happens in New York and a quick turn around, like in the futures market where you are not waiting months, or years sometimes, could be exactly the right thing to help. Besides, the $500, while a significant gamble right now, is affordable right now. It might not be in 2 months. She decides to give it a try, mainly because Jim says so.

Since there is no news source in Valdeolmos, Jim calls daily from the cantina, where the nearest phone is, for updates on the price of orange juice futures and 2 weeks after the purchase, they sell them for a total of $750, less the brokerage fee. Marta is impressed, allocates the profit to remodeling costs and some kitchen needs like a woc and some pots and pans, and a set of Valdeolmos original dishes, hand made.

In the glow of her purchases, Marta agrees to a more adventurous futures purchase that

Ben has explained, this time to both Jim and Marta, at the same restaurant. This time, instead of $500, they buy $5000 worth of sugar futures that will likely mature within a month. If the deal is as good as the orange juice one, they will likely have enough in the bank to support the family until the apartment building sale. Smiles all around, Jim and Marta leave the meeting heading to Torrejon Air Base to pick up Xochitl from School. Madrid is feeling pretty good just now.

What a difference 2 weeks make. The $5000 is gone. There is suddenly an abundance of sugar on the market depressing the price, thus the futures, and the Tucks' sense of well being. When Jim gets the word from the telephone, he sits, he starts making rather urgent local enquiries about possible funding sources, all with negative results. It is not good. There is no funding from the States in the near future, there is little in the Madrid bank account, and Marta does not even know yet. Just then, Marta walks in the door.

"Isn't it time to get Xochitl? Why are you still here?

"Marta, the money is gone."

"What are you saying? What money?"

"The sugar futures money. It is gone. I have been trying to find replacement money, but no luck so far. I have been a little distracted."

Marta sits on the wooden chair next to the door and does not say anything for an age, until, "Xochitl now. We can talk on the way to the school. Lets go."

"As usual, you're right." And then they are away. On the ride, Jim describes the telephone call he made to Ben. Ben had been rather cheerful in his response, while Jim was silently suggesting Ben count his lucky stars for being in Madrid rather than Valdeolmos. Ben was less cheerful when Jim suggested what might have been a better response and that Ben had been remiss in not letting Jim know, since he had the information considerably before the phone call. The quality of menace in Jim's voice also managed to break through Ben's rather dense response to the point that he recommended he and Jim have lunch sometime and abruptly hung up.

Marta listened intently, as usual. Then stated the obvious, "We don't have enough left to get us to Christmas."

"Maybe, if we are very frugal, we can get through Christmas. There are no presents this year, none. Right?"

Marta is quiet, then sadly and sagely nods assent. It is her favorite celebration. It is nearly crushing for her to admit the obvious. Then, she gets her head back up and says, "So, we need another plan. What are you thinking so far?"

"I am thinking that we have a little finca, and maybe we could find something to raise since it was a farm anyway."

Marta is obviously pondering the situation, then says, "We have 2 stud animals that are pure bred. Perhaps we could breed and sell pups, if we had pedigreed females."

Jim is nodding, "Plus we really enjoy the dogs. I'll check going prices this afternoon. Pups take a while. If the females bred today the pups would be born around

Christmas. Wonder if there is anything with a quicker turn around?"

Marta suddenly sits up a bit straighter and looking at Jim, "Rabbits!"

"What? What are you talking about?"

"A standard meat served in this part of Spain is rabbit meat. All the local restaurants, the restaurants with mainly Spanish clients, serve rabbit. Here in the village the young men all go out with their guns, mainly on weekends, and shoot rabbits. You have heard them."

"Indeed I have. Sounds like goddam World War III first thing every Saturday morning. Only thing I enjoy about the Catholics is that they won't let them hunt, where they can be heard anyway, before first mass on Sunday. So, what's the idea with rabbits?"

"Actually, I think we should do both, breed the dogs, and make pens for rabbits, get rabbits and breed them for the market. Their turn around is much quicker than the dogs, but they are inexpensive so we have to have a lot of them. The biggest expense is setting up the cages and the first buying of stock. We have plenty of room for cages, yes?"

"Yes. Do you know where to get breeding stock of rabbits?"

"I do. Chayo, ah, Maria Rosario, whose sister helps with our house cleaning sometimes, knows who has the rabbits."

"OK. Here's the deal. We need a definitive number for the cost of start up for raising rabbits. We can divide the work. I will find a plan for rabbit cages and get a cost for 30 cages. That will be one female per cage, I am guessing. You can talk to Chayo and find out the cost of breeding females and a couple of males, and what they eat, how much, and so forth. Oops, here's the air base gate. We'll include Xochitl. Some of her friends may be able to help with construction. It's going to cost more money and we need some cash. I'll write to a few folks back in the States. They have good info, and maybe can help with the cost of construction."

With their sticker in the windshield they get passed quickly through the gate since they are now known by nearly all the sentries. Xochitl is waiting at the curb, but is smiling.

"I was beginning to wonder. Where you guys been?"

"Sorry, bud. A few complications arose today, and delayed us. You OK?"

Her smile is still there. "Sure, Papa. What complications, anyway?"

"Well, the family is in a spot of bother, financially. Marta and I invested money in a fund expecting to receive enough return to tide us over financially until the apartment building in New York sold. The return was expected to be high, which means the risk is also high.

We bet wrong, and the money that had been in the bank for us to live on, after remodeling the house, is gone, well a lot of it is gone. Found out this morning after you went to school. We have been working on solutions, none of which seem to offer immediate relief, and it's getting closer to Christmas. Marta loves Christmas, you get a kick out of it as well. This year is going to be a pretty thin year for Christmas. Not only do we have to find ways to make some more money, we have to save it as well, avoid spending on anything that is not absolutely required. Understand?" Marta's face is downcast, but her head is bobbing up and down in agreement.

Xochitl has just sat and listened, the smile long gone. Then she says, "So, what ideas have you come up with to make more money?"

Jim leans back in his seat, starts the engine and pulls away from the curb to leave the base and head home. His face is mostly a mask except for the slightly ironic smile on his lips. "You don't know how much I was hoping you would ask something like that. Good one, young lady. So, ok, here's what we have thought so far. We can use the dogs to breed females and sell pups, and we can raise rabbits for the community meat market, maybe even for restaurants in Madrid. This is where you come in. We'll need help to make cages for the rabbits. We'll need probably 30 cages. You and some of your mates could help constructing them." By now they are well away from the base, driving home.

Back in Valdeolmos Jim starts a letter writing campaign to friends and acquaintances in the States, essentially outlining an investment opportunity in letters outlining current events in the Tuck family, occasionally suggesting that his unknown whereabouts is actually a good thing, at least for a while. Xochitl enlists some of her classmates into the project as amateur-hour construction help while Marta is scouting the least expensive building supplies for 30 cages and locates a source for breeding rabbits. Xochitl added to the team has helped divide the work, and the project is well underway.

Within a month, there is a rabbit farm in the building at the back of the property behind the house. Jim's next task is marketing the product, first locally to housewives, then further afield into Madrid, with recommendations from Tony, and even some from Ben, with whom Jim is somewhat reconciled. Full reconciliation is not likely given Jim's typical obstinacy, but they can't afford to avoid taking advantage of all assets.

The first lot of production rabbits has been completed within 3 months from the erection of the cages, and the proceeds pay for the startup costs, without the reimbursement of the few investors from the States. Christmas was, as anticipated, thin on celebration, using home made decorations on an improvised tree that had no gifts under it; a very difficult Christmas for Marta. Now, they have made it through the cold of Winter, Spring brings new hope to the house, the does are impregnated again getting ready to cash in on the next sale. Maybe then they can afford to repay some of the investment money and buy a couple of pedigree female boxers for their dog breeding business.

One morning in March, Jim goes out to the rabbits to feed, and discovers one of the does is dead and two are looking puny. Several others are not looking keen and refuse the food he leaves for them. The four males are in a cage of their own, three are perky enough but one is looking droopy like the females. He calls Marta in his urgent voice and she responds quickly, coming out into the shed.. "Look what I found this morning." He lifts the dead doe and Marta's hand goes immediately to her mouth.

"How are the others," she asks?

"Check them out. See those over there, the three cages straight across? Those females are looking sick and won't eat. Go look."

Marta reluctantly goes across the yard to the other side and looks into the cages Jim pointed out. Opening one door, she pulls out a limp rabbit. "This one is also dead."

Jim slumps down onto the nearby bench. "What the hell's going on?"

Marta brings the dead rabbit and puts it with the other one, sits next to Jim, and says, "It is a disease of rabbits. I know it from Mexico. How are the males?"

Jim says, "Three are fine, one looks like those females over there."

Marta looks up at Jim with the saddest eyes he has ever seen. "In two days they may all be dead. What can we do? In Mexico, they all died." And she slumps down, puts her head in her hands and cries.

Xochitl is at school, so she won't find out until this afternoon. Jim says, "This isn't Mexico, it's 1964, not 1934. We have to get these to a vet. Find out what's wrong, find what must be done to fix it."

This brings Marta back around and she responds, "I'll get a basket for these two, you take the sick buck out of his cage and put him in one by himself. We must, at least clean the cages the sick rabbits are in"

"Now you're thinking again. I'll take these two with me and stop at the vet on the way back from getting Xoch."

Now, it's Jim's turn to slump. "Just when we thought we had a way out. Goddamn it!"

"Yes, it is bad. We can not give up. There is so little money left in the bank."

Just then, there is a knock on the front door of the house. "We expecting anybody?"

Marta sits up, "No, not I know about. I will see who it is."

A minute later she returns saying, the woman from the cantina says you have a phone call from America. Who in the world has the number to call?"

"Just one person I know of. I'll go see."

"Jeem. So good to hear your voice, but it is very light sounding."

"Kai, I can hear you fine. Is there a problem? It seems problems are coming in bunches just now."

"That is better. I hear you now. No. No problems. I thought you would like to know that the apartment building sold yesterday. The net receipt will be $48,000, about. The papers will be signed Monday next week, and the money deposited in your account that day. I expect you will be able to get money from that account by Wednesday next week. I thought this news may be helpful to you. I will take my money out before putting in your account, OK?"

Jim has deflated onto a bench seat at the bar, head in his hand, then after several seconds realizes he needs to respond to Kai. "YES! Yes, that is fine. For sure to take out the amount you have earned my friend. Please send the completed paperwork to the address we gave you, OK? Oh, Kai. Thank you very much. I must go tell Marta now. Goodbye."

"Goodbye Jim." And the phone is handed back to the barmaid as Jim is heading out the door, erect, bouncing on the balls of his feet.

Jim nearly flies through the front door, leaving it wide open, jogs the length of the hallway and bursts into the gloomy backyard as Marta has just dispatched another doe, its back legs between her strong fingers, hanging down in front of her. She looks to see a radiant Jim Tuck loping across the yard toward her, arms wide open. "Put that dead thing down, woman. Give old Jim a hug!"

She recoils with the dangling dead rabbit still in her hand and says, "What in the world, Jeem? You are crazy or something?"

"Yes, crazy. Crazy it is. Crazy, HUH! Yes, more than a bit crazy, I think."

Marta looks at him then, lays the dead rabbit with the other two, "Why are you crazy? Who was on the telephone?"

"Kai has sold the building. Net return is $48,000, less his commission. It will be in the bank next week. My heart is overflowing!"

Marta just stands there a moment, then stumbles back to plop down on the stone step behind her. As quickly as she thumps down, Jim has scooped her up and swings her full circle before standing her in front of him, giving the biggest kiss he has exchanged with her in years. Marta is then clinging to him, sobbing in relief, then they both sit down and are very quiet. Marta breaks the silence with, "That is very, very good. As sad as I was, that is how happy I am now. Oh, Jeem, this is very good news."

Jim releases her, still holding her hand, then says, "I think it would be good if we continue with finding solutions for the rabbits, even with this money coming. I'll take these three does to the vet. Glad you weren't too efficient. Maybe we can save the sick ones, yes? **AND**, we should have dinner in Madrid, I think."

"I agree, for both."

"Yes, I agree it is terrible, but, I think the vet may have some ideas. I want to tell the Alcalde what the problem is, see if anyone else had the same problem. Better yet, he really likes you, you ask him while I am getting Xoch and seeing the vet." With that, he gives one more quick kiss, full on the lips, grabs up the basket of dead rabbits and heads to ,and through the door. Marta hears the front door shut, then goes to change her clothes, brighten herself a bit and heads to the house of the alcalde.

Xochitl is somewhat distressed at the news about the rabbits, delighted with the news about the sale, happy to indulge in a restaurant meal since it has been many months since it was possible. She's even interested in what the vet has to say when they stop with the rabbits. The virus is indeed common to the countryside. It is one of the reasons the wild rabbit population stays in check. There are treatments, drugs, that can help some and a sample is given to Xochitl to carry. It is not cheap, but the vet says there are less expensive versions in the UK and the USA. Armed with treatments for rabbits, renewed energy and determination the two head back to Valdeolmos to get Marta for dinner in Madrid.

During dessert of flan Xochitl looks up at Jim and says, "Poppa, do you know what I think would be really good to have at the house, that I think we could make ourselves?"

Jim puts his spoon down and says, "What?"

"A swimming pool."

Marta's spoon nearly falls out of her hand. She catches it and says, "Xoch. We don't have money or space for that sort of thing. That is too much."

Jim starts to say something, but Xochitl's hand comes up and she says, "It was too much yesterday. Maybe not today. You and poppa know how to do all sorts of things. There are lots of people here in the village that could help with the construction and who need the work, and the cost will be nothing like it would be in New York.

Nothing like that. If I do the planning work for making an estimate, and you can confirm that it is correct and reasonable, will you agree?"

Jim can't help the half grin on his face while Marta is trying to find another argument, but then raises her head to look at her baby girl and says, "OK. Bring the plan, and the figures, and we'll see." Her voice is firm, Jim smiles again, and when Marta glances his way, he just nods. Looks like we are out of the rabbit business and into a swimming pool, just in time for summer.

Even though the ground is nearly as hard as concrete the first 20 centimeters deep, the excavation for the pool is done by hand over the period of a month. The interesting aspect of the area is that ground level inside the wall is higher than outside, so a person standing inside the back yard can see over the wall, but not the reverse. Digging down for the depth of a pool for swimming barely makes the bottom of the pool below the level of the street outdoors, which eases the engineering problems for drainage. To keep as much of the pool out from under the several trees in the yard, a triangular shape is decided, but still long enough on the long side to swim laps.

Jim takes his pick of several local applicants for labor, Xochitl enlists weekend help of some of her classmates with the trade off being use of the pool, and Marta feeds the lot as needed. Jim even did his share, or what he deemed his share, of the digging. The pool was not large, maybe 10 meters on the long side, but that is still a lot of digging to be done, as well as creating a drain for emptying it. The entire excavation went through April, with several days off for rain. The drain is laid, and the bottom concreted during early May, but the more complicated concreting is delayed until June when it is warmer and the rain is less likely. For this, Jim gets three local men for the labor, and Marta is designing the tiled edging to be applied during the final stages of applying concrete to the walls of the pool. Jim designs the elevated apron surrounding the pool, which will also be tiled, but the tiling will not be fancy like the edging. The entire project is finished in time for the end of the rains, which comes in June. To finish the entertainment options for the area, Jim constructs a large barbeque pit, outside the exterior kitchen door, just in front of the ancient well. The overall effect of shade, pool, well, and cooking facilities makes the area incredibly inviting.

To celebrate their relieved financial situation as well as the opening of the pool, each of the three family members makes a list of invitees with the final tally being nearly a hundred. Of course, the workmen who participated are asked, but most decline. Working in the Granja la Maja is one thing. Visiting is quite another thing. Marta invites a few of her acquaintances from Madrid, as well as three women from the village. Since two of them are wives of men who had worked on the pool, they decline. It's not likely the wife would show up when the husband already declined. The third is a local artist friend who frankly doesn't care what any of the men decide. Jim starts with Tony Arizza and his wife Carmen, finds out that Joe Purcell is in town, and invites him. Joe, the Hollywood cinematographer, is a hoot and should liven up any gathering. Several others are eventually included, but Ben is not. Jim can hold a grudge. Of course, the previous owner is invited, and he graciously accepts. Xochitl invites her whole class of 21 senior high school students. Several have steady dates who will come as well, and they make the largest single contingent at the party.

Jim buys a pig to roast, Marta arranges with the wine merchant for a cask of red wine. Those attending will more than likely contribute to the drink menu. Marta bakes bread, cooks rice with Xochitl, they deplete the local market's supply of fresh fruits and vegetables. The impending celebration is obviously the talk of the town. With the buzz accelerating, two of the men who had refused originally recant and ask, meekly, if they can still come with their wives. Assurances are given and gratefully received.

Cars begin arriving in the village about 4:30 for the official start time of 5p.m. The limited area in front of the house quickly fills this Friday evening, and later arrivals start parking all around the perimeter of the plaza, some even as far away as the cathedral. There must be 35 cars in a village that, at most, has entertained two at a time. It is a fine, dry July evening, cooling off a bit once the sun is down. The traffic through and around the village has raised considerable dust that settles on the cars as souvenirs of the visit to the countryside. Marta is the greeter for most, with Xochitl stepping in to greet her high school mates. Joe Purcell arrives only knowing Jim. Marta sends him into the backyard after a buss on each cheek and Jim lets out a bellow heard in the front of the house, creating a grin on Marta's face. Standing, leaning on the side of the open front door, looking over the scene out front, she is suddenly wistful and smiles an even deeper smile, appreciating the wild ride that has gotten her to this place and time. From danger, to collapse, to poverty and ruin and arriving at a truly beautiful place creates magnitudes of gratitude. "Wonder if Jim or Xochitl appreciate this as much as I do?" With that musing, seeing there are no arrivals in site, she walks through the house and out the back to join the festivities, laughing at the young people splashing away in the pool. The local guests seem taken aback a bit, standing together to one side, Jim is turning the pig on the spit with Purcell jabbering away in his ear. She waves at Tony and Carmen, fills five goblets with red wine and walks over to the restrained group of villagers to distribute them. She smiles, thanks them again for coming, handing each a goblet. After the first drink, these apparently shy locals start loosening up, begin talking more animatedly with Marta, one of the women returns to the cask and refills three of the goblets. The party is under way.

CHAPTER 4

The Land of Spaghetti Westerns

Two of the immediate benefits of the pool party are from Jim's conversation with Tony Arizza. First, the English language paper in Madrid just lost its food critic, responsible for providing the expat community with updated information on the municipal restaurants, as well as on a few from out of town. Jim is onto that almost before Tony finishes the tale.

Second, Tony has Hollywood contacts. He lets Jim know about the current trend in Hollywood of finding location filming sites that would allow shooting a feature film less expensively than in the US. Because of the nature of the countryside, the genre typically discussed for filming in Spain is westerns. A few have already been successfully completed in Italy, in the southern area where the landscape duplicates the arid US Southwest. As such, they are dubbed Spaghetti Westerns. Jim starts communicating with a few contacts he still has in California, as well as directors he knows in New York. Ever since he went looking for financing of the "rabbit enterprise" among friends in New York and other US locales, he has become less wary of communicating back to the States. His letters early on had requested secrecy from US folks simply because he was not sure how diligent the IRS would be. Now that there has been enough identifying information out there, floating around the mail and telephone communications, to say nothing of the sale of the apartment building, that if those minions at IRS were interested, he surmises he would have heard from them by now.

Jim goes after the newspaper food critic job as he has conducted every other campaign, straight on. He takes Marta to three different restaurants over a period of two weeks, writes a compare and contrast of the dining experiences then takes the final article to the paper for a meeting with the managing editor. He probably has more writing experience than anyone else who might be applying, and is fairly certain he is the only one applying with an example of a proofed article ready to publish. He's correct, and he gets the job, which pays almost nothing, but allows regular dinner dates with Marta where he can record the experience, and provide the restaurant valuable advertising, assuming they rise to the occasion.

Nearly all do. Just enough places do not measure up to allow him to maintain an appearance of neutrality. And poor pay or not, it provides some financial support for the family.

Some of the California correspondence bears fruit, and he discovers that there are several productions in planning for shooting in Spain. One is anything but a western. It is the biographical film about Patton with George C Scott, some of which will be shot in Spain. Two others in early planning are 100 Rifles and Valdez is Coming, all with name actors and performers. 100 Rifles won't be filmed until 1967, at least a year or more, but he maintains contact with the production company, and is able to provide valuable on- site logistical assistance for several companies, ingratiating himself into the working groups of at least those three. In true Tuck fashion, he wangles appearances for himself in Patton and 100 Rifles, and Marta gets on the cast list in Valdez is Coming with a part as a brothel owner. There will be lots more about these later.

Purcell is now riding the Tuck coattails, and cashes in on some of the film production contacts. Being a filming technician, he's good at the details of production, but not as great at schmoozing, organizing, creating an entire production. At 60, Jim can still energize rings around Joe as well, so the Hollywood Spanish connection devolves to Granja la Maja, in the pueblo Valdeolmos.

Marta is in the front of the house, sweeping in the living room when she hears, "Marta, Seniora, Marta!" The screech is coming from the familiar direction of the cantina cum telephone exchange, so Marta is pretty certain there is a call. The cantina is essentially the answering service for Tuck enterprises. She puts the broom in the corner and heads out the front door to shout across the plaza.

"Si?"

The bar maid makes the universal sign of a telephone with her hand to her ear, waving Marta over. Once inside the cantina, she indicates the phone in the booth for her and she nods. Marta enters the doorless booth where, as long as the conversation is in Spanish, the news of the day for the village is produced. "Si? Esta Marta aqui."

"I am sorry, I do not speak Spanish. Do I understand correctly that this is Marta Tuck, Jim Tuck's wife?"

"Yes it is. Whom am I speaking with please?"

"This is Averil Underwood, manager for preproduction of a Hollywood film, The 100 Rifles. I understand that your husband has had communication with the producer and might be available for local logistical assistance. Is that correct?"

"Yes, it is correct. Jim is in Madrid until 7p.m. today, so he is not available to talk today. Can he talk to you tomorrow?"

"Won't it be easier to talk this evening? We are on a bit of a tight schedule here."

"This is the only telephone service we have, here at the cantina. It is for all calls, so it will be difficult later today."

"Why is that? It seems a simple situation. I'll just call again after 7p.m."

"I am sorry I didn't explain better, Mr. Underwood, but this not our home. The cantina does not often accept calls after 5p.m. local time here. That is in an hour, I do not expect Jeem to return before that."

"You're kidding! You mean you are incommunicado for telephone after 5:00? Every day? Like, what do you do in emergencies? This is extraordinary!"

"In emergencies, the policia have a radio to call official offices to help, like ambulance, hospital, other police, tow truck, safe driver for friends who can not drive home after a party here at our house. There are a few people here in the village they will provide that service too. They are very nice people, the local guarda. Rarely the cantina phone works after five p.m. So, we are not completely without communication, as you can see. Shall I tell Jeem you will call tomorrow?

If so, what time. I am sure he will want to talk with you."

"Sigh! I suppose. It is extraordinary. Here it is, the 1960's and Spain has yet to advance into the 20th century. Alright! 2p.m. tomorrow, your time. Please have your husband available. Good day, Mrs. Tuck!"

"So nice to speak with you, Mr. Underwood."

"Humph!" Click.

"He was not very polite at all, Jeem. I would say he was impatient and rude." Jim is back and the family is at the dinner table in the hallway.

Jim puts his fork down, sits and rubs his right temple, thinking. "OK, so a Mr. Underwood from California wants to talk about us helping with a Hollywood film. What was the name of it?"

"Something about rifles. The connection was not very good and he talks very fast.

Xochitl is watching and chimes in, "Now that I am a bona fide high school graduate, do you think I could get a job with the film company?"

"No idea, crumpet. Let me talk to Marta a second. So, was this fellow rude enough to make you not want to work for their business? Is that what you are telling me?" Jim's eyebrows rise in question.

Marta is quiet for a minute, then says, "I am not so tender that I can not deal with a rude American. I am not saying that." She is sitting very straight, her head is a bit forward, jaw jutting forward a bit. Jim knows the posture well.

"It's OK, you know. You don't have to take crap from anyone. None of us do." With that, Jim casts a quick glance Xochitl's way, then continues, "I am just asking for confirmation, or wondering how much of a neanderthal this Underwood fellow is, that's all. Is that fair?"

The Marta stance softens considerably, she leans into the back of the chair, then says, "I understand. I just did not like his tone, or words. To answer your question, no, we need the money, it will be interesting if we can get the work, I am not opposed to the idea. I just hope this fellow is not around much of the time. OK?"

"Fine. I'll talk to him tomorrow. Two you said?"

"That's what he said. It seems he must not be calling from California, because it would be 5 a.m. there at 2 p.m. here. Do you think anyone would call at 5 a.m?"

"Doubt it. Maybe he is dumber than he sounded, or maybe you're right and he's in New York or something. We'll see tomorrow."

Jim is swirling the red wine around the large glass, sitting at a table in the cantina when the bar maid answers the the phone, "Si? Quien es? Quien se quiere? No intiendo. Momento."

"Senor Jeem, esta un Americano. No intiendo que," and she holds up the phone for Jim to take. He motions for her to set the receiver onto the bar with the cord running into the booth. She clunks it down, with slightly more force than required as Jim ambles over to retrieve it.

"Tuck. Who's this?"

"Is this Mr. Jim Tuck in Valdeolmos, Spain?"

"Yes it is."

"Hold the line for a moment for Mr. Underwood."

Buzz

Click, "Hello, is this James Tuck? Hello, hello"

"This is Tuck. Who the hell is this?"

"This is Mr. Averil Underwood with Paramount Pictures, New York offices. I spoke with your wife, I believe, yesterday, arranging this telephone interview. I believe you and our producer have a mutual contact, a Colonel Arizza who is currently stationed near Madrid. Is this accurate?"

"Well, I can't vouch for the accuracy of your name, but I do know Colonel Arizza. He is at Torrejon Air Base. I also know an Underwood person, or someone claiming that identity, spoke to my wife, Marta, yesterday, and left her a bit perplexed as to how someone could be that rude to her on the phone. We are used to gentler, more refined conversation here in Spain, but I imagine that is not universally understood in US society. Am I making myself reasonably clear, here, Mr. Underwood."

"Uh, um, um, … it sounds like there may have been some misunderstanding Mr. Tuck. Yes, I was the one who spoke to your wife yesterday, hoping to be able to contact you, but I, uh, I sincerely regret any offense she may have taken. None was intended I assure you."

"Well, perhaps there was not a great telephone connection to our small pueblo out here. We'll just leave it at that, shall we?"

"Indeed, indeed."

"Now, how can I be of assistance, Mr. Underwood."

"Please, you can call me Averil."

"Fine Mr. Underwood. Now, as you were saying, I might be helpful in some way?"

"Yes, of course. So, we are in the preproduction phase of a major project, with much of the filming scheduled for Spain. The immigration and logistics arrangements from this end have already been made. We need some local resource who can assist with travel, scene selection, some accommodation, and various other detailed arrangements and your name came up. I understand you have some experience with live theater and other productions here in New York. Is that correct?"

"Yes, of course. I have been involved in a few productions there, and I can provide a list of contacts for you if you wish. I have been living here in Spain nearly 3 years now so do not have extensive knowledge, but there are others I can contact for additional assistance if needed. My permanent residence is here in Valdeolmos, which is about 30 kilometers outside Madrid. As you have experienced, some communications can be problematic, but to date we have managed quite well here, with a reasonably active professional and social life. I suggest we have a more formal exchange of written communication using my poste restante at the Hilton Hotel in Madrid central. Communication there is secure, reliable and relatively immediately available. If you will be so kind as to forward me some more details of the services you need, remuneration you see as appropriate and the current production schedule you plan to use, I will return a response the same day as received with information and confirmations you might require. Does this seem appropriate?"

"Quite. I will forward the letter today. Do you have any idea how long the mail takes to get there from New York?"

"It seems 4 to 7 days is average. Occasionally shorter, but rarely longer."

"Fine, I will send you a letter with the details of the needs for our production in Spain and hopefully hear from you by this time next week."

"We appreciate your call. Bye for now. Ciao."

"Ciao it is." Click.

"Well, it looks like we are in the filmmaking support business, for now." Marta's head comes up from her printmaking, in the loft upstairs. Red paint spatters her nose and cheek, which broadens with a smile.

"It seems the rude man was nicer to you, no?"

"I had a few words with the fellow, and it seems I didn't piss him off too much. Hopefully he is a fast learner, in case you have to talk to him again. Don't know if he was nicer to me or not. He understands, I think, that he might have handled his conversation with you a bit differently. They are hard chargers over there. Almost forget that part of New York or US life. Miss it sometimes." With that there is a wry grin slightly twisting Jim's mouth as Marta makes a face.

"I do not miss it one bit, or one day. None. Clear?"

"I know, I know! I understand you have found paradise here in this fairly cool sanctuary. Not suggesting anything. OK? Oops, gotta get Xoch. Back in a few." And he is down the stairs and out the door.

At the gate to the air base, the traffic is backed up significantly further than any time Jim has passed through. The guard at the gate looks at the decal, asks Jim for identification, examines the back seat and is generally officious to the max. "I don't recognize you. You new here?"

"Not new. Reassigned from the MP's. Things have tightened up significantly since the accident."

"Accident? Not sure what you're referring to. A problem on base? Are the high school kids o.k?"

"Not on the base. Kids are o.k. On your way, Mr. Tuck. NEXT!" And with a fairly imperious wave he moves Jim forward.

"Xoch, you heard anything about an accident"?

"Where you been, Poppa? It's all over Madrid by now."

"You may have lost sight of the fact we live in Valdeolmos?!"

"Big plane crash on the coast. It was an American military plane is what I heard. I bet Tony can tell ya."

"I'll have to ask him. In you get. More news on the family front. I'll fill you in on the way home."

In fact, Jim never gets to get any info from Tony about the 1966 B52 crash on the Spanish coast, causing an international incident, requiring the under water recovery of a hydrogen bomb and the extensive cleanup of 2 others that broke up on land, ruining local farm land for years into the future. Nope. Tony is quite unavailable while he ramrods the cleanup efforts, and once his schedule allows visiting again, there is no discussion of the incident. Even with inside contacts, living in the region, Jim's nose for news gets him only what the newspapers and radio offers. It's immensely frustrating for someone used to informing others, but is soon lost in the hubbub accompanying entry into the US film industry.

CHAPTER 5

In Jim's Words

While we are awaiting the effects of the Tucks' adventures in the film industry, I have decided to insert an unpublished work, in Jim's own words. I was given a couple of yellowed, type-written pieces by Margaret, Jim's widow, to use if it seemed appropriate. This work seems nearly, but not quite, completed. Jim was actively editing the work when it was stored away. I have attempted to keep it exactly as it is on these yellowed pages, making a few corrections for clarity when the editing was incomplete in some way. Here's as good a spot for it as any. Jim's own description of some of the Life of Valdeolmos, in the 1960's.

All the Living Creatures

By Jim Tuck

date unknown

Against the whitewashed front of our house, beneath the tall barred windows are two large, limestone boulders and a solid, sawed elm tree-trunk. I was given the tree-trunk, when I admired it, by Ramon, the provincial road tender. He receives a huge load of firewood each Fall from the province as part of his annual emolument. But, the origin of the stones is unknown. Tio Nicholas says that my stones, as well as a few others which are scattered around the village have been here "por todo la vida". Which means for all of a lifetime and is the villager's maximized concept of an extended period of time. Despite the erosion of centuries, both rocks reveal the faint impress of hammer blows and chisel scars. I speculate they came from the ruins of a Roman, or late Moorish, hilltop fortification at Torrelaguna, some twenty miles away. The blunted V-shaped stone could have been the capstone in an archway, and the rounded one a Roman war ball for rolling down the steep slope into the massed ranks of an Iberian attacking tribe.

The stones were probably trundeled to Valdeolmos in creaking, springless ox carts by Serranos, the half wild mountain people who inhabited the slopes of the distant Sierra. Their ancestors still work the ancient limestone quarries and supply the valley villagers with hollowed-out stone drinking troughs for their animals.

My rocks, and the others around the village as well, and my tree-trunk, are for sitting in the sun, a pass-time daily observed by my older neighbors, and myself, throughout the year. Para calientar los huesos, or, to warm the bones they say. The seats are placed strategically; the capstone is at the southeast corner where it avoids the chilling blasts that sweep off the snow covered Sierra in Winter, and yet captures the enfolding warmth of the morning sun. The war ball and the tree-trunk flank the entrance to the gallery, and are for afternoon sitting. Here, the Summer sun is cooled and filtered through our leafy green acacias, which semicircle the front of the house, and when the trees are bare the seats are bathed in a liquid light until the sun drops behind the purple-hued Guadarramas in the west.

When the weather permits, which is about ninety percent of the time, it has become my custom to go out to the capstone just after dawn and drink two or three cups of coffee.

Here, I find moments of glory. The long shadows make soft, slowly repeating patterns across the plaza. The swallows and sparrows whirl and swoop across the plaza and the housetops. The air is clear and fresh, as though cleansed by the night breezes, and it carries the sharp smell of wood smoke from the newly made kitchen fires. The aromas of frying sausage and freshly made coffee reach me too.

The pueblo women make coffee with great care for the beans are expensive; a pound costs nearly half a man's daily wage. Real coffee has been known by the villagers for the past ten or fifteen years; formerly they drank an ashy, sour-tasting concoction that was extracted from a mixture of roasted acorns and barley. But, with Spain's new affluence, practically every family disayunos, or breaks the night's fast with it.

I have copied the village's way of making the brew, and it tastes nothing like the insipid stuff we drank for so many years back there in the States. We grind freshly roasted beans to a coarse powder which is loosely packed into a fine mesh bag. Boiling water is poured through it slowly and the coffee is allowed to drip into a pot of freshly boiled milk that has been brought from Jesus's cows the evening before. Incidentally, we extract more than a pint of heavy cream from each three quarts of milk.

By the time I have finished my coffee, the village has come alive again. The plaza in front of the house is drenched in sunlight and the first creatures have sallied forth from the houses or corrals to celebrate the dawn of a completely new day. For, the village expires, at nightfall, into a sort of dusk to dawn hibernation.

The hours of darkness portend an ominous time for a people dominated by thousands of years of traditionally working and living between luz y luz, or sunrise and sunset. All work and all chores are rigidly scheduled to be finished and out of the way before light ends. Although electric lights came to the pueblo in 1922, this custom is still vigorously followed when possible. With the darkness descends surprising vestiges of centuries of superstition and fear. Few of the people under fifty continue to believe in brujas, or witches and warlocks, but a generation or two ago, everyone was convinced of their existence and presence in the village.

And the legend persists. Old Aunt Filomena, who is well into her eighties and looks like a witch was supposed to look, assured me that if I had come to Valdeolmos before the installation of electricity, I would have seen the witches on moonlight nights flying through the air, perching confidently on the edge of the church belfry and holding wild meetings on the cropped grass of the prado. But the witches, she assured me could not stand the vibrations emanating from the electric wires. Since they were strung, the flying has ceased.

The evil eye, el ojo malo, is another scourge of the night. Nearly everybody in the pueblo believes this spell, which must be cast when the sun is down or hidden, is responsible for those aches and pains which do not respond promptly to prescriptions of the local doctor. Young children are thought to be particularly vulnerable. Though both men and women have the talent of bestowing el ojo malo with a specially bold and penetrating stare, its chief practitioners are thought to be the gypsy women. Consequently, the Gypsies are very well treated when they pass through Valdeolmos. But an unwritten law requires them to set up camp and eat and sleep outside the village proper if they decide to spend the night here.

Curiously, the villagers believe that el ojo malo does not require evil intent on the part of the starer. For this reason, maybe, I have found it most difficult to catch a villager's eye when conversing after sunset. In compensation there are many remedies and defenses against el ojo malo, and most seem to work. The most popular are religious medallions worn around the neck depicting the Virgin or one's personal Saint. If the evil eye is bestowed despite the medallion, rubbing the afflicted part with dried thyme, which is common in our countryside, will usually break the spell.

I heard so many stories about the supernatural power of el ojo malo that I decided to make a first hand investigation of the mystery. Ever since my arrival in the village I have been friendly with Senor Leander who is King or leader of a small clan of Gypsies living in Torrelaguna. They buy, sell and trade animals and visit Valdeolmos and the other valley towns six or eight times a year. Now it should not be presumed that any particular tact or dissimulation was necessary on my part in my discussion with Senor Leander. One of the most rewarding qualities of the people of the Meseta is their frankness. Vamos a hablar con cosas claras they say, let us talk of things clearly. Over a bottle of local white wine, chilled in the stream behind his house, I told Senor Leander candidly that the villagers suspected some of the older women of his clan having the power of the evil eye.

"Sin duda", without doubt, "Don Jaime," he admitted. "They have lived a long time and are very accomplished. But they do not cast nearly as many spells as we receive from the old women in the pueblos."

The upshot of our conversation was that the Gypsies were more sinned against than sinning. And this was true also of the few witches I tried to track down in the pueblos without electricity. Yes, the old women would admit, there are still flying witches, but they lived in an adjacent town.

The other superstition pervading the village about the dangers occurring in the darkness is the dread of the night air. There is no skepticism among the young or old in the belief that disease and sickness and even death can be carried by the night winds. Marie, the wife of Diego, told me that once when she was a little girl she was carrying a lamp into her parents' bedroom and a viento malo, a bad wind, entered the lampshade and broke it into a thousand bits. "What luck, my mother said, that the wind went into the lamp and not into me," Marie related.

In the beginning I often wondered how a people who belong to a modern European culture, read, albeit inadequately, and who live within 20 miles of one of Europe's most sophisticated capitals, could continue to hold such beliefs. But then I remembered that, back there in the city, hotels rarely have a 13th floor, few people walk under a ladder happily and three on a match is really asking for trouble.

Superstitions die slowly and the Valdeolmos night is hardly begun before the children and dogs are collected and the harsh rasping of the wooden doors on the cement sills announces the closing of the houses. The windows are tightly shut and solid wooden shutters are forced into place behind them. The women and children and dogs sit in the kitchen and watch television and await the return of the menfolk from the village's three taverns. By nine thirty in the Winter and an hour or so later in the Spring and Summer the taverns are empty. The heavy doors crunch open to admit the men and then are closed again till sun-up.

The village is shrouded in a moon-like silence. Not a ray of light escapes to the street. Not a sound comes from within the houses. The radios and TV sets are muted.

The babies are quietened with the teat or a pacifier. The educated dogs sleep quietly in the corrals. Whoever is forced by some absolutely unavoidable errand into the street scurries nervously along as though pursued by demons. "This is no time for talking, Jaime", I am told flatly when I attempt to delay them with conversation. "Vamos a costar," let us go to bed, and they rush off to complete their mission. The last meal, la Cena, is eaten and they are in bed by eleven thirty or twelve. They sleep like the dead, totally apart from the world about them.

Only the most persistent thundering on a door with a heavy stone -- a recourse at moments of acute emergency -- will bring a sleeper to his shuttered and barred window. Then the conversation will go like this;

"En el Nombre de Dios, who is it?"

"Yo", or me, the traditional village answer by a knocker.

"Which me?"

"Jaime."

"Which Jaime?" Though I am the only Jaime in the village.

"Jaime of Marta." Long silence.

"Bueno, que pasa, Jaime?" Or, good,, what's happening, Jaime?

"Your brother is sick and wants you."

"My brother is sick?"

"Yes, your brother is sick."

"Esta seguro?" Are you sure? More agitated conversation with wife.

"Si, hombre, your brother is sick."

"Caramba! I am coming." And reluctantly he will emerge.

There are, however, two infringements on the silence that startle the householders immediately back to consciousness. When their dogs bark in the corral, they awake and listen for the source of the dogs' alarm. When the dog stops, they at once fall back to sleep. Other people's dogs, however, rarely disturb them. When the church bell is rung, slowly and continuously, the entire pueblo comes awake in an instant. Before the third or fourth peal has reverberated through the still night, the doors are flung open and the men are in the street running. For the bells at night have only one meaning -- fire. And this the pueblo fears more than witches, thieves, disease or the evil eye.

But life goes on in the darkened, noiseless town. There is the echoing of a hoot owl nesting in the church tower. The sharp cry of a night hunting bird as it swoops across the pueblo hunting. The chirp of frogs carried from the arroyo on the light night wind. And, in the Fall and Winter, the sounds of the wind itself as it blows from the Guadarramas and sweeps the Meseta.

Intermixed with these sounds is the silent padding of the village cats, hunting and mating on the rooftops. There are legions of them; every family admits to owning cats but they don't know how many. During the daytime, the cats live in the dark corners of attics beneath the rooftops. Here they sleep and tend their young in noble isolation. At dusk they go out to hunt, for few of their masters provide food to sustain them.

For the cat in the Spanish pueblo is not a tart to be pampered or spoiled. Rather, like all the other animals, he is part of the social organization with a specific task to perform; the killing of rats and mice. In return, his master provides him with relative freedom, housing and a very occasional bowl of diluted milk or leavings from the midday meal. The cats respond in kind; only rarely does one permit itself to be picked up or petted, even by the children. But they do their job with admirable efficiency; the rats and mice exist, but we rarely see them.

These village cats are highly developed predatory animals, and on moonlit nights I spend hours tracking them around the village and through the fields and, with the aid of binoculars, watching them hunt and mate. Their movements are sublime and rarely in nature has beauty and utility combined as in this most elegant of animals.

We have owned many cats, usually males. But our Valdeolmos felines have been proud and mighty warriors compared to the cringing, supplicating, highly bred, pedigree slaves we had back in the States. I started the line with Saber Tooth I, an independent, ferocious tiger who once brightened a morning on the capstone by depositing at my feet the biggest rat the pueblo had ever seen. We are presently partners with Saber Tooth IV.

The village cats seldom die natural deaths. They wound each other mortally in their desperate mating battles. The dogs take a toll as do the traps the villagers set for rabbits. But this is as it should be. Any great cat remains an untamed and undomesticated animal. His nobility emerges because he is free and unassociated with a "master". In nature, the hunter is always hunted and our Valdeolmos cats, tied to this code, live and die with pride and dignity. It never ceased to amaze me how, in the morning, my most valiant battler, Saber Tooth III, would return from his nocturnal foray and stalk like the veritable king of beasts into the kitchen for his bowl of milk and play the role, for my enjoyment, of an innocent house pet. His great yellow head would be crusted with dried blood, his ears ripped and mangled and his powerful leontine body raked with deep scratches. As long as I ignored his wounds, he permitted me to pet and stroke him. But the instant I attempted to assert my authority and doctor him, he fled to his sanctuary among the beans in the barn in the corral. There, his "at home" wife and he would lick his wounds safe from masters and veterinarians, as wild animals have done through the millenia.

Victor and Consuelo rise to milk their cows just after dawn. For years they have sent milk to several village families, who have emigrated to Madrid, on the seven thirty bus that goes to the capital each morning. At this hour in Winter it is still quite dark and Consuelo greets the new day tremulously. I have watched Consuelo tremulously greet the Winter mornings. The dim bulb in the streetlight illuminated only its immediate area, and the plaza in front of her door is still quite dark. First, the heavy iron bolt at the top of the door is pulled back, then the heavy iron bolt at the bottom is released. Finally, the big iron key is turned and the door is unlocked. She wrenches it ajar a few inches and stares into the darkness suspiciously. As her eyes adjust to the dark, I come into sudden focus. "Dios mio, Jaime," she exclaims, "you have scared me!" But she recovers her dignity quickly, picks up the milk cans and, reassured by my presence, walks forthrightly to meet the bus.

With the first light in the east, I wrap myself warmly in my ankle-length sheepskin coat and go back to my capstone for my second cup of coffee.

CHAPTER 6

When Dougie Met Jim

"Marta!"

"Jeem. Why are you yelling? I am right here in the kitchen!"

"Sorry. Couldn't see ya. Look, it's 12:30. The film folks will be arriving in an hour or so, and this pig is not cooking fast enough." Jim is tending the spit outside the kitchen door, making sure the slowly roasting pig doesn't burn on one side. "Could you bring some more firewood for the pit? I need to build the fire a bit or we're never going to eat this evening."

"Yes. I am coming in a minute." Marta comes through the door with an armload of small wood pieces that Jim piles under the roasting animal, the flames rise and the sizzling increases. "How many did you say are coming tonight?"

"Not sure. At least twenty. Probably a few more. I don't think many villagers will be here, other than the alcalde, maybe. Too late for them. Might get a few dinner eaters earlier. Free food seems to bring them in sometimes. Maybe a total of 30 or so.

"Oh, Purcell is coming and bringing some new blood to the hacienda. Some fellow from London, works in advertising, artist of some sort, Joe says. Actually, he arrived yesterday driving from London, via Czechoslovakia. Apparently has a few Czech bullet holes in the back of his Zephyr. Ought to be an interesting story or two in there. Name's Douglas Cown, or Corcoran, no, Chowns. That's it. Likes to be called Dougie for some godawful reason. You got enough tortillas and corn for 30?"

"Plenty, and I will cook rice as well, but not until people are here."

"Good. Don't want rice glob. I told Tony to make sure people bring their own wine, or alcohol. But, to make sure, Maria, at the bodega is drawing off a bucket full for us. Can you collect it in half an hour? Or, I can get it if you'll tend the pig."

"You get it. I'll take care of the pig. It'll be heavy enough to need your arm. It will be a big bucket, I know. I have to get back to the corn."

"Fine. Just don't let this pig burn."

The following is Doug Chowns' (Hijo de Jaime to the villagers) own story of his arrival at the Tucks' in Valdeolmos, in his own words.

My long road back to Madrid.

Autumn leaves and fallen crab apples crushed beneath my tyres, a straight tree-lined road ahead, a 1968 blue sky early morning in Austria now so long ago in my memory. Autobahn overnight, a long drive south from Ostend Belgium where I had landed from the cross channel ferry late afternoon having left home in Buckinghamshire England the day before. I was on assignment. I needed a mission.

Like a droplet on a window pane just a mere trickle of water following gravity, finding its way, I was being pulled across Europe a vast landscape. My unexpected retreat from a cliff edge and destruction in Madrid three months before had made me a willing agent to take on the unknown. Suddenly out of assured income, a smart downtown apartment and a high powered lifestyle required an urgent change of direction. After three months of safety recovering, the tension had been relieved, responsibilities at home lessened by positively "going for it" - taking the opportunity. A vague plan in the head to re establish back in Spain where I had been forced out by circumstances beyond my control leads to suddenly "up and away" at 4pm one summer afternoon.

Three months earlier, with no warning, my Madrid office had been sold to our parent company directors in New York, the staff fired and the safe emptied. Accountant Antonio Luengo shattered. The New York directors ignored me in the elevator on my arrival at the office, only for them to later discover they had bought a lemon. Worse, their Iberian associate was still their partner in Portugal ... and they could do nothing about it since he held unexpected cards as GM of the manufacturer of the Colgate Palmolive products in Portugal as well as Distributer and Market Research consultant. Colgate were later amused. I was suddenly out of a job, no longer creative director.

Life's twists and turns can change all in a second. Little is predictable even when one believes all is well - change of circumstances and the impossible can happen. In Spain I had to cut my losses fast. The safety of my family a priority necessitated a hasty return the same day to England. Our furniture went out the 2nd floor windows into an American Express container in the street. Three hours later, we left by car and a thousand mile road trip north as the container doors shut. With our parents in England two days later, they asked few questions and took us in while I regained our home from our tenant nurses.

As a well paid high flier and international ex jet-set executive, I had to expect the unexpected, cut losses and remain positive. On applying at London job interviews, my heavyweight track card resulted in only polite "we would like you but " So, treading water and anxious, I received a proposal from a Swiss photographer and friend, Rene Groebli. We worked together for many years on my commissions. He heard of my plight and proposed I should be involved in a Kodak Cologne Fotokina light show he was producing for Kodak Stuttgart.

Available, I was introduced to Electrosonic their commissioned Greenwich London special FX designers. The problem was to transport thousands of delicate, die positive colour transparencies from Kodak Hemel Hempstead to Kodak Stuttgart. The problem was easily solved when I proposed I drive them myself by road, free of courier and customs. My car was loaded with Portabello Road market antiques for friends' new mountain home, the 80 ready loaded Kodak carousels, and included a meter-high cabinet musical box with an impressive silver metal playing disc bigger than a very large dinner plate behind a glass door. Uncovered, it stood in view upright on the back seat. No questions were asked at frontiers, my British Ford Zephyr had Portuguese and Espana insignia. Ahead of schedule, I drove another hour to Linz and spent the night.

Like that dribble of water, I was finding my way as miles opened up before me - I was following my nose and within 48 hours I would deliver the loaded carousels to the team at Kodak Stuttgart.

A Scottish Country dancer friend, a German woman who was au pair locally in the Chiltern Hills, who I had even Piped away at Victoria Station when she returned to Germany, lived locally in Stuttgart. I asked a German- speaking office secretary to phone her for me. Her mother answered and became very upset, the secretary was shocked. My friend was dead, shot in Czechoslovakia. Eventually her mother calmed after the unexpected request for Susanne, and finally understood I was a friend from England. She invited me to dinner. At dinner, I discovered that both my friend and her husband had been shot while demonstrating against the Russian invasion. I understood that they were part of a visiting Freiburg choir when the Russians took over.

A difficult dinner-for-one resulted until I realized the mother had Czechs in the next room. We shared my steak before an incoming Chech telephone call. There was a problem, a need to extract more family stranded on the northern Austrian frontier near Aigen im Muhlkreis, less than an hour north west of Linz, only 80 miles or so, I thought, from my night before. With six cylinders and a full tank outside I offered the obvious before I resumed my journey south to Zurich. I guess I was open to living dangerously.

My brief excursion was better than a screen writer would have dreamed up. At dusk, having parked the car in dense woodland forest inside the Austrian frontier off to the side before the frontier post on a forestry road, I crossed, on foot, an unguarded and unfenced frontier. From forest to meadow to rendezvous was a short distance, maybe a kilometer, to a deserted boat landing on the southern side of the Lipo. A father and daughter, with no English, waited as a small boat departed back due north into the night. Returning back but off the road we regained the meadow field I had come over, and back into the forest and across the border into Austria where my car waited. Now, in total darkness, we had avoided a farm and the road frontier well lit checkpoint beyond to our right. Now, I had to circle back and join the dead-straight pine tree lined main highway only half a kilometer south of the frontier post, not a good feeling as I wanted to put as much distance as possible between myself and the Czech border, and be as far away as quickly as possible. A foot patrol must have been curious, perhaps hearing my engine to the south, close on my arrival under two hours before. I started my engine, slipping the clutch at the same time, the car shot forward, I punched the headlights, trees flashing past and lose gravel and stones hitting the car bottom - a thud sounded behind my back.

The musical box must have had a penny lodged in the slot - it fell into the brass clockwork as the bullet hit the music box. The silver disk sprang into life, and, accompanied by bells and sweet timpani "God Save the Queen or King" no less filled the car interior. My passengers were terrified - I could only laugh rather hysterically.

Calmed but reassured, country lanes turned at Linz into Autobhan with Germany less than an hour ahead at Salzburg where a frontier Guard signaled me to pull over well away from the brightly lit portico where other cars were being turned inside out. My headlights full on, the guard approached capped and greatcoated. I opened my door keeping one leg inside as my passengers made themselves scarce under a blanket in the left front seat-well. The guard, realising I was a stupid Englander driving a right hand drive car with Portuguese registration and Espana identification, launched into verbal abuse walking back and forth in my headlights. His tirade prohibited inspecting the inside of the car or being aware of my hiding passengers. So critical was he about me, his diatribe finished, he waved this stupid Englander on.

In a pre-arranged drop at a beer garden an hour later in Munich, I delivered my cargo outside to anxious waiting relatives. The least known or said the better,

I again dipped my clutch without formalities before they spoke and quickly regained the road to Constance and Wintethur. By mid morning I was in Zurich on familiar roads to the Morgentalstrasse studio and friends pleased to have their antiques for a new home in Glaritz. Next day, refreshed, came Geneva, Grenoble, Lyon and Avignon, Perpignan and the mountains into Spain and Barcelona. I passed through the junction on Calle Diagonal at Tusset and Balmes where I was, years later, to work, and headed for Zaragoza and Madrid. I had had an overnight stop in Lyon and a sleep in the car en route. I enjoyed long drives.

Tired, I went to my old apartment in Madrid, knowing Joe Purcell would be in the basement, a Californian, a minor film producer and friend who hoped to have work from me. He agreed to put me up. Next morning he said we were going in my car to a pig roast out in the campo. His Citron dos cavallios was not big, and with his girl friend, my car was a treat. A Mexican food event as a wind-up for the cast of two westerns that my future hosts had work in - A Hundred Rifles, and Valdez is coming.

Joe said the cast had become friends of these congenial and interesting Americans, Jim and Marta Tuck who each had small parts as extras, Jim as a locomotive engineer in Hundred Rifles and Marta as a remote desert brothel madame in Valdez is coming. Marta, an Aztec by birth, had married Jim years before in California, later to live in Woodstock, New York state and later New York City. Joe's connection, he said, was that his mother, Marta Tuck, and Steve McQueen's mother used to babysit each other's children in LA. In good spirits, he filled me in on the Tucks as we headed northwest from Madrid into the Campo towards where they lived in a large old hacienda. The main road runs north in Provincia de Madrid north of Guadalajara, then the caratera highway, the main road to Burgos in the north. After a few kilometers only, at San Sabastian de los Reyes, we made a right onto a country road heading east through olive groves and tilled red soil in a rolling series of crests, crossing the south-flowing Jarama river. Jim later told me this was where Britian lost the cream of its university intelligencia in 1936. They were machine gunned here, at the river crossing.

At Fuentes la Saz, a small Pueblo to the north, we bounced through a crossroads at Alghete Alalpardo, the houses brilliant white against the sun baked red soil. Poor homes built right up to the road surface, where animals shared the interior earth floors. We passed churches with chains hanging on the walls waiting for women to drag them by their ankles at the celebration of San Isidro. Spanish earth, dry and dusty for months without rain would, at the first shower, burst out in a perfume I know of in no other place on earth.

A broad open landscape appeared with isolated Pueblos, each with its own customs and way of life hardly known to each other before cars. A burrow stood, ears up and wearing a tatty straw hat under an olive tree munching quietly. The empty single-lane tree-lined road crested to show a Pueblo hill town ahead, the church and tower clearly visible. Dung and olives, the Sierra Madre north on the skyline snow crested above a clear unblemished haze. Tall autumn poplars, comforting and yellow against a deep blue sky. In Portugal, houses are better kept, blue painted corners and everything in its place - in Spain, not so. Crumbling, whitewashed brickwork or hollow ceramic tile was common since the construction of a boundary wall was the first priority of ownership with iron gates and inside the wall, pots as large as a man.

Roadside Fascist Falange spears announced our entry and arrival to Valdeolmos. No dull green clad Guardia to be seen on their horses, rifles slung broadside over their shoulders, their shiny black hats with a flat upturned brim at the back. The Zephyr 6 cruised in causing heads to turn, anything and everyone came to Valdeolmos to see Jaimie. Not famous in their minds although many seen on the Bodega TV, nobody other than Franco would be a surprise. The Valdeolmos locals, all poor peasants, had no idea what year it was, some had never been to Madrid 30 Kms away. Valdeolmos was still 17th century isolated in Spain, the women in black, the men mostly shepherds tending their sheep like their fathers. They milked their sheep for cheese at night after a long day walking a large circle. They still wore yards of cloth around their stomachs and their coats like a cape over one shoulder, a stick in their right hand, a clod of soil to throw in the other.

The big old White House with rejas on both windows, our destination, had people gathered. I parked with others in the shade under a row of Acacia trees. In front, two large boulders as seats each side of the centered open barn door. People were moving around elegantly, the women in smart Italian pants and the men in white pleated Mexican shirts. The background sound, Pearl Fishers, was loud on a gramophone and the cool of red flag stones where many guests moved clutching Rioja red wine, smiling and relaxed. We could hear the slap slap slap of Mexican-faced women at the back in the kitchen making tortillas and enchiladas as only Mexican women can do, hand to hand amid smiles and laughter. Marta, a tallish elegant Aztec woman in her late fifties was in charge, smiling with colourful back chat in Manhattan American accent, her arms waving as she talked and laughed. I liked her instantly. Back in the hall below framed posters from stage productions in Woodstock were well known faces from the movies. Now they were about to become drinking friends as the afternoon progressed.

Glass in hand, I explored the dusty book-shelved front room with its creative black and white pillow tick curtains and extensive long play vinyl record collection. A large brick fireplace was built into the end wall. A soft afternoon light filtered through the single iron reja window set into a half meter thick wall. Back in the hall, a large paneled Spanish door featured as a table with many seats around it, far too few for today's gathering. Beyond the kitchen, another carved old doorway in the whitewashed wall opened to a patio garden and Pozo - the well - close to the kitchen. The well was a low, circular, stone, hip-high wall with towering decorative black ironwork with a pulley wheel and rope centrally for a bucket over the well mouth. Today, the wooden cover was still in place as a bench top for a large charcoal b-b-q where a spitted suckling pig was nearing perfection. A speciality food critic in Madrid, the host was a great lover of good food and had it almost done to a perfection. He was basting while holding court, a cigarette in one hand and an olive oil brush in the other as he turned and applied this day's special fare from his own special mix of herbs and spices. My host, Jim, was sort of unusual. Normally the Spanish are very formal, he was not.

Clad in rumpled, clean, un-ironed scruffy light trousers and shirt, several day's growth of uncut beard and a waving head of white hair, this was my unknown host. As people seeking the garden and pool edged past in this congested small patio space with a picturesque hundreds of years old well, in the middle, I wondered how do I introduce myself? It was made easy - someone had told him I was with Joe, and that I was a young English creative director returning to Madrid from London by road via a mid European adventure - of sorts. Without a thought "My boy..." he loudly said as he put his arm around my shoulders ". all this is yours when I die". I felt welcomed.

Joe was animatedly talking with Sumner Williams, a tall Californian and Piccadilly nightclub owner who looked after his Uncle Nico's investments from a Tony Curtis/Widmark Vikings feature film. Apparently the set-up of the movie industry was similar to the making of Doctor Zhivago, recently completed at Estudios Roma. All original negatives were cut by Spanish editors prior to leaving Spain, the studioi and film profits to finance a car factory, Barrera Dodge, while clubs, restaurants, and other industries were encouraged. Overseas investment was important as Spain transitioned to the modern world and tourism, especially attracting the Spanish and Italian speaking California-based film industry. Use of all-Spanish facilities and crews made financial sense as did the free export of the edited negative film.

Two spaghetti westerns were underway, 100 Rifles featuring Raquel Welch, Burt Reynolds and ex gridiron star Jim Brown which was what this afternoon was about. Another underway, Valdez is Coming with Burt Lancaster and Frank Silvera was also well represented in the attendees. Jim in one, and Marta already measured, to her amusement, for "her rags" in the other. Small parts as extras featured as part of their lifestyle bringing them in touch with the kind of internationals they enjoyed, but also as friends and contacts as these actors and filmmakers became famous stars and directors.

Frank Silvera, a delightful Jamaican and co-star with Burt Lancaster smiled on as Jim eloquently made me his heir above all others - the suckling pig then removed to be tenderly jointed and carved, the best bits reaching Jims mouth as he elaborately performed for his guests who had gathered around holding plates. Some already had tamales and chili. Several of Jim's rabbits were roasting "Conejo asada" a local campesino delicacy, always available on Sundays at selective rural river crossings, very cheap with crusty bread and red wine. The local peasant neighbors, the shepherds and their wives and families, all unseen, peeped over the high orange tile topped wall. Only Peely, the Tucks' maid and her daughter would come to La Granja to wash up and clean the kitchen and house when guests had departed. They were proud to be servants and would have been offended or embarrassed had it been otherwise.

This event would be village talk for months and likely also their way to mark the year. Only Gaston the priest, Guardia, Alcalde and the school teacher were present from the pueblo itself. Only they would have known or needed to know that it was 1968. A year of change in the world.

Frank Silvera, not as his film part Diego, but a Shakespearian scholar was discussing the merits of King Lear with Jim. Both were amazed and delighted with each other, the popular brand 403 brandy was flowing. Dorothy, I was told, was Mrs TWA Cargo, writers Elmore Leanord and Roland Kibbee, Greek, had brought their stylish campasino Spanish boots for safe keeping. Artist Dimitri Perdikidis and sister-in-law Fifi, his wife Helene were watching their children in the pool. Phil Yorden, I understood, was the Director and was the key production mogul. Burt Reynolds I did not know until later as he was not a star I was aware of. Among other unknown faces, director Tony Grimes, Maralyn Schawartz and Jerry Goldsmith who wrote

The Sound of Music. Richard Eder from the New York Times had turned up after phoning Alalpardo 68, the Centralita, the telephone exchange,and at that time the only village telephone that acted as a way point for incoming Americans and the Pueblo's single telephone that served the Tuck family. We chatted and I have his card. I met Jim Brown later but don't specially remember him that day. A quiet Englishman and his girlfriend, Mary Adams, turned out to be El Ingles, the bullfighter. Quiet and serious, a friend of Jim's daughter Xochitl, Henry Higgins talked to me about his UK art school at Guildford Art England, the least likely Torero Matador I could imagine.

Although Joe had pointed out on our way where Anthony Quinn was staying he was not there as far as I remember but his "Fixer", Poli, an energetic Spaniard who could organize and fix anything on location with the locals was there. Like Quinn, Burt Lancaster was elsewhere, or had looked in before we arrived - people arrived and departed all the time - much to the bemused locals' expectations.

Charismatic Tony, an actor of mixed birth and religion was chatting up a smart single southern schoolteacher from Torrejon American school. Tony made a superbly American Indian at half the cost of a real one when made up and dressed. Japanese also worked as Indians because they were cheaper and available. To cast a film, one only had to go to the Elsa Frigor Milk Bar near Colon where extras lined up daily, dressed and ready to work. Many were actual Vaqueros, as their hands showed.

The famous mingled comfortably for hours that late afternoon. "Su casa", the warm invitation was readily accepted. Gaston, an illegitimate son of Don Domeque the millionaire Jerez and Rejoniador, and an intrepid proud horseman of the Spanish School was well versed in English. Thirty years old, he lived with his partner close by, a few doors away, also in the Plaza. Casually dressed in off white, he approached the pool to admire it and its bathers' antics, but as he leant forward his glass eye dropped out - slowly it rolled to the deep end. Everyone became silent and quite spell bound. A pregnant pause in the afternoon, it lay 2 meters deep looking up at us - then splash! - soon recovered, Gaston just popped it back in saying Gracias to the bikini clad retriever. Conversations immediately recommenced without comment.

Mexican Americans, Tony Arizza, and his always smiling wife Carmen, she now free of the kitchen and making Tamales, had their very bright 20 year old son Monte back-chatting Jim with academic word usage. Jim told Monte that his pediatric novice dance steps needed attention. Monte's brilliant response was to Jim's delight. I discovered later that Jim had known Monte's father, Tony, since the Philippines. Monte later went to Cambridge University as a 21 year old Tutor of Spanish History. His quiet but very experienced Dad, an ex-USAF Colonel, had been involved in managing the clean up and negotiations surrounding the B52 accident on the beach in Spain, complete with extracting the hydrogen bombs it had been carrying. His Basque heritage and excellent Spanish made him the USAF Officer who was the ideal choice.

The Harmonica solo of Bob Dylan singing Mr Tambourine Man filtered for the fourth time through the house from the front room where Ed Mann, a filmmaker and wife Marylyn sat drinking strong coffee from large red tin enamel mugs with a Californian arms dealer. His wife, I was told, was skeet shooting champion from maybe Arkansas. Their Hollywood tigertail born daughters Robyn and stunning Dale both had been at school with Xochitl presently gathered up to no good getting a high together in Xochitl's bedroom with classmates Chilean Dennis and Dorothy's talented guitarist blue-grass singer son, Jack.

Such was Granja La Maja a Mayors house on that afternoon in Valdeolmos, the Valley of the Elms.

As guests departed, Marta cornered me keen to show me her hand painted scarves. She took me upstairs to her studio work space. An empty upstairs packed with all kinds of things, Jim's writing office was directly above their bedroom. Marta had many chiffon hand-painted very long high fashion scarves, each hours of work. Experienced in printing processes and marketing, this creative director, who had enjoyed the silk screen process at art school fifteen years before, said, "Too labour intensive. You will never cover your time. You must silk screen fabric print them in runs of twenty or thirty at a time."

Marta responded desperately that she didn't know how, would I help and teach her?

That started our association to set up "Creaciones originales estampados a Mano" - Mano was to become our brand name for one off original creations; scarves, high fashion gowns, shifts, shirts and expensive culottes. Anything was possible and we could utilize the many unemployed Pueblo women who were available with sewing machines as maker uppers.

CHAPTER 7

Delights and Disasters

"Jeem, come up, come up. Come see what we did!"

Marta's voice is ringing from the loft where she and Dougie had just finished silk screening 20 scarves and enough material for a dozen unique dresses in the time it would usually take for her to finish one hand painted fabric. As Jim's head appears above the top step he sees Marta applying one of her patented hugs to Dougie's neck as they examine the hanging printed fabric that is draped around the perimeter of the loft, engulfing Jim's "office" space.

"My god. What have you wrought up here?"

"Isn't it marvelous?" Marta is literally dancing along the line of printed fabric. "We did all this this morning. Look at the table. It is grand, yes? Dougie is a magician, a sorcerer I think."

"Nothing magic about it mate. Just silk screen process. Allows much better efficiency of production, but still can be considered hand made. These are Marta's designs and I just transferred them to silk screens. Jim, we have to talk. This is good stuff. It needs to be properly marketed."

"You got ideas, boy? What are you thinking?"

"These have to dry to make room for more. We'll clean up here a bit and come down. Morning tea is in order, I think. You put the coffee on, OK? We'll be down in about 10."

Sitting outside near the well, cups in hand, the three friends are bantering back and forth about how to advertise Marta's work, and perhaps how to produce clothing in quantity so there is reasonable income for the family. Dougie points out that the Hilton shops in Madrid could probably take additional stock, especially if production could be increased.

Marta is thinking aloud, "What if some of the compasenas could be organized? They all sew their own clothes anyway."

Jim responds, "Well, you would be the one to do the organizing. Why don't you, now that you have enough fabric to start?"

"OK, I will. I'll talk to them this afternoon."

Dougie continues, "There is bound to be a wider market for the garments, in particular. I'd introduce them to up market locations with foreign tourists. That's who is buying at the Hilton downtown. Widen the area you are serving."

Jim is sitting quietly. Then his head comes up with, "Alicante. There are tourist boutiques over there on the coast, for sure. The crush for this year has passed, but there is an influx, particularly from the UK, in December for Christmas. We have time to explore the coastal towns for outlets. You want to come, Dougie?"

"I am away as of tomorrow. Marta has the printing system down already, so you people don't need me and work is calling. I have to be in Barcelona for 4 days, back to Madrid, and then may need to be in Lisbon, which is not confirmed. Short answer is can't, but I would love to hear what you find. I agree, the Hilton downtown is not sufficient outlet for the volume Marta deserves. Have you thought of the US?"

Marta and Jim exchange quick glances, and Marta perks up with, "We thought of it, but our finances will not support that kind of travel. Maybe someday, eh Jeem?" The smile says it all. In spite of the tug of her beloved Spain, Marta has nostalgic affection for New York.

"Someday, indeed. Dougie, we don't have to get on a plane to explore possibilities in the US. How about a brochure, or small catalog we can get to possible outlets in the city?" That was New York City, the only one worth considering for either Jim or Marta.

Doug sits a moment, then smiles at Jim with, "I have my camera with me. Lets get some shots of garments and finished prints before I leave. I'll plan to be back in 2 weeks, the weekend and they will be printed by then. We'll start working up something then. What do you think?"

Marta is reservedly excited, "I think Alicante is good, a good idea. I can not go for a while. I just started the women on a new batch of clothes and must do the inspections regularly. But we can talk on the telephone while you are there, Yes?"

"OK, yes." Shifting his focus to Dougie, "You're going to break that chair if you don't stop wiggling, boy. Get your camera. Let's get to work. Marta, go select the dresses you want to advertise, and half a dozen scarves. You two are still sitting there, lets get going." The last is with a smile over the gravel phonation. The three are off and if not running, at least they are moving quickly.

Two days later, Dougie has left for Barcelona, Marta's samples have been selected and this morning, the car is packed and fueled for the drive to Alicante. Standing in front of the house, Jim yells, "Marta, it's at least a four and a half hour drive, I need to get on the road. OK, I'm leaving, I'm gone, now." Jim is doing the gravelly yelling from the front door and ready to step out when Marta comes running from the back of the house, silhouetted by the light from the open door to the back yard.

Breathing heavily, she hands Jim a small cardboard box, "This is your lunch, mi amor. It is a good one. This is exciting, yes?"

Taking the box, Jim wraps one arm around Marta's waist and ignoring the few passing people in the plaza, gives Marta a large kiss. "I am sure it is worth the wait. I can still get there in daylight and maybe get to one of the shops on the list this afternoon. Hope they are open this time of the year. I'm off." With that he releases Marta's waist and heads to the car. The windows are down so he drops the box onto the front passenger seat, walks to the other side and gets in, with a wave over the top of the car. Marta gives a little jump and a return wave as the car backs up, turns and raises a small dust cloud as it crosses the plaza. Jim's on his way, marketing again. He enjoys driving, so anticipating the trip has been a pleasure.

Objectives, priorities, plans all have given the last few days some meaning. He hates to admit it, but he misses Xochitl since her move to London with David, her beau. Seems she has forgotten them in Valdeolmos since she left. No calls, which is not too surprising. But, no letters either. That's been harder. Back on track, boy. There's work to do.

The out-of-season accommodation in Alicante is reasonably priced, a good thing, and Jim's two days have been productive so far. It is mid afternoon, but the waning sun still provides a lot more heat than it does mid day in Valdeolmos. This temperature is quite agreeable. Parking the car at the pension where he is staying, he walks into the lobby and the clerk waves him over to the desk. Handing Jim a message paper he says the call came at about one p.m. Thanking the clerk, Jim walks to his room while opening the note. He is reading while standing at the closed door, and immediately turns and walks back to the lobby. "I must call my home in Valdeolmos. I need to use the telephone."

The clerk has a distressed look on his face as he responds in Spanish, "We are not permitted to call long distance on the phone. Only the owner has this ability. I am sorry."

"Shit," is the first English word coming out. Then its equivalent in Spanish, plus much, much more. Finally Jim is quiet and asks, "Where is the post office and public phone?"

"It is near here. Only three blocks to the right. You will see the sign over the walkway, left side of the street. You can walk faster than drive, I think."

With a nod and a half smile, Jim leaves through the open door and walks right. After waiting his turn through two others, Jim gets access to the small booth and places his call to the cantina in Valdeolmos, communication central for the village. The mistress of the bar answers and Jim identifies himself. After the necessary pleasantries, then an explanation of where he is and why Jim finally uses his command voice and asks to speak to Marta.

"Si, uno memento," and the sound of the receiver hitting the countertop comes through loud and clear. Next, there is the familiar screech of a banshee as the woman yells through the front window and across the plaza for Marta.

Immediately, the receiver is lifted and Jim hears, "She is coming, quickly I think. She is not happy at all. Do you have trouble at home, Senor Tuck?"

"I don't know. That's why I am calling." This exchange is, of course in rapid fire Spanish, and before the woman can get another set of questions going, Marta's voice comes through the phone.

"Jeem, oh, Jeem. The rabbits are dying again. PLEASE come home now." That last sentence ends with the sound of Marta's fast breathing and a short sob.

Jim's mind begins racing. "Damn, damn, damn. Have you given the medicine we got from the vet?"

"Si, yes!. Of course I have! Do you think I am stupid?"

"No, no, no. You are not stupid, never stupid. You've never been stupid your whole life. You know I know better. It is just the first thing I could think of. That medicine worked the first time. Any idea why it is not working now?"

"I don't know. All I know is, there are five sick rabbits, two dead ones and I have given all the medicine now. I don't know what to do. It is terrible!"

"I am coming home. Can you get a way to go to the vet with one of the sick ones? I can't get home today before the vet closes. I will be home tonight."

"I will try. Perhaps the alcalde will let me use his car. I don't know. Oh, Jim. I thought we fixed this problem. Oh, damn, damn, damn."

"OK. Look, it is difficult, yes. Go see the alcalde, get to the vet if you can. I am leaving as soon as I pack the car and get notes written to the shops I scheduled for tomorrow. I think the pension will deliver them for me. I'll be home as soon as I can." With that he hangs up, and goes to the counter to pay for the call.

The drive back is much less pleasant. The rabbits have provided a small but steady income and food source for the house. Just when they need cash to launch Marta's boutique offerings, they are going to lose a source of income it seems. Life in Valdeolmos is certainly full of ups and downs, like everywhere. But the downs are more threatening since their finances are so precarious. Another damn, damn, damn starts coursing through his head as he is driving. He's never been an hysteric, but it's close now. "Calm down, boy. You have weathered worse. Find the possibilities, the constraints, make a plan. Hmm." The Low growl actually soothes his mind, and the road returns to full focus.

It is after nine p.m. when he arrives at the house. Marta is in the shed in back, sitting on a sack of rabbit food, rocking and crying. Looking, she sees Jim in the doorway, and slumps a little further. Jim walks right up, lifts her under the arms and whispers in her ear. Looking up, she says, "They will all be sick or dead in 2 days, Half are sick now, there are eight dead. The vet can not fix it he says. This virus is worse than the other one.."

Jim gently pushes Marta back and looks at her grief stricken face. "I was thinking all the way here. I was thinking that there must be something we can do. We always have before."

"Yes, I know. We can always succeed, somehow. Until now."

"Did we fail in New York? No. We had big problems, but we stuck together and found a way. Maybe we can find a way this time, too."

"There is one way, the vet said. Kill all the rabbits and bury them. Do not let any of them get away, and do not handle any other animals without washing our hands with alcohol or bleach. That is what he said."

Jim drops his hands, and sits on the sack of rabbit feed. His head droops. When he looks up, "Can we get anything for all this rabbit food? We have three bags, forty kilos each. That is a fair amount of money right there, and the cages and equipment.."

"Anything the rabbits have been near must not get near other animals. We have to burn it all, after we kill the rabbits."

Jim now droops, about as low as Marta when he found her. They both sit for quite a while, not talking, Jim growling from time to time. Then Marta says, "Oh. Dougie is coming tomorrow. He will be here two days before going on to Madrid. I already told him about the problem with rabbits and he said he could help us do whatever needed to be done. He also wants to talk about what you found in Alicante."

"Another pair of hands could be helpful. Alicante my ass. What a mess!"

Marta, sits quite a bit straighter, looks at Jim full in the face, "Alicante may be what saves our asses."

Jim's head jerks toward Marta, he looks her straight in the eyes, then sits nearly as straight as she is sitting. "You are astounding, woman. I must be the luckiest guy alive. Lets go to bed, I am tired."

"Si. And we have an early, ugly day tomorrow."

"Yes, early and ugly"

Dougie parks at the front door and comes through the eternally open double door, yells, "Hello the house!" Nothing but quiet in response, then he hears a thud coming from the back yard and walks quickly down the hall to the open rear door. In the back, he finds Jim standing holding a rabbit by the hind legs then presently whacking it on the head with a small club, crushing the skull and breaking its neck, all the while tears streaming down his cheeks. Marta is at a separate table, repeating the action, but dry eyed. There are two wicker baskets full of dead rabbits with two more, one each by Jim and Marta, half full each. Jim drops the rabbit corpse into the basket, looks at Dougie, asks, "What the fuck do you want?"

"Just to help some way, if I can."

Jim's face mellows somewhat, "Sorry kid, not feeling the best today. Look at the carnage. Awe, damn, damn, damn. Start the fire in the pit, will ya? Gotta burn these, as well as the cages, the contents of the shed that will burn. Everything. Can you do that?"

"Sure, I'll get it going and then do whatever."

The funeral pyre sends black smoke over the plaza toward the cantina and smells that no one appreciates. Soon, the word is out and there is a line of mourners leaving contributions by the open front door. One container of tapas has a note attached asking if Marta will still be able to provide rabbit meat to the cantina. She takes the food into the kitchen, wiping the soot off her hands and brushes her hair back so some order is restored to her appearance, then walks to the cantina. The owner is behind the counter where Marta greets her. Tears are flowing as she thanks her for the food, and tells her that all the rabbits are gone. They can not afford to get more because the disease will kill them too, and their money is needed for other things now. The owner comes from behind the counter and hugs Marta long and strong, whispering in her ear that it will be better, certainly. After an eternity, Marta straightens, as she is a head taller than the owner and kisses both her cheeks. "Gracias todo mi amiga." With that she turns and leaves the cantina, back to the house across the plaza. Her walk is a bit faster going than it was coming, her heart slightly lighter. The black smoke is still rolling out from behind the house, but the wind has changed and it is now blowing out over an empty field. Small blessings.

Using the donated food stuffs, the three rabbit morticians sit at the table in the hallway, eating silently until a few wines have gone down when Dougie asks, "So, what happened in Alicante. Haven't heard anything since I got here."

Jim gives a short, sharp report about the shops visited and the responses he received and the conversation takes off. Soon Marta is chiming in with some of her plans for production and slowly a plan starts to rise, literally out of the ashes. Two more glasses of wine and Dougie produces some paper and a pencil, making a written record of agreed ideas, a list of the most promising shops contacted so far, jotting down the names of the nearby towns of Denia and Javea. Nearby is relative since they are on the other side of a headland hill from Alicante and there is a significant drive involved getting there, but all three agree that it would be good to include them in the exploration of possible outlets.

The next day, Dougie is off to Madrid, and Jim and Marta start the clean up of the yard. Jim gets Paco to do the wheelbarrow pushing once they are full. There is a small ravine nearby that receives the ashes and unburned bits. By mid afternoon, they are finished and both indulge in a long soaking bath as light colored smoke from the wood burning hot water heater once again drifts across the plaza. There is an early evening to bed in order. Both are very tired, emotionally and physically. The physical effort has used up quite a bit of the emotional energy of the disaster. Suddenly, Jim is back up and Marta says, "What are you doing? It is late. Aren't you tired?"

"I'm exhausted. That's why I forgot to feed Sancho and Pedro. Be right back."

A few minutes later, Jim slides back into a quiet bed, listens a minute to the regular breathing from Marta, and finally falls asleep.

Breakfast is interrupted when Xochitl leaps into the kitchen with a mighty, "Ta da!" Both Marta and Jim's heads jerk up from the porridge at the same time, but Xochitl's exuberance vanishes with the looks on their faces. "What's the matter?"

Jim says, "Sit down, Bud. The news ain't good." With that he gives a shortened history of the events over the last two or three days. Xochitl's slump into her chair deepens as the story progresses. "So, we are well and truly out of the rabbit meat business. The fortunate part is that I had some success on the trip to Alicante. Going back, probably today, to finalize with two of the shops and try to expand into neighboring towns. Denia and Javea are nearby, sort of. You want to come to the coast with me for a couple of days? Can't pay you, but the company would be nice. Marta needs to be here to get the production increased. No rabbit farm income means alternatives must be exploited quickly."

Xochitl is quiet for several seconds. Her head comes up with tears in her eyes. "I am so sorry, guys. I didn't know. David and I were in the mountains, just got back last night. Yes, Poppa, I want to come with you. The reason I popped in was to let you guys know that David has work in London. We are due to go quickly. We won't go before I can make the trip to the coast with you, OK?"

Both Marta and Jim had realized that Xochitl's independent nature was bound to result in her leaving Valdeolmos and Madrid. There is a saying, probably more than one, about bad or difficult news coming in bunches. "You want breakfast? Get a bowl. There is plenty there." Typical Marta response.

As they eat, the conversation turns away from disasters to possibilities and plans. Xochitl gives more details about where they will likely be living in London, the network that is already there, some of whom are her friends from Madrid, David's work. "Guess what?"

Jim finishes his last bit of porridge, and looks at Xochitl, eye brows elevated, "What?" It comes out more growly than intended, but he has been blind sided by Xochitl's pronouncements enough to warrant a bit of concern.

"Well, you know that David and I have been together for almost a year now, right?" Two heads nod in response. "And you know we really adore one another, tons, right?"

Two slow nods in response.

"Well, we decided, before we leave for London, we want to get married, right here at the house. Can we, huh? Good idea, right?"

So there is the rest of the story, of what was driving this morning's excitement. Marta leans over and gives Xochitl a long kiss on the cheek and straightens up saying, "Of course we can have a wedding here at the house. It seems we may need to hurry with the plans, right?"

Jim stands, crosses to the other side of the table and plants a big kiss on Xochitl's forehead, then the gravel starts rolling up from his chest and out of his mouth. "Hurry is not quite the word I would have chosen. Seems there is precious little time available. We'll be away to Alicante at least 3 days. When are you and David due in London?"

"Ah, don't know for sure. He hasn't signed any contracts or anything, just accepted the job. Guess who put in a good word for him? Come on, guess."

Two heads swivel in ignorance, saying, "No idea," nonverbally. "Bob Dylan. You know him? Bob Dylan, for Christ's sake. He's getting very popular lately. Guess he remembers me, eh?"

Neither Marta nor Jim register the name immediately. The looks on their faces are transparent for their ignorance. "Oh, come on! I told you about him more than a year ago. I was in London visiting, met this fella, we had a few laughs. He took me to a couple of gigs. Remember? I wrote to you and told you I was a groupie? Explained all about what a groupie was. Remember?"

The light bulb goes off with half smiles showing. "Well, I stayed in touch with him, writing a few times. Told him about life in Valdeolmos, in Madrid, then let him know David and I wanted to live in London. Told him about David's work. Then when David applied for this job and we thought he had a chance of getting it, I told Bob and by golly he went and talked to the owners of the company. Must know them or something. Anyway, pretty great, huh?"

Jim sits back, smiles a full smile now. "Networks are very good, indeed. Yes, great is a good description."

Marta is nodding in agreement, then says, "What will you be doing to make a living?"

Xochitl suddenly stops wiggling in her seat and looks at her mother. Silence. "I haven't decided yet."

"Now would be a good time to decide. It is better if you can take care of yourself, isn't it?"

Now the smile on Jim's face is really wide as he watches these two women, the loves of his life, engage. Xochitl looks at her mother, then looks down at her empty bowl. A small swallow, then, "You're right, again. Don't you ever get tired of being right?" The last is with a smile on a face full of recognition and irony. "I have some ideas, but have been so excited about London, David's job, friend's waiting for us, I seem to have lost track of a couple of things, eh?"

"Not to worry. You would have realized soon." Marta's quiet comment is effective.

"Would have been better to think of it on my own, eh?"

Jim chimes in, "Glad Marta could help. Let's get ready for Alicante. Do you have clothes for a couple of days?"

"In my room. I'll pack a backpack and be ready. Hey, can I try out the phone? You guys got one put in, right? I want to let David know the plan. Marta, can we make a date for the wedding before Poppa and I leave? Who will do the ceremony? Lots to get done, right?"

Marta nods agreement to all, Xochitl jumps from the table and heads into the front room where there is a black telephone on it cradle sitting on a small table next to the sofa. A wire come through the front wall of the house, near the floor, to a small black box on the wall then another to the phone. She stands and stares for a few seconds, then returns to the kitchen. "How does it work? I mean, what do I dial to call Madrid?"

"Just lift the receiver. Listen and someone at the post office answers. Tell him the number you want to call, put it down and he'll call you when the connection is made. It's sort of like being at the booth at the post office, but we can do it here. The days of the cantina visits are numbered." That last is accompanied by another smile.

The attendance at Xochitl and David's wedding is enough to require the space of the back yard to accommodate everyone. The Mexican flavor added by Marta's dress and food after adds to the spice of the day. It is a civil ceremony presided over by someone Jim does not know, but recommended by Tony, from the base. Tony is there with Carmen, and dance in the open area behind the well to the music of the small local band enhanced by a few of Xochitl's artistic friends from Madrid. The air is festive, and Tony's dancing with both Carmen and Marta, and finally with Xochitl is Spanish to its core. Jim doesn't dance, never has, but watches in rapt attention. The women are all smiles as they swish around the floor. An Argentine tango starts and many fill the floor, except Tony comes over to Jim, chest heaving a bit and points to the far corner near the swimming pool.

By the time they reach a slightly quieter spot, Tony's breathing has started to slow and he raises his glass to Jim, whose tumbler of red wine is still half full. "Salud, amigo. Your health, your family's health and prosperity, y adios amigo. I muster out beginning of next month, Friday the second to be exact."

"Congratulations my friend. I knew it had to be sometime soon. Just didn't realize how soon."

"I know. We have been working on the paperwork for a while, as you can imagine. It was classic hurry up and wait, and the NOW! Just got word yesterday myself. Since we were going to be out here anyway, I figured I would let you know in person."

"Well done on all counts. So what happens from here? Do you have plans?"

"That first weekend next month, we fly to Bilbao to catch up with family for a few days, then to D.C. to finish the paperwork, visit local friends, do the registrations required for foreign residence and mailing address for all those lovely retirement checks then back to Bilbao to settle. That's where we want to stop."

"You have any Bilbao contact information now? Wouldn't mind the chance to stay in touch, you know."

"Just the mailing address, or, I mean I will have the mailing address soon. It will be a post office box in the city, but that is one of the things we need to accomplish while we're there. I'll send it to you directly once I have it, don't worry."

"Not worried, old salt. Just interested, if you know what I mean. It's been quite the ride, eh? I am happy you can settle where the roots are still alive."

"And you? Is this the end of the road for you, dusty little Madrid suburb?"

"So far, it has been a suitable if somewhat difficult sanctuary. Not sure the winters will be to my liking in a few years because they aren't now. But, we are fairly settled here. Still have our dogs, and each other as well as our local network. The alcalde is as close to having a local friend as we are likely to get, and his influence helps smooth things we need to do, like expand Marta's fabric and clothing business."

"How is that going, by the way? I hear by the vine that you have been to the coast a couple of times now, looking for sales opportunities."

"Your vine is accurate, as usual. I still don't know how you manage it. Anyway, we have at least three boutique shops over there, ready to take Marta's garments and scarves; two in Alicante and one in Denia. You been to Denia?"

"Yes, many years ago. I remember it being a rather sleepy location. Is there enough business opportunity for the things Marta makes?"

"It must have been several years since your visit. It is a strong tourist destination along the coast, more quaint than Alicante, but during high season there is quite a bit of traffic. I enjoyed the visit over there. Last trip was with Xoch and she liked it as well, and that is saying something."

"It looks like we are both embarking, eh? It's good to be starting with the new. You agree?"

"Couldn't agree more. In addition, the rabbits disaster set us back a bit financially and the new opportunities in Denia and Alicante look like they will certainly help offset the losses."

"I am glad. Have you thought about trying the futures market again? Might be helpful under the circumstances." That question jerks Jim's head up, and a fierce light appears in his eyes. "Not suggesting anything. Just wondering. Relax, mate. Relax."

Jim's shoulders slowly slump back down. "We don't have play money any more. Never did quite recover from that experiment. You would find my hide on the wooden gate out front, personally tacked up by Marta if I suggested it. No, we won't be going there."

"Understood. Say! I hear the production for Patton is underway. You involved?"

This brings a large smile and the lights in Jim's eyes are now twinkling. "Yes, we have been involved in some of the logistics, plus I have a bit part. Get this; I am the archbishop of Palermo, meeting Patton on the steps of the cathedral. The shooting is day after tomorrow at the Royal Palace of Madrid. The area will be cordoned off but I imagine I can get guests in. What do you think?"

"Day after tomorrow. Tuesday, eh? I'll make room. Get me a pass, or whatever I need to watch. I gotta see Tuck as a priest. Unbelievable. Or, better not be or the thing won't work, right? Ha! You met any of the people involved, any of the stars?"

"Nah. Just logistics personnel and got fitted for my smock and outfit. Met the producer for about 37 seconds, but he doesn't bother with the underlings as a rule. It is pretty cut and dried, and huge. It's a lot bigger than Hundred Rifles or Valdez. A lot bigger. So, it is business for sure. Not much fooling around. I will see what I can do tomorrow when someone will be in the office at the Hilton."

The day for shooting Jim's scene is bright, sunny and a bit breezy. Just right. The smock that is his costume is several layers, and brings out the sweat in no time. Jim is placed on his high backed chair at the top of the stairs. Just then, the director comes over for his first and only conversation with Jim. "We want a reaction from Patton when he arrives to kiss your ring. Think you can get one from him? Remember, you meet him at the landing in the middle. You speak English don't you?"

"Yes, I can get a reaction from him, yes, I remember where to meet him, yes, hablo Anglise." The director's head jerks up at that, receiving a beatific smile from the "Bishop". Straightening, he yells at the one hundred or so people congregating on the set, "Places everyone. George, where the hell is Scott?"

Below, at the bottom of the stairs a fellow in a US army uniform stroles into view. "I'm here. Ready when you are. Up to the first landing, correct?"

"Right." The manager takes over instructing the film crew. Jim is sitting, sweating, waiting for his cue. George C. Scott has retreated to the right, just behind several extras in uniform and the scene begins. Soldiers at attention provide crisp salutes as he strides briskly forward to the bottom of the stairs, then begins his ascent. Jim stands and begins walking down, arriving at the landing before "Patton" arrives, and is standing waiting. As George C. Scott arrives to present himself to the bishop, he bends forward to take the bishop's hand and Jim quietly says, "Do you know how the bishop gets the very important general up all those stairs?" Scott hesitates a moment mid bend forward and Jim says, "He offers to rape him." The general's head jerks up to that same beatific smile Jim graced the director with, then very professionally completes the required bow and respectful kiss of the ring, which the bishop regally accepts. After the submission, the two subjects on film complete the ascent to a waiting set of chairs at the top from which they review the parade honoring the saviors of Palermo, the US army. With the parade started, the director halts the filming and the crew begin preparing for the next scene, with Jim quietly filling Gorge Scott in on the director's instructions. That gets a belly laugh out of the "general" and Jim's responsibilities are finished for the film. There is no after party scheduled for Valdeolmos as there was for One Hundred Rifles, but it has been fun, as well as paid a few bills.

Back at the Ganja la Maja, the production of garments and printed fabric for scarves and various uses has kicked into a higher gear, with four or five village women assisting with the sewing of garments, but Marta exclusively printing and cutting. Spring is in full swing and Jim has already made several trips to the coast, each time wishing he had Xochitl along. The half dozen outlets he has organized in Alicante, Denia and Javea, Xivia on the map, have been good outlets, even during the lower tourist season. A modest profit has been realized from sales to date, and he and Marta are looking forward to high season, that starts in a month or so.

Back in Valdeolmos, Dougie has arrived and is deep into cutting new silk screens, examining finished garments and prints and helping to set up additional production facilities. When Jim arrives from his trip, Dougie and Marta are in deep discussion. When Jim enters the living room, Marta jumps up and blurts out, "Oh, Jeem, Dougie is leaving! He's going back to England."

Jim stops in the doorway, looks at the two, then asks, "When?"

"Flying out Monday, day after tomorrow. Meg and I have decided to simplify, reconnect, go somewhere simpler. Her brother lives in New Zealand, and he has convinced us both it would be a good move."

"You have a plan?"

"A bit of one. It's not fleshed out yet, but we will do that once I get back to the UK. What I want to do is make certain that Marta and I have a firm understanding and arrangement for expanding her reach. I am proposing a joint venture with me organizing the South pacific region and the two of you expanding Spain, Europe and the US. Her stuff is quality, perhaps of interest to a boutique clientele, but still the upside is practically boundless. We were just talking about a name for the enterprise. You should get in on this."

"First things first." With that, Jim heads into the kitchen and Dougie and Marta can hear the clink of ice falling into a glass, pouring sounds and then Jim rejoins them in the living room. "The name will have to be in Spanish, right?"

The planning is suddenly in high gear. A Spanish name, but what's the rest of it? It is fabric, printed for sure, clothing, mostly women's apparel, originating from Valdeolmos. Let's see, and the conversation goes around and around. Doug offers, "OK, what is the most important aspect of the product, what will the public appreciate?"

There is quiet, then Jim points out, "Each piece is unique, and made by hand."

Marta chimes in, "The tourists are our largest market right now, and they will want something that is only theirs, unique, but will want handmade creations, for sure. Wait, hand made, that will also give us a logo, yes?"

Doug's turn, "Unique and handmade creations."

"Jim huffs a bit, "Way too long. It has to be short and sweet. I like the logo idea, for sure."

"Creationes is the Spanish version. What about the creationes? Handmade, a mano. Creationes a Mano. A colored hand is the logo. What do you think?"

There is quiet again, then Jim and Dougie both say, "Fine, good…" Doug says, "There are negative interpretations of a red colored hand, blue is bad for trying to duplicate."

"Black," Jim says almost automatically. "Black has connotations, I know, but it is also mysterious, and easily duplicated. Black."

Dougie and Marta just look at one another, nod, and the three shake hands across the table. Then Jim breaks out the red wine and the celebration of a new enterprise is begun. Doug commits to getting a logo printed, the brochures updated and Jim announces the next trip to the coast; Alicante, Denia and Javea. It will be two weeks, which should just be enough time to have the new brochures to distribute on the trip, as well as at the Hilton in Madrid.

The next day, Dougie is gone again, but has arranged to visit on his way out of Europe to the southern hemisphere. With new brochures in hand, both Jim and Marta start hammering away at marketing, the sales take a jump from minimal to modest and there is a bit of money in the account again.

"I'll be there this weekend. Won't have much time, but enough I think." It is three weeks since Dougie left and the efforts at getting Marta's business expanded has even taken the time Jim would have given to the food critic writing for the paper in Madrid.

There have been at least two calls that he had to refuse, and the editor noted that if there were many more the paper would have to find another critic, as much as they did not look forward to that possibility. Jim soothed the ruffled feathers as well as he could, which was pretty well, and said he would be available the next week, for certain.

The voice from the front of the house, "Hello the hacienda!" tells them Dougie has made it back. They are ready. Jim strolls down the hall and provides a large abrazo to the well kitted out young fellow in the doorway. There are three large pieces of luggage at his feet that they push to the side of the door and Jim takes Dougie's arm in his as they return to the kitchen. The stop is short, as they collect two sizable bottles of wine, three glasses and exit to the right of the well to a waiting table. Marta has set the table, and Jim has left the roasted piglet intact for quartering at the table. Potatoes au gratin, steamed vegetables, a pitcher of cold water and the smells rise deliciously. A quick kiss on the cheeks is exchanged between Dougie and Marta, who then motions to Dougie's place next to Jim. "This is astounding. How did you manage to time this so well, and so much food. I AM starving, for sure. Oh, a million thanks to you both."

"This must be a good memory, yes? You will be missed, and so far away. But we will see one another again, I am certain. Yes, Jeem?"

"Hunh! Let's eat." And a wry smile escapes, with a wink at Dougie. The meal is exquisite, and the conversation catches everyone up to current status on families, business and personal health. After dinner, Dougie's luggage is moved into the room he usually occupies and Marta takes him upstairs to see the production. "You have been busy. This is impressive. I have saved room in one of my suitcases for samples to take with me. It will be important to have actual pieces as well as a current copy of the brochure to show in New Zealand. You realize I won't be arriving for close to a month, right?"

Marta nods. "You mentioned stopping other places, like Australia. We just did not know details. It is OK.

We will look forward to your safe arrival. Let's go back downstairs. You can pick the pieces you want to take this evening. When do you leave Madrid?"

"The train to Lisbon is day after tomorrow, in the afternoon. So, two days here. Not long, but long enough, I think, to allow us to make some plans. Yes?" Using the Marta "yes" allows a chuckle from both and they start back down to the hallway.

With Dougie's departure, Xochitl off to London, Tony Arizza gone, no filming prospects for the near future, life in Valdeolmos settles into as close to a routine as it ever has been. The dogs, Sancho and Pedro, never actually got a mate for breeding boxers, but did become elevated to new status with the reduction in other distractions. Whenever Jim is around, they are right next to him, Pedro nuzzling and Sancho with tongue hanging out. They like to feel they are the scourge of the local cat population, but none of the local cats, including the one that frequents the Tucks, seem to pay any attention. The foxes and stray dogs in the fields are a much greater danger than Pedro and Sancho. Jim is regularly walking them in the barren fields, keeping them away from Paco's sheep, but strolling far and wide. Marta enjoys the quiet company they bring to the workshop. So, Valdeolmos life is now much more attuned to a pampered dog's life.

The summer high season has just finished. It is 1973 already, Jim is completing his tour of Alicante, Denia and Javea, retrieving some of the unsold garments, negotiating next year's arrangements, planning with each outlet for the coming low season, but season's that see some tourists from colder areas right through the winter. At the last stop, there is a call and Jim is summoned to the phone. "Alo," thinking it is likely a Spanish speaker.

"Jeem, oh Jeem. Get home now. Come now, please!"

"Marta, slow down. What's the matter? I can hardly understand you."

"Oh, Jeem, the dogs, Pedro and Sancho, they are very sick. I don't know why, but they can't move. I must have the car to take them to the vet. Hurry, please!"

"Sick, sick how? When? I don't understand."

"This afternoon, not long after they eat their dinner. Then they started gagging, and then they throw up, and now they don't move very much. I am very afraid."

"Can you get the alcalde's car to go to the vet?"

"He is away to Toledo this week. There are no cars left in the village. Oh, oh, oh."

"I am coming. See if you can make them drink water, OK? I am coming."

Jim thanks the shop owner, says he must leave immediately, leaves the unsold garments uncollected from that shop, and is in the car and away while the shop keeper is waving to the disappearing vehicle. The Volvo has been a good car, but is tested now, as are the rural roads heading inland. Slowing only slightly through the villages and towns on the way, Jim is pulling up in front of the house three hours and fifteen minutes after leaving the outskirts of Alicante. Marta has heard him drive up and is dejectedly walking through the front door, no greeting, no arms open to receive him. Out of the car, Jim walks up to her, lifts her chin and asks, "How are they?"

Marta bursts into tears, "They are both dead."

The news hits Jim hard enough to cause him to sit on the stone to the right of the doorway. "What happened? I don't understand?"

Marta is sobbing so strongly she can't talk, so Jim stands, takes her hand and they walk into the house together. They make their way straight down the hallway and out the back door past the well and under the nearest tree to the pool. There they are, both dogs, very still. The first time in many years Jim has not been slobbered on immediately when he arrived in the house. The dogs lips are pulled back from their teeth in grimaces, as if they did not die easily. Jim slumps down at their heads, and strokes each one, as if the tenderness could revive them. Tears are streaming down his cheeks, he throws his head back and bellows a wail, a sound

Marta has never heard from him in all these years. Then he rocks, slowly forward and back, and continues to cry, unabashedly, all the while stroking the unresponsive heads on the ground. The evening turns into night, the wake over the dead dogs continues. Both Marta and Jim are out of tears, but both continue to rock on the ground by the dogs.

Finally, Marta says, "We must go in now. Stand up, Jeem." Jim looks up at her, then his head falls forward and he doesn't move. "It is time, now, Jeem. Come with me."

Jim looks up, his head starts to fall forward again, then he says, "Right," and stands with Marta's help. She wraps one arm around his waist and holds his hand with the other, and leads him indoors. "Do you want a glass of wine?"

"No." And he disengages and walks down the hallway to their bedroom, through the door and closes the door behind him. Marta pours herself a wine glass full of red wine and sits at the table in the hallway. It is going to be a long night.

Awakening, Marta turns and notices that Jim's side of the bed is empty. It is early morning, so the light is dim through the window. Then she hears the scrape, thunk, scrape sound from the rear of the house. Throwing on a terry cloth blue bathrobe, she leaves the bedroom and starts down the hall, stepping to the rhythmic scrape, thump, scrape coming through the back door. She stands in the doorway, watching, as Jim uses a spade to scrape loose dirt from the ground and then dump it into a large hole. Stopping, he looks up, the right side of his lips rise into an ironic smile, then he looks down and starts again, scrape, thump, scrape, thump. Marta walks over and asks, "What time did you get up?"

Scrape thump, scrape, thump, scrape thump, pat, pat, pat. Standing more erect, he looks at her and just says, "Don't know." Scrape, thump, scrape, thump, pat.

"I'll make some coffee. You want some?"

"No." Scrape, thump, scrape, thump. Marta turns away and walks into the kitchen to boil the kettle, glancing over her shoulder as she walks through the door. Scape, thump.

She sits on the right hand stone, while Jim sits, out of the morning sun, on the left. There is quiet, except for the few shepherds leading their flocks out of town for the day, accompanied by bleating when a staff urges stragglers along. Jim's head is bowed, Marta is sipping her hot coffee, neither is speaking. The sheep are gone, nothing is moving in the plaza and neither are Jim and Marta. Inertia reigns. Suddenly, Jim is up, reaching for his staff leaning against the door frame, and says, "I need to talk to Paco." And away he goes. Marta sits and sips, watching his back as he strides away toward the open fields.

Lunch is nearly ready when Marta hears the front door open. Peeking into the hallway, she sees Jim lean his staff in the corner then start his way down the hall. Looking up, he sees the peeking Marta, and he uses both corners of his mouth to create a small smile. Marta comes out of the kitchen door and stands in the hallway waiting Jim's arrival. When he comes close, she opens her arms and he silently walks in. They stand in the quiet embrace for an impossible period, Marta not wanting to ever stop. Finally, Jim leans back and says, "It smells good in there. What are you making?"

"Paella."

"Ah, no wonder I was ready to come back."

"It's ready in about 5 or 10 minutes. You want to wash up?"

"Sure. I'll be back," and a definite smile crosses the space between them.

Lunch is mostly quiet, but Jim does give a short recounting of his finding and talking with Paco. Apparently, the shepherd had been more determined that morning and was quite a distance from the house before Jim caught up with him. The outcrop of rock near the grazing area was good for sitting, and Paco was his usual quiet self as Jim related the disaster with the dogs. Once Jim had finished, Paco's sorrowful face turned up toward Jim, and he made a small wail, causing the sheep to jostle and move slightly away down the hill. Then Paco looked at Jim and said, "The dogs had poison. I do not know the name, but it kills rats. I think the dogs ate rat poison. I am so sorry, Jaime. It is so sad."

That was it. The conversation was finished, apparently. Several minutes of silence later, Jim stands, shakes Paco's hand, turns and walks back to the village. "Where the hell did they get rat poison?"

Marta leans back, wipes her mouth with the napkin and takes a sip of wine as she thinks. "Pepe was away from the bakery when I went to get the leftover bread for dog food. A young boy I don't know was there, and when I explained what I wanted. He looked a bit strange, but went to the unsold bin and found only one loaf. I asked if that was all there was because I usually got at least 3, sometimes more. He seemed a bit annoyed, but I smiled my best smile and he said to wait a minute, went in the back and came with two more loaves, really old ones, with bite marks on them. He said he had seen them near the back door and back window. They obviously were not going to be sold, and they were a bit chewed up, so he just gave them to me. I thanked him, brought them home, broke them up into the dogs' bowls with some meat and they ate it all. What do you think?"

Jim sits quietly for a minute, then stands and says, "I'll be back."

"Where are you going? I should come with you, yes?"

"No. Not long. I'll do the dishes when I get back."

Determined striding across the plaza gets Jim to the bakery in less than five minutes and he stands in the doorway, shifting from foot to foot while the shop keeper finishes with his customer. He looks at Jim fidgeting, then gives his polite, "Good day, Jaime. How are you?"

"I am well, Alejandro, thank you. And you?"

"Yes, I also am well. I am sorry to hear about your troubles. You must have been very upset." Nothing is sacred, or secret in the village.

"Thank you for your concern. I have a question, if you do not mind." Just then a mother with three small children, twins and a larger child, swarm into the shop and she bustles up in front of Jim asking for bread and three small cakes. She gives Jim a glance, half a smile and a, "Good day, don Jaime."

Jim retreats a step, to avoid the children mostly, smiles his most generous smile, and returns the greeting. Collecting her goods, the mother and children swarm back out of the shop and Alejandro, shaking his head, half smiles and says, "You had a question, Jaime?"

"Yes. I suspect you have difficulties with rats from time to time, even with all the village cats. How do you control them so they do not ruin your business?"

Standing a bit straighter, the shop keeper looks strangely at Jim and says, "That is so strange that you should ask. I just had to put out more rat poison and bait this morning. My nephew was here yesterday and kept the store when I went to Madrid. His mother collected him before I got back and when I returned to lock up the shop, I found that the bait I had set out two days ago was gone. So, I had to put out more. The poison is strychnine, very powerful, and I have to be very careful with it. I have not had a chance to ask Pepe what happened. And now you came in, and… Oh my. Jaime. How did your beautiful dogs die?" The look on Alejandro's face is agony, waiting for the answer.

"Poison. What did you use for the bait?"

Alejandron suddenly sits and his hands come to his face. He is rocking slightly back and forth, then whispers, "Bread." When he looks up, tears are streaming down his cheeks. "I am so, so sorry Jaime. I can not bear it. I am sorry. Oh, oh, oh."

Jim just stands there, slightly unstable, then walks around the counter, stands Alejandro up, and holds the man in a long embrace. They clutch one another and are still embracing when the next customer comes in. Seeing the scene, he just turns and leaves without speaking. Jim releases the embrace, wipes the tears from Alejandro's face, then from his own, turns and leaves.

Back at the house, he tells Marta the story and they both cry for quite a while. It is dark by the time they both surface from their grieving and move to the living room, each with a glass of wine. Jim lights the fire, and when they sit on the sofa facing it, the emptiness of the carpet on the hearth hits them again. No dogs filling that warm space. It's another long night.

Work, for both, is therapeutic and Marta's apparel business is actually paying many of the bills as well as providing a source of cash for local women helping to sew and construct garments. Marta is the sole printer/screener and creator of the designs. Jim's contacts in Madrid keep him busy at the Hilton Hotel as well as writing for the English language paper. The pain of the dogs dying is receding just as a letter from the states arrives. Marta claims it from the cantina and since it is addressed to the both of them, opens it on the way back to the house. Jim's typewriter is clacking away upstairs as she comes through the door with, "Jeem! There's a letter. From Alger. Come down." The clacking stops, a chair scrapes across the floor and the footsteps behind descending the stairs.

"What's Hiss bothering us with now? Looking for a return on his rabbit investment?"

"No, no, no. He says, oh, go ahead, read it."

Taking the paper, Jim squints at the small handwriting, but starts smiling almost immediately. Looking up, he says, "What do you think?"

"Yes, yes, yes. Ten years is long enough, I think. It would be so good. And, they insist on paying for the plane tickets, putting us up, organizing get- togethers. Oh, it would be so nice, and Christmas! We could have Christmas, like before. Oh, yes, yes, yes."

"I wonder how many are involved in this? It's not cheap, by any means. Hiss has some money, but not a lot. Hmm." The hmm actually is more of a rumble, or growl, but Marta recognizes it for what it is, satisfaction. Their friends in New York are supporting a trip home for them. It is a wonder. "Ugh!" A pained look crosses her face.

"Don't you like the idea? What's the matter?"

"No, I love the idea. Just one of my female pains, I think. Not to worry. It's October. We need to plan things. I will start dinner. Ugh!"

"You sure that's just female pains? You don't look good."

"No hay problemo, mi corazón. Ah, see. All gone. Now to make dinner, and we can talk more. OK?" The smile is wide and real as she bounces down the hallway to the kitchen, a definite lilt in her step. Jim bounces up the stairs to answer Alger Hiss's letter.

At dinner, the conversation is animated, the food barely tasted, as they contemplate Christmas in New York. Then Jim gets quiet for a minute, looks at Marta and says, "Macy's, Bloomingdale's, Nordstrom's."

Marta stops chewing for a moment, looking at Jim, then smiles, nods and says, "That's my Jeem. Ah, what a chance we could have there. The women of Valdeolmos could be famous all over the world if we could sell to those big places. Do we sell to all?"

"No, exclusivity is key here. We get the best deal, but any one of them would be good. We must restrict the size of the project or we risk not being able to fill the orders. That is one reason to make it an exclusive deal. It helps to sell the item as much as the quality. The store becomes the sole outlet for an exotic item and people respond, especially in New York. The garments still have to be good, but they are. They are the best, already. So, making the offer an exclusive one will help sell it. The brochures must be updated. I'll do that. Damn, wish Dougie was here. Anyway, you concentrate on the samples you want to take with us. Get creative, my sweet. We're off to sell to New York City, and see wonderful people for Christmas!"

The atmosphere in the house has gone from gloom to radiant sunshine. The industry in the printing area and from Jim's typewriter raises the Fall temperature in the house. Things are heating up just as the air is cooling off. New brochures are created over the following 3 weeks, printed and sent off to strategic contacts in New York, people whose networks can get them entry to buyers at the various stores. Networking has never looked so good. The positive energy reinforces Marta's creative spirit and the silk screens developed and tested now vary from Aztec to Peruvian, to Castellano with even some Basque thrown in to honor Tony and Carmen Arizza. The only thing that slightly, only slightly, dampens Marta's enthusiasm, is how often she finds herself required to sit down with fatigue or to take some aspirin for her lower belly pain. Then, it subsides and she is off again.

The American community in Madrid invite Jim and Marta to the hilton for the annual Thanksgiving celebration, and they readily accept. They have, at times, had several guests to Valdeolmos to celebrate, but this year the place is in absolute uproar preparing for the trip, so the respite is appreciated even more. The conversation around the room is mostly about Nixon, this Watergate nonsense, as some put it, or the criminal conspiracy, as Jim puts it. There is spirited conversation, and Jim has never been shy when an argument is nearby, so the energy is lively during the evening, as well as distracting. The ride back to Valdeolmos seems shorter than usual, but both are tired and no need for wine before bed. Christmas is coming.

Luckily, they have enough saved to afford the fees for extra, and overweight baggage. They warned the Hisses to bring a large form of transport. Everyone within the

New York network is aware of the commercial aspect of this visit, but not deterred. The trip, transfer of luggage, which all arrived with them, the trip back to Manhattan, the hugs, hurrahs and toasts are exactly as anticipated. Dinner at Kai's Chinese restaurant is scheduled and the Hisses and Tucks are treated as royalty. The center of the restaurant is cleared of tables, one large table erected and the few remaining diners watch as the Tuck entourage is feted in royal style, as if Chinese mandarins had invaded. Most of the way through the meal, Alger's wife glances at Marta, then rises from her place and goes across the table to her. Marta's face is grim with pain and she is doubled over. Jim and Alger had been arguing politics and had lost track of the women. As soon and they notice, Jim is out of his chair and at Marta's side. "What's wrong? You in pain? What's the matter, for crissake?"

Alger's wife gently presses Jim's arm saying, "Calm yourself, Jim. Lets concentrate on Marta quietly, shall we?"

Marta looks up, tears in her eyes, and says, "I need to leave. Let's go home. I feel awful."

Kai is hovering nearby, his amazing ceremony and celebration going to hell, but his beautiful Marta is worse. "Did my food make her sick?"

Jim stands more erect, looks at Kai, "Never your food, my friend. Never your food. Perhaps she is too tired. I am sorry, but we must leave. I will talk to you tomorrow. Thank you for a wonderful evening." While Jim is calming Kai, Alger and his wife are assisting Marta out of her chair. Jim gets the coats and other winter gear while Alger summons the taxi and his wife helps Marta to the door. Marta sits on a chair in the lobby while they open the door to the taxi that had been at the stand outside. As they leave the front of the restaurants, Kai is last seen, downcast, wringing his hands. Marta is gasping slightly and whispers to Jim, "Hospital. Something is wrong. Hospital."

"OK, sure. We'll go to Bellevue. Driver, can you get us to Bellevue emergency entrance soonest, please?" The four of them exit the taxi at the emergency door, Marta barely able to walk, assisted by Jim and Alger. That night is another one with no end.

Next morning, instead of the scheduled followup meeting at Macy's, Jim, having sent the Hisses home, is conferring with a surgeon about a plan. Marta is next on the schedule and the current diagnosis has an obstetrician- gynecologist as the lead physician involved. He is the one Jim is talking to now. "First I remember was probably October, but only rarely did I ever see her resort to pain medicine after that. It was obviously painful for her that one time, but it was nothing like this."

"Mr. Tuck, I suspect your wife, Marta is it?" Positive nod. "I suspect she has been hiding quite a lot, for quite a while. What did your doctor in Madrid say about the condition?"

"There is no doctor in our village, and we rarely see any in Madrid. The expense of private doctor visits is something we don't do often, especially when it seems to be something that goes away fairly quickly. So, no doctor in Spain, really."

That produces a frown, a nod, and then, "Well, we will see what this brings. We can't tell at this time what the extent of the difficulty is, but uterine cancer can spread as it is a highly vascular organ with an excellent blood supply that can transfer cells elsewhere. We'll just have to see. I will talk again, after surgery. We should be finished and she in recovery in about two hours. Have you had any sleep?"

"No. Not an option at the moment."

"Well, the cafeteria is now open. It opened at 7:30, so perhaps some coffee will help. I will have you paged to return here when we can talk more." With that, the white coated physician is off, down the hall and disappears into a double door marked No Entry. Jim turns, then walks to the reception area for surgery and asks the person behind the counter for directions to the cafeteria.

"Xoch, it's your dad. Listen, I have some difficult news. Can you talk?" The transatlantic call is adequate and he can hear her well enough. He just is having a hard time telling it again. Two days of relating the impossible has taken its toll, but Xoch needs to know now.

"Sure, Poppa. What's up? I don't have any money to spare, but I can at least listen."

"It's not about money this time, bud. Listen carefully. Marta is very sick, as in not going to get better. We are still in New York, but arranging to return to Valdeolmos, probably before the week is out. We'll be back right after New Years."

"What do you mean not going to get better. What's she got? Marta is never sick. How bad could it possibly be?"

"The worst it can be, Xoch. She has uterine cancer that has spread. They did a hysterectomy here at Bellevue, on an emergency basis, but there is evidence of the cancer having spread to many, many other places. I don't want to make a list here on the phone. It has gone too far to be treated. She's not going to get better. She knows it. She wants to go back to Valdeolmos, now. I think you should make arrangements to get there as soon as you can."

Silence. Then, "Oh, Poppa. I can't think. How did this happen. What!? No! It can't. No! No! No!" Sobbing then the sound of the telephone receiver hitting the floor. Sobbing in the background as Jim grinds his teeth, waiting. Finally the receiver is lifted, "I'll be there day after tomorrow." Click. Tears wet Jim's cheeks. How the hell did this go so wrong?

The New York Tuck support network swings into gear and the return to Spain is swiftly and efficiently organized with Jim making as many plans and decisions as he can, and are necessary for staying sane. The return is accomplished immediately following the New Year, 1974. The plane is met by Xochitl in Madrid, as well as several in the Madrid Tuck network, and Carmen and Tony Arizza. Marta smiles for all as she is delivered by wheelchair to the international arrivals salon. Xoch has brought the Tuck Volvo to the terminal and the family and luggage, minus a few suitcases that had held samples of garments left in New York. There are three vehicles in caravan that pull in front of the house in Valdeolmos, Marta is assisted into the house in the borrowed wheelchair and several of her local friends from the village immediately liven the kitchen with evening meal preparation. It is eerily quiet until Marta calls from the bedroom, "It's pretty damned cold in here!" That produces the portable gas heater, extra blankets and at least four pairs of hands to remedy the situation. The hustle creates considerable noise and focused activity and a large smile from Marta, everyone's reward.

With women working in the kitchen, the room warming from the heater and Jim upstairs on his typewriter, Xochitl sits on the side of the bed, holds Marta's hand and they talk quietly, with tears constantly in four eyes, occasionally down the cheeks. Finally, Marta sits a bit straighter and says, "I need to check on the kitchen. These women are likely to mess things up since they don't know where stuff is, where it is supposed to be. Help me up, please, and leave that wheeled thing in the corner. I can walk around my own house." That sets the tone for the duration. Marta as in-charge as she can be, smiling as often as she can, and caring people working hard to keep it that way, as long as possible. Tony and Carmen decided to stay in Madrid for the night rather than burden the household, but intend to return tomorrow. The third car in the caravan from the airport was the alcalde, a real friend of both Jim and Marta. He and his wife are still at the house, the wife in the kitchen, the alcalde in the sitting room in front of the fireplace with a glass of wine and functioning as gatekeeper for the house. Many villagers want to visit, but he turns most away, gently, recommending a visit another day. The relatively smooth exit from New York, assisted by the New York network, is duplicated in the reentry to the village assisted by the village and Spanish network. Friends are important.

Days fold into weeks, and the course of Marta's illness is obvious. She is soon rarely outside the house, then rarely outside the bedroom and the bed, but the village is constant in its support, as is Xochitl. She is everywhere, and seemingly always available for Marta or the others. Jim is not pushed aside, but finds it hard to feel functional, given the amount of help constantly around. Finally, he takes his staff, his cape and hat and wanders away into the fields, finding Paco whenever possible. Mostly, they sit and say nothing, or talk about particular sheep, the next holiday, the weather, then nothing at all, quiet. Arriving back at the house, the first stop is the bedroom. Opening the door, he appreciates the warmth of the air, and of the group that seems to be in constant attendance. As Marta has lost her ability to care for herself, the group has gotten larger, constantly changing, usually quiet, but smiles responding to smiles from Marta. The door opening and Jim entering produces another Marta smile, as well as one from Xochitl, and suddenly the room is nearly empty as the helpers, except for Xochitl, leave for other chores. There is dusting, clothes washing, sweeping and many other details of home life to attend to. Walking to the side of the bed, Jim bends down and gives Marta a long kiss, with his hand behind Xochitl's shoulder, giving her a squeeze at the same time. "Jeem, what day is it?" Marta looks at him awaiting the answer.

"It's Tuesday, I think. Right, bud?"

"Wednesday, Poppa. February 13th, Wednesday."

"Oh, right. Thanks. Missed a few days I guess."

"I seem to be missing more lately. I never ask any more. No wonder I still feel cold. February is always the coldest month. Could you turn up the fire a bit, Jeem?"

"Sure. Oh, it is on full amount. Let me get you another blanket."

"No, no more blankets. I can hardly move now. Too heavy. Is the electric fire upstairs? Maybe we could use that."

"I'll be right back."

"No, Poppa. You stay here. I'll get it."

"Look, bud. I have been looking for things to do for a while now. Let me, OK?" The one sided smile appears in the right corner of Jim's mouth.

"OK. You get it."

"Thanks, Jeem."

That's the conversation that has overtaken the house the last couple of weeks. Very utilitarian. Not much personal stuff getting said. Safe talk. The room gets warmer with the electric fire added to the gas heater. A blanket actually comes off the bed, making Marta actually a little more comfortable.

Friday night, Jim comes into the bedroom to see if Marta needs anything before he goes to bed in the back, the room Dougie usually used. Marta is awake, with a bit of a grimace, but a smile nonetheless. "Hello, my sweet. Can I get you anything?"

"No. Please just sit. Siente te, aqui." She pats the edge of the bed near her head. He comes and sits, stroking her very thin cheek, pushing her thick hair back from her forehead. "Ah, that feels very good. I like it. I love you, Jeem. You are a good, sometimes difficult man, but the best man for me."

"I love you , too, amiga. You are a grand woman, and a friend."

"Si, we are friends. Please stay with me this evening. I feel I need you here. You can come under the covers. Do you know where Xochitl is?"

"For me, under the covers would be too hot in here. For you it is good. Xoch is upstairs typing something. She said she would be back down not too long from now. Do you want me to get her?"

"No, when she comes, it is OK. Come and hold me, please."

"Are you OK? Is something wrong?"

"No. Things are nearly right, now. Come hold me." This last is accompanied by a strong grimace.

"You are in pain. Let me get you something. Where is your morphine?"

"No. No morphine, just now. Maybe when I need to sleep, not just now. I want to see you, feel you, hear your gravel voice clearly. No morphine now."

Jim slides into bed, on top of the covers, and his arm is over Marta's chest with his hand on her cheek. "Ah, yes. This is good." Even that is with a grimace, which is hard for Jim to accept, but keeps his suggestion to himself. "Ah. I like this feeling. I can not feel it so well with morphine. This is better. Ugh!"

Jim jerks up onto his elbow saying, "Are you sure? You OK?"

"Si. Very OK. Please Call Xochitl now."

Jim slides back out of bed and climbs the stairs across the hall. "Xoch, Marta is asking for you."

"One more sentence. Almost done, Poppa."

"Now, I think is better. Come now, please." Xochitl pauses her typing, looks at Jim, slides the chair back and they descend the stairs from the frigid to the sweltering.

"Are you, OK, Momma?" It's the first time in years Xochitl has used Momma.

"Si. I think I need you and Poppa nearby just now. I feel it is important. I told Jeem no morphine for a while because I want to see you and hear you clearly. It seems important. Jeem is uncomfortable with my pain, but it is OK. Will you be OK?"

Jim is back lying on Marta's other side, Xochitl is sitting on the edge of the bed. They haven't been three-in-a-bed for years. Marta occasionally gives a grunt, sometimes a small snuffle then they return to their abrazo, an intimacy they have not had for some time. The conversation ranges widely, mostly about the future, a few memories, some good, some difficult, but everything significant. Suddenly, Marta says, "I think now is a good time for the morphine." Jim slides out of the bed and retrieves the capsules and a glass of water. "Three please."

Jim hesitates, looking at Marta who simply smiles a slightly crooked smile, nods her head and, "Please."

Jim hands the glass and three capsules to Xochitl, slides into the bed beside Marta and supports her head as Xochitl helps put the capsules, one at a time, in her mouth followed by a drink of water. After the third drink, Jim lowers her head to the pillow and he slides back down beside her. Xochitl puts the empty glass on the table and sits back down, holding Marta's hand in hers. None notice, but the hour has changed and it is a new day. "Te amo, Jeem. Te amo. Ah, my sweet girl, te amo tambien, todos. Te…." The sound of a long slow exhale is followed by a slow, silent inhale and she is asleep.

Hours before sunrise, both Jim and Xochitl are aware that Marta's breathing is very quiet. In fact, she is finished breathing. Jim slides out of the bed, reaches for and holds Xochitl for a long, long time. The first of the village women appear at the door of the house, silently enter as usual so they don't wake Marta, and make their way toward the kitchen, and to start the wood burning hot water heater on the back wall of the house. There is slight bustling about at the back of the house, and Jim releases Xochit who sits back down placing her head on Marta's chest, and Jim makes his way down the hall to the women. "Marta has died," he says, in Spanish. The women stop mid activity, put down their things, except the woman starting the fire in the water heater. Hot water will be needed, for sure. Each villager stops at Jim's side, raises a hand to his cheek, then departs. Finally the fire is going and the last woman departs, in the same fashion. The house is quiet, cold and quiet, Jim slowly returns to the bedroom, strokes Xochitl's hair as he passes by, and turns off both heaters. He returns to the kitchen, retrieves a bottle of wine and two glasses and comes into the bedroom, pours the wine, hands one glass to Xochitl and states, "To the finest of women." They both drink, then Jim leaves for the alcalde's house. He needs to be told first. The rest of the village will know in minutes, but Jim must be the one to inform the alcalde.

Marta is buried with the entire village, along with much of Madrid it seems, in attendance, at the cathedral in Valdeolmos, just as she wanted. The preparations, communications and accommodating of friends is nearly completely distracting for both Jim and Xochitl. Finally, Xochitl says, "Poppa, I have to get back to London. Have to."

"I know, bud. You go. I am OK. I really am."

Xochitl looks at him, with the glass in his hand, and simply says, "Bullshit." Next morning she is away, with Jim seeing her off at the airport, driving home to quiet, cold, inactivity. It is a cruel winter.

Wine and cigarettes, cigarettes and wine. Throw in an occasional hard boiled egg, crust of bread, goat cheese, back to cigarettes and wine. Occasionally wandering the dusty streets, more often dawdling in the open fields, very occasionally sitting with Paco and his sheep, but rarely saying anything to anybody. Jim's wardrobe could be easily described as early scruffy during the good times. Now the village is lucky the winter weather forces him to cover it in many layers. The conversation around the village revolves around the apparent rapid descent of don Jaime into the land of lost souls. Solutions are few until the cantina owner mentions the fact that his dog just had a litter of puppies. The sudden possibilities become obvious, and two other people note their dogs also had puppies. The plan is made, and late in March, Jim answers the forceful knock at the door with a louder than usual "What?" or "Que?" No Response, so he returns to his attempt at reading and suddenly the knocking is repeated. "Arrgh!" The gravel could fill a dump truck. No return sounds, so he pushes himself up from the sofa in front of the fire and heads to the door. "This better be good! I am not pleased!" Opening the door, he notices - nothing, no one there. "AArrggh!" and he is about to slam the door when he hears whimpering. Looking down, there is a woven basket with 3 puppies in it with a note. Translated, it says the writer hopes he will carefully care for these puppies. They need a good home. Thank you. "Thank you, my ass. Who's dumping dogs on my doorstep?" About to slam the door shut, he looks down at the raised ears and expectant face of one of the puppies. The other two are nuzzling into one another, but this one is alert and watching his every move. Jim stops, looks at this brown, nondescript puppy and it cocks its head to the left and jumps to all four feet, tail wagging as if to say, "Nice to meet you. How do you like me by now?"

"Oh my god, what the hell am I going to do with three dogs?" He lifts the basket and the alert puppy immediately is at his face, licking vigorously. The other two are much less forward, slightly fearful, but this one is all over him. Carrying them into the house he starts talking, "Where the hell did you guys come from? How can I take care of three of you? Don't you know I don't have such a great track record with living things in this house? Dogs, rabbits.... Oh well, you hungry? You're a young lady, aren't you?" The alert pup is wagging head to toe. The other two are hanging back a bit, but affected by the first one's enthusiasm. "Names. You guys need names. OK, you're bright enough, sort of a bloom or blossom compared to these other ones. Hmm, flower, eh, Flor. That's you. Let me see you other two," and he reaches down to gather another one. "Ah, a male, you're a male as well. Two boys and a girl. All brown, but different personalities, for sure. Still wonder where you came from. Different parents, that's for sure. Look at you three. OK, you're Flor; you, you'll be Beto, and You're Rudy. Why? Why not. Settled. Now, something to eat."

Jim has the three pups enclosed in the back yard so he can have a vigorous walk this morning. The pups have grown on him. Flor is definitely his favorite, but the other two have their moments, and the three get along quite well. Heading to the door, there is a knock that makes him hesitate, then open the door, worried there will be more offerings. Paco is there, standing in front of the door, his dog watching the sheep while he is at the door. They greet one another, then Paco reaches into his pouch and retrieves a puppy and hands it to Jim. Jim jumps back saying, "No, no. Tengo tres ahora. No, no."

Paco simply walks straight up to Jim and thrusts the puppy onto Jim's chest, turns and whistles to the dog and is away with the sheep. "What the hell? Do I look like the SPCA? Where are these things coming from?" He holds the pup, which is obviously from a sheep dog litter, another male, and closes the door. Raising the dog up to eye level, he looks at it. "You are ugly, muy feo, so you will be Paco. I gotta put the word out, no more dogs. How the hell am I going to feed four of them. These guys are bound to get fairly large." With that he heads to the back yard and deposits Paco in the pen with the other three. The sniffing and posturing lasts about ten seconds, then they are romping with each other, then racing in a circle around the perimeter of the pen. Jim watches for a moment, then walks into the kitchen to look for more stuff to feed them. "This may not be easy," he says.

It turns out to be easier than he thought as offerings intermittently show up on his doorstep from time to time. Leftover bread, mutton stew, paella, all sorts of examples of the generosity of the villagers of Valdeolmos. The wine and cigarettes are now regularly interspersed with reasonable meals, at least every other day. The clothes line now regularly has washing on it, the pups are getting bigger and follow Jim everywhere. He takes them into the fields with him regularly now, and occasionally walks around town without them on leashes. The local cats stay hidden on their walks, several villagers wave as he goes by with the dogs, especially when they are all on their leashes. It is often comical, with Jim trying to keep them untangled. April and may become much more pleasant months because of the temperature, but also because of the company. Sunshine was never so appreciated.

"Come on, boys. Come and get it." The four bowls are laid in line and the sound of pounding paws announces the dogs coming around the corner of the building, dripping wet. "Been swimming again?" With that, Jim strolls over to the pool and looks at the evidence. Wet at the far end where the steps are, mud settling into the deep end. "Ugh!" Then, another, "Ugh" as Jim leans forward with a grimace, leaning onto the back of a metal garden chair. Sweat starts forming at his hairline, and he sits, bending way forward. "Goddam it. What the hell's going on?" No answers, just snuffling from the dogs noses deep in tier bowls.

"You have a significant stomach ulcer, Mr. Tuck. I understand you have had significant stress lately. You smoke, if you don't mind the comparison, like a chimney, your diet is sporadic at best, except for the wine. You are doing yourself in." The doctor is one Jim hasn't met previously but is seeing at the clinic at the British American Hospital in Madrid. The referral was from his GP on the outskirts of Madrid, and from the posture and facial expression Jim is displaying, not going well.

"As a matter of fact, I do mind. What the hell do you know about my "stressors", and I have been smoking since I was 12 years old. Never had these abdominal pains before."

"Cumulative effects I am afraid. As far as your stressors are concerned, your GP was very helpful with background information."

"Son of a bitch. Last visit to him."

"How would you expect a reasonable diagnosis from me without appropriate background information?"

"What the hell do you call that, reasonable? That's not reasonable, that's just bullshit."

"Your descriptors are as advertised, colorful. But, nevertheless, my opinion stands. You have a significant stomach ulcer that may not be treatable with medication."

"So, what treatment are you suggesting, eh?"

"For now, medication and diet change, behavior change. I suggest we try this conservative approach for a month. If it fails, you will need surgery."

The growl is pure gravel and comes out, "Surgery my ass. Nobody is cutting on me."

"Of course, that would be your decision, but it is my opinion that surgery will likely be necessary, probably before this Fall."

"Like hell. Thanks but no thanks. I'll let myself out. You have my address. Send the bill." With that Jim is up and out the door leaving the surgeon sitting with pen in midair and a baffled expression on his face.

Driving back to the village the conversation goes something like this with himself: "Stressors my ass. Sure, Marta's gone, Xoch is no longer here, but for Chissake, I flew in China with the Japs shooting at me. Ditched in the ocean on the way to Manila, dodged a murderous Mexican husband. Stressors, what the hell does he know about stressors? Stop smoking? You must be kidding. No more red wine? Ha! OK, so I'll eat better. Cut out the spicy stuff. We'll see who can handle the stressors. Damned incompetent bastard."

September arrives with cooler weather at night, warm dusty days, the dogs fully grown teenagers now, and Jim vomiting blood. The cramps are worse. Pride stowed, he heads back to the surgeon's office for another appointment. Three days later, he is in recovery at the BA Hospital, with a very attractive English speaking nurse from England at his side when he becomes aware of his surroundings. "Have I died and heaven is real? Don't tell me, you're an angel, right?" Even through the post anesthetic haze his gruff pronunciation is clear.

"Of course. I just have my wings folded under this white outfit, and this hat is for show. How are you feeling, Mr. Tuck? My name is Emily and I am your nurse in recovery."

"Recovery? Oh, right. I let that incompetent bastard cut on me afterall, didn't I? I must be getting weak."

"Well, I don't know much about your typical fortitude, but from the operative report I read, I would say you got back to the surgeon in the nick of time. Your stomach was in a bad way. The damaged portion is gone now. Hopefully, you will be able to prevent a recurrence in the remainder. Your nurse on the floor will begin your reeducation process."

"Reeducation?! What the hell are you talking about?"

"Calm down please. Those stitches can come apart if you get too rowdy. Calm, I say!"

Jim lies back, resting his head on a small pillow, turns his head away so as to not have to look at his angel. "Now, now, Mr. Tuck. Let's not get all moody, shall we?"

"I think it's your time to go, isn't it?"

"No, not really. I just need to take a few vital signs, fluff your bedclothes and make sure you are comfortable. Then I am off to the next customer."

"Arrgh!" The growl is deep and meaningful. The taking of blood pressure, temperature, pulse and respiration rate is quickly accomplished and Emily is away to the other side of the curtain to the next patient in recovery.

The process of becoming upright requires a full three days, then there are short walks with the Spanish speaking nurses' aides. These become more frequent and Jim is enjoying the company, while slowly warming to the nursing staff, Marianne in particular. From the USA, she has been at the hospital for six months, is learning Spanish at night classes and every bit as attractive as Emily, who actually stops by Jim's bed from time to time. Chatting up good looking women, ever more frequent walks with the aides, getting further from his bed each day, all make the required stay at the hospital as pleasant as it could be.

"I think perhaps three to five more days here at the hospital should be sufficient recovery for you to be able to be discharged to home. You live alone, is that correct?"

"Correct." The response is with eyes down and relatively quietly delivered. This brings the doctor's head up from his recording in the patient notes.

"How are you feeling?" The blunt end of the pen he is using is between his teeth as he examines Jim's appearance.

"Sore, a bit. Otherwise fine. Well, relatively fine. I'll be better in my own bed, with my dogs."

"Yes, I am sure. So, does that sound reasonable to you? Three to five days more, then home, to," examining the paperwork, "Valdeolmos?"

"Yeah. Peachy. Sorry doc, I am just getting a bit stir crazy lately. I need more activity. Yeah, fine, three to five more days." With that, Jim stands and waves as he retreats from the doctor's clinic room, back to his ward. Instead of returning to his bed, he walks to the end of the room where there is a small table and two chairs under a large window. The view is of the mountains at the edge of town, the peaks of some already white with snow. Winter is coming. "Fucking cold winter, again." He sits in the right hand chair and stares at the mountains.

"Excuse me."

Jim gives a start and turns to see another angel in white. "Yes?"

"Are you Mr. James Tuck?" The rather erect woman looking down at him is holding a patient record and he sees his name written on the tab.

"Yes, as a matter of fact I am. Who are you?"

"Ah, yes. I am Margaret Wiley, your nurse as of this afternoon."

The lilt reminds Jim of Ben in China and he asks, "Australian by chance?"

"Yes, as a matter of fact. Is that a problem for you?"

"Not at all, not at all. Here, have a seat," and he pushes the chair opposite back for her.

"No, that would not quite do. I was told you had seen the doctor and would be back in the ward soon. I wanted to have the chance to meet you and inquire as to whether you have any particular needs at the moment."

"Not at the moment." Jim turns and looks out the window at the Navacerrada mountains. There is an extended silence with Margaret allowing it to finish. "Marta loved those mountains. She used to take Xochitl up there for skiing every winter, right through into the Valdeolmos Spring."

Margaret winces slightly, "Marta is your wife?"

"Was. Died February."

"I am so sorry. It must still be a very fresh discomfort."

"Fresh? Yes, I'd say fresh is accurate."

"And Xochitl?"

"Our daughter. She finished high school here, is 28, married, living in London. She was back for a bit during Marta's final days. Left right after the funeral. The whole village was at the funeral, people I had never met. And Arizza came, a buddy from way back, Basque, ex-Air Force. Quite the event for such a small pueblo, small church. Nice folks up there in Valdeolmos. How long have you been here? I don't think I have seen you before. Probably would have remembered." This last is with the Tuck smile.

"I have been here at the hospital about 3 years now, enjoying most of it, don't mingle much with the ex-pat community. I enjoy traveling about, seeing the sites around Spain, learning a bit of the language, slowly. I read better than speak. Otherwise, my life is fairly vanilla at the moment."

"Vanilla is a special flavoring when used properly." This produces another bit of color in Margaret's cheeks.

"It has been nice having this chance to chat. Perhaps I can do a few of the necessary vital examinations when you return to your bed. It's been a pleasure, Mr. Tuck."

"Why, Margaret, the pleasure was all mine. I will be back to my bed shortly." Both corners of his mouth rise, as do both eyebrows.

Margaret retreats into the ward with the paperwork and is thinking, "His profile didn't mention recent widower, just significant illness, but he seems rather pert at the moment. Wonder what the rest of the story is." Jim is watching closely as she retreats, the smile never leaving his face.

CHAPTER 8

New Chapter

"So, you're leaving today. You seem happy."

"I am happy. Been cooped up in here long enough, Margaret. Feels like escaping prison, almost. I have let a couple of the other nurses know about my departure and have invited them, and am inviting you now, so a celebration lunch. What do you say?"

"I'd love to, except I don't finish until two this afternoon. Is that too late?"

"It was just the time I was thinking of. There is a fine cafe two blocks from here, main street, opposite side, Finca de Toros. You know it?"

"Yes. It is actually one of my favorites. I stop on my way home, often, for something to drink and a seafood sandwich. Sounds good. Right after two p.m. I will still be in uniform, if that's OK."

"Of course. You look quite good in that uniform."

Now the color can't be hidden in her cheeks so she turns quickly with a, "See ya there."

Jim is at the cafe when Margaret arrives, alone at the table. "Where are the others?"

"Apparently neither could come today, but I have extracted promises from them of a visit to Valdeolmos while the weather is still agreeable, maybe next weekend. I asked, on your behalf, if there was room for you to come as well and received an affirmative from Emily. It's her car."

"I could have asked, myself, but thanks for the effort. Emily is a good sort. We often have traveled together. I think I saw Cadiz with her. So, good enough. Next Saturday. I have not checked the roster, but I am pretty sure I have Saturday off next week."

"I hope I did not overstep my bounds with the ride thing."

"No, I guess not. I am just fairly used to making my own arrangements. Not to worry. I'm starving."

"Good. Oh, not good you're starving, but good there are no hard feelings. Food. Yes. COMIDA!" is the shout and a waiter appears almost instantly. Lunch is very good today.

Margaret is waiting at the curb when Emily drives up, Marianne in the passenger seat in front. Margaret climbs quickly into the back door as the hooting starts from delayed drivers. The car is away as soon as Margaret sits and she lurches back into the seat from the acceleration. "Whew! That's a getaway! We could be robbing banks."

"I hate those assholes honking behind me all the time. You'd think they would grow a bit of patience, but little boys right to the end."

"Not so little, though, right?" Marianne is half turned toward Margaret. "I don't remember the last time we were able to have a day out together, do you?"

"I think it was March, at the equinox festival. Or, did we go to the Prado together in April? Not sure."

"Prado! That's it. I tend to avoid those festivals. The smacking lips, whistles and occasional hand on my butt gets to be too much, fast."

"Got that right. Bet it's the same assholes who honk in traffic." Emily is sitting over the steering wheel in combative mode.

"I'd say, how about we smooth out the conversation a bit, relax on the day off. What do you say?"

Emily and Marianne look back and forth at each other, then all three burst out laughing. "Relax it is. Valdeolmos, here we come. How far is it, by the way."

"Mr. Tuck said about a forty-five minute drive from the hospital. The last bit is dirt road into the village."

"You still doing the Mr. Tuck thing? We have been using Jim for a couple of weeks."

"Mr. Tuck just seems more appropriate. For heaven's sake, he's at least thirty years older than any of us."

"Yeah, but it's a short thirty, gotta tell ya." Emily winks at Marianne who turns in her seat and asks directly, "You mean he hasn't suggested any extracurricular activities to you? Wow! He's been hittin' on Em and me for at least a couple of weeks."

"I should say not. Hmm. Should I be insulted?"

That brings a laugh from all three as the car passes from the outskirts of town into the countryside.

Jim is in the garden at the open spit, turning a suckling pig over the pit. Tony Arizza brings two glasses of wine out as Jim continues the turning by hand. "When you gonna modernize this operation? Still turning this thing by hand is quaint, but max inefficient."

"My boy, this is meditative. Plus, I get to make sure it is done to perfection. What time is it?"

"Don't know. Hold on. Carmen!"

"Si?"

"Que hora es?"

"Una y media."

"OK, the girls should be here in half an hour. I have it all set up for weekend entertainment. Live music tonight, cantina in the morning."

"You got the cantina to operate on a Sunday morning? How did that happen?"

"Tony, my man. When's the last time I failed to sell an idea? By the way, I am thinking that it's way past time I had live-in company in this place. Especially with Winter coming on. Ha! Anyway, I have decided, one of these lasses is it, the new lady of the house."

"Oh, yeah? Which one?"

"The first one that gets pregnant."

The clink of the wine glass against the whiskey tumbler accentuates the point, and the two glasses are drained simultaneously."

The car pulls up in front of the house, next to a dirty white Volvo and a flashier Renault. Getting out, the three women look at one another then the scene in the plaza. It is dusty, quiet and a couple of dogs ambling toward the far side of the open area. Across the way and higher sits the cathedral, backlit by a clear September sky. "The wine is inside, ladies." Jim's wide open arms beckon the women indoors and they accept the invitation. The little entourage makes its way down the hallway and out the backdoor to meet Tony who is manning the spit and smiling.

Cordial greetings are exchanged all around, except Carmen seems quiet, then excuses herself from the group to return to the house. Jim watches her leave, looks at Tony and asks, "So?"

Tony has been busy basting the beast and says, "So what?"

"What's up with Carmen? Haven't seen her this quiet since I can remember."

"Jim, don't be so obtuse. You've invited three very attractive young women into Marta's space. Marta was Carmen's best friend. What do you expect?"

"You really think that's it?"

"Jaime!"

"All right, all right. You're probably right."

"Right about what? Did we miss something?" The women are gathering around the fire pit as the evening approaches and the air is cooling, but have no wine.

"About the fact that you lasses are without glasses. Ah, you didn't realize I could be a man of poetic letters, did you? Carry on with your excellent cooking, Tony. The ladies and I are for the kitchen. After you." The three young women are herded into the back door of the house and the spit maintains its regular pace with Tony at the handle.

Inside, Jim is gathering drink orders, all white wines, pulling glasses down from the shelf, and peeking around the corner of the kitchen door to see if he can spot Carmen. Nowhere in sight. "Now, you are all armed and ready, we can explore the rest of the house. Directly across here is the spare room, once occupied by my young friend Dougle, of English extraction, recently relocated to New Zealand with his family. Down the hall on the left is the lounge with our central heat." They peek into the room that is fairly dark, but observe the walls of books and the large, silent fireplace awaiting the winter. "Across here is the main bedroom." They see a large master bed, more books and Jim notices there is no Carmen. "Now, we will explore the upstairs." The three women precede him up the stairs and when they reach the top, there is Carmen, caressing the silk screen table, wistfully looking at the hanging printed fabric along the wall. "Did you meet Carmen? Tony's wife and a good friend for many years." Carmen, stands slightly more erect and each woman introduces herself. "Carmen helped Marta often when she was printing fabric. They spent many hours here together. And over here is my office, of sorts, where I write and do our correspondence, uh, my correspondence." That brings a small cloud to his eyes, and a large one to Carmen's. Quickly, he moves on to, "Dinner will be ready in half an hour, I think. See you downstairs, yes?" Carmen responds with a nod and half a smile to the three young women. The four return to the ground floor and make their way out the back door. The smells of dinner are strong and suddenly the appetites are even stronger. "We'll tour the rest of the grounds after dinner. Can I get some help to set the table in the hallway?" Three heads vigorously nod and they are back into the kitchen, the table is pulled away from the hallway wall and two more chairs retrieved from the living room while hand made plates and bowls are set for six around the table.

The meal is a smash, and before the dessert of flan, Jim gives a quick guided tour of the plaza, pointing out the cantina, the house of the alcalde, and notes the shutters being closed, doors shut, and village closing down as the sun retreats. "This place is quiet as a tomb, except for a couple of excitable dogs, until first light in the morning. We are anomalies wandering around town, but the villagers are accustomed to the foolish foreigners by now. As a matter of fact, Marta was typically welcomed into homes, even at night."

"Why was that?"

"Because, after several years, we were able to put a telephone in the house. It used to be in the cantina, but now, often as not, we, or I, serve as the nighttime message resource. I am liable to get a call after dark to get an urgent message to one of the villagers, primarily the alcalde, who still does not have a phone. Marta was very happy to provide that service and the villagers showed her their appreciation, frequently. She is missed." The silence is extended while the three women are trying to think of what to say, until, from the house comes, "Dessert! Who's ready?" Three hands quickly go up, and they are off again, on their way back to the darkening house.

The conversation in the car returning to Madrid wanders from the upcoming holiday season through to the weather and finally to the apparent virtues and vices of one James Tuck. No conclusions drawn among the three women, but thoughts and imaginations are swarming. The village was a delight.

"Margaret, I suspect it may be past time for you to address me as Jim." The phone call at the hospital was unexpected, and true to form, Margaret had acknowledged the caller formally.

"Alright, Jim it is. It's nice to hear your voice, actually. Are you in town?"

"No, but coming for a follow up visit today, and thought perhaps a late luncheon could be in order. Interested?"

"Of course. Same place, same time?"

"Done. See you there. I will probably arrive before you as my appointment is at 1:30, and I think you do not finish until 2p.m. Correct?"

"Correct. See you then."

Emily, Margaret and Marianne have, occasionally, exchanged notes and found that each had been contacted from time to time over the last couple of months, contacted by Jim Tuck that is. The shared experience was that he was charming, solicitous and attentive. Other details were omitted.

At lunch, the conversation drifts toward future meetings, and Margaret offers the fact that she has purchased a small car so has independent transport now. It is early December and the offer of a weekend in the village is made, and accepted. The company is as good as the weather was difficult. The "central heating" of the house is on full blast, roasting the side facing the fireplace and freezing the other. The dash from the warm to the frigid bedroom is almost comical. "You have been living in this Winter experience how long?"

Jim is silent for a moment, "It is a bit difficult, isn't it. Yes. Anyway, we came in the Fall of '63. Bought it soon after arriving, so eleven years or so. Why?"

"Do you enjoy this? I mean, really now."

"Really, now? Actually, these bones are beginning to complain a bit. But, the village offers many amenities, and the place is paid for. All in all, it's worth it, to me."

"Understood. Just wondering I guess. My flat in Madrid is cool, for certain. But this is cold. For certain. Helps make my flat more attractive, even when cool. Ah! But that makes this place more attractive. Where did you learn to do that. Oh, Jim. Oh dear. Ummm."

December is a cold but busy month. The car park in front of the house is now home to a small Italian car that everyone recognizes. The trip from the house to the hospital is no more than forty-five minutes in slow traffic time, and Margaret has managed to change her duty hours to three night shifts a week, nine p.m. until nine a.m. By the time she is on her way back to the village the morning traffic has diminished, and there is little traffic at night. Things are settling in, when Margaret brings the coffee to the table on a Sunday morning and says, "I thought it a good idea to get a pregnancy test at the hospital Friday. The results came back yesterday. Merry Christmas."

Jim's cup is halfway to his mouth and stops in midair. Slowly, slowly it returns to the table, then he looks up, smiles, opens his arms and Margaret settles onto his lap.

The word gets out to the village immediately that there is to be a wedding in the cathedral, an important wedding. The buzz around the plaza is constant and there is a sense of expectation, even in the frigid January air. Several of the village women greet Margaret as she strolls to the market, smiling as they extend their congratulations, asking about the date. In Spanish, she tells each one, "The fifteenth, a Saturday, day after Valentine's Day." with a wink and a smile.

Tony Arizza is almost more excited in anticipation than Jim. Carmen, Tony's wife and Marta's best friend, not so much, but she keeps her own counsel. Tony is talking to Jim on the phone, "You bet. Best man it is. Always have been best."

"My ass. Utilitarian, but best? Ha!" Jim is nearly back to his old irascible self. "When you coming over?"

"I am in Madrid now. Came yesterday. Figured you would need someone to hold your hand for a while. Gotta head back to Bilbao for a few days, but back at the apartment here early February. Not to worry, I will be available for any crying on my shoulder needed."

"What an ass you are sometimes. But, useful, I'll admit. A useful ass. Now that's a picture I can hold onto. Say, do you have any connections with the bishop in Madrid?"

"Sure. Why?"

"It seems there is a slight glitch in plans. Margaret is a certified Catholic, but I'm not. Seems I need to get certified to be able to use the cathedral here in Valdeolmos, so I need to talk to the bishop. An introduction would probably help."

"Halfway around the world and 37 years later and I am still pulling you out of trouble?"

"Why not? It's a talent you have nearly perfected. Trouble shooter for the world, and me. How about it? Introduction, and maybe some ideas of what it will take to get me certified as Catholic?"

"I'll see what I can do. Gotta get it done soonish since I have to be back in Bilbao next week. I'll get back to you this afternoon. Stay near the phone. Don't wander off in some love sick reverie. Got it?" The smile on Tony's face penetrates the phone line and stares at Jim as he forcefully replaces the handset into the cradle.

"What's that all about? Something upsetting you?"

"Nah. Just Tony doing his imitation of an asshole." Jim's smile eases Margaret's nerves, at least a little.

"Can he help with contact with the bishop?"

"Probably. That boy has his fingers in all the local pies. Anyway, he says he'll look into it, and has to get it done now since he has to return to Bilbao next week."

"Next week! What about the wedding? He's best man!"

"It's OK. Listen for a minute. He knows about the best man thing. He has it under control. He'll be back first of February, or thereabouts. It's OK, alright?" Jim strokes Margaret's back, letting his hand drift down a bit, which gets a playful swat, then Margaret's shoulders relax some.

"I'll admit I am a bit tense."

"Yes, a bit."

"But, I want this to work well, I want the village women to accept me here. I want Carmen to be a bit more friendly. There just seems so much to get done, and Mother doesn't get here for another two weeks."

"It is going to be fine, Margaret. Believe me. I will admit that Marta cast a large shadow in Valdeolmos, but it will not erase you. Not at all. Time, my dear. Give it some time."

It is five in the evening, the sun going down, the cold sliding under the door when the phone rings. It is on the small table in the hallway, so Jim has to leave the living room and the roaring fire to answer it. The routine is automatic now, wrapping himself in the wool blanket and pulling the woolen beanie down over his ears, raising it back up off his right ear.

"Tuck."

"Arizza. Got your appointment. Got a pencil?"

"Don't need it. Shoot."

"OK. Day after tomorrow. Luncheon at the bishopric. You know it?"

"I'll find it. Time?"

"Eleven thirty, sharp. Don't fuck it up. Got any Chivas?"

"Chivas? What for, for crissake?"

"His eminence has a particular taste for it, apparently. Lubrication for the conversation, shall we say."

"Damned expensive lube, but it is what it is. Anything else?"

"Nope. I'll be there. Meet you in the parking area in back of the building. Camouflage the bottle. See you at 11:15, back of the bishopric day after tomorrow. Dress up, dude."

"Right. Who the hell you think you're talking to, anyway? Thanks." Click.

"Was that Tony?"

"Yeah. Day after tomorrow, lunch with the bishop. He says I need to bring Chivas Regal."

"What? A bribe?"

"No, lubrication for the conversation. Now listen. I suspect I know what's going to be required."

"Sure, you have to be baptized Catholic."

Jim's eyes go wide, brows up, the old half smile showing. "You knew this was going to happen?"

"Certainly. It is a constant anywhere for the church."

"Well, it's a goddam nuisance, and this is the closest thing to a state secret you've ever entertained. Yes? Understand? No breathing a word, to anyone."

"Sure, sure. But any Catholic will know what the requirements are."

"But there are many, particularly back in the States, who do not, and need not. It would ruin my good name. Particularly Hiss and company. Mum's the word, right?"

"Right." and Margaret is back on Jim's lap.

Suddenly it is February. With the local priest on board for the ceremony, Margaret's mother arrived from Australia, Arizza's back from Bilbao, local women occupying the kitchen as well as their kitchens, bunting up around the house, flowers in every room, Jim's turkey roasting in the oven, Mother's trifle overwhelming three large bowls, all is ready for the reception following the service in the cathedral. Margaret is all in white. Not a long flowing gown, but tasteful and with lots of lace and ribbons. Her jacket is fur trimmed and necessary given the weather, but goes well with the dress. Jim is in a dark suit, white shirt with string tie, black brimmed hat and his lined woolen cape. He is actually dashing in a fashion. There is one bride's maid, Emily from the hospital, and the best man, Tony Arizza. The entire entourage can walk to the cathedral, but Margaret is driven in an open carriage pulled by two white horses. Paco is the driver, and splendid in his scarlet, ancient outfit.

The service is mercifully short and the women from the kitchen leave before everyone else in order to set out the food. Margaret's mother speaks no Spanish, but appreciates the solicitous nature of the locals as they greet her, mother of the bride. When he can, Tony makes himself available to translate for her, as does Margaret occasionally. Back at the house, the cask of red wine is sitting on the large square rock to the right of the front door and Jim is holding court, cape, hat and walking stick in place. The turkey is on the table in the hallway, ready to be carved. Surrounding the turkey are local vegetables, potatoes, bowls of paella, and a crock of mutton stew, brought into the house with great fanfare from the home of the alcalde. A separate table holds the service for the meal, plates, cutlery, glasses, and the three bowls of trifle.

The glasses have mostly been distributed among the revelers who repeatedly visit the cask of wine by the front door. Each time they come by, they salute don Jaime, who returns the salute with the requisite sip, or gulp, from his glass. Jim is the only one with a whiskey tumbler for his wine, but by now no one notices. It is starting to get a bit rowdy. Margaret's mother suddenly emits a small screech that brings Margaret to the hallway from the bedroom where she has gotten changed. "What's that matter, Mum?"

Her mother is standing somewhat speechless and can only point to the table with her trifles. There, three of the villagers, each with one of the serving spoons, are dipping and eating, as if the bowls are individual servings just for them. Margaret calms her mother with a soothing hand on her shoulder, walks over and whispers to one of the women busily eating. The women responds with a slightly shocked look on her face, "Si? Verdad?"

"Si," is all Margaret needs to say, and the three villagers meekly return the serving spoons to the bowls, with serious dents in each of the trifles. Margaret is soothing their slightly wounded pride and returning the situation to normal when the husband of one of the women from the kitchen seizes the platter with the turkey still in its entirety, and holding it overhead, dances in the hallway toward the front door crying, "Pavo! Pavo! Pavo!" As he reaches the doorway, Paco, the carriage driver, steps up with Tony and suggests the reveler have a drink while they replace the turkey on the table. Margaret glances over to where her mother is standing, white as a sheet, with a small tremor appearing at the corners of her mouth.

"Mum, how about a lovely gin and tonic?"

Her mother looks at her wistfully, as if thirty years of Margaret's life go flashing by, and simply nods. The two women walk slowly into the kitchen, arm in arm, where Margaret makes a very generous G&T. Tony does the honors of carving the turkey, Jim rings the bell over the gateway to announce it is time to eat, and the crush of humanity fills the hallway, all smiles, slightly wobbly, and Margaret and her mum peeking from the kitchen door. Margaret slips her arm around her mother's waist, gives a squeeze and says, "I am very happy, mum. I'm glad you are here to share this with me."

Her mother's head leans onto Margaret's shoulder as she says, "I think I am happy to be here. My glass is empty." It is filled again, immediately, and the evening progresses at pace. The dinner is more than successful, Carmen almost appears happy a couple of times, Jim holds court all evening and almost everyone gets some of the dessert.

Success, even when Margaret's morning sickness gets in the way of eating much. No one notices, except her mother, who by now is privy to the news. It is a closely held piece of information as far as the rest of the village is concerned. Society has some restrictions and decorum, here, that have already evolved in the city. Both Margaret and Jim realize that the less that is known locally, the better. The villagers are certainly not stupid, but they also know how to maintain an impression of normality. Besides, no one wants to mess up the fun at the dinner. And they don't.

CHAPTER 9

Newspaper Man

While the last year has been a whirlwind of tragedy, recovery, discovery and new possibilities for Jim Tuck, the world has continued to turn whether he is attending or not. Geopolitics are his passion, and an enormous upheaval has occurred right in Jim's neighborhood, the Carnation Revolution in Portugal. "Franco must be pissing himself." Tony Arizza is his usual avuncular self, marvelously succinct.

"We can only hope. Word is he is on his last legs. This may send him over the edge."

"What are you reading about the current situation? It seems that there is still a great deal of unrest, particularly in the military. It's been nearly a year and they can't get the thing settled down."

Jim leans back, takes a sip from his tumbler, and "There is quite a bit of demand for radical reform that has built up over the last fifty years. That's longer than Spain's wandering in the autocratic wilderness. It'll probably take several years to settle. Have you seen any English language coverage of it?"

"My ass. Not a word locally and the New York Times doesn't seem to think it exists, at least the paper I get at the Hilton. Everything that is coming out of Portugal is in the Spanish papers, and you know that's censored. I'll bet you fifty bucks that you can't find half a dozen in the Hilton crowd who have a clue."

Jim responds, "No bet, mate. I'll admit, I wasn't paying much attention myself last year." Tony just nods agreement. "But, I think there may be economic difficulties that the local expats, who have invested in Portugal, have no inkling about. I mean, the retornados, the Portuguese expats coming back from the colonies are overwhelming the employment market, driving down wages, using up the savings that downgrading the wars were supposed to give the government. It's a mess over there, and not a word in the local rag."

"Well, what the hell ya goin' to do about it?"

"Me?"

"Yeah, you! You're the newspaper man. Mr. Zamboanga Times."

The moment is quiet as Jim swirls the remaining ice cube in his glass. His kitchen table holds one empty bottle, which he returns to the counter and retrieves the second. "That's interesting, actually. Been busy for a while. My head has not been aimed at the usual target for over a year. Hmm. Portugal in April. What are the chances?"

"Nature abhors a vacuum, my friend. So does the news cycle. I suggest it's time to climb back in the saddle. History is calling, louder than food criticism at the moment."

"You're damned right, as usual. I think I'll make a call to New York."

Tony is curious, "Anyone in particular?"

"My letter writing has kept me in contact with several over there. How about you? You know anyone influential, especially at the NewYork Times?"

"A couple. They were in and out with filming crews a couple years ago. Carmen and I are here until Sunday. I'll call from the Hilton. Our apartment phone is crap, worse than your antique. How about we talk tomorrow, you tell me yours and I'll tell you mine."

"Two, in the lounge. You good to drive back?"

"Absolutely. Ever seen me not?"

"Yes, that's why I asked." That accompanies a firm whack on Tony's back and he is gone out the front door.

At precisely two, next day, Jim saunters into the lounge at the Hilton where Tony waves him to the seat next to him. Jim is carrying a copy of the local English language weekly, which he casually plops on the table, headline up. "Well there's the extent of the coverage of the Portuguese revolution for English language folks here in Madrid. Hopeless. You have any luck calling New York? I just talked to Hiss who was the most helpful. It seems even he is having difficulty getting anyone to care much. Vietnam is sucking all the air out of the news cycle. But, he has found someone who may have the influence to send a body there, no pay, but expenses covered."

Tony casts a wary eye at Jim and asks, "You interested in working for free? Since when?"

"Since I have not been this close to history since China. Expenses covered, I can wander around with press credentials. This sounds like fun."

Tony takes another short sip of his beer, then looks at Jim, "Well, fun it is then. You can have Hiss contact my guy, here's his name and number, and maybe they can get something organized soonest."

The expenses turn out to be for gas for Jim's Volvo, hotel for two weeks and starvation diet food expense. Jim loves it. The two weeks turn out to be two of Jim's best. He alerts Tony as to when articles may appear in the Times so Tony can save the relevant paper from the Hilton newsstand. Many a glass of red wine is consumed with Jim relating the backstory to the fairly brief articles that appear. Margaret enjoys the story time nearly as much as Tony, but hers comes with juice.

CHAPTER 10

Family Man

That summer is a hot one, and Margaret's schedule at the hospital, Monday, Wednesday, Friday nights reduces the misery at work, but not at home as she expands into motherhood. She now negotiates much of Valdeolmos as the mistress of the house, the Granja la Maja, and her obvious pregnancy simply cements her position. There's nothing like expecting a baby for endearing you to a very traditional village. Gifts, usually in the form of food, appear weekly on the doorstep, and Margaret even enjoys some of the conversations with the local women, invariably about family, babies and motherhood. Spanish is becoming much easier.

It is Wednesday night and Margaret sees Marian obviously in a rush to make it to the maternity ward. "Got one cooking with gas," is her comment with a wave.

"Talk after?" Margaret hasn't selected anyone to assist with the birth yet, and likes Marian. The hope is that they can work together on this birthing project. A thumbs up is returned by Marian just before rounding the corner and out of sight. Margaret returns to her paperwork.

"So, how are you feeling?" Marian looks fresh as if it is the middle of the afternoon, not the middle of the night.

"Feeling pretty well, actually, now that I am not so sick. How did it go in there?"

"Great. Everything was really good. I still wish fathers were allowed in during the birth, but she did well with us. The assistants were cheering her on, in Spanish. She's a trooper, for sure. Transition to hard labor was fairly quick and she wasn't pushing more than forty-five minutes. Just like a champ, and it was her first."

"I have to admit, I am a bit nervous about this birthing process. This is my first," as she pats her rounding abdomen, "and having taken the extra midwifery courses does not seem to be lessening my anxiety. I don't have anyone to assist yet, and was wondering what you're doing in September."

"Fine in September. Only have six scheduled for that month. You realize that this amazing thing you are doing is not about reading it in a book. It is all about doing it, relaxing into it. There is nothing you have to teach your body about this event. It knows exactly what to do, even the first time. Are you anxious because you don't really know how you can take it? Whether you can?"

"Hmm. I suppose that is exactly it. So, you can be my midwife? I would really like it if you could.?

"You bet. We'll make a schedule, get started Friday. You're on Friday, correct?"

"Correct. So, how about I come in at eight and see you here, before my shift?"

"Just what I was thinking. I am pretty certain I will not have a conflict that evening. So, first, that anxiety is absolutely normal; second, you might carry some anxiety with you right into the birth, but we'll try to avoid that if we can. Third, once the real event gets started, you will be so focused on your inner self that there will be no room for anxiety. However, the more confident we can get you ahead of time, the easier it gets during the birth. It's sort of, you get what you anticipate, at least a bit. Those good ole hormones flow a lot better from a confident brain. That's just a fact, so we'll work on it. I was wondering how Jim is about your pregnancy."

"He is actually excited about it. He has an older daughter, who is almost my age actually, but lives in London. He enjoyed her quite a bit I know. Misses her. He is a writer, a publicist, a bit of a renaissance man, but not sure what sort of support he can be through the process. I am sure, though, that he is looking forward to being a father again."

"That's helpful. OK, I'll see you here, at the nurses' station, eight p.m. Friday, and we'll get started. Have you completed the birthing sheet for the hospital yet?"

"Whew! Somehow I completely forgot that one. Do you have one readily available?"

"In my bag. Hold on a minute and I'll bring it on my way out."

Thus begins that holy relationship between midwife and potential mother, the relationship that has repeated itself over hundreds or thousands of years. Margaret's shoulders visibly relax, and she takes up the birthing form, her pen, and enters the biographical data about herself and Jim at the top, address, contact details, birthdates, nationality, and away she goes.

September is thankfully cooling off a bit. Margaret is working right through the first week, big as a barn, and Jim has asked a couple of times if she thinks she should stop soon. "Look, I am perfectly capable of managing these slow nights at the hospital. There is hardly anything going on at night, less the last few weeks. I have to get up and move around to make sure my circulation is still going. The baby is moving quite a bit. No problem there. Everything is just fine. Women have been having babies and working for a long time, OK?"

"Alright, alright! Just asking, OK? Jees! You getting touchy?"

"Touchy! What do you mean touchy?"

"Margaret, my love. Let's step back a bit, shall we? You are feeling fine, correct?"

"Fat, bloated, but fine, yes."

"Alright, we'll leave it at that. It must be getting a bit difficult getting behind the steering wheel. How about I drive you into the hospital and come and pick you up?"

"Absolutely unnecessary expenditure of petrol. Sure, it is a bit tight there, behind the wheel, but not too bad. I can do it. How about this? I'll finish Friday next week, OK? One more week then I will begin my confinement."

"Confinement? You are going into confinement?"

"Well, that's what delicate flowers do before birthing their babies, right?"

"Listen! I take it all back. You can work right through the delivery if that's what you want. Is it? That what you want?"

"Silly boy. Of course not. No, I will tell them I will work through the twelfth, then we'll concentrate on getting ready for the baby. How's that?"

"Fine. Good plan. The twelfth is Friday a week, right?"

Smiling now, sliding her arm through Jim's, Margaret slides closely in beside Jim, murmurs slightly, almost the sound of cat purring, and that is that. The twelfth arrives much sooner than either could have imagined and Margaret's send off from the hospital is warm and supportive. Arriving home, she uses three trips to the car to move all the gifts into the house.

The next week is busy with finishing the baby's room, which is essentially the living room so the fire can be used to warm the baby at night. The bedroom is across the hall, immediately available if and when needed. In the midst of making the baby bed, Margaret suddenly sits down and calls, "Jim! Whoa, Jim!"

He comes up the hall at half trot and looks into the room. "Yes. Something?"

"Definitely something. Can you call Marian?"

"Really? It is now?"

"Not sure, but I need to talk to her. Something is going on and she'll want to know, I want to know."

"Alright, alright. Right away. OK, OK." And Jim is bantering away as he heads to the telephone stand in the hallway.

"Marian, hello. This is Jim Tuck, Margaret's husband. Yes, I am sure you realize I would be her husband. Anyway, she needs to speak to you. Hold on, here she comes"

"Hi. Oh, I have been pretty good. I was just making the baby's bed and got quite a contraction. Had to sit down actually. Breathing gently helped, but still, it sort of interrupted conversation." Pause, "That strong, yes."

Margaret and Jim meet Marian at the maternity ward at the hospital at about seven p.m. as it is getting dark. Jim follows behind the two women carrying the overnight bag with Margaret's belongings. As they climb the stairs to the next floor, Margaret stops, grips the railing and bends forward, releasing a rather obnoxious noise. "Are you OK? What's wrong? What's the matter?"

Jim is jostling up and down the stair next to Margaret as Marian quietly slips her arm around Margaret's waist, looks at Jim and says, "This is OK, Jim. It's OK. Right Margaret, OK?" Margaret is quiet now, returns to erect and holding the railing, nods to Marian, then to Jim. "Then, let's get you to your ward, shall we?" Calmly, Marian boosts Margaret up the last three steps and they make their way to the ward. Just before the door into the room, Margaret holds a hand up, stops, bends forward and releases another call of the wild. Jim steps back, looks at the two women, and shakes his head.

"I take it that this is another OK event?"

"By all means. It also means you may have a baby this evening. Don't go far."

"Far. I'm not going anywhere. Where did you think I was going?"

"I presumed you had read the hospital rules already. You have a reputation for being a thorough man. This is an all women's ward. Only women and male physicians are allowed in. You can't come in past the doorway. So, wherever you go, don't go far."

By now, Margaret is again erect and Jim asks, "Did you know about this ridiculous rule? I suppose you did. You work here. Why didn't you tell me?" His angst is obvious.

Margaret lays a hand on his neck, nods her head, and says, "Of course I knew. It was second nature to me and I simply lost track of it with everything else going on. Be calm, Jim Tuck. Everything is OK. I'm getting tired standing here, Marian."

"Off we go then. I will come back and get the bag, Jim. Just leave it by the door. Off you go."

"Guess I will be at the cafe across the street from the hospital entrance. Cafeteria here closes at seven. Come get me if you need me, or sooner." With that he levels the firm Tuck gaze on Marian' face and then, for Margaret, a large smile. Margaret gives Jim's stubbly cheek a last stroke and the two women enter the ward toward the far end. Jim turns and walks back down the stairs.

"Say mate, what's the date today?" Jim is addressing the bartender, just after ordering a tumbler of red wine with ice.

"Eighteenth of September. Why?"

"May have a kid born today. That's all."

"So, we are wetting the baby's head, are we?" The British accent is not lost on Jim, and he relaxes onto the stool at the bar.

"Hope so. We'll see. Odd, I am nervous as a whore in church. Haven't felt this worked up in thirty years."

"Really. Yeah, I get a few expectant dads in here from time to time. If you don't mind my noticing, you seem a bit worn around the edges for having a kid."

"Worn is right. Second time around. First wife is gone, first kid is grown. It was nerve wracking the first time, but nothing like this."

"So, what was going on thirty years ago that got you riled up the first time?"

"Ah, just flying around in China for the nationalist Chinese. Was there almost a year."

"Really? Had a buddy whose dad flew for the Flying Tigers. That the bunch you are talking about?"

"Those are they. Interesting times mate. Interesting times." The bartender is obviously an expert at strategic deflection and Jim is at the bottom of his tumbler, getting a second, relating the time he landed without power in the middle of a firefight, at night. Now, there is no time, just stories, until Jim, into his third tumbler, spots a hospital orderly looking around the room. Jim waves his hand, slightly uncoordinated, the orderly comes and asks if he is senior Tuck. Jim nods and the orderly says that madame Marian says it is time to come, now. They turn to leave and suddenly Jim returns to the bar and leaves a generous tip with the cost of the wine. He is perfectly aware of the service provided by the amateur psychologist behind the bar.

At the top of the stairs, Jim stops and the orderly indicates a row of chairs just down the hall. One chair is occupied; Jim sits at the end furthest from the occupant, who is slumped leaning back on the wall, chin on chest. A snore indicates the fellow is not that worried.

Ten minutes, or less, later, a door opens shedding light into the gloomy hallway. Down the hall comes Marian, a bounce in her step, a grin on her face. "Well, Jim Tuck, you are the proud parent of a bouncing baby girl. Both mother and daughter are fine. They will be out in about twenty minutes, and we'll come right down here. Don't get excited when you see Margaret in a wheelchair. Standard hospital protocol since new mums can be a bit woozy at first. Lost a bit of blood, but nothing unusual. As I said, we'll be down here in less than half an hour." With that, she gives Jim's right cheek a bit of a pinch and is off, back into the birthing room."

The twenty minutes test Jim's patience to the limit, and he ends up standing and pacing to expend energy. His slumbering compatriot opens one eye, watches for a moment, and gives a slight nod and smile then another snore. With that snore the birthing room door opens and Margaret is pushed by Marian, down the short hallway, right up to Jim. She pulls the wrapping down from the baby's face to introduce a brunette haired bundle with eyes wide open and one hand on the breast she is suckling. Jim says nothing for several seconds, then, "Irene seems good, don't you think? It was one of your favorites, and she looks like an Irene I'd say."

"She looks exactly like an Irene. Yes." The tired smile from Margaret is returned by a completely sobered one from Jim, a stroke of her cheek, and a kiss on her lips."

"Irene Tuck, welcome to the world. How are you feeling?"

"Tired. I want to be at home, but I think overnight here would be good. What do you think?"

"I think, under the circumstances, you should call this shot. If overnight here is good, then I will be here first thing tomorrow. You think they will want to get you out before the next shift comes on, before nine?"

"Most likely. How about you get here in time to take us home at nine, and I will have the paperwork done, or Marian will, ahead of time so we can leave straight away."

"Nine it is. Have a good night. Love." Another kiss and away he goes, a slight skip in his stride, two steps at a time going downstairs.

Jim basks in the new father accolades, especially from the older men in the village who do not disguise much of their envy. He is excited to see Xochitl, visiting from London, bringing baby gifts and warm, if slightly distant regards to Margaret. While she is there, Tony arrives with a bottle of excellent red wine, a malbec from Argentina, that does not last long. Margaret is able to hold court welcoming villagers and exhibiting the baby for a short while, in the living room/ nursery, the fireplace going full blast, then she disappears into the bedroom and Jim continues on with Xochitl and Tony.

"So, Carmen couldn't make it? Where is she? She OK?"

"Poppa, you are not as dense as you act. Carmen was Momma's best friend. Margaret is great. Everyone can see that, but she is not Momma. I understand, and I think you do too. So, behave yourself. Only one bottle, Tony?"

"You kidding, young lady? I'll be right back. Just thought I would start with the good stuff while we can still taste it."

Jim is looking Xochitl up and down as Tony exits the kitchen. "You really think that's it, about Carmen?"

"Poppa! You remember at the wedding?"

"Sure, what about it?"

"The reception. I guess you were outdoors most of the time, with Paco and the locals, plus Tony. But, Carmen was inside here, and she and a few of the women from the city were off by themselves, just outside the kitchen door. They were all very polite, very, if you catch my meaning. Margaret had plenty of company, the village women, the colleagues from the hospital. But Marta's friends kept to themselves. It is hard for Carmen. What the hell! It's hard for me. I miss Momma, terribly sometimes, and so do they. They are not mean, just not over the loss. Didn't you notice any of that?"

"Actually, no, I did not. Feels sort of stupid, now, that it was so obvious and I missed it. Do you think Margaret noticed?"

"Of course she did. She's a nurse, Dad. Her job is to read people's body language. Of course she did. She's too proud to mention it, and very strong. You picked a winner, Poppa."

Jim's arm encircles Xochitl's waist and he kisses the top of her head. "What a woman you have become. Do you feel like you get on with her OK?"

"She's a bit straight laced for me. I suspect I stretch her coping abilities sometimes, but all in all, we are OK. We are just about the same age, you know."

"Now that you mention it, yeah, I guess you're right. Hadn't thought about it."

"Poppa! You are starting to worry me a bit." The mock surprise on Xochitl's face brings a gravely chuckle to Jim's chest, and a firmer squeeze from the encircling arm. "You ought to check in with her, don't you think? She's been going strong much of the day. Wine can wait a minute."

"Right you are, again. Tell Tony,…"

Tony Arizza has silently entered the conversation, "Tell Tony what?"

"To hold off opening the next bottle for a couple of minutes. I need to check on the new mother." With that, Jim claps Tony on the shoulder, gives a wave to Xochitl and is down the hall.

"What was that all about?"

"Poppa is just doing a little catch up work with Margaret. Did you realize Carmen was not that excited about the new wife, nor the new baby?"

"I had an idea or two. I expected she would snap out if it soon enough. Look, you're spending the night here, right?" Xochitl nods. "I have to get back to Madrid. We are heading back to Bilbao in the morning. I suspect Jim will be occupied for a bit, so give him these," handing three bottles to Xochitl, "and tell him I will call from Bilbao, maybe day after tomorrow. Bye, kid."

"Bye to you, old man. Ha!"

"Old man my ass."

"Yeah, it is getting to be dragging a bit. Bye."

Tony sets the bottles on the kitchen counter and is away. Xochitl opens the nearest one, retrieves a tumbler, and an ice cube from the freezer and pours a generous portion for herself. She sits at the kitchen table, twirling the tumbler between the palms of her hands.

Jim is up early and starts coffee in the kitchen. Xochitl comes in from the small bedroom across the hallway, hair tousled, flannel pajamas at least one size too large. "You're up at the crack of dawn. You and Margaret have a reasonable night? How are you handling this middle-aged parenthood thing?" The crooked smile says it all. Xochitl is somewhat enjoying Jim's obvious distress.

"Enjoying? Enjoying?! You are a diabolical child." The gravel that usually accompanies rhetorical flourishes has now been delivered by a dump truck. "Aargh! If I had a full hour's sleep last night it would have been astounding. Not a wink, young lady. Not a wink."

"How's Margaret?"

"Sound asleep, thank you very much. Dawn brought sleep inducement for that child. Dawn, mind you. Here, you make this coffee, and do not scrimp on the ingredients. I will be on the sunny stone out front." With that, Jim applies heavy footfalls onto the stone flooring and heads to the front of the house. Outside, he surveys the plaza, the early morning activity of the locals, Paco urging the belled sheep forward out of sight into the fields beyond, the relative quiet of the village awakening.

Sitting onto the sunny rock at the side of the door, he inhales deeply, the sounds and smells of the village filling his face, and then as he exhales, his shoulders lower, his face relaxes, and he rolls his first cigarette of the day. Before it is lit, Xochitl appears with two steaming cups and they share the sitting surface of the stone.

"Sounds like the first night was not so easy, yes?"

"Not so much, no. There must be a reason people are the most fertile in youth."

Turning to Xochitl he asks, "You considered having kids?"

"Considered, as in given it some thought?" Jim nods. "Certainly, and the outcome of my musings tells me that I am not the maternal sort. I am rarely in one place for very long, even married to David, it is not a relationship that deserves children. I don't deserve children. Nope. Not in the cards for me. Why, if you don't mind my asking, did you decide to do this again?"

"It is in my cards. I just forgot that the first card laid is a joker. Ugh! Anyway, I'll live through it. Margaret is a great mother. The baby has these amazing moments, maybe three so far, when she is obviously looking and concentrating to the maximum. The other twenty-three hours and thirty minutes are taken up sleeping, crying or on the breast. I suspect I enjoy conversational kids more than nascent ones. Don't get me wrong, I understand enough to realize this changes quickly. It's just that I'll enjoy her more when she's conversant. At least, that's the way it seems now. I look at the locals here, each family with more than two children, sometimes many more than two. Then I think to myself, exactly your question, 'What the hell am I getting myself into, here?' A nap, a meal, and we'll be on to the next chapter, I imagine. No disparaging. Nope. Just sleep deprivation. Ah, Hark! What sound beyond yonder window breaks? Here, take my cup back will ya? Duty calls." Xochitl smiles a straight smile, accepts the cup as Jim rises and enters the house, turning left into the bedroom.

"Can you take her for a minute? I need to go to the bathroom." Margaret leans forward projecting the wrapped bundle toward Jim who accepts it, raises Irene to face level and looks with an extended gaze. Margaret slides out of bed, wraps the bathrobe tightly around herself and quickly sidles out the door and down the hall, Jim still looking intently at a baby face staring back at him. In a moment, he sits on the bed and cradles the bundled baby in his arm making cooing sounds that could just as easily come from a quarry.

When Margaret reenters the room, she sets the squirt bottle on the bedside table and sits with a sigh. "You OK?"

She looks at Jim and says, "Given I birthed a baby yesterday, I'd say I am doing quite well. The nether regions are still stinging so the spray bottle helps reduce the sting. I am tired, just so you know. Other than that, fine." This last is accompanied with the slightest of smiles.

"Just asking. Hoping things are returning toward normal, that's all. Don't get your panties all tightened up."

"I am really tired, Jim. Maybe if you and Xochitl could watch her for a bit so I could get a nap, how about it?"

"Sure. Not a problem. Lie down there, get wrapped up, cozy. We'll be in the kitchen. Not to worry, got this covered." With that, he stands with the baby, leans over and gives Margaret a quick kiss on the cheek, and heads out the door, closing it behind him. In the kitchen he announces, "We have baby duty for a while."

"How long? This a regular thing, now?"

"Just until Margaret has nap. May be a regular thing. Why? It's your sister after all."

"Look, poppa. I don't know diddly about taking care of babies. Never been around them, don't have the inclination. As in none."

"I realize that. It's not at the top of my list either, or wasn't. It's where we are, now. Get used to it. You can start with holding her while I make another pot of coffee. You want some as well?" Handing Xochitl the bundle, she reaches, takes it at arm's length and walks with elbows fully extended to the other side of the kitchen table, and sits, arms still straight out.

"Sure, I'll take some, as long as you're offering."

"She's not radio active, for crissake. Bundle her up against you." Just then a wail starts from Irene. "See, she needs cuddling, not long distance affection."

"It's the affection part that seems to be the problem."

"Work on it young lady. You have done more difficult in your past. Much more difficult." Xochitl brings the baby in closer, still crying but quieting some. Then Irene is next to Xochitl's chest, resting in the double cradling arms, looking up and the crying stops. "Well done. Knew you had it in you."

"This is weird, poppa. Doesn't feel normal at all."

"Doesn't have to. Just do what needs doing, and the feeling can come later. Talk to her, OK?"

"What do I say? She doesn't understand anything."

"So, how do you expect her to understand anything later if you don't talk to her now? Marta and I talked to you all the time. I couldn't wait until you could talk back. Nearly got that wrong. Hard to get you to shut up sometimes. Anyway, you get the point, right? We're a family, right?"

"Right. And I need to get back to London. Planning to fly over on Friday. I talked to David and there is plenty on at the moment, so my presence has been requested."

"Friday it is. Until then, talk to your sister." The coffee comes to a boil and the filtering starts. Cream from the fridge and sugar on the table. Jim and Xochitl spend the next hour trading baby holding and coffee drinking across the table.

The next few weeks are full of occasional visits from Madrid friends, locals dropping by with food offerings, almost establishing one routine after another, each one changed within a day or two. The minority rule applied, a baby in the house demonstrated how the minority of one held precedence. Margaret developed a roster of nannies from the village, and soon enough they began spending time in the house, along with the weekly cleaners. By the time Margaret returned to work at the hospital, Irene had gotten used to each and the return was almost a relief; almost.

As Fall turned to Winter and the temperature dropped, the routines in the house began to revolve around the living room/nursery and the fireplace. Meals are now eaten there, an extra lamp is brought in for better light for reading, an improvised bottle warmer is set up next to the fireplace, they hardly leave the room. Jim and Margaret are sitting on the sofa facing the fire, Irene on the thick carpet in front of it, not too close, not too far away. Turning their heads toward one another they speak simultaneously, "You know, this cold is no fun - I don't think I want another Winter here - Wonder what Alicante is like now - How about selling this place?" They fall onto each other laughing, then sit straight.

"Do you really think selling this place is OK?"

Jim looks at Margaret and says, "These bones are complaining. Valdeolmos is nearly a suburb of Madrid now. It's not the dusty little nothing place it was ten or twelve years ago. I suspect this property would do well on the market, now. May be the best thing to do. What do you think?"

"It has been a lovely place to be, Jim, but it has ghosts, for me anyway. The villagers are fantastic, but I really don't like the cold here in the Winter, and summers are blistering hot. If you think it could sell for enough to get something nearer the coast, then I say we do it."

"I am off to Madrid tomorrow. I'll stop in at the Hilton. There's a great message board there, plus there are a few at the hotel who might be interested. Thursday tomorrow, so you're here, right?"

"Right. Wow. Pretty sudden, don't you think?"

"When it's time to go, it's time to go. No need to be messing around. Get it done." And, they're off.

CHAPTER 11

Shift to Warmer Places

November winds are perfect reminders for Thanksgiving in the US, but just cold in Valdeolmos. It's a Thursday, so Margaret is home, having been back to three days a week for two weeks already. Suddenly, Jim comes crashing through the front door, leaving it wide open, arms windmilling away, shouting at the top of his lungs, "He's dead! The son-of-a-bitch finally died. He's dead, dead, dead!"

There is a sudden wailing from the living room/nursery and Margaret thrusts her head through the door. The look on her face would turn most men to stone. "Stop your yelling!" she hisses. "Irene just went to sleep. Her nap is an hour late, my nap is an hour late. Hush!"

Jim stops in mid stride, quietly lowers his foot, slides up to Margaret and gives her the biggest kiss they have exchanged in ages. "Sorry, sorry." The smile is still ear to ear on his face and Margaret quietly leaves the living room and closes the door to keep the heat in.

As they move down the hallway toward the kitchen, Margaret looks up at Jim and asks, "Now, what in the world was all that caterwauling about? Oh, before that, go and shut the door, please. It's Winter, you know." Margaret continues toward the kitchen, listening for noises from the nursery while Jim returns and closes the front door.

"So, what was that noise? Hmm?"

Jim is standing, arms akimbo, legs spread to shoulder width, head erect and quietly, but forcefully exclaims, "Franco died this morning, at the hospital, in Madrid. The wicked witch is dead, dead, dead."

Margaret holds the boiling water jug in mid air, on its way to the coffee urn, then slowly begins pouring. "I had heard he wasn't well, and that he chose the BA Hospital. Certainly got the noses out of joint at the other ones. But, didn't hear how ill he was. Where did you hear this?"

"I was walking across the plaza and the alcalde came walking very quickly from the direction of the cantina, smiling as if he were the cat that just caught the canary. He told me. He received a call a few minutes earlier, from the hospital. Seems aspects of the old information circuits are still active. Anyway, the country is finally free of the asshole."

"What, practically, do you think this will do for the country? I mean, all his cronies are still in place. Won't they simply carry on?"

"They could, but they want to make a buck as much, or more as anyone else, and realize that keeping the country in the social-political dark ages holds back economic progress. First thing I expect will happen will be attempts at reconciliation with resistant parts of the country. That's us. The village still does not have a municipal water supply, the road, the last two miles into town, still is not paved, the plaza is not paved, locals have great difficulty making ends meet. Valdeolmos is a quaint throwback to bygone days, largely due to official policy. Why, you know, but let me restate it. They were republican during the civil war. Franco has a long memory, very long. Now, Franco's gone. No more curfews, removal of development restrictions, help for our plans to move to the coast. In addition, the son-of-a-bitch is just dead. Hallelujah!" That last was a near shout, and brought a near beaning with a large wooden spoon Margaret was holding. Hands in the air, Jim bows before the spoon, "Mea culpa, mea culpa." Margaret gently taps him on each shoulder, and Jim delivers another passionate kiss.

"Jim, you realize what next Thursday is, one week from today?"

"No, what? Wait, this is November, right? Thanksgiving? Really, already? Oh, wow! What a celebration!"

"How about we make a list, make it, at least, a partly-shared meal, make it middle of the day, Saturday the 29th. Next Thursday is the 27th. No one will be able to come on Thursday, so how about Saturday?"

"Yes to all. Saturday it is. It will provide a marvelous advertising opportunity as well, advertising for the house and property. I'll put together a single fold brochure and get it printed for distribution that Saturday. Hmm, wonder where I can get it done with a picture. I got it. Anyway, there will be a door prize almost everyone coming will be interested in."

"Door prize?"

"Remember what's under Dougie's bed? I'll go get it."

Jim returns in a few moments and is standing in the doorway with a rusted Falange symbol, the clustered band of arrows placed by the Franco forces, at the entrance to Valdeolmos, to remind them who won the civil war. Jim had confiscated it a few years ago, on one of his more adventurous evenings, with only Paco and one or two others in the village knowing where it was, who had taken it. The room stayed locked whenever the cleaning ladies were in the house, just in case, and the floor dusted only occasionally. Actually, Margaret had forgotten it was there. "You are going to use that as a door prize at Thanksgiving? This soon?"

"Perfect timing. Plus, it'll make the weekend memorable, and we can get rid of the thing. I don't think anyone here in the village wants it. I will give you good odds that the remaining one on the post by the road will be gone before next weekend. Yay, us!"

Tony takes Jim out the back door at the Thanksgiving celebration, after the roast pig has been demolished and the after dinner port is in all the glasses. "A friend from the Hilton crowd called me today, this morning. Seems he knew I was coming out here this afternoon. He has a proposition, from a small group that may be interested in the Granja la Maja. He wants me to act as go between. Why? No idea. Anyway, I said I would talk to you and get back to him."

"Talk about what? You know we are trying to sell the property. It could go in two lots, or all in one lot. The house can be had on its own and the property behind separated out. I cleared that with the alcalde already. So, what?"

"Don't get your knickers in a twist. Look, I think the fellow has a group together in order to make an offer."

"Does he have any idea what we paid for this place?"

"None. I have kept it quite confidential. The 12 years since you got it have had a lot of changes, and now with Franco gone, this area will develop rapidly. It's less than an hour drive to the Hilton. In today's world, that is standard commuting distance. No one in the village would understand that, but everyone in the Hilton crowd understands it. So, they see investment possibilities, and you need to change your orientation from selling a house to the prospect of a development property. Know what I mean?"

Jim is quiet for several seconds, then, "I've been here too long. I used to do this for a living, for crissake. Thanks for the lesson. So, you going to give me the name of this mysterious contact, or do I have to beat it out of you?"

"Neither. The fellow will call you, himself, tomorrow afternoon. I'll talk to him tonight, when I get back to the apartment. Carmen's waiting for me there. We'll get together with him and a couple of others at the bar in the Hilton. Most business in Madrid is conducted there. I'll let him know you'll accept a call. You thought about what you want for the place?"

"No, as a matter of fact. Let me get Margaret and we can group think this while you're still here. Hold on." Jim looks into the kitchen, doesn't see Margaret, starts to call for her, thinks better of it and goes through the kitchen into the house. Two minutes later he and Margaret are coming through the kitchen and out the back door. Both are much more bundled up than previously."

"Jim says you have some interesting news for us, about selling the house?"

"It's about selling your property, yes, but also about your mindset. Look, it is simple. Things will start to change very rapidly, now that Franco is gone. Valdeolmos will cease to be the sleepy, dusty native village, soon. There are already people I know who know about this place, for any number of reasons. A small group is interested in this property, largely for investment and development purposes. The village is about to become a bedroom suburb of Madrid. You and Jim want, or better yet, need warmer surroundings. It's a perfect fit, right timing, win-win, whatever you want to call it. But you have to have your heads screwed on straight so you don't get screwed."

Margaret is pondering Tony's little soliloquy, shifting her weight from one foot to the other, then asks, "So, if there is one group wanting this place for investment, there must be others, right?"

Tony and Jim look up, then at one another, then Jim smiles and looks at Margaret. "Yes, that's likely. Well done. How about that Tony? Do you have some special interest in this particular group?" With that, Jim's eyebrows go up, and so does Tony's back.

"What the fuck you sayin? You think I'm playin' you? What?"

Jim quickly raises both hands, leans back and quietly says, "Of course not. We're friends. Aren't we?" This is delivered very quietly, but forcefully.

Tony's back comes right back down, and he continues, "Yeah, yeah." His voice is now several decibels lower and he says, "Look, I took it wrong. OK? I got out of line. Margaret, you're a sharp cookie. No doubting that. Excellent point. Look, I'll let the fellow know to call your tomorrow, but hint that you have been talking to others. Actually, you remember Ben, the futures fellow?"

Now it is Jim's turn to raise the hackles on his neck, bow his back slightly. "What about him? Lost quite a tidy bundle to the guy. About broke Marta and me."

"I know, I know. But, this may be a way to get a return on that losing proposition. If the locals think he is interested it will immediately hike up the value of the property. Whaddaya think? Want me to slip him the information that this place may be on the market soon?"

Jim's shoulders return to horizontal as he says, "Fine. But if he wants to play, he'll have to bring cash."

"Fine. But to allow for Margaret's idea to play out, there needs to be another player in the mix, yes? Doesn't even have to be an active one, just one that others think is active. Right?"

Both Jim and Margaret nod, then Jim puts his arm over Tony's shoulders and he walks him through the kitchen and out the front. Nearly everyone has left and Margaret is conversing with some of the stragglers before rejoining Jim and Tony at Tony's car. She walks up and leans over to place a large kiss on his cheek. Tony looks up and smiles, "What's that for?"

"For being a friend, and perhaps helping us get to warmer surroundings with something left over. See ya later, Tony." Margaret gives a parting wave and heads back into the house.

"I'll be looking for a call tomorrow afternoon. Take care of yourself fella."

Tony slides into the driver's seat, closes the door and extends his hand toward Jim, who takes it. 'See ya later, bud. Thanks for the celebration. Hope this works out the best.?"

With that, he starts the engine, backs out into the plaza, turns and disappears into a cloud of dust as he leaves the village. Jim reenters the house, gets a full glass of red wine and begins herding people out of the house. Thanksgiving is over, the next chapter is about to begin.

"Tuck." It is at half gravel level, given the probable caller.

"Hello, Mr. Tuck. This is Alistair McDonald. I am calling from the Hilton in Madrid where I am staying at the moment. I believe Mr. Arizza may have alerted you to my call today."

"Tony said someone would be calling this afternoon, correct; although he neglected to mention your name."

"As requested, yes. You sound as if you may have origins in the United States. Am I correct?"

"You are, Mr. McDonald. I am a US citizen, but have lived elsewhere fairly consistently for quite some time. How, can I help?"

"Ah, I suspect the question is how we can help one another. I suggest we have a meeting, assuming the information about your interest in selling your property is genuine."

"It is genuine, and face to face is always the better medium, in my experience. I recommend the cantina, here in Valdeolmos, tomorrow at noon. It does not open until eleven, serves a reasonable paella, and the wine is acceptable. If our discussion seems fruitful, then we can walk across the plaza to the property and you can see the real thing for yourself."

"Noon seems fine by me. I will not need sustenance, however I will be accompanied by two other interested people, Mr. Alexander and Mr. O'Sullivan. Both are men of means and actively looking for investment possibilities. The three of us will see you at noon, tomorrow, at the cantina, then walk over to view the property."

"We will walk over to the property if our conversation has seemed acceptable to each of us, now four by my count, and if my daughter, who is four months old, is not likely to be disturbed by the commotion. I have learned over a reasonably brief period of time, to avoid unnecessarily antagonizing my young wife by irritating the child. Are those stipulations acceptable?"

"Of course, of course. All understood. Very clearly stated. Tomorrow then?"

"See you then. I will be at the cantina when you arrive. Good afternoon."

"Good afternoon, indeed." Click.

"Did you hear?

"Sure. I just was not aware of your trepidation where my feelings and reactions were concerned." Margaret can demonstrate nearly as ironic a smile as Jim.

It causes Jim's hand to come up and caress her cheek as he says, "I gotta use some control mechanisms to maintain some sort of advantage, don't I?" His smile is genuine, and they both chuckle. "What do you think needs doing to put the place in its best light?"

"I will tidy upstairs a bit, if you can bring some order to the garden." Her use of the term garden instead of yard reminds them both of her Australian origins.

"Right you are. Is Esmirelda here to watch the baby while we are busy?"

"She's been here for the past half hour. I'll head upstairs after telling her what the schedule is." And they are off and sorting.

Jim calls Tony that evening, in Bilbao. "So, Mr. McDonald and two colleagues are coming for a meeting tomorrow at noon, at the cantina. Whaddaya know for sure?"

"OK. So McDonald has gotten to you. The three are from Boston, seem to be fairly sharp pencils in the box, realize that Franco's departure represents opportunity, as of now their first investment priority is real estate. I happened to overhear some of their conversation the other day and butted in. McDonald wanted to make the first contact, likes his chances in negotiations, so I agreed to keep his identity confidential. Now, this is the juicy part. The conversation I overheard centered around developing rental residential property, so I am guessing they are not only interested in the house, but the entire package for a project. They have already received a plot of the house and land, so have the dimensions of the package."

"You have any ideas of price I should be talking?"

"No details, but given the nature of the market in Madrid at the moment, I think it is at least six figures."

"Madrid! This isn't Madrid. You know that."

"Look, buddy, you still are not thinking clearly, appreciating the situation. This time five years from now

Vaaldeolmos will be incorporated into metropolitan Madrid. Believe me. You are not selling a single family dwelling in a dusty village to someone who wants to get away from it all. THINK!"

Jim pulls the handset away from the side of his head so Tony's shouting doesn't injure his ear. "OK. Look, they are coming at noon tomorrow. When can you get here?"

"Me. What do you want with me? You're the marketing expert. You talked your way into free meals at the best restaurants in Madrid. What do you want me for?"

"You're my good luck charm."

"I can get an early start, say six a.m. and be at your place by eleven latest. You better have your best version of coffee ready."

"My pleasure. Eleven in the morning it is. Do some price research before you come, OK?"

"This is going to cost you, bud."

"Five percent of the gross, how about that, covers the referral and research help."

"I may get there a bit earlier. Manyana, bud." Click.

"OK. Tony's coming in the morning. He'll be here about an hour before the meeting, hopefully with some pricing research for similar properties. Who do we know who might have information for us?"

"Let's think about the guest lists from the wedding, and Thanksgiving. There must be a few who can help or have good advice." Margaret and Jim develop a short list of people to call in the morning. It's getting a bit late this evening. Margaret promises to ask at the hospital in the morning, then again when she goes to work in the evening. There are several people who have just moved to Madrid from overseas who could have data on costs of rentals as well as purchasing property.

At ten forty-five, Tony bangs on the front door, with the smell of freshly brewed coffee coming clearly from inside. "Si, entre amigo!" The door might not even been there the voice was so clear.

"I am in. Coffee smells great." Tony is walking briskly down the stone floor of the hallway. At the door to the kitchen, he says, "Aren't you afraid of waking the baby, or something? I didn't expect all that bellowing in the house." He and Jim exchange a quite abrazo and Jim hands him a village crafted mug, coffee black.

"Family is out visiting this morning. Margaret and I did a little researching last night and earlier this morning. What do you have?"

"You first. I want to see what you found." Tony sits at the table in the hallway, cup in hand. Jim sits next to him and slides a small stack of papers toward Tony. Putting the mug down, Tony scans the first three sheets fairly quickly, then "That's it?"

"So far. What the hell did you expect. I am afraid McDonald will have the advantage here, if we don't have better data."

Smiling that prize winning smile that Jim still remembers from their first meeting in Manila, Tony reaches into an inside pocket in his jacket and extracts a folded sheaf of about ten or fifteen sheets. "What I got actually matches yours quite a bit. I just found more of it. Here are seven properties with land that sold, or are for sale, around Madrid, here are rentals in central Madrid, first mile out, five miles out, and rural." With that the majority of the sheaf of paper hits the table. "Now, for the coup de gras, here is the current rental cost to investment capital figures from a friend whose office is in Bilbao, but has extensive business in Madrid." The last sheet of paper hits the table, and Jim snatches it up.

"With our acre and a half, plus the house, I would guess that a decent sized apartment complex could be developed here. Lets say, just for argument, there would be twenty apartments constructed and two or three flats within this house. Twenty three flats, or apartments. The rentals, out here in the boonies, …" Tony's hand had come up and Jim jumped in, "I know, I know! I agree that Valdeolmos is destined to be a commuter community for the city. Hell, Margaret does it now, working at the hospital. I was using the boonies term loosely, with you and me. It won't come up at the meeting. OK, no idea what they are thinking about number of rentals, etc, etc, but we know it is a development project, not a residence. So, let's just put a few numbers into the equation, shall we? Twenty three units, rentals out here in the next year assumed to be, what?" They shuffle a few of the pages, find the figure. "Investment to rental conversion is…" Some more papers are shuffled, Jim's pencil is rapidly scratching on a blank piece of paper, and then he lets out a short whistle, looks at Tony, and the two of them smile.

"I said I thought six figures would do it. I just had no idea which six. This is pretty good, Jim."

"Pretty good. This repays the losses on the futures gamble that went bust, the rabbit ranch bust, likely gets us another place free and clear. How close to this do you think I can get it?"

"Knowing who the players are helps. Have you had any luck with background information from the States?"

"None. Something might show up today, but not in time for the noon meeting. Today will be exploratory. We'll keep it that way, that and a tour for them to see what they are buying. Margaret didn't want to be here, and we figured it would be better to have Irene elsewhere during the tour. They will obviously see the set up for the nursery, and that might be helpful. No idea about that one. It is what it is. This is good information, buddy. Thanks. You wanting to be at the cantina with me?"

"Nah. This is your show, and I don't want to spook them. They still don't know we are connected, and it's probably best we keep it that way. I will be back after I see them leave. You got this."

"Yeah, I suppose I do. Margaret and I also put together a list of other possibly interested parties, just in case. But these guys seem to be the best bet, for now. Fine. I'll see you here once they leave. What's the time?" Jim pulls out his pocket watch as Tony looks at his wrist. "If you don't want them knowing you're around, you better go. I'll head over to the cantina now. I like being ahead of schedule."

"Later, mate." Tony puts his cup into the sink, heads back down the hallway where Jim lets him out the front door. Waving to Tony as he pulls away, Jim notices a large black sedan entering the plaza from the other side, dust kicking up slightly behind the back tires. Tony has pulled down the side street alongside the house and exits the village on the side of the plaza opposite where the sedan was slowly making its way forward.

Closing the door behind him, Jim walks briskly to the cantina as the sedan passes out of sight behind the building on the side of the plaza. Jim ducks into the gloom, smiles at the woman at the bar and nods toward the door letting her know their guests are arriving. She brings a tray with four glasses and places them around the table. Jim lets her know he will order whenever he knows what the others want. Nodding, she returns to the bar, and the doorway darkens as the first of the three well dressed visitors enter. Jim rises, welcomes the group to the village, McDonald makes the introductions and Jim calls the owner over to deliver the drink orders. Two coca colas and two red wines. The obvious disappointment Jim can see on her face is missed by the others who are taking in the quaint ambience of the cantina.

"Welcome to Valdeolmos, gentlemen. I hope your drive was pleasant. You passed through some historic countryside, both modern and ancient history abounds in the area. My wife is a nurse at the BA Hospital and makes the trip three times weekly, and usually finds it pleasant."

O'Sullivan speaks up from behind his coke from the other side of the table, "It certainly passed more quickly than I imagined it would. The scenery seems a bit barren this time of the year."

"It is barren just now. Winter can be cold, for sure, but the last few centuries have been relatively kind to the locals. I suspect you'll find that the population of this area enjoys some of the greatest longevity in Spain, indeed in the Mediterranean. I did not realize it when my first wife and I moved here in '63. A bit of research and observation made that fact obvious. However, if you don't mind my saying so, it does not appear that any of you three are anticipating moving to Valdeolmos; not in the near future anyway." With that, Jim's classic raised eyebrow raising query is applied and he waits for a response.

McDonald takes the lead in responding with, "Astute observation, Mr. Tuck."

"Jim, if you please. I am more comfortable with Jim."

"That's fine, Jim it is. We have noted that for some time, Spain has been underutilized for investment, especially by investors from the USA. We also noted the passing of Franco." With that he glances around the room with a slightly wary expression on his face.

"This was, is and forever will be a Republican village. No one within the village, and certainly within earshot, mourns Franco's passing. I assure you that you can speak freely. You noted the falange symbol when entering the village?" Three heads nod in unison. "That was one of a pair, the other disappeared a few years ago, but both were erected punitively, by the government, as a reminder to all which side these locals supported in the past. The remaining symbol is scheduled for removal soon. Date uncertain, but things are changing, for sure. Go on."

"Thank you for the background. We are not naive as to the history of the area, but did not appreciate the symbolic meaning. At any rate, through some of our contacts, we discovered that your place had a bit of land with it, was of historic value, and perhaps was coming open onto the market. You seemed to confirm that, so we adjusted our schedule in Madrid to be able to examine the property ourselves as well as discuss possibilities with the owner, yourself."

"So, it sounds like we are on the same page so far. And you, Mr, O'Sullivan and Mr. Alexander, are of similar opinion?"

Two heads nod in unison. Alexander then asks, "Do you mind discussing your reasons for leaving the village now?"

"Not at all. My wife is quite a bit younger than I. We just had a child, little girl, in September. They are away visiting a friend in order for us to explore the property at our leisure. Anyway, Margaret feels being closer to the coast would offer a warmer climate, specifically in Winter, and I am in agreement. Also, I am not certain how much longer we will be resident in Spain, and Margaret is interested in advancing her nursing career and is exploring educational and employment opportunities outside Spain. We would not implement any of these options soon, so, in the interim, we are exploring warmer surroundings for the next couple of years, warmer in Winter to clarify. This seemed an auspicious time to test the waters, so to speak."

"We appreciate your candidness, Jim. Perhaps we have stumbled onto a possible win-win situation, for all of us. May I ask if you have outstanding obligations concerning the financing of your place here in Valdeolmos?"

"I do not."

"Perhaps it is time for us to explore the property?"

"Off we go then. I will come back later and reimburse the cantina."

"Oh, no, no, no. We insist." With that Alexander rises and heads to the counter and the owner. He places a fifty dollar bill on the counter, smiles and says, "Gracias." The aproned woman behind the bar reaches for the cash box to make change and Alexander raises his hand, "No, no, no. Aqui esta todo. Para ti. Gracias" With that he returns to the table where the other three are waiting. As they turn to leave, Jim glances at the woman behind the bar and winks, and her smile is larger than Jim has ever seen it.

The short walk to the house is punctuated with a running description of landmarks, first being the cathedral on the hill. Jim explains that Marta, his first wife, is buried there, allowing the information to sink in a bit. Yes, there is real sentimental attachment for him here in Valdeolmos, at the cathedral and within the house itself. Just as they reach the door to the house, Paco comes around the far corner, waves at Jim and sends a greeting. "The village shepherd, or at least the primary one. His name is Paco. We go back a few years, now." Smile, with a touch of sadness in the corners of his mouth.

Opening the doors, both sides, without a key required, offers another silent piece of affirmation about the nature of life in the village. "Come right in, gentlemen. We will go straight to the back, first." And he leads them to the back door, which he opens widely into the back yard. The tour goes through the yard, through the farm sheds, past the pool, along the wall back to the house and to the right past the well, through the kitchen door and into the kitchen. He demonstrates the fact that it is a fully functioning kitchen, including electricity, the hand made pottery plates, mugs and various kitchen bowls are on full display in their racks. As the guests are examining the wares, the phone rings in the hallway and Jim excuses himself. "How is it going?" asks Margaret. "Are you finished soon?"

'Going well, I'd say. We just started the tour of the house and are in the kitchen. Well done, by the way, displaying the plates on the rack at the wall. Nice touch. No idea when we are finished here, but not long."

"Thanks. Just impatient, I guess. Irene is napping at the moment, so we are in no hurry to leave here yet. I was just bursting, a bit, wondering. Good luck with the rest"

"Thanks my sweet. I will call there when we finish here. Bye."

Returning to the kitchen, Jim says, "Sorry for the interruption. My wife, Margaret's, curiosity got the better of her. Do you have any questions so far?"

"How secure are the utilities here? I see you have the basics, but sometimes in rural areas they can be interrupted."

"To date," knock, knock on the wooden countertop, "we have had no interruptions of service. Water service will not be interrupted since the source is an artesian system with its own natural pressure supply and the water is pure as you can get. It is certainly better water than is available in Madrid. Electricity and telephone I can not tell you are as secure as the water; however, to date neither has been interrupted due to weather or any other reason. I suspect the future will be even brighter as I understand that upgrading both the power grid and the telephone service is scheduled for within the next two years. That information is fairly reliable, but I am sure you understand it is not guaranteed."

As the conversation has been progressing, the foursome have left the kitchen, examined the small bedroom across the hall and walked past the telephone in the hall toward the living room on the left. "As you can see, there is a baby in the house. Her name is Irene and I think she is now almost three months old. Not yet talking, unfortunately, but soon, we hope." That brings a gravelly chuckle as a postscript, and the three tourists exchanging glances. "The fireplace provides plenty of warmth for the lounge, but the rest of the house needs help in the winter." The group makes its way past the bookshelves and sofas, climbing the stairs.

"Up here is my office area, and the remnants of my former wife's boutique clothing business. You'll note a few of her hand printed pieces still hanging along that far wall."

The three guests, make their way past the silkscreening table to the hanging pieces. McDonald says, "I have seen this material, or something similar. Yes, this black hand logo I have seen, in New York. My wife was excited by some dresses she found at Macy's, and they each had this logo. I think she actually brought one home."

Jim is quiet for several seconds. "My first wife, Marta, made the designs and created the garments, on her own. We have a friend who helped set up the printing process, and we had gone to New York for Christmas, visiting Macy's actually, when Marta was diagnosed with cancer.

She died less than two months later. I just haven't gotten rid of everything of hers quite yet."

The extended quiet is not even uncomfortable. No one knows what to say, then Jim straightens and says, shall we go back down?" The silent parade to the kitchen gradually returns the group to near its previous tempo and the four sit at the kitchen table to finish the discussion. "Do you have any questions from what you have seen?"

"This is incidental, I believe, but it seems the ground level in the garden area is above street level. Am I correct?"

"Mr. Mcdonald," Jim is interrupted fairly rapidly.

"Ian, if you please, Jim."

"Ian it is then. Your observation is astute. Yes, ground level in the garden, or back yard, is one and a half feet higher than ground level in the street. We suspect that is because it was used for many, many years as paddock area for farm animals, sheep and cows, perhaps horses as well, when this was the main house for the primary farm in the village. Also, you noted the swimming pool we installed. The dirt from that excavation added to the height a bit. You have a keen eye, it seems."

"Thank you, but it was rather obvious that it was much easier to see over the surrounding wall from inside the garden than it was when we arrived on the street. It was just a curiosity, that's all. No further questions from me. Gentlemen?" Two heads turn side to side in the negative. "So, I think we will bid you adieu. I will contact you prior to Friday next week. Good day."

The four stand simultaneously and Jim accompanies them to the front door. Standing in the door, Jim waves to the retreating car and then closes the door. It is no sooner closed than the phone rings. "Well, buddy. How did it go?"

"Tony. You been spying on me or what?"

"Or what, fella. I got eyes everywhere, you know that. Now, how was it?"

"Fine. Nothing too dramatic. I got, maybe, a bit too sentimental when I took them upstairs. I need to get rid of the last of Marta's stuff, no doubt about it."

"Maybe it allowed them to see a human being rather than just a vendor?"

"Or made me look weak. We'll see before Friday next week. McDonald is to contact me before Friday."

"On that note, some of my people report enquiries from an investigating firm in New York. Seems someone has been checking up on you, and by extension, Marta. Thought you oughta know. McDonald, Alexander and O'Sullivan are from Boston. At this point, they seem to be completely legitimate, but tough. I would expect some additional maneuvering prior to serious price negotiations. That's my take on it."

"Can you send me hard copy of what you have. Maybe leave it at the concierge at the Hilton. He collects material for me from time to time."

"Done. Best of luck, bud. Keep me posted, yes?"

"Yes." Click.

When Margaret and Irene return, Jim is subjected to the efficient extraction of a full history from a practiced nurse. The details, including the upstairs interactions are delivered in sufficient detail that the discussion is fairly brief. Jim also relates the phone call with Tony, and Margaret asks, "What was your estimation of their intentions and legitimacy?"

Jim leans back in the chair in the living room, in front of the active fireplace and thinks for a moment. "You think they may not be legit?"

"I have no idea. It would not surprise me to find that they are not, but I certainly hope they are honest and ethical."

"I think they are as honest and ethical as any investor I have dealt with in the past. I suspect they may play hardball, or try it anyway, but within the bounds of tough business exchanges. How's that?"

"Fine. I am just glad you are the one handling this. I trust you, Jim."

That brings an arm encircling Margaret's shoulders and a kiss on the top of her head, and a sudden screech from Irene who happens to be hungry. Business life is immediately exchanged for family life and the evening proceeds as normally as it ever has.

Jim retrieves the packet of information Tony left at the Hilton concierge and studies the backgrounds of the three investors. The information is scant, but leaves Jim with the same impression Tony had conveyed, tough but probably legitimate businessmen. Then Wednesday afternoon, the phone rings and Margaret answers, "Hello, Margaret Tuck here."

"Hello Mrs. Tuck. This is Ian McDonald. Perhaps your husband has mentioned me. We met last week to see your place. I regretted not having the opportunity of meeting you at the time."

"Yes, of course, your name is familiar, Mr. McDonald."

"Please, Jim and I have reached agreement on using first names. I hope you and I can do likewise."

"I prefer the slightly more formal, if you please Mr. McDonald. It is just my background as well as my work if you please. How can I help?"

"Yes, certainly, uh, Mrs. Tuck. Yes, certainly. Hmm, anyway, Mrs. Tuck, I promised to contact Jim, or Mr. Tuck if you will, before this Friday. Is he available?"

"I am sorry. He is out of the village until about five thirty. Are you calling from Madrid?"

"No, I am actually calling from my office in Boston."

"Well, it is three in the afternoon here, as you probably realized. My husband will return in about two and a half hours. Can you call again? It is just that making overseas telephone calls out of Valdeolmos is still difficult, otherwise I would offer for him to return your call."

"Certainly, Mrs. Tuck. I will call at, say, six p.m. your time? Would that be convenient?"

"Excellent. Pleasant speaking with you, Mr. Mcdonald."

"And you Mrs. Tuck. Good bye." Click.

Ring, ring, ring, "Tuck."

"Ah, Jim. Glad I was able to get you this time."

"Ian, that you?"

"Yes, of course. I presume your wife told you of my previous call."

"She did. I take it you have made some progress in your due diligence?"

"Quite a bit, actually. I have to tell you, we are especially interested in your place. It seems to tick a lot of our boxes, so to speak. We are prepared to make a generous offer."

"How nice. And what, in your estimation, is a generous offer for Granja la Maja?"

"For what?"

"That is the official title of the property. I thought you might have run across it in your due diligence efforts. Bit of a surprise you didn't realize it. Whatever, what was it you thought would be generous?"

"We, our small group that is, are prepared to pay cash, in the amount of $52,000.00, to whatever bank you nominate, subject to the appropriate exchange of ownership paperwork. I assume you have legal representation there?"

The silence on Jim's end of the conversion is extended. Finally, McDonald breaks into the space and clears his throat, "Are you there, Jim? Did we lose connection?"

"Mr. McDonald. Why, in god's name, have you been wasting my time?"

"Jim,…"

"Mr. Tuck to you. What the hell is this nonsense? You wasted my time, my wife's, an entire day lost touring your useless band around my home. Disgraceful. Good day, Mr. McDonald!"

"Wait, wait! Hear me out."

"Why? So you can waste more of my time?"

"I think you should hear me out. We did our due diligence, as I said, more in New York than in Valdeolmos as a matter of fact. We understand that the circumstances of your departure may have been extreme, a Mr. Sylvano's name came up, there seems to be some strange financial transactions related to air conditioners, perhaps the internal revenue service has interest in your whereabouts. We thought that, under the circumstances, a rapid sale, for cash, might be in your best interest. Were we mistaken, Jim?"

"McDonald, you're in Boston, are you not?"

"That seems irrelevant."

"Not to my friend, Tony Sylvano, and his organization. You see, Tony is actually a valued business partner in my past. His telephone is immediately available to me, as we speak. His gratitude for the profits from past successful business transactions with me, and his wife's affection for my first wife, Marta, is widely known around New York. The fact is that his cousin lives, and works, if I can use that term - works - in Boston. Among those fellows, family is very important. Our conversation has continued long enough, Mr. McDonald. I am hanging up now. Tony Sylvano is my next call, and from today onward, I recommend you watch your back, Mr. McDonald."

"Wait, Mr. Tuck. Wait, just a moment. I think, perhaps, we got off on the wrong foot, here. Just a minute, please."

"A minute is about thirty seconds more than you have. Speak."

"Alright, alright. I realize you seem upset."

"Upset, you slimy son of a whore! You call me and threaten me in order to steal a property for less than a third its value, and you expect accolades? I will, from the future proceeds of the sale of Granja la Maja, forward flowers to your widow. Have a wonderful day, asshole."

"Now, now, now. I can see you're upset."

"There's that word again. Bye."

"WAIT!"

"Ten seconds."

"I will call you back, within the hour, once I have conferred with my colleagues."

"You have exactly fifteen minutes from now." Click.

"Jim! What in the world was that all about? I have never heard you speak to anyone like that."

"Margaret. The idea that these fellows are tough negotiators just got expanded to new dimensions. Ian McDonald is a snake in a suit, tried to threaten me with my history in New York, the whole rapid exit, brought up Tony Sylvano's name as if to leverage me with threats from the mafia. The man has absolutely no idea who he is negotiating with. I'll sic Tony and his cousin Vinnie on him so fast that he'll pray for the simpler days of penury. IRS no longer gives a rat's ass about me or they would have flagged my passport and had me when Marta and I went to New York. No, the bastard touched several nerves. This place is worth at least three times his puny offer, he knows it, but made the greedy mistake of his life. Now it's ten minutes before I expect a return call from him. I think we'll do OK from this sale. Maybe better than OK."

Margaret visibly relaxes, then says, "But what if he doesn't call?"

"Then, more than likely we sell the place to someone else. The investment opportunity is obvious to more than just McDonald and company. And McDonald can spend the next year or two looking over his shoulder, maybe paying for bodyguards, maybe carrying a touch more worry than he has in the past."

"You are diabolical, Jim Tuck." Ring, ring, ring.. "Hello, tuck residence, Margaret speaking."

"Ah, Mrs. Tuck. cough, cough. So nice to hear your voice. I was just speaking to your husband, and I wonder if he is still available?"

"Why, hello Mr. McDonald." Margaret gives Jim a large thumbs up, smiles then says, "Why yes, he is here, just in the kitchen getting each of us a glass of local wine." Wave, wave, wave at Jim pointing to the kitchen. "Can you hold on for a minute?"

"Of course, I'll hold." clunk, Margaret indelicately places the receiver on the table as Jim quietly makes his way into the kitchen. Two minutes later he returns with two glasses, one a locally produced ceramic wine glass, the other a tumbler, both half full, the tumbler clinking a large ice cube. They clink their glasses together as Jim picks up the receiver.

"Tuck."

"Ah, Mr. Tuck, so good to speak with you again."

"Bullshit."

"Now, now. I believe our previous conversation ought to be placed into the dustbin of history. Here, let me see if I can correct any misperceptions you may have taken from that first conversation."

"Give it your best shot, but I suggest it should truly be your best, if you fully understand my meaning."

"Yes, yes, indeed. In any case, I was able to confer with both of my colleagues, and the figure I quoted you, you accurately deduced as a third of what might be reasonable, and my error was not pointing out that the figure mentioned was what each of us was willing to contribute, so indeed, the amount was about one third the total. In order to avoid any further hard feelings, and perhaps hasten the completion of our negotiations, we have concluded that an additional ten percent, each, might be helpful. How does that sound?"

"Call it an additional fifteen per cent and I think we may have a deal."

Cough, clearing of throat, and again, then, "Fifteen may be harsh."

"I suspect not nearly as harsh as Vinnie Sylvano."

"Yes, yes, I see your point."

"I bet you do."

"I think I can convince O'Sullivan and Alexander of fifteen per cent. I suspect so. Yes. In addition, we realize that you intend to relocate to warmer climes, and it just so happens that O'Sullivan has a cousin in London who is suddenly interested in selling the vacation home he has been building in Javea. Do you know Javea, on the coast, near Alicante?"

"Quite well. Tell O'Sullivan to call me tomorrow, this same time. I think we may, finally be on the right track, Mr. McDonald. I appreciate your promptness and alacrity. My lawyer will contact yours, who is…"

"Price, O'neil and Porterhouse, Boston."

"Fine. And I will speak to O'sullivan tomorrow." Click. No good bye, farewell, have a good day, nothing.

"Interesting. I think we may have just sold the place and found another in Javea. We'll know more tomorrow. Negotiate from a position of strength. Yes." Clink, the glasses bump in celebration."

While Jim has been conducting property negotiations, Margaret has been reading old nursing journals at the hospital, and some she brought home. The education, professional development bug has been at work and she begins a letter writing campaign to determine how she can become qualified at a higher level of nursing than the diploma level qualification she now holds. Their conversations have been full and frank, as is often described in diplomatic circles. But, to his credit, Jim recognizes Margaret's need for professional development despite the generational difference in their ages. His career is behind him, hers is starting. What to do? Whatever it is, they need to do it in warmer winter weather. Neither has much love for frigid temperatures in the house.

Following the O'Sullivan call the next day, Jim and Margaret bundle up Irene for the four hour drive to Javea, Xabia to the locals. The address is 60 Vaca, up a terraced hillside from the village center. The house is obviously under construction, no landscaping, one terrace wall collapsed, surrounded by similar properties with varying sizes of land and fruit of all sorts. Being winter, some of the trees and plants are difficult to identify, but the vineyard next to the house is obvious, and there does not seem to be an owner at home there. As they stroll around the property, a reasonably fit man with salt and pepper hair comes across a garden to say hello. After introductions he says, "I had heard that these folks may not be returning and the property up for sale. There is no sign, but that's not unusual. No traffic to speak of past here. If you don't mind, what is your interest?"

Margaret's shoulders rise in irritation, but Jim smiles and says, "We are currently in Valdeolmos. It's cold there, warm here. Thinking about changing. You? Are you visiting or permanent?"

"Me? Oh, permanent, I assure you. Not a snow bird, no indeed. My word, what an awful descriptor. No, retired two years ago, from Leeds. Won't go back on a bet, except perhaps for a visit. Agree whole heartedly with the warm versus cold preferences. Yes, indeed."

"Glad we got that one settled. Not certain of a timeline for us, but I am talking with people with interest in this property, and we have decided to sell in Valdeolmos, so I expect it won't be long. I see there are a few odds and ends of completion as well as repairs needed. Do you have local contacts who might be capable?"

"Indeed. The trickiest may be the terracing wall. I have seen some constructed and one repaired and I would not want to try it on my own. I did quite a bit of construction in Leeds but nothing compared with this. There is an older man, expert in the field it seems, who I know of. Perhaps I could be of assistance there."

"Splendid!" Jim has slipped ever so easily into the vernacular of the future neighbor. "Well, we have a bit more wandering to do. So pleasant to make your acquaintance. We will talk again, I am certain." A quick handshake and Jim leads them to the back of the house.

"I was more than a bit put off by that fellow. Seems rude to be butting into others business, don't you think?"

Jim smiles again and rests a hand on Margaret's arm as she holds Irene. "You are, as usual, correct. He was a nosy busybody, but also likely our neighbor of the future. Softly, softly, catchee monkey. I am liking this place, by the way. What do you think?"

"We haven't even seen the inside of the house, Jim. But, actually, I like it so far as well. Can we get in?"

"I was told it would be unlocked. Lets see if they were bullshitting us." Click, turn, the door swings open and there are now two smiles. The house is truly Spanish- Mediterranean with floor to ceiling tiling in the kitchen and bathroom, tile floors throughout including the three bedrooms, plenty of room in the kitchen and a large front door that gives direct access to the large front porch or deck. Standing there on the deck they can see that the most of what requires finishing is the landscaping. "And the pool will go right there." Jim is pointing to the front left of the front yard. Margaret smiles as Irene is wiggling to be put down on the sun warm deck.

"It may be a mistake to come on a warm sunny day, but this feels heavenly. I am almost sorry to go back to Valdeolmos." Margaret leans into Jim, Irene sitting at her feet.

"Agreed. I think this is for us, young lady. How about you?"

"It's hasty, but I agree. Lets go."

The closing of the house and bustling back into the car takes only a few minutes. The ride back takes four and a half hours, but it is time well spent in planning. Everything from finalizing the selling and purchasing to making the move to the first things to do in the new place is discussed, some in minute detail. Once the next morning comes, the telephone and typewriter are both humming. Banks in England see most of the transfer of funds regarding both Granja la Maja and the Javea property. The differential is significant so that even though Margaret will not be working and bringing regular income into the house, they will have funds to live on, for quite some time. The uproar agitates the four dogs, but Jim is able to satisfy some of their anxiety by daily long walks in the fields around the village. Margaret gives two months notice at the hospital with multiple departure events planned by staff, some spontaneous, some formal. Jim, ever the diplomat, spends considerable time with local friends and particularly the alcalde, with whom he has become close. Just about every other day, there is a small gathering at some time in the cantina. Often, Jim pays the bar tab for everyone, but many times, someone pays his.

Two months passes in a moment and the house has been packed up onto two medium sized trucks using all local labor. Abrazos and bessos abound as Jim and Margaret finally climb into the car, Irene in her makeshift car seat already. Backing up the car away from the house, in front of the waiting trucks, Jim turns toward the exit of the plaza, looks left and one final wave to the alcalde sitting on the stone at the right of the doorway. The wave is returned, and they are away.

Among the piles of boxes and containers being unpacked in Javea, Margaret recovers two thick packets of nursing journals and three textbooks, donations from the hospital. These are placed first on the bookshelves, before anything else has been sorted among the books. The bookshelf is next to a small desk holding the recently installed telephone and the typewriter. The office is now in the living room. The urge to sit and study is nearly overwhelming, but, first things first. Unpacking continues, the kitchen is put in order, a bed made up as is the crib, and the day is called with candles and wine, Jim's tumbler is full, Margaret's glass is ceremonially small. It's going to be good. The dogs agree, since they are now fed and arranged around the bed on the floor.

CHAPTER 12

Return to the States

Javea is exactly what they thought it might be. Warm, friendly, inexpensive and labor intensive early on. The division of labor is almost along traditional lines with Jim working outdoors and Margaret more involved in taking care of Irene, now an active toddler, working the garden and studying. The immediate neighbor seems to rarely be home, but the fact that there are vines heavy with grapes does not go unnoticed. Margaret wanders among the vines almost daily, selecting the best, ripest grapes of various varieties, bringing them home. Jim seems to have some creative recipes for grape dishes, mostly desserts, so he appreciates the largess.

One sunny morning, before the rush of activity had started, there is a knock on the door. Pushing three of the boxes still unattended out of the way, Margaret opens the door. "A very good morning to you. I am your neighbor, just there, and thought it best if I would take the opportunity to introduce myself."

Looking in the direction indicated, Margaret gets that sinking feeling everyone has when caught out. She is thinking, "Oh God, the grapes. He's going to be so upset. Oh no." Her smile is slightly crooked as she calls Jim from the bedroom.

"Hello sir, madame. My name is Allistair McClean, of Devonshire and occasionally Javea. How do you do?"

Jim glances at Margaret, who is studying Mr. McClean, then says, "We are doing quite well, actually, Mr. McClean. I am Jim Tuck and this is my wife Margaret, recently of Valdeolmos."

Margaret raises her hand for shaking hands and says, "Mr. McClean, how very nice of you to come over."

Shaking first Margaret's hand, then Jim's, McClean is saying, "Very nice to meet you both. As you may have noticed, I make it to Javea on a very sporadic basis, even though I enjoy it immensely. I have found, by the way, this neighborhood to be quite safe from theft, if that has worried you. It can, in areas of Spain, be problematic, but I have not found that here." Margaret's insides squirm a bit, Jim slightly shuffles his feet but his smile is fixed.

"Thank you for that assessment. We have just recently arrived and not had much interaction with the locals, some but not much. That is welcome news, is it not, Margaret?"

His nudge with the elbow springs Margaret's voice to action with, "Very, indeed, very welcome. Would you like a cup of tea or coffee, Mr. McClean?"

"Ah, thank you so much for your kind offer, but I am expected in the village I am afraid. I Just wanted a quick hello, in case I have to depart soon, and to make certain you know you are welcome to harvest from my vineyard as much as you desire. Coming as infrequently as I do, I am afraid the fruit often rots before I can attend to it, and I would be very happy if you would avail yourselves, perhaps make some wine even, but, in any case, feel free to harvest. I would actually appreciate it knowing someone was frequently roaming my property. Theft is rare, but not unknown, if you get my meaning."

Jim's hand comes back out as his arm encircles Margaret's waist, "We appreciate your generosity and will be sure to make good use of it while you are away. Very nice to have you as a neighbor."

The sun is rising, the coffee is on the small round table on the veranda at the front of the house, Margaret is bringing the baguettes and jam while Jim wrestles with Irene in his chair. It is not entirely quiet since the birds are chirping and the bees in the blossoms are humming, but those "noises" are music. There is no money coming in, but the house is paid for and the savings from the equity from Valdeolmos is keeping them going. It is slightly worrying, but only slightly, given that they have not been cold for a while. The dogs have settled in and the new dog food, local fish, is inexpensive. It only requires a hike down the hill to the village and the fish market. Both parents are happy, busy and Irene enjoys whatever Spanish speaking company comes along; it is her first language. The last home improvement project has started and is evident with the fresh dirt piled in the front yard; it's another pool.

The local expert Jim used to repair some of the terrace walls was excellent, if older than the surrounding hills. Still, the old Spanish gentleman nearly out worked Jim during his instruction sessions. Now, Jim has the primary role in laying out and creating the pool. His hard won expertise is noted by visitors. Off center to the left and squeezed into the minimal flat landscape available it will testify to the pool loving nature of the man creating it. Local labor is, as usual, inexpensive and the digging phase is nearly complete. This morning the coffee conversation is not about the pool appearing in front of the house, but of the results of Margaret's exploring the continuation of her nursing career. As usual, her letter writing campaign has been thorough, inclusive and only partially successful. The number of places that simply did not respond at all is astonishing, but on she plunges. "What criteria would you place high on a list of optional places for us to relocate?"

There is no hesitation in Jim's response, "It's gotta be warm."

"Hmm, guess that leaves out Robert Gordon U. in Aberdeen, eh?" The eh is delivered with a bit of a wicked grin.

"Didn't know it was in the running. Ugh!"

"Ha. Never was, really, but their program looked interesting, it is well thought of and English speaking. So, sent them a letter. It's important to be complete."

"Aargh! Not that important. Now, what reasonable places have you heard from?"

"Well, I finally received a reply from Augusta, Georgia in the US. It seems they are fairly clued-in to educational requirements and the needs of older students. What do you think about Augusta, GA?"

"Only thing I know about it is that they put on an annual extravaganza glorifying the rich and useless called the Masters golf tournament. Most misogynistic, racist public event in the country, other than NASCAR racing. But, it's warm, not too big. What do you think about the educational institution?"

"Well, they have been exclusively the ones answering all my questions and have put me in touch with the nursing board of Georgia. So, things seem to be moving along with them. I can't say the same for many of the others. I could do my education in Australia."

"That's too far from anything, anyone worth knowing. Warm is good, but distance is bad. Lets explore this Georgia thing. I have a friend in one of the towns in Georgia, Milledgeville. It was actually the first capital of the political entity called Georgia. There is a lot of history to explore there, for sure. So, are we settled on Georgia?"

"Not so fast. There are other options needing study, I think I need to see and speak to people in the highest priority options, to clear up remaining questions."

"You thinking of traveling over there, to the States? When?"

"Well, sooner is better. I want to go maybe September, after the new school year has started but before it gets cold there. What would you need to make it easier here, for you, while I am gone? And don't worry, I will plan to be back before Irene's birthday."

"That's good. As far as my needs, not much; full time nanny, cask of red wine, get Harold over here every other day for Irene's swimming lesson, another cask of wine." Margaret hears the acceptance and notes the half smile advertising her success. Her arms open wide as she sits on Jim's lap. The cuddle lasts quite a while.

Holding nearly-three-year-old Irene's hand at the airport, both Jim and Irene wave goodbye to the airplane as it taxis down the runway. The observation lounge has large windows at the Madrid airport, nearly floor to ceiling, providing an excellent view of activities on the runways. "Know what I'd like right now?" Jim is looking down at Irene as she is wiggling slightly in his grasp.

"What?"

"Ice cream. I think an ice cream cone would be good right now. How about you?"

The wiggling increases to the point that Jim has to lift her onto his hip and head down the stairs to the area with vendors. "Dos helados por favor."

"Si! Un para ti y un para su nieta?"

"Nieta? Mi hija!"

"Sorry, sorry. Two ice creams. No problem, no problem." Irene is looking up at Jim with a quizzical look on her face. She knows very well Jim is her dad, not her grandfather, so is not making much sense of the interaction.

"Not a difficulty, Bud. It's OK. He just made a little mistake, that's all. Maybe he got a bit confused with my white hair, eh?" Jim ruffles Irene's hair as he says it, leans down, and she ruffles his. There is no difference in the appearance of either head before or after the ruffling. Standing back erect, the vendor hands Jim two ice cream cones and Jim passes the correct change to him, turns, hands one to Irene and they walk away, hand in hand, other hands occupied, with no backward glance toward the errant vendor. Irene gives a half skip or jump, can't tell which, and they start down the stairs next to the escalator. Irene stops before stepping down.

"No aqui. Alli," pointing at the escalator. Spanish has been her first language since starting to talk.

"Si, hija, over there, for sure." She understands both languages, but speaks Spanish most often. They take the escalator down to the ground floor and the exit. Discovering Irene's preferences has never been a difficulty.

Down the escalator, out the door and home. It's a four and a half hour drive from Madrid airport to Javea, so after unlocking the back door, entering through the tiled kitchen, Jim retrieves the leftovers from the refrigerator and takes the food to the front veranda where the afternoon sun is behind the mountain, but still warm. Sitting at the table with plates for the two of them, they had just started eating when the phone begins ringing. "Damn." Jim leaves Irene at the table and answers the phone at the small table in the living room. "Yes!" in a not very pleasant voice.

"Jim, is that you?"

"Of course it is. Who's this?"

"It's Margaret, you big dummy. I just arrived at Alger's house. He collected me at the airport, now called JFK, and brought me here for the night. Why do you sound so grumpy? Where's Irene? What time is it there? Talk to me."

"Alright, alright. One at a time, will ya? Hold on. Irene, mom's on the phone. Come here." There is a scrape of a chair on the veranda, "She's on her way. Sorry about the grumpy. I thought it was an annoying interruption to our dinner. Here she is." Jim puts the hand set up to Irene's ear with the mouthpiece in place for her to talk.

"Irene, it's mommy. Como estas hija?"

"Bien, bien, momma. Donde estas?"

"I am in the United States, in New York City. That is where the plane went when it flew away. Our friend, Mr. Hiss took me from the airport to his house where I met his wife. I am fine. How are you?"

"Tengo ambre, momma. Quiero comer. Bye!" With that, she's off, back to the veranda and her food.

"That was quick."

"Well, we just sat down at the table when the phone rang and since we didn't stop on the way back, she has only had juice and some water since this morning. No wonder she's a tad hungry. No worries, though. Are you OK?"

"Certainly. A bit tired, but Alger and Priscilla are as nice as can be. They send their love. How are you?"

"Tired from the drive, hungry as well, but that can wait for a few minutes. Do you have cash to reimburse them for the calls?"

"Yes, plenty. Remember we got some in Madrid before I left. Anyway, they keep saying not a problem, but I will keep track and give them something. My day tomorrow is pretty full with meeting the nursing registration people in the morning and then getting bus tickets for Georgia and Florida. I sure wish you were here with me."

"You can handle it, I am sure."

"I don't doubt I can handle it. I just would like to have you two here as well. OK. Wanted to let you know I am here at the Hiss house, made it OK. How about I call again before I leave for Georgia?"

"Sure. We'll be around. Any idea when you'll call?"

"Let's say day after tomorrow, noon your time."

"Excellent. Ciao."

"I love you Jim."

"I know. Talk to you later." Click, and there is a full smile on Jim's face as he returns to the veranda.

"How about a quick swim before we go to bed?"

"Ice cream first?"

"Of course. Couldn't have said any better myself."

As Margaret advances her professional development in the US, Jim and Irene develop their routine in Spain.

Having a part time housekeeper helps Jim have the time to take the walks, often with the four dogs along, to get their food, fresh fish in the village down the hill, or explore the side of the small mountain at the back of the house. Today was the mountain. Jim's cigarette habit is starting to get in his way of keeping up with Irene on the hillside, but she calls the dogs along as she bounces up the embankment, Jim trudging behind. Finally, she hears, "Bud, wait." Looking back, she does not see Papa, but then he staggers around the bend of the path, sweating, and she smiles.

"Si? Esta bueno?"

"Momento, momento. Consado."

As Jim climbs next to Irene, she bounds up four or five more steps and hears a growl, "Wait!" With a frown, she nimbly comes back and sits beside a very sweaty and panting father.

"Are you sick, Papa?" She is now looking at Jim with a worried expression.

"No." Puff, puff, groan. "Just a momentito, pro favor."

"Si," and she pops up and rubs one of the dogs around the muzzle, then steps over the next one to begin picking flowers that are still blooming. A bee flies out of one and startles her.

"Careful, chica. They can hurt."

Now she has a fistful of flowers and Jim, still sweating, but no longer panting says, "OK, now we swim. La piscina, si?"

"Si!" And off she goes, helter skelter as a near-three-year-old can. End of this month is her birthday, but her physical abilities are well ahead of her years. By the time Jim arrives at the house, she has already gotten the flowers in a jar of water and on the kitchen table. The colors blend well with the tiles, making them almost disappear. Irene is sitting on the edge of the pool, at the shallow end, where the water is at the top of the pool rim. As usual, she has no need for clothes in the pool, and Jim strips right there ready to jump in.

"You did very well, waiting for me before getting into the pool. Well done. Momma would be proud of you. OK, uno, dos, TRES!" and they hit the water at the same time, sending it sloshing out and down the drain along the driveway. The waves simply rise up at the other end, which is at least nine inches above the water. Another unique Tuck pool at home. The cool water is glorious after the hill walk. Jim does the fatherly thing and flings Irene about in the water to her glorious screeching.

Porridge for Irene, with raisins, cinnamon and brown sugar, eggs and toast for Jim. The swim, and climb before breakfast have them both hungry. Finished, Jim pulls the stool over to the sink. He washes, hands the soapy item to Irene who dunks it into the rinse water and puts it in the dish drainer to drip dry. Dishes done, Jim lifts her off the stool and says, "How about we go find some fruit to pick next door. We will have fruit salad and yogurt for lunch, and maybe oatmeal cookies. Que dices? What do you say?"

A slight squeal, with a slight leap, and Irene is off for the woven basket used for collecting fruit. It is hanging behind the open kitchen door. Bag in one hand, her brown little hand in Jim's, they head through the living room and out the front door to the next door neighbor's. The orchard there is abundant, with even some banana plants, many citrus trees, of course the grape vines that are now nearly bare and half a dozen papaya. There are enough options that they can be selective, so the lesson today is how to select the best from all the possibles. It becomes a game with Irene on Jim's shoulders so she can reach the fruit on the trees, making a selection but looking at Jim to see if it is a good one. A shake of the head and she looks again, a nod and it gets picked. Within half an hour they have tangerines, grapefruit, oranges, one papaya, grapes and several guava. The basket is now too heavy for Irene so each holds one handle and they carry it back together, stepping over and around a lot of fruit that has already fallen onto the ground. No wonder they were offered the chance to come pick whenever they wanted. The neighbor is not due back until next week. Almost a shame to see all that fruit wasted, but the fruit salad today will be magnificent.

It is early afternoon and Jim examines the dog food bin in the refrigerator. "Hey, Bud. Wanna walk to town with me? We need more fish for the dogs."

"See Felipe?" The family friend in Javea is a favorite of Irene's. The fact she gets to rummage through his pockets for candy probably has something to do with that. "Si, Felipe and pescado. The fish market is near his house. Let's go." Irene puts her sandals and hat on, Jim gets his sunglasses and woven basket and away they go, Jim with his polished walking stick, Irene running as much as walking, the four dogs in the house. They always want to go, but keeping four dogs and one very active almost three year old out of trouble is a bit much for one adult; especially when the adult has people to see and talk with as well.

The descent into town is significant, but less than a mile, downhill most of the way. Jim greets several familiar faces along the way, Irene waves at everybody. "Do you know all those people, chica?"

"Know?"

"Conoce lo?"

"No."

"Why are you waving?"

"I like it. I am happy."

"Oh. Good idea." Jim starts waving at everyone as well, and the two of them wave their way all the way into the center of town, at the seashore and the fish market. Jim negotiates for the trash fish on the back counters, has several kilograms wrapped in newsprint and starts looking for Irene. "Damn. Where the hell has she gotten to? IRENE!, BUD! CHICA!"

"Ah, su hija? Ella esta alli." The woman at the next stall points out toward the waterline.

Jim shoulders the bag of fish and exits the doorway looking left and right. Off to the right, near a boat tied at the pier, there is Irene in full blown conversation with what appears to be a fisherman whose arms are waving in emphasis. They are going back and forth as Jim strolls up. "Buenas dias."

"Buenas dias, senor. Ella esta su hija?"

"Si, mia. Porque?"

"Porque creo ella esta muy inteligente."

"Hi, Bud. This nice fisherman seems to think you are pretty smart. What have you been talking about? Ciao," and Jim takes Irene's hand as he leads her away.

"Pescado, y perros, y frutas."

"Fish, dogs and fruit. That's very interesting. Was he a nice man?"

"Si, pero no tiene hay perros."

"That's OK. Some people don't have dogs. Maybe he is away too much to have dogs, if he has to go fishing a lot. It takes a long time to catch enough fish to make money." Irene is quiet for half a block, holding Jim's hand as they walk up the uneven cobbled street.

Suddenly a loud beep comes from behind them causing both to jump, and Jim leads her to the side of the street allowing a small truck to pass. Irene waves, but the driver does not wave back.

"Now, Felipe?"

"Si, ahora, a Felipe." Irene gives the classic Irene hop in response, maintaining her grip on the last two fingers of Jim's right hand. They are thick fingers, but also getting a bit tender and Jim winces a bit at the strain from Irene's grip while hopping. The wince is confined to his face and Irene doesn't notice, occasionally hopping along. There is more smiling than wincing evident on Jim's face, should anyone be looking.

The sunny street has little breeze so the temperature is up and they are both sweating by the time they reach Felipe's house on a cul de sac. Rounding the bend, Jim calls out for him and by the time they are at the door, it is open and both are invited through to the back, out the back door onto a veranda under an arbor and facing the sea. Felipe offers Jim tea, which he accepts, offers Irene a juice, which she also accepts, and invites her into his kitchen to help. Plenty of hopping from veranda to kitchen, and before the pot or cups or glasses are addressed, Felipe steps back so Irene can begin her examination of his various pockets. Luckily, he is wearing his work apron, for doing some woodwork, and it has four pockets immediately available, all empty except for a few nails. Bending down, he gives her access to his shirt pocket producing squeals of delight as she retrieves two wrapped hard candies. "Un para Papa, si?"

"Si," and she runs back out on the veranda to share with Jim.

"Mira. Papa. Dulces."

"I see, chica. You are a lucky girl, no?"

"Y, uno para ti."

"Gracias," and Jim holds out his hand for his share of the loot. Plopping one wrapped candy into his palm, Irene pivots and runs, hops back to the kitchen to "help". Jim looks at the candy, smiles and puts it into his shirt pocket. It'll come in handy later.

The tea party is a success and the pair depart with their burden of dog food fish, heading up the hill for home. Going up is significantly slower than down, with a few stops to rest Jim's shoulders and Irene's short legs. She is taking at least two steps for each of Jim's one, and climbing three times the height, for her body size, that he is, so her work uphill is tiring. Jim manages to keep track of her fatigue and strategically "requests" a couple of stops to rest. His natural inclination to get it over with as soon as possible is sidelined for the moment. Watching Irene's effort brings out a certain respect for her, and he is appreciating the opportunity Margaret's trip affords.

At home, the fish are unloaded into a large pot and set to boil. Another pot has rice cooking, to be mixed with the fish for the basic food supply for the dogs. Four sizeable dogs can consume quite a bit. Roaming around the kitchen, they indicate they realize what's cooking on the stove. After several bumps, trips, and stumbles, Jim loudly announces, "Out! Dogs out!" creating a mass exodus for the front of the house. Looking at Irene's wide eyes, Jim simply notes, "It's better to cook without dogs. They will eat soon enough." Irene solemnly nods assent, creating a wide grin from Jim. "Let's go swimming while the dog food cooks, how about it?"

"Si!" and Irene's clothes are off before she is through the living room. Out the front door, down two steps, then standing on the side of the pool while Jim, without clothes, catches up, the splash, into the shallow end. Jim cannon balls into the middle and the next half hour's activity is settled.

The next two weeks are full of walks to town, hill climbing in back of the house, fruit picking, planting flowers and fruit trees and almost every other day, a call from Margaret. The bond between father and daughter is sealed with nightly reading of books, mostly with lots of pictures, and mostly in Spanish. Irene is as bilingual as a kid can get, even with a slightly American accent to her pronunciation of Spanish.

Margaret's return flight is scheduled to arrive mid afternoon, so Jim arranges with friends for an overnight in an available apartment in Madrid, arranges for the housekeeper to feed the dogs, leaving her the house key. Irene knows that mommy is coming today, but has no patience for the four and one half hour ride to the airport, nor for the delay in the plane's arrival time, so by the time they spot Margaret coming through the international arrivals, both Jim and Irene are relieved at the change in attention. Frowns and growls turn to smiles and leaps and the first thing Irene says when Margaret is in ear shot is, "I am almost three."

"Yes! You are, my sweet. How are you?" The hug lasts long enough for Margaret to reach with an available hand to grip Jim's who is behind Irene. No way he was going to get between those two. The smiles don't stop as the reunited three make their way through the throng to the car park, stow the luggage and drive into the city.

The apartment is in the middle of the city, with its own off street parking below the building. The family, including Irene, have visited here a few times in the past, so the place is familiar and almost like home. By the time the travel materials have been deposited in the living room, Irene is announcing she is hungry. Looking at her watch, then asking, "So, what time is it now?" to correct her watch from US east coast time, Margaret then makes the change and says, "No wonder she is complaining. It's way past her usual dinner time. Let's go eat. I ate about two hours ago, on the plane, but the poor thing must be starving."

"As is this poor thing, " as Jim points to his belly and Irene gets the point.

Leaping up for Margaret's hand, "Comida! Comida!" loudly erupts from Irene.

"Si, hija. Ahora." Margaret scoops her up into her arms and they head out the door for the elevator. "We'll go eat now, for sure," and the three head down the elevator and out the door, around the corner to the cafe.

Dinner is nearly chaos with Jim and Margaret trying to exchange current information, Margaret more than Jim, and Irene constantly finding another important piece of information to give, or ask for, whenever the thought pops up, no matter who is saying what at the moment. In spite of the uncoordinated, disjointed flow of the conversations, it soon is apparent that there are very real possibilities for Margaret to advance her career, and they will most likely be fulfilled in Georgia. Irene receives confirmation that she will indeed be three years old in one and a half weeks, the half week being most difficult to explain. Margaret takes a napkin and draws a grid, putting numbers on a calendar, highlighting the date today, and circling the date of her birthday and they count the days. Giving her the napkin to examine more closely, Margaret says, "I will need to take one course related to psychiatric nursing, abnormal psychology, and there is one available at a small college in the city of Savannah. Once I take that, and pass the registration examination, I can work as a nurse. There seem to be a few places available that I will be writing to in Augusta. There are several hospitals in the city, the nursing school is there as well, and there is inexpensive housing not far outside of town. I think.."

"Mom. Mom. Mom."

"Yes, dear. What is it? I am trying to talk to Poppa."

"Can Felipe come to our house for my birthday?"

"Of course. No hay problema."

"Bueno." And Irene is back into her ice cream dessert.

"So, it looks like the state of Georgia may be it? I have never considered that as a place to settle. Augusta is the home of that bourgeois sporting event, the Masters golf tournament, isn't it? What a waste of agricultural space, and, from what I have learned, about as retrograde as you can get regarding the development of human society."

"True, the Masters is played there. I don't know anything about golf, don't care. That's not what attracts me there."

"But, it may be an indication of the ambience of the place, don't you think? Would you want Irene to grow up in that sort of environment?"

"She'll grow up in our environment. It won't offer you a lot of intellectual stimulation, I suspect, but it is not devoid of it either. Besides, you like to travel, so visiting from there is a possibility, maybe even back here to Spain, or the UK, or wherever. I think this can be a very good move, Jim, and, it is warm, nearly all year around. Very warm some months, for sure. And humid. From what I understand, July and August may be brutal, but tolerable. No severe cold, and the cool can be dealt with by central heating that is truly central. It's a good opportunity, Jim."

"I hear ya. Augusta, Georgia. I will never get Alger down there. Hmmm."

"Poppa, soy consado."

"OK, bud. We'll head back. Tomorrow, we'll go see Felipe, OK?"

"Si!" And Irene is out of her chair and half way to the door."

"Irene, wait!" Margaret is out of her chair and intercepts Irene just before she is out the door. Jim heads to the cash register to pay for dinner while Margaret and Irene open the door together, walk out and stand watching the traffic on the street in front. Ten minutes later they are back into the vacant apartment, Jim herds Irene into the bathroom to brush her teeth and Margaret is unpacking the travel bag for her night gown. The terminal stages of Tuck in Spain are now in full swing.

Jim is on the phone with the deputy director of the British American Hospital in Madrid, Margaret's former employer. "Yes, we are making plans to return to the States. I think it was Margaret who told the director of nursing last week. Is there something I can help you with? Just curious? Why the question?"

"No, it is not idle curiosity, Mr. Tuck. I have a colleague in Devonshire who is in the process of emigrating to Spain and he has asked me for advice or assistance in exploring the housing market. Perhaps I could be an intermediary should you plan to sell your place there in Javea. He expressed particular interest in property near the coast, which describes your situation, I believe."

"Indeed it does. Sorry if I was a bit testy. Things are more than a little hectic at the moment. Yes, of course you can consider yourself an intermediary. You have our telephone number. The address is 60 Vaca St, Javea, Alicante. My full name is James Tuck, my wife as you know, is Margaret, again Tuck, nee Wiley. We are, indeed, interested in liquidating our assets here in Spain. The property comes with a Volvo car that is serviceable but not pretty, and four dogs if wanted. If the dogs are not required, they can be rehoused. I have developed a small brochure featuring the property with relevant details and several pictures. I can mail one to you at the hospital if you like. Once again, I apologize if there was any offense to my initial outburst."

"Absolutely no apology required, but appreciated. I look forward to receiving your brochure. Goodbye Mr. Tuck."

"Bye. Margaret! We may have a lead for a sale of the property!"

The last bits of tidying the house and gardens complete, Jim and Margaret wait for the arrival of the hospital official who has agreed to an onsite review of the property for his friend in the UK. The week since making the appointment has been even more hectic than before, but Irene has cooperated with voluntarily accompanying the housekeeper for trips to the village, taking the dogs for walks up the hillside with Xochitl who arrived two days ago and spending nearly the entire remaining time in the swimming pool. Her dog paddling has nearly turned into a regulation swimming stroke in the past two weeks, now that she is a full three years old.

The sound of the automobile engine rises up the driveway, arriving just before the car turns into view. It is a modest white Mercedes, and pulls into the parking area behind the seriously off-white 1961 Volvo sedan. Exiting the car, the tall, distinguished man with salt and pepper hair and casual clothes closes the door and strides purposefully toward the veranda where Jim and Margaret are waiting. As he is passing the pool, a small voice sturdily calls out, "Hola!".

"Hola to you. Como estas?"

"Muy bien, y usted?"

"Muy bien, tambien. Gracias. Your daughter, I believe?"

Jim extends his hand saying, "And semi-official greeter. Jim Tuck, this is Margaret."

"Ah, yes, I recognize Margaret. Stanley Hawthorn, Mr. Tuck. Nice to see you again, Mrs. Tuck. And may I recommend a raise for your semi-official greeter? Well done." With that there are smiles all around as the three adults retreat indoors where tea and biscuits await.

"Me too, me too." Irene clammers out of the pools and races after the adults, assuming correctly that some of the biscuits might be for her. The wet trail dries quickly in the breeze, and Margaret assists Irene into dry clothes.

"I must say, the brochure does not do you place justice. This is quite lovely. How long have you been here?"

"A little over a year now. We managed several improvements since the place was somewhat unfinished when we bought it, but for the most part it was as you see it now. It is freehold, by the way, without incumbrances so to speak."

"Perhaps Irene would care to show me some of the rooms. What do you say, Irene?"

Irene is looking expectantly at Jim, then Margaret, then back at Jim with questioning eyebrows. "El quere mirar la casa. Te gustas? She understands more English than she speaks, but can still get tripped up with secondary conversation."

"Si."

"OK. Take Mr. Hawthorn and show him your room. My older daughter, Xochitl, will be back shortly, so you will have the chance of meeting the entire family. She is living in London now, but lived in Spain several years including her last year at high school. Go ahead, take Mr. Hawthorn to see your room."

"OK."

Hawthorn is about to get in his car, after handshakes and a hug for Irene as a small Fiat comes up the gravel drive and stops with a slight skid beside the Mercedes. "Sorry, I got tied up at the gallery in Alicante." Xochitl is calling from her open driver's side window, then she slams the door shut she strides over to Hawthorn. "Xochitl Tuck. Poppa said someone would be here today to see the place and I promised to participate. Missed it, I'm afraid. What did ya think." All this while vigorously pumping Hawthorn's hand.

Leaning slightly back, but smiling at the sight, Hawthorn replies, "I was, indeed, hoping I could meet you, Miss Tuck. In answer to your question, I am quite positively impressed by the property, the family and the opportunity for my friend in London. I understand you are now resident in London as well."

Xochitl, in her flowing blue, red and gold dress that brushes the ground, sleeveless with a belt, black Spanish hat with gold chin strap that almost contains her cluster of hair, large sunglasses and bare feet flashes her largest smile. "That's great. It is a peach isn't it. My Husband, David, David Green by the way, has been to the top of the mountain three times I believe. We adore this place, but time waits for no one, eh." With that she firmly drives her fist into his left shoulder causing the slightest of winces.

"Unh. Ah, where did you say you are living in London, by the way, Mrs. Green is it?"

"No. Xochitl Tuck is the name. Mrs. Xochitl Tuck. Tuck is good enough for my Mom and Poppa, I'll keep it thank you. Soho is our home. I am there when not here. David travels quite a bit. He's in India at the moment. It is his business that keeps him on the road. Management consultant, working for an international consulting firm. I'll be heading there once Poppa, Margaret and the lovely Irene are away. So nice to meet you." Her hand comes up again and Hawthorn instantly takes half a step back while accepting the handshake.

Jim has watched the conversation anticipating some of the interactions and is not disappointed. As critical to the sale as his relationship with Hawthorn is, having an activist daughter who takes no back seats from anyone is even more important. The door on the Mercedes shuts quietly and the engine starts. As the car reverses, Jim is beaming for several reasons as he waves an energetic goodbye. Hawthorn returns the wave then is gone down the hill of the driveway toward the paved road below. "Now for a lovely celebratory tumbler from our best cask. Xochitl!"

"Yes, Poppa?"

"Get three glasses out, an ice cube in my tumbler, and fill 'em for a toast. We're coming in."

"Righty ho." Jim chuckles at the obvious reference to their guest.

Once Hawthorn's glowing report is received in London, the negotiations and developing the particulars of financial transactions begin, most of which take place out of sight of the Spanish tax authorities. A joint bank account is opened in London for James and Margaret Tuck, a specified amount transferred from the buyer to that account at the same time a bank transfer to the Tucks at their bank in Madrid. There is a significant difference in the amounts, with the transfer of title mentioning only the Spanish bank funds. Final plans are made as the legal fees, taxes and disposition of chattels are settled. All the while, a sea freight crate is being prepared and decisions about what to take, what to leave behind, what to try to sell or donate are constantly being made. The well worn Volvo goes with the house for a nominal fee. Title and insurance are fiddled so it appears that no change has occurred. Foreign cars can not be sold in Spain, and the Volvo is definitely a foreign car, still with its French plates.

Xochitl is very helpful with both Irene and the many, many details that need attention. She even helps decide which precious artifacts get packed to go, and helps with the distribution of the four dogs. No single family seems interested in housing them all, but Flor and one of the boys do get to stick together, and the other two will go to good rural homes, good as far as Jim can tell. As the last dog is collected, he waves to no one when the car descends the driveway out of sight, then turns and marches deliberately into the kitchen. He grabs a half a roast chicken, left overs from two evenings ago, and a full bottle of wine, places them on a tray with half a round loaf of brown bread, a bread knife and retreats out the back door onto a small patio. Sitting at the table, he first takes a long draw from the wine bottle, no glass, straight from the bottle, before putting it down deliberately, cutting a slab of bread and then tearing off a chunk of cold chicken. Best comfort food in the world. Yes, he's going to miss those four dogs, but they just did not fit into their new chapter. Grovetown, Georgia, next to an Army base for god's sake, is their next stop. Jim Tuck, country squire, sounds good. Julio Matunkup in the Philippines pops into his mind, which he immediately shakes off. Sentimentality is for fools. Still, it sounds good. His local Georgia contact, of long standing, has some options that are well within their budget, even with a few months of no income anticipated. November in Spain, Christmas in England, January in Georgia. Things are really rolling along.

The bill of lading for their sea freight is to the freight office in Atlanta, for now. It will be updated later. The house is locked up and Hawthorn has the keys for his London contact, who has not seen the house himself, and whom Jim and Margaret will never meet in person. The final financial arrangements have been completed, as telex communications from banks have confirmed, and Xochitl is leaving for London day after tomorrow from Malaga while the family carries on to Lisbon, then to London. They spend part of the time in Lisbon acquiring winter clothes for their stay in the UK, even though it will only be the month of December. These last two years on the Spanish coast have removed much of their wintertime climatization.

London is a whirlwind, and the social whirl is well underway when the new clothes meet their test. Near blizzard conditions descend through the midlands and as they are driving back toward London, their small car, on loan from one of Xochitl's friends, becomes stuck in a drift on a remote country lane. No amount of rocking the car forward and back with shifting the gear box into second then reverse and back is effective in dislodging them from the three foot deep drift. One last lurch backward and Jim stops the engine, looks at Margaret, who is more than a little concerned, and then at Irene, who is obviously excited about the opportunity to get out into all that white stuff.

"Well, isn't this a fine mess we've gotten into. What do you think, Bud?" He raises his eyebrows when he looks at Irene, who is fairly jumping up and down in the back seat.

"Jim, how are we going to get out of this? It will be dark soon, it is absolutely freezing, and we're stuck."

"All an accurate recitation of the facts, my dear."

"Jim! I mean it! This is dangerous. What about Irene?"

"It seems she has this figured out already and is ready to go."

"Don't play! What are we to do? I don't like this at all."

"Not playing, my dear. Just making certain as much positive energy is applied to the situation as can be. How about you, Bud, you ready to go find a solution?"

"Si, vamos!"

"I agree, let's go. We are obviously not going anywhere in this car at the moment, no shovel in the trunk, I looked. That means we have to stick together, and think together, and we have to get out of the car to do a full assessment. Out we go." The doors of the car are difficult to get open while pushing against the snow drift encasing the sides, left side higher than the right, but they all three make it out of the car and slam the doors shut. Once out, they button all buttons up to their necks, scarves wrapped tightly around their necks and insulated hats in place.

Once bundled to Margaret's satisfaction, Irene starts walking down the track left by the tires on the left side of the car, just her head and shoulders showing above the top. "Not far, pumpkin. I want to be able to see where you are, got it?"

"Got it." And off she trundles three steps then launches herself into the drift along the side of the road and banked up against a stone fence. Suddenly, she stands back up, shaking her head causing snow to fly off left and right. "Ooo. That is too cold!"

"That's how snow is, sweety, it is very cold, like from the freezer at home." Margaret has arrived by her side and is busy brushing off Irene's face and head.

"Pushing Margaret's hand away, Irene replies, "Solamente, Mommy."

"I know you can do it yourself, sweetheart." Irene's hand gives Margaret's hands another push and she finishes brushing off her upper coat and hat.

Jim has been circling the car and then joins Margaret and Irene in the tire tracks. "It needs pulling out. There was a farmhouse half a mile back up the road. I recommend a family trudge to get some assistance. I suspect a family fronting up on a doorstep will be more likely to receive assistance than a lone adult. What do you say? Off we go."

"Yay!" Irene is now literally jumping up and down.

"Irene, best you don't get your feet too snowy. They will get wet and very cold. Those shoes are not made for hiking in snow." Margaret begins fussing over Irene's long pants, coat and hat attempting to make sure she is properly protected, and Irene's hands are rapidly interfering. "Irene, stop."

"No, solamente, Momma. OK. Myself." With that she deliberately stomps a foot into the snowdrift, filling her shoe.

"Irene, listen to your mother! We have to do some walking, now. Let's go." Jim leads the small band back up the road, staying in the tire tracks and out of the deep snow.

After about five minutes, there is a small wail, that gradually gets louder. "Poppa, soy frio. Mi pies son frios."

"True. Momma said don't step in the deep snow, I said don't step in the deep snow, and you stepped in the deep snow. Snow is cold, and makes feet wet. Yes?"

"Si, yes. I don't want this!"

"Of course not. Momma and I knew you would not want it. And now you know how we knew, because our feet got cold in the snow when we were little. Now, yours are cold. See that house there? That is where we are going. That is how far you need to walk. Off we go." There is a small farm house near the road with a barn behind, and there is a light in the front room of the house with smoke from the chimney. The three trudge on, the small wailing getting a bit louder as they go.

On the front porch, under a small roof, Jim firmly knocks on the door as Irene's complaint starts becoming seriously loud. Footsteps approach the door, and it opens to a gush of warm air escaping onto the porch. Irene is suddenly silent and a balding man in a thick cardigan sweater, thick woolen trousers and socks on his feet asks, "Hello, who's this then?"

Jim extends his hand and while shaking the man's hand says, "Jim Tuck, wife Margaret, daughter Irene, recently of the Spanish Mediterranean, here in lovely England for Christmas with friends and in a spot of bother."

"Ah, half mile down the road, you're into a drift, are you not?"

Jim releases the hand, steps a half step back and says, "Svengali is it? How did you know that?"

"Better come in a moment. I have to put on some proper boots and some winter duds. Come in, come in, all my heat is getting out." The family stomps their feet on the porch and step into the warm house. Blowing on bare hands, they move into the living room and Irene sits right down on the floor and pulls off her shoes and wet socks. Neither Jim nor Margaret notice as Irene is behind them, but the farmer sys, "Nelson Blaylock's the name, and it seems your daughter intends to stay a while, eh?"

Turning around, both Margaret and Jim gape at barefooted Irene, then Margaret immediately squats next to Irene and says, "Irene, we will have to go. You can't have bare feet. Jim!" And she is pleading for help looking back up to Jim.

"Yes, I bet those wet socks and shoes felt pretty bad didn't they Bud? Not a problem. Get those feet warm a minute while I talk to Mr. Blaylock here." Margaret is not amused, but starts wiping Irene's damp feet with a small towel Mr. Blaylock has handed down to her.

"I should put into council for traffic control and snow relief work. Every winter, that bend in the road produces at least half a dozen requests for help out of snow drifts. Ladies, you stay here, and Dad and I will get your car out of the drift. Warm those feet, Bud is it?"

Margaret corrects him, "Irene, actually. Bud is a pet name, I'm afraid. Irene."

"Aha! Irene it is. Come along, Jim, we'll have you out in a jiffy."

Jim and Nelson exit through the kitchen and trudge through snow half way up to their knees to the shed housing the farm tractor. Taking down a length of chain with hooks at each end, Nelson motions Jim to the step on the right as he climbs the left and deposits the chain behind the seat. The diesel engine rumbles then catches developing a chugging rhythmic sound and the tractor heads down the lane half a track over to the right to widen the drive space. At the car, Jim takes one end of the chain and hunts on his hands and knees for a place to secure it along the rear axle, suddenly noticing the welded loop on the rear chassis placed there for the exact purpose. Nelson has turned the tractor around and backed up near the back of the car just as Jim stands, brushing snow out of his face, hair and off the front of his coat. The other end of the chain is looped around the axle of the tractor, and Nelson says, "You get in the car and start her up. Once I have you back a bit, put it in reverse and come on out into the road." Jim waves confirmation, opens the driver's door and sits, closing the door and starts the engine. There is a slight jolt as the slack comes out of the chain, then the car simply is removed from the drift.

After they are in the middle of the road, Jim flashes his lights and they stop to remove the chain. Nelson says to follow him up the driveway as he again widens the diving area for the car, which is parked behind the house in a sheltered area. Margaret hears the stomping on the back porch and opens the door. "That was quick."

Jim smiles as he comes in. "It is much simpler with the right tools." Both express their gratitude as Irene chips in, "I'm hungry."

Laughing, Nelson says, "How about chicken and rice. Have some leftovers in the fridge I need to get rid of."

Margaret looks distinctly uncomfortable, then says, "Oh, I think you have done way more than enough already. We couldn't possibly impose."

"Yes we could. Chicken and rice sounds great. Thanks. Right, Bud?"

As Irene nods her head, Jim massages Margaret's shoulder with a whispered, "A gracious acceptance goes a long way sometimes," and gives Margaret a squeeze.

"Perhaps a little would do us all good, thank you so much, Nelson." Jim nods, and smiles, and Margaret sits at the kitchen table with Irene on her lap.

Warm, fed, unstuck, the family bids Nelson Blaylock goodbye with Irene waving from the back seat through the rear window as they travel down the driveway. On the road, Margaret looks at Jim and says, "I have always been fairly independent, you know."

"I know. I like it, actually, your determination and self reliance. Sometimes accepting help graciously gives the giver as much as the receiver gets. That's all I was saying, and Nelson seemed to enjoy feeding us, almost as much as getting the car out of the snow drift."

"Agreed. And, Irene was hungry, so…"

"So, indeed. I estimate about another two or three hours to 'home'."

"I think I will use some of the time for some more study. I have that registration examination in New York in two weeks, right after New Years. I still don't feel ready, but every little bit helps."

"Fine. There is still enough daylight to read, I suppose. Irene looks like it is nap time, anyway." Irene is on her side with her head on a stuffed giraffe, eyes slowly setting. The rest of the ride is gloriously uneventful.

The next week and a half is full of Christmas gatherings, a visit with the purchaser of the house in Javea, two dinners with Xochitl, one of which David is able to attend, and the time to leave for the States arrives. The small entourage of well wishers accompany the family right to the departure gate, the flight is called, hugs all around and the three trundle out the door to the awaiting bus that carries them to their plane, small bags and stuffed giraffe and all. As cumbersome as it all seems, suddenly they are in the air and on their way to New York, and the awaiting Alger Hiss.

Back on US soil, for good probably. Negotiating customs and immigration with a curious three year old is a challenge Jim has never had in the past. His amazement is the only thing holding off an eruption of his temper. When the customs agent insists on opening the giraffe, Margaret immediately interposes herself between Jim and the unsuspecting bureaucrat. She has not seen that level of redness in his face in the past, nor the pugilistic hunch of his shoulders as he is about to lunge at the agent and get the whole family embroiled in a losing hullabaloo. Irene looks at Jim and asks, "Que passa, Poppa?"

The sound of her voice, and Margaret firmly face to face against his chest have the desired effect. "No passa nada, chica. No hay problema." He leans to the side and strokes her cheek, only to hear the sudden wail she lets out as the belly seam of the giraffe is sliced open with a razor blade.

Margaret sweeps Irene up into her arms and Jim growls in her ear, "It's OK, bud, it's OK."

Margaret strokes Irene's hair as she wriggles and squirms and wails some more, reaching for her giraffe. "Momma will fix giraffe, don't worry. He will be fine. It's OK." And she gives the agent a glare he is not likely to forget.

"That was completely unnecessary, you realize. Completely."

"Ah, sir, the current war on drugs demands certain protocols be followed to stem the flood of deadly drugs into our country. Surely you understand that." With that, he hands the mutilated giraffe back to Jim and is about to wave the next victim up to his counter.

Jim takes the giraffe, pushes stuffing back into the belly, looks at the agent and replies, "Bullshit. You expecting a flood of drugs from the belly of a stuffed giraffe? Your mother have any children that lived? You are a model bureaucrat, which means a poor excuse for a human being. Officious while dumb." Margaret is gently but firmly shouldering Jim along the counter, trying to calm Irene and avoid a fight while closing luggage back up so they can get out of the customs area and to the awaiting Alger.

"Jim, please get this one closed, will you? It is too full for me after the examination by these lovely people." With that she shoots the agent another withering glance, holding a wriggling Irene, a partially destroyed giraffe and closing a small suitcase with her free hand. Jim nods, gets the suitcase closed, gathers the luggage onto a cart and they are away. Irene's feet finally hit the floor and she wants her giraffe.

Margaret says, "Mommy has to do a little fixing at Mr. Hiss's house this evening, then you can have giraffe back. He will be just fine. Right?"

Both Jim and Irene look at her, and both nod, and they are suddenly out of the international arrivals area and facing a waving Alger Hiss. He ushers them toward the taxi stand where they join the line for the next available taxi. "You three look a little tired, or stressed. Am I right?"

Margaret and Jim glance at one another, then both emit small smiles. Jim says, "A bit, but no more. So nice to see you, my friend. So nice. Oh, and if anyone is taking a poll, the US has the worst customs and immigration in the world. Just sayin'. We're fine. Ah, we're next." And they are back in the USA.

Four days in New York and not a leisure moment among them. Margaret preps and then takes the national nursing registry exam, but only after hours of review. Jim takes Irene to various haunts in Manhattan including the last apartment he left nearly sixteen years ago. The taxi slows as Jim explains that he lived there a long time ago, with Xochitl and Marta. Irene has heard many stories, mostly from Xochitl when she visited, about the mysterious Marta. Xochitl always referred to her as momma when talking to Irene, even though she addressed her as Marta when she was with her years ago. Irene understood the difference between Margaret, her momma, and the fact that Xochitl had a different momma. The poppa was the same. Late in the afternoon, while Margaret was still taking the exam, Jim took Irene past the Chinese restaurant and introduced her to Kai, who instantly won her approval. Something about him appealed to her and she even listened intently as he was instructing staff in Chinese, as if she could understand. Jim made reservations for that evening, for five which included the Hisses. As far as Jim knew, Alger and his wife had never been there before and deserved the experience. After a quick drive-by of several of the apartment complexes he and Marta had restored, Jim has the driver return to the Hiss residence. A fidgeting three year old is poor company when wallowing down a sentimental lane. Margaret's taxi pulls up as Jim and Irene exit theirs, and the reunion is very pleasant to see. Jumping up and down is an Irene forte.

By the time the family has finished with New York, the real estate market around Augusta has been thoroughly explored via telephone and personal contact communications. A tentative plan for buying a small piece of land outside of town, two acres maximum, with a dwelling has taken shape and there are three appointments made with two different agencies before they board the plane to Atlanta. Alger Hiss accompanies them to the airport, seeing them off at the gate with a wave, a hug for Margaret and receives a kiss on the cheek as a farewell from Irene. Grand compensation.

Atlanta airport is busy, getting busier every year. Collecting baggage is blissfully easier than at customs and they are away to the automobile rental stalls within the terminal. Margaret takes charge as she is carrying the cash at the moment, approaches the counter and says they would like to rent a car here in Atlanta and return it to the airport in Augusta. "No problem, Mam. There will be a small additional fee, but I think you will see it is not difficult. Name?"

Margaret provides her details as the primary driver of the car and as they are finishing the clerk says, "Credit card please. We just need it for security purposes. Nothing will be charged until the car is returned."

"I'm sorry. What did you ask for?" Margaret is rifling through her purse to get the cash she thought she would need to provide as a deposit against the rental fee.

"Credit card. You have a credit card with a major lending organization?"

"I have no idea what you're talking about, young man. Credit card? Seems nonsense to me. I have money with which to rent one of your cars. What is this card thing you are talking about?"

"Mam, you must have a credit card in order to rent one of our cars. I am afraid that is a company policy."

'I don't give a fig for your company policies. I don't work for this company. We just need to rent a car. Do you, or do you not rent automobiles here? Are you trying to tell me you cannot accept money for renting a car? This is absurd!"

Jim has been grinning ear to ear slightly behind Margaret, then slides up beside her and offers, "Young man, we have been resident overseas for some time, about sixteen years actually. Well, I have anyway, and just this week returned to the country. Other countries do not, yet, entertain as cavalier an attitude toward personal debt as is present in the US, thus we have not had the opportunity to beggar ourselves as many have here. We have, however, been able to save a sizeable nest egg with which we can pay cash for your vehicle, should you be willing to move this interminable process along. What say you?" This last is delivered with a sizeable upper crust London accent.

The young fellow is now blushing considerably, stutters that he must consult his supervisor and stumbles away from the counter. Shortly, an obviously older man comes from a door to the left, sizes up Jim and Margaret, and is about to speak when Irene bellows, "I'm hungry!" in her best, new found English pronunciation. The week in New York has worked wonders on her spoken English.

"I know dear. We have a little more business to do with this nice gentleman and we'll get something." With that, Jim's attention returns to the supervisor, with the young clerk behind his left shoulder, out of the line of fire. "So, we were about to rent one of your vehicles, I believe."

Not missing a beat, the supervisor says, "And what sort of security were you thinking of providing, seeing that you will be driving away in a $10,000 vehicle of ours?"

"We will provide ten percent of the value of the car as security, assuming the rental fee is reasonable. Margaret, would you give this gentleman a thousand dollars as I watch the apprentice complete the receipt for the same?" The supervisor nods, turns and hands the clerk the rental agreement form,

"Just put the deposit on the line labeled card number, have them initial it, you initial as well, and they should be good to go. Fair enough, Mr. Tuck is it?"

"Quite right." That is again from upper crust London. Funds exchange hands, drivers licenses recorded, even though Jim's is years out of date, address in Georgia, using Jim's contact in Milledgeville, keys passed over with the receipt, and they are away, finally.

Irene gets fed, as they do, then they do not drive to Milledgeville, the original capital of Georgia, but to a motel in Augusta. The motel is at the intersection of interstate twenty and Washington Road, the main thoroughfare into town. It has been a long day, and after settling into the room, they treat themselves to a Chinese dinner at one of the several Chinese restaurants nearby. Ignoring the fact that the food does not meet Kai's standards, they finish, return to the motel, and collapse into their beds, Irene qualifying for a cot that has been rolled in. The next few days will again be full.

Of all the places they tour over the next three days, the Grovetown property on two acres up on an elevation with pine trees in the yard ticks most of their boxes. It has some land, it is out of town, it is elevated where it can catch some breeze in the summer. Summer is likely to be hot. There is a ride-on mower that comes with the property, but the grass is meager at the moment, and probably needs work in the Spring. On the negative side of the ledger is the fact that Grovetown is not one of the more desirable locations to own property. Which leads to the positive factor that the property is very affordable. It will be a cash deal, which is making the sellers as well as the agent drool. Back on the other side of the equation, four of five neighbors are military stationed at Fort Gordon, just down the road, which may have something to do with the type of dwelling it is, a factory built three bedroom house, low ceilings, aluminum siding, small screened porch in front, sitting up on concrete block pilings. It is locally referred to a double-wide, as in double wide trailer. Factory built is a euphemism for trailer. This one being larger than most barely overcomes the fact that it is as flimsy as the Granja la Maja was solid. One has the feeling that it might blow away in a stiff breeze. But, it is cheap, available, and ticks the rest of the important boxes. The deal is done, papers signed and the shipping company is contacted with the address for delivery of the sea freight. Home sweet home.

Next on the list of necessities is transportation. Don Jaime insists he needs something larger to be able to haul supplies for the "farm", so it is a large station wagon type vehicle, while Margaret sticks with a small car, a Toyota this time. They are cash deals again and the rental car is returned ahead of schedule, allowing a bit of a refund.

They move in over a two week period, trying to finish in time for Margaret to be at class in Savannah for her psychology course, required as a prerequisite for entry into the Medical College of Georgia bachelors of nursing course. She has been assured of a job at Doctors Hospital, assuming she passes the national exam she took in New York. The enticing part of the Doctors Hospital position is that they offer tuition reimbursement for nurses who want to develop their careers by enrolling in courses that will enhance their qualifications. Margaret's initial qualification is a diploma degree from Australia, and the hospital looks very favorably on her desire to acquire a university-based qualification. So, she will be able to obtain a bachelor's degree at the hospital's expense while supporting the family with her salary, assuming she passed the registry exam, and assuming she passes this psychology course required to enter the nursing program at the Medical College of Georgia. Lots of assuming there, lots riding on her academic success. Oh, and she has to pass the nursing courses in order to qualify for the reimbursement. No pressure.

They are into the house, and Margaret is suddenly off to Savannah, waving to Jim and Irene as she drives down the driveway. "When's Mommy coming back?"

Jim lifts her and strides back into the house, out of the cool breeze. "We get to go see Mommy soon. We'll make a calendar and mark the days, OK?"

"When's Mommy coming back?"

"Hmm, seems I am not being clear. Here, look at this. You know what this is?" Jim has laid out a wall calendar on the floor for them both to examine.

"No."

"This is called a calendar. It helps us understand when something will happen. Look." Jim circles the date for today and explains how each number is another day. Then he circles the coming Friday and they count the days between. "So, we get to see mommy in five days, right? Four sleeps and we get to see her again. Understand?" Jim stands there, expectantly while holding up four fingers.

"When's Mommy coming back?"

"Arrgh! OK, OK, don't cry. I didn't mean it. Shhh." And Jim lifts her and cuddles her for a while. "In a while. We get to go see Mommy. We have to go in Poppa's car, but it is a nice ride, not too far, and we get to see the ocean. OK?"

Irene slides down Jim's leg, feet hit the floor and she is out the door, but before the screen door slams shut, she says, "OK." She's away.

The fairly dilapidated fencing around the property is the first to receive attention that first week. Don Jaime intends to have animals on this little finca, and a secure fence is essential. The hired handyman has excellent skills at setting posts and stretching field wire, so by Friday noon, most of the work is finished. Irene has been right in the middle of the activity all week, slowing it perceptively, but not seriously as she tried hammering, "helps" stretching the wire, "assists" lifting the gate onto the hinges. At noon, Jim pays the handyman cash, understanding full well what achieves a less costly repair, and he and Irene have lunch, showers and put the small bag into the car before driving out to Savannah.

Irene sits in her elevated car seat in the back, as usual, but sitting is not exactly what she is doing. Finally, Jim pulls the car to the edge of the road, turns and says, "We are going to see Mommy soon, IF you are buckled into your seat. Understand?"

A modest, "Si," rises from the back of the car, there is quiet until the click of the seat belt is heard, Jim checks the outside mirror and pulls out into the driving lane while growling, "Todo bien."

It only requires one potty stop on the two and a half hour drive before they pull into the driveway of the residence where Margaret was staying. Irene is unbuckled and out the door in a flash while Jim is collecting the various water bottles, empty juice containers, oreo sleeve, and the overnight bag from the passenger footwell beside him. As he lumbers up beside Irene, she turns with a seriously pained expression saying, "Mommy's not here. Arrgh!" The high pitched emission is a grand duplicate of one of Jim's.

"Hold on a minute. How do you know she's not here?" Asking a three year old for evidence seems perfectly natural.

Two sniffles and Irene responds, "I did this," she mimes knocking on the door, "and nothing happens. Mommy's not here."

"Hold on, who's that?" Margaret's car is just turning into the pine needle covered driveway and Irene is off like a shot.

Opening her door, Margaret unsuccessfully braces herself for the onslaught and nearly falls back into the driver's seat. "Wait a minute, Irene. Let me get out of the car." The door slams and Irene leaps. The two are one for quite a while, with a couple of tears coursing down Margaret's cheeks, none on Irene's.

Putting Irene down, she beckons them into her living quarters, a one room efficiency with everything in one room except the toilet and shower. Jim unpacks the take-away food he bought at the potty stop, putting it on the counter, the trash goes into the trash can and the overnight bag onto the bed. All set. Margaret's first order of business is to boil the jug, and second is to sit for Irene to climb back onto her. They are in for the evening.

The weekend is full of tours, sea food, discovering the parks that are all through the town and two trips to the beach. Jim is actually impressed with the historic preservation evident in the town, and agrees that the oysters are the best he has had in quite a while. It looks like these weekend visits may be more pleasant than he thought. It is a worthwhile effort. While there, he mentions the progress made on the fencing and the new gate, then proposes, "I think a few ducks would do the place well. How about you? We talked about getting a few animals for the land. Hmm? Whaddaya think?" That's followed by a small chuck onto Margaret's shoulder. Jim's getting frisky again. Irene is fast asleep on a pallet on the floor.

Margaret looks at Jim, smiles, then offers, "Ducks? What do we know about raising ducks? What do we do with them?"

"Eggs. We eat the eggs, and if the urge strikes, a duck. How about it?"

"Oh, Jim, I just don't know. I am not dead keen on the idea."

"Well, I can see that. But, just as an experiment. Might work a treat, as you say. Nothing ventured, nothing gained. There are several more of those in here. Cliches are great, don't you think? How hard can it be? We've done more difficult things. Come on, let's do it."

"Oh, Jim. I know you're going to do it. Try to keep it as inexpensive as possible, OK?"

"You know it. You'll see. Finca Tuck. It's going to be so good. Right, Bud?"

Irene stirs slightly and Jim responds, "See, even Irene agrees. Grand. Finca Tuck will be well under way by the time you get back. When is that, actually? Remind me."

"Seven more weeks, Jim. Seven. The course gets out a bit earlier than some of the others. I should be able to start at the hospital in May. Oh, I passed the exam I took in New York. I had the results forwarded to Savannah State and got the letter just before you arrived. I got so excited to see you two I nearly forgot to tell you. I called the Director of Nursing at Doctors already. So, a new finca, a new job, a new education. Go get the ducks, Jim. Onward and upward." There is a long kiss and a longer embrace, and Jim gathers up the sleeping Irene, bundles her into the car for the ride back to Grovetown.

The second week of life in Georgia is full of project completions, visiting various farm supply stores nearby, installing a small chicken/duck shed in the back corner of the lot and finally, purchasing seven adult ducks, one drake and six females. All seven are enclosed in a single container, on loan from the supply store, to be returned the next day. On instruction from the staff at the store, Jim has already put out food and water for the ducks by the coop before bringing them home. He drives through the gate, closing it behind him, backing his vehicle up to the shed. Out the door, Irene at his side, Jim lifts the tailgate, opens the cage and he and Irene stand back as the ducks creep forward, they flutter down to the ground, one after another. Waddling with white tail feathers flitting back and forth, they start exploring in front of the shed, find the water bowl, and two immediately jump in, flutter around, drop a large amount of duck poop and climb out for food. Two more climb in and repeat the process, but the water is now filthy. Jim retrieves the water hose, tips out the two ducks and the water and refills the large bowl. Irene asks for the hose, and stands holding it as the bowl fills, spraying the last duck from time to time. Jim smiles, Irene gives a screech of pleasure, and Jim turns the hose off. Finally, all seven ducks are around the feed trough and Irene and Jim climb back into the vehicle and drive it out of the field, parking next to the house.

After dinner, Jim and Irene return to the front porch, Jim with a glass of wine, Irene with an iced tea and occupy two of the three rocking chairs. The sun is nearly down and they are watching the tranquil scene across finca Tuck. The ducks are gathered in a small cluster, no longer at the feeding trough, but gradually fluttering their wings more and more, until suddenly all seven raise into the air and circle the shed once, then fly off down the hillside. Jim's hand has his drink near his mouth, frozen in place, and Irene jumps up and runs to the screen. "Poppa, poppa, the ducks. Get the ducks. POPPA!"

Jim slowly stands, puts down his glass and walks to the screen door. "Come on." He takes Irene's hand, puts her drink on the small round table by the door, and both slowly descend the steps to the gravel driveway. Crunching their way to the opposite side of the drive, Jim lifts Irene onto his shoulders and they look down the hillside. No ducks, but Jim notices the small pond at the bottom of the hill, behind a house facing the unpaved road leading to finca Tuck. "Into the car, Bud. Let's see if we can find our ducks." They slowly drive down the road and stop in front of the house, about half a mile from theirs up the hill.

Climbing out of the station wagon, Jim opens Irene's door and helps her down, closing the door behind. As the car door closes, the front door of the house opens and a greying woman comes down the stairs of the house toward the road. "Hey, y'all. How y'all doin'?" She is smiling, but obviously curious.

"Evening, mam. I am Jim Tuck, this is my daughter, Irene." Jim releases Irene's hand and she waves, with a small smile.

"Poppa, I don't know what she says."

"It's alright pumpkin. That's just the way people who live here talk."

"Can they talk English?" Their conversation is quiet, but the woman obviously has heard and smiles.

"Ah talk purdy good Anglish, darlin'. It's just ma own kaand. Ah'm Emma Lou Watkins. Ma husband Walter is eeuhn town, comin' back latuh. Y'all dun moved inta Seargent Prentices's place up duh heel, raaht?"

Irene looks at Jim, looks at Emma Lou, then says, "No intiendo, nada." Shaking her head, she turns back toward the car, opens the door, climbs in and closes it.

"Not to worry. We just moved here from Spain, Spanish is her first language, so various English dialects are still difficult for her. No offense intended."

"Ain't none takin'. Dahlin' little thang. What can I doo fo ya?"

"Glad to hear it. I expect you get folks who have been from all over from time to time. Hope we can be good neighbors. The reason for the visit is that I brought home seven ducks for our little spread, to start raising some eggs and perhaps more ducks, and all seven seem to have flown down to your pond, or at least that is what I suspect. I wonder if I could take a look in the water out back."

"Corse ya kin. No problem. Cum on back." With that she gives a wave, and heads to the side of the house. Jim turns and waves for Irene to follow along. The car door opens, she climbs out and slams the door, trotting up to take Jim's hand. Looking up, she sees Jim smile, so she smiles back, gives a skip and the three head to the rear of the house.

There is no fence so they walk straight back through a few peach trees that are not yet blooming and arrive at the shore of a small pond, about one acre in area, and out there in the middle are seven white ducks swimming in a small circle in the gathering darkness. The three are standing there and Emma Lou says, "Yip, thar's seven awraat." Just then, one duck suddenly disappears into the water. "Oops, 'fraid a thaat. Won't be too minny tuhmarrah, fer sher."

"What just happened to that duck?" Jim is wide eyed, still holding Irene's hand. The six remaining ducks are fluttering toward the shore of the pond, and a second duck disappears. "

What the f.., uh the heck was that?"

"Snappers. Three uv 'em in theah. They luv duck meat."

"Oh my gawd. Well, I guess, you folks have as many ducks as there are left once the turtles are done. You have a lovely evening, mam. Come on, Irene, lets head home."

"POPPA! Get the ducks!"

"Ya cain't git them theer ducks, dahlin'. Ahm sorry, but it's the way uv the animuuls." Irene looks at Jim, eyebrows up like, what did she say? And then lets out a wail.

Picking her up, Jim says, "Emma Lou is right. She says there is probably no way to get the ducks back now that they have a home in the water. They like that new home. It's like a huge water bowl, right? Remember how they liked the water bowl and jumped in? Well, this is now their water bowl." Jim studiously avoids mentioning the fact that there are now only five ducks instead of seven as they make their way back through the peach trees to the car. "You have a nice evening, Emma Lou. See ya later."

"Y'all cum baack ta see us naow, heah? Sorry 'bout dem ducks. Tanks fuh cumin, baa." With that last salvo, Jim and Irene are back into the car, give a wave, and drive back up the hill to "home".

"Poppa." Irene is in her seat in the back of the car as they drive back up the hill.

"Yes, Bud. What's up?"

"I did not understand that lady. She talks very funny. Can she speak Spanish?"

"I don't think she speaks Spanish, precious. She speaks Georgia. It is how a lot of people who live here talk. It is the way they grew up talking, and their parents talked that way. For years and years. It is English, but not the way we speak English. Understand?"

"No. Why?"

"Why what, my love?"

"Why do they speak English that way when it doesn't sound like English?"

"Ah. It is the same reason we talk the way we do, Bud. It is the way they heard it as kids, like you heard Paco talking Spanish, and Imelda when she took care of you when mommy was working. You heard them talking Spanish, and it was OK, right?"

There is a long silence from the back seat, and the car pulls into the parking space in front of the house. Turning off the engine, Jim turns and looks at Irene, his face asking the question. Irene finally looks back at him, from staring out the window and says, "Si." They both break up laughing and exit the car.

Just then a large pick up truck pulls into the driveway and stops behind the station wagon. Jim is holding Irene's hand as the doors to the truck open and two young men with close cropped hair, in army fatigues come toward them. The taller fellow waves his hand and says, "Hey, y'all. We're livin in the next place, raht uhp the draavwey. Thought we'd cum dawn and say hey."

Jim looks at Irene, who shrugs, then raises a hand to the first fellow with, "Hey, back. I am Jim Tuck, this is my daughter Irene. Just moved in." Irene gives a small wave of introduction for herself.

"Billy Bob Thornton. Thisheers Hinree Johnston, of the Macon Johnstons. His daddy was my daddy's bist frin. Nasstameethcha." Henry comes forward and also shakes Jim's hand and Irene gives him a wave as well. "Wheer y'all fruhm?"

"We moved here from Madrid, about two weeks ago."

"Is that Maydreed near Jeckeel Ahland? Not shur whur that Maydreed ees. Ain't hurd uh it."

"No, it's not near Jekyll Island. It's not in Georgia, actually. It's in Spain."

"Spaayn, lakh in Yurp, Spaayn? Whoo, that's purdy damned fur."

"Yes, it is like in Europe. I was living there for a while, just came back with my wife, Margaret and my precious Irene here. Where you fellows from?"

Henry responds, "We bin livin here in Joagah all a awr laavs, cipt ayt baysuk trayinin in Tixus. Wint an cum back, an heeuh we ahh." Big smiles on both servicemen's faces.

Jim glances at Irene whose eyebrows are both way up and her eyes are large with questions so Jim responds with adequate interpretation for her. "So, both you fellows left for basic training for the army in Texas and came back together, I suspect to Fort Gordon. Is that correct?" Irene's hand gives Jim's a gentle tug.

"Yip. Bout raht. Thisheers jis abaht thuh bis playees in duh wurl, so wha leev unywhur ilse. Raht?" With that exclamation, Billy Bob looks at Henry, and both heads bob up and down in agreement.

Jim gives Irene's hand a little tug, smiles and says, "Well, I suspect you may be right. It seems quite the welcoming place, and I suspect we will be well satisfied living here. Glad to meet the neighbors. Thanks for coming by, guys. Gotta go feed Irene here. Wife's away in Savannah at the moment so we are having some father and daughter time. Stop by any time. Bye now." With that, Jim gives the two guys a small wave, Irene copies him and they climb the stairs to the porch as the two young men climb back into the truck and slam the doors. With the porch screen door open, Jim and Irene give one more wave to the guys before going through into the house.

"Poppa. I can't understand anything. This is hard!"

"It will get easier, for sure. But, you're right. It may be just a tad more difficult here than other places. Actually, I am beginning to wonder if life on a finca is quite right for us, or me. It certainly would be more difficult here, yes?"

"I don't understand."

Lifting Irene onto his hip, he holds her with one arm and tweeks her cheek with the other hand. "Sometimes, neither do I, poppet. What was I thinking? Anyway, tomorrow, maybe you and I could start looking for a place that is easier, for both of us. Want to help look?"

"Yes! Tomorrow?"

"Si, manana. Tiene ambre?"

"Si! Can we eat now?"

"Well, let's make it easier, OK? We will go find some food someplace. We'll have tacos, OK?" A large jump, then two hops indicate agreement and the two are back out the door.

That evening, with Irene well asleep, Jim writes to Margaret giving the full adventures of the day, including his conclusions, as well as Irene's, and says another letter will be coming in a few days outlining possible options for alternative housing and ideas for unloading their current property. Problem solving mode has quickly replaced the sense of disaster. Fort Gordon, with its military turnover and subsidized housing options for servicemen might just prove to be part of his escape solution. Escape is the order of the day, that's for sure.

It is two weeks since the duck disaster, the introduction to the neighbors including Irene's pointing out the obvious; they have nothing in common with the folks living around there. Back visiting Margaret in Savannah, Irene sound asleep on the pallet, Jim and Margaret are closely examining various real estate brochures for the Augusta area. Jim has already started his marketing campaign at the fort, utilizing two or three local contacts including his long time connection in Milledgeville. He has already had two calls, and one drive by. No one has stopped by, yet, but there will not be a sign by the roadside as he does not want to irritate the neighbors.

Margaret is holding a brochure open to a picture then asks, "Where is Evans, Georgia?"

"Why?"

"Look here. This is intriguing. It looks like a log cabin, but is two stories, and apparently is made from wooden telephone poles. It says it is in Evans, Georgia. Any idea where that is?"

"Here's the map of Augusta and environs. Any indication of direction from town?"

"Let's see. West, it says west of town."

Jim runs his finger along a major street going west out of Augusta, Washington Rd. it reads and lifts his finger to look back at the town center but then glances back at the map. "Here. Here it is. Evans, Georgia. Damn, that's a fair piece from town."

"How far is it from Doctor's Hospital? Can you tell? Let me see."

The two are pouring over the map when Margaret exclaims, "Look at that. It is not far at all, from the hospital. That's critical, don't you think? That's where most of my driving will be going, commuting to work, and it's on the same side of town as this property."

"Well, would you look at that. If that's not an interesting coincidence, I don't know what is. Who is the realtor?"

"Century 21. Doesn't give a name of an agent. Why?"

"It may be a difficult property to move and no one really wants it. Hmm. I'd say, this may be first on my activity sheet for Monday. The first one for you will be verification of your position at the hospital. We'll need a mortgage for this one until we sell Grovetown. Any one actually, so even if this one is not it, we can't guarantee we'll have the equity from Grovetown before buying the next. We have some money still, from Javea, not much, and you have another three weeks here before there is any chance of starting at Doctors. Gotta save that nest egg for now, right?"

"Of course. One step at a time, or maybe two. We'll check out this Evans property, finish the improvements to Grovetown, organize the start date for Doctors. I have my job offer here with the rest of my professional papers. You take that with you when you go back, if you have a chance to talk to a bank. This is, as usual Mr. Tuck, a bit exciting. More than a little scary. Onward and upward."

With few serious hiccups, a deal is struck for a two story log house among the trees off Washington Rd. in Evans, Georgia. Within two months, the much improved property in Grovetown is sold, as investment property to a firm renting temporary housing to servicemen at Fort Gordon. The sea freight shipped from Spain can finally be completely emptied, with gnomes, keepsakes, sculptures, a yoke from an oxcart, paintings, posters and books spread over the downstairs of a fairly dark, but deliciously rustic log home. The crate from the sea freight becomes raw material for bookshelves that start in the living room, work their way into the kitchen and in the upstairs hallway. The large kitchen partly accommodates the enormous table installed with bench seats on either side. The atmosphere is just right for some serious entertaining, at some time in the future. Now, Margaret watches from the door of the house as Jim starts pacing off the dimensions of, what else, a pool, across the drive and out from under the pine trees. "Here we go again. Guess we're home, for sure." She shakes her head, and comes back in to fix Irene her lunch on a Saturday. Savannah is a memory, her job has started at the hospital, and Jim Tuck is creating another swimming pool. All's right with the world.

The End

Epilogue

It's a Sunday, probably in March or April, 1982. My family and I have recently moved to Augusta, Georgia, where I will be teaching physical therapy at the Medical College of Georgia. We, my family and I, have begun attending the Unitarian Universalist Church of Augusta for the Sunday services after which there is a social hour. Today, I have decided to give the social hour a miss and take my coffee to explore around the premises. Soon, I find myself in a small courtyard, with a central granite water feature that is trickling away, bench seats around the fountain and on the other side of the fountain sit two white haired gentlemen in animated discussion. I note that there is one other visitor to the courtyard, sitting to one side in rapt attention to the conversation that seems to be center stage. Always up for a bit of entertainment, I join the spectator, who nods his approval, and sit with my coffee. I find that the two gentlemen are Fred and Jim and that this is their regular domain on Sundays, after church; their schtick so to speak.

Fred is becoming more animated in his description of a controlled tail spin maneuver in a WW1 vintage biplane, explaining it as his invention, one he taught to flying recruits as a combat flying instructor. My companion spectator explains that Fred is in his early 90's and is well known to the church, although he never attends. Jim is a generation younger, the husband of one of the members of the church board, drops her and his daughter off before church and picks them up after, usually. He, likewise, has not darkened the door to the sanctuary. Just then, there is a mighty growl, obviously from Jim as he allows as how that maneuver is bull shit. "Look it up, look it up!" is Fred's retort.

"Don't have to look it up. I had enough experience flying bombers in China for the Flying Tigers to recognize bull shit when I hear it." Then, he is away into one of his stories, in between puffs of his omnipresent cigarette.

Those apres church exhibitions became a regular event for me, even after Fred was no longer able to attend. They launched my relationship with Jim Tuck, one that lasted years, and ultimately provided the motivation to write some of them down. This project began in 2011, and is still going in April, 2022, in Niantic, CT. Books two and four are written. Books one and three await. Il l'chaim.

DAR

David A. Rohe (Dave to most) is a retired physical therapist and teacher whose only other publication was a text book written in collaboration with his boss in the 80's. His experiences living in Central Africa, Asia and Egypt provided the perspective which drove the need to write about Jim Tuck. There is something about a larger than life existence that requires recording. As noted elsewhere, this writing project is in 4 parts with the first part published being book 2; inspiration from Star Wars duly noted. Starting to write for the public in one's seventies seems a tad foolish, but perhaps no more than planting trees whose shade will never be enjoyed by the planter.

Here's to Dave's foolishness, and his family: Wife Sharon, kids Jo Ellen, Jennifer, Adam, Sarah and Will. Go forth and prosper.

Dave and Sharon

www.ingramcontent.com/pod-product-compliance
Lightning Source LLC
Chambersburg PA
CBHW020651010826
48969CB00012B/141